The sound of a loud crash turned his blood cold. *Emma!*

The front door was wooden, old, with a flimsy dead bolt. Thunder boomed, and Reed took advantage. He rammed the door with a well-placed kick.

It shuddered and gave way.

He entered the house, his flashlight moving over everything. His breathing was ragged, but the hand holding his weapon was steady.

Which way? Upstairs or toward the back of the house?

He paused, straining to listen. There. A noise coming from the kitchen. He raced down the hallway. Someone was coughing.

His flashlight caught a dark figure bolting out the back door. Reed swung to his left. Emma sat on the tile floor, one hand holding her neck. Her face was red and her long hair stuck out in all directions. Relief replaced the terror in her expression when she caught sight of him.

Lynn Shannon
and
Heather Woodhaven

Moving Targets

Previously published as *Following the Evidence* and *Tracking Secrets*

LOVE INSPIRED
INSPIRATIONAL ROMANCE

LOVE INSPIRED®
INSPIRATIONAL ROMANCE

Recycling programs
for this product may
not exist in your area.

ISBN-13: 978-1-335-42459-4

Moving Targets

Copyright © 2021 by Harlequin Books S.A.

Following the Evidence
First published in 2020. This edition published in 2021.
Copyright © 2020 by Lynn Shannon Balabanos

Tracking Secrets
First published in 2017. This edition published in 2021.
Copyright © 2017 by Heather Humrichouse

This edition published by arrangement with Harlequin Books S.A.

For questions and comments about the quality of this book, please contact us at CustomerService@Harlequin.com.

Love Inspired
22 Adelaide St. West, 40th Floor
Toronto, Ontario M5H 4E3, Canada
www.Harlequin.com

Printed in U.S.A.

CONTENTS

Lynn Shannon writes novels that combine intriguing mysteries with heartfelt romance. Raised in Texas, she believes pecans and Blue Bell ice cream are must-haves for every household. Lynn lives with her husband, two children, an extremely spoiled dog and a turtle who hibernates half the year. You can find her online at lynnshannon.com.

Books by Lynn Shannon

Love Inspired Suspense

Following the Evidence

Visit the Author Profile page at Harlequin.com.

FOLLOWING THE EVIDENCE

Lynn Shannon

For we walk by faith, not by sight.
—*2 Corinthians* 5:7

To my husband. I'm thankful to be walking through life with you by my side.

ONE

Emma jerked awake.

She automatically reached for the baby monitor on her nightstand. No cry or whimper came through the speaker, only the slight shushing sound of Lily's steady breathing. Her muscles relaxed. The baby was fine.

A bolt of lightning streaked across the sky, followed by a loud clap of thunder. The storm must have woken her.

Before Lily came along, there was nothing Emma couldn't sleep through. Now every creak of the house disturbed her, a side effect of motherhood. Of course, recent events also had her on edge. The threats...

Emma squeezed her eyes shut and forced the thoughts away. If she started pondering her new troubles, she'd never get back to sleep.

Texas storms could be fierce, and this one was no exception. Rain pounded against the roof. Wind whistled around the corner of the old house, a hollow, mourning sound.

A shiver raced down Emma's spine. She tried to snuggle back into her pillow but something felt off. Wrong somehow. She extended her leg, parting the covers near the foot of her bed. Warmth caressed her toes but no solid form interrupted her progress.

Where was Sadie?

A low growl came from the bedroom door.

Emma sat up. Her eyes hadn't quite adjusted to the dark, but she could make out the large blot of her dog near the doorway.

"What is it, girl?" Emma whispered.

Sadie didn't turn her head. Her body was rigid, the hair standing up on the back of her neck.

Fear, sharp and instinctive, coursed through Emma. The Labrador wouldn't behave that way if it was just Vivian, her sister-in-law, moving around.

Lightning momentarily lit up her bedroom and the corresponding hallway. No one was there.

Emma strained to listen beyond the sounds of the storm. It was impossible. The rain was coming down in curtains, the thunder as loud as a sonic boom. Sadie's ears twitched, and another warning growl rumbled through her chest. This one was sharper and more urgent.

Emma needed no further convincing. She threw off the covers and grabbed her cell phone. She hit the first number on Speed Dial.

A woman answered. "Heyworth Sheriff's Department."

"My name is Emma Pierce." She ran to her closet. "I live at 125 Old Hickory Lane. I think someone has broken into my home."

"Did you hear someone break in?"

Emma cocked the phone between her ear and her shoulder. Her hands shook as she pulled a small box from the top shelf. She ignored the dispatcher's question. It would be too complicated to explain Sadie had alerted her. "I need deputies sent to my home immediately. 125 Old Hickory Lane."

"I'm sending them now."

It brought Emma little relief. She lived in a rural area. On a good day, she was twenty minutes from the sheriff's department. With the storm raging outside, it might take twice that long for deputies to arrive.

"Do you know who is breaking into your home?" the dispatcher asked.

"I can't talk right now," she said. "I'll call you back in a moment."

"Ma'am, stay—"

Emma hung up and fished a Taser out of the box. Her late husband had bought it as a security measure, an extra precaution when she left vet school late at night. She'd almost gotten rid of it when she moved to the countryside, but Mark's warning had stopped her.

You never know, sweetheart. You might need it.

She gripped the Taser with a shaking hand, simultaneously rising from her crouch and tucking her cell into the pocket of her pajama pants. Sadie followed her into the hall.

Emma had spent sleepless nights running this scenario through her mind. The threats from her cousin Owen were escalating.

When Uncle Jeb unexpectedly died and left Emma almost his entire estate, she'd been flabbergasted. Her mother's brother had been one of the last living blood relations she had. They'd talked on the phone regularly, had been as close as two people living on opposite sides of the country could be, but never did she imagine he would pass over his only child, Owen, and give her the lion's share portion of his estate.

It'd taken only one meeting at the lawyer's office to understand why Uncle Jeb hadn't left the property he loved so much to his son. Owen bounced from odd job to odd job, from girlfriend to girlfriend and spent most of his time with his hand around a liquor bottle. It would've taken him a few months to destroy what Jeb had spent a lifetime building.

Owen hadn't taken the news well. Her cousin had flown into a screaming rage at the lawyer's office. Shortly after Emma moved into Uncle Jeb's home, the hang-up phone calls began. Flowerbeds were destroyed and patio furniture broken. Minor annoyances became increasingly frightening when the phone calls took a more threatening tone and someone attempted to poison Sadie. After that, Emma reported it all to the sheriff's office. Her complaint hadn't been taken seriously.

Would Owen go so far as to break into her house in the middle of the night? She feared he might.

She entered Lily's room. The glow from the nightlight glimmered off the little girl's hair and the curve of her cheek. Emma picked up her daughter, nestling the child's face against her shoulder. Lily stirred but, thankfully, remained sleeping. As silent as a shadow, Emma flew to her sister-in-law's room.

"Vivian," she hissed.

The other woman muttered something in her sleep. Emma placed Lily down gently on the bed before shaking Vivian awake. When her sister-in-law opened her eyes, Emma held a finger to her lips. "I think someone's in the house."

Vivian's eyes widened and her body went stiff.

"Take Lily into the bathroom and lock the door." Emma pressed her cell phone into Vivian's hand. "Speed Dial 1 is the sheriff's office. Deputies are on the way, but you should call them again."

Vivian grabbed her wrist. "Where are you going?"

"To check it out." Emma secretly hoped whatever had caused Sadie's reaction wasn't cause for serious alarm, but she wasn't taking any chances.

Vivian's gaze dropped to the Taser in Emma's hand. "Please…be careful."

Emma gave a sharp jerk of her head. "Bathroom."

Vivian flew into motion. Within moments, the bathroom door clicked closed. Before leaving Vivian's bedroom, Emma rested her hand against Sadie's head. The dog's fur was soft against her fingertips. Sadie glanced at her and Emma could almost hear the animal's thoughts. *Take me with you.*

"Stay," Emma whispered. "Guard."

If there was an intruder in the house and he managed to get past Emma, he would have to go through Sadie to hurt Lily or Vivian. The Labrador would fight to the death to protect her family—especially Lily. She'd been trained to.

Emma slipped out into the hall on silent footsteps. Her heart pounded against her rib cage. Possibilities played in her mind, the images flashing like her own personal scary movie. She was no innocent country girl—she knew full well the horrors people could inflict on one another. As a search-and-rescue volunteer, she'd seen it up close and personal.

Father, please help me be strong. Give me the ability to protect my family if necessary.

She paused at the top of the stairs. Her senses were

on high alert. Warm, moist air washed over her and the rain seemed louder, like a door or window was open. She swallowed hard and gripped the Taser a bit tighter before edging her way down the staircase.

Bang!

She jumped and bit back a shriek. Her hands went numb. The wind screamed through the house, rattling the windowpanes.

Bang. Bang.

Trembling, she took a deep breath and rounded the banister. The sound was coming from the kitchen. She raced down the dark hall, her slippers silent against the wood floor. She paused at the entrance to the kitchen and peeked around the doorframe.

One of the large glass panes on her bay window was broken, the shards scattered across the tile floor. The wind screeched again, rocking a cabinet door forward before slamming it closed. Water from the rain mixed with the glass on the floor. Was that…?

She stepped forward and caught a glimpse of leaves on the floor. A tree branch.

Heady relief washed over her. No one had broken into the house. The storm's high winds had simply thrown a branch through the glass. She lowered the Taser. A streak of lightning lit up the kitchen, making it as bright as midday. Emma saw them a fraction too late.

Muddy boot prints.

Something moved out of the corner of her eye. Emma spun. The Taser flew from her hand and a cookie jar on the counter shattered as the intruder tackled her.

The storm was a bad one.

Sheriff Reed Atkinson sat in his favorite chair on the

screened-in porch and watched the rain batter against the barn. Wind whipped tree branches back and forth, the thunder so loud it vibrated in his chest. Lightning bolted from the sky, striking a nearby tree. Reed sucked in a breath as a limb cracked. It crashed to the ground, narrowly missing the barn's roof by inches.

Close. Too close. He made sure there weren't lingering sparks, but the rain drenched any fire before it could start. Reed settled back in his chair. He checked the time. A little after one in the morning.

He'd already called the sheriff's department and placed himself on reserve. The standard units were working, but with a night like this, sometimes an extra hand or two became necessary. Everything was quiet when he spoke to his dispatch operator, Mona, and he hoped it stayed that way.

Still, he couldn't manage to sleep. Insomnia and Reed were old friends, albeit grudgingly.

The anniversary of Bonnie's disappearance was this month. His sister had been gone for a year, and there hadn't been a single phone call or email from her. Not even a letter. Her social security number hadn't been used, her bank accounts and credit cards remained untouched. Reed had been a cop long enough to know her case probably wasn't going to have the happy ending he wanted.

Yet, there was a niggle of hope he couldn't snuff out that she was alive. It's what kept him digging. It also kept him awake in the middle of the night.

Reed rose from the chair and stretched. Maybe he would try to lie down anyway. As he crossed the threshold into the tiny living room, his cell phone rang. The familiar number on his screen flashed and his heart skipped a beat. Dispatch.

He answered, his voice gruff but authoritative. "Atkinson."

"Sheriff, Emma Pierce contacted me a few minutes ago." Mona spoke in a rush. "She inherited Jeb Tillman's place."

"I know who she is."

A simple sentence that didn't begin to encompass the complicated relationship between Reed and Emma. They'd had a serious summer romance ten years ago before reality and different life goals sent them in opposite directions. Since Emma's move back to Heyworth last month, Reed had done his best to avoid her. A ridiculous notion, considering the town's size. It was smarter to be polite.

Still, when he'd spotted her in the grocery store last week, the rush of emotion had caught him off guard. Reed had turned on his heel and walked the other way.

"She thinks an intruder has broken into her house," Mona said.

Reed's chest clenched. Emma was a widow with a small child. That made her an easier target for criminals looking to steal.

"I've dispatched the closest unit but with the storm, they're more than thirty minutes out," Mona continued. "Since you—"

"Got it."

Reed's ranch bordered Emma's. He could be at her house in less than five minutes—a huge, potentially life-saving time difference.

"How does she know someone is breaking in?" Reed shoved his feet into worn cowboy boots.

"She didn't say. I tried to keep her on the phone, but she hung up, claiming someone would call me right back."

"Contact the unit and let them know I'll be on site," Reed ordered. He didn't want to be accidentally shot by one of his own men.

"Will do."

He hung up and pulled on his holster along with his jacket. Within moments, he was sliding into the seat of his pickup truck and flying down his driveway.

Possibilities raced through his mind. Violent crime was almost nonexistent in their county, home invasions extremely rare. In this storm, she could have heard the wind rattling the house or had a tree branch shatter a window. Both of those would've sounded as though an individual was breaking in. An honest mistake. It'd happened before.

But what if it wasn't a mistake? It was always the question Reed asked himself whenever he rushed to a potential scene. He treated every case with absolute seriousness. Reed knew, better than most, even small towns like Heyworth had their darker elements.

God, please help me get there in time. Let her and her family be okay.

It'd been a long time since they'd dated, but if Emma was anything like the woman he used to know, she would be first in line to protect her loved ones. Reed battled against the images of her hurt or worse…

No. That wouldn't happen.

His headlights sliced through the darkness. The old country road was unpaved, narrow and rarely used. It was also the shortest route between his ranch and Emma's property. His tires ate up the gravel and it pinged against the undercarriage. He was going dangerously fast, but he couldn't slow down. If something happened to Emma or her family, he would never forgive himself.

Out of nowhere, another truck appeared, racing toward Reed. The vehicle had no headlights on, bouncing down the road at a reckless speed. Teenagers? His office had had a problem with racing on these back roads, but since Reed had become sheriff nine months ago, he'd cracked down on it.

A sick feeling twisted his stomach. Or could this be Emma's intruder? The truck was coming from the direction of her property. Reed tried to make out the make and model of the vehicle, but in the rain and the dark, it was impossible. He honked his horn, but the truck didn't change paths. It barreled down on him.

A blinding light filled Reed's windshield, obscuring his vision. The driver had turned on his brights.

Reed jerked his wheel to avoid colliding with the other truck. His tires hit a slick spot and fishtailed. His heart jumped into his throat. He tapped his brakes, managing to bring his truck back under control before it skidded off the road and into the woods.

In his rearview mirror, the other vehicle disappeared. The driver hadn't even slowed down.

Shaken and angry, Reed allowed himself half a breath. Under normal circumstances, he would do a U-turn and arrest whoever was driving, but he didn't have the time for that now. He had to get to Emma.

He raced the rest of the way there. Before making the turn to her ranch, he killed his lights. If the intruder was still inside the house, Reed didn't want to alert him that law enforcement had arrived. That was a good way to turn a home invasion into a hostage situation.

Rain instantly soaked the shoulders of his jacket. In his haste to leave, Reed hadn't taken his hat. His hair became plastered to his head, water running in rivers down his face and into his collar. The grass was slick under his boots. Mud splashed the cuffs of his jeans as he ran to the front porch.

He scanned the front door and the closest windows with his flashlight. Nothing. Everything looked locked and secure. Lightning streaked across the sky, and above his head wind chimes danced. He needed to go around the perimeter of the house, look for signs of a break-in. The back door maybe—

The sound of a loud crash turned his blood cold. *Emma!*

The front door was wooden, old, with a flimsy deadbolt. Thunder boomed, and Reed took advantage. He rammed the door with a well-placed kick. His heel screamed in protest, but the wood splintered.

"Come on, come on…" He focused his energy on the weak spot he'd created. He slammed into the door again. It shuddered and gave way.

He entered the house, his flashlight moving over everything. A banister leading upstairs. A dining room to his right. A living room to his left. His breathing was ragged, but the hand holding his weapon was steady.

Which way? Upstairs or toward the back of the house?

He paused, straining to listen. There. A noise coming from the kitchen. He raced down the hallway. Someone was coughing.

His flashlight caught a dark figure bolting out the back door. Reed swung to his left. Emma sat on the tile floor, one hand holding her neck. Her face was red and her long hair stuck out in all directions. Relief replaced the terror in her expression when she caught sight of him.

Reed bent down, scanning quickly for blood. How seriously had she been hurt?

"Go," she choked out. "I'm okay, and he's getting away."

Reed dashed after the intruder.

TWO

Reed's boots slipped on the mud and the grass as he rounded the corner of the house. Rain pelted him, and he blinked to clear his vision. The intruder was already across the yard, headed for the safety of the woods.

"Police!" Reed shouted. "Freeze!"

The dark form paid him no heed. Reed raised his gun, but the man was a quickly moving target. Reed had no shot. Within the span of two heartbeats, the intruder disappeared into the woods.

Reed wrestled with the need to give chase, but the rain and the dark put him at a distinct disadvantage. It wasn't smart to go into the woods without backup. Smothering his frustration, he pulled out his phone and hit Speed Dial while jogging back to the house.

Mona answered before the first ring finished.

"I need every available unit to my location. I also need an ambulance." He barked out his orders and a brief description of the suspect. Not that it was much. Male, roughly six feet, wearing dark-colored clothing and a ski mask.

He hung up and entered the kitchen.

Emma had turned on the lights, bringing the attack's

destruction into full focus. A tree branch had obviously been used to break the window. It lay discarded. A shattered cookie jar was partly on the counter, the rest on the floor. A Taser resting on the tile sent a fresh wave of adrenaline through him. Had Emma been attacked with it?

She was standing with her back to him, one slender hand clutching the wall as if it was the only thing keeping her standing. Her breathing was raspy. There was no blood on the floor or on her clothes, but it didn't necessarily mean she was okay. Shock could be covering the pain.

Glass crunched under his boots. She turned at the sound of his approach. Her face was ashen, her eyes huge.

"It's okay. You're okay," he reassured her. He scanned her body for wounds, stopping at the sight of the red marks around her neck. His jaw tightened in anger. "Did he use the Taser on you?"

"No." Her voice came out barely above a whisper. "Just his hands. The Taser's mine, but he knocked it away before I could use it."

Other than the marks on her neck, Emma was remarkably whole. A few minor cuts from the glass on her arms. Her pajama top and bottoms were wet from the rain. Her whole body trembled. Whether from cold, fear or shock, he couldn't tell.

"The ambulance is on its way." Reed took off his coat. The outside leather was wet, but it was layered and would help warm her until the ambulance arrived. He draped it over her shoulders.

"Is he gone?" she asked.

"Yes." He pulled a kitchen chair around and gently led her to it. "Where's your daughter?"

"Lily is with my sister-in-law, Vivian. They're upstairs."

"Wait here."

Reed tore down the hall and ran up the stairs. A rumbling growl drew him up short.

A dog was standing in a doorway, teeth bared and hackles up. There was no doubt the animal would attack him if he went closer.

The stairs creaked as Emma came up behind him. "Stop," she rasped. The dog immediately ceased growling but remained at attention. "Good dog, Sadie."

"Can I move past her or is she going to bite me?" Reed asked.

"Sadie will only attack on my command now."

He took her word for it. The bedroom was empty, but he could hear the sounds of a baby crying on the other side of a door. Reed rapped on the wood. "It's Sheriff Reed Atkinson. Can you unlock the door, please?"

The lock clicked. A blond woman emerged, cradling a red-faced child. The vise around Reed's chest loosened, and he took his first deep breath. Vivian and the baby appeared unharmed and although Emma was hurt, her injuries were minor. Things could've been so much worse.

Thank you, Lord.

Vivian spotted Emma standing in the doorway and rushed around Reed.

"Thank God, you're all right." Vivian started crying. "I was so scared. When I heard the banging—"

"We're okay." Emma wrapped her arms around Vivian. "We're all okay."

Sadie joined the group, standing as close to their legs as possible. Emma took the baby, shushing her. Lily was gorgeous, with her mother's dark hair and eyes. Her chubby arms were wrapped around a stuffed lamb. Seeing Emma holding her little girl twisted something in Reed's gut.

"What happened?" Vivian swiped at her tears before tilting Emma's head to get a look at her neck. "You're hurt!"

"I'm okay. Reed stopped him before…" Emma's voice trailed off and her grip tightened on the baby. "Unfortunately, he got away."

"He won't be free for long," Reed interjected. "Whoever did this will be caught, I promise."

Emma spun toward him, her eyes widening. "Really? So it took him breaking in and attacking me before you decided to stop ignoring the situation?"

Sadie, sensitive to her owner's temperament, growled, and Reed eyed the dog with trepidation. He held up his hands in a sign of surrender. "I know you're upset—"

"I'm not upset. I'm furious." Her cheeks flushed. "Tonight could've been completely avoided if you'd taken the threats I reported seriously."

Reed stiffened as her words registered. His gaze snapped to hers. "Threats? What threats?"

"This is your last warning. Heyworth is not your home. Leave or you will be hurt."

The voice coming from Emma's cell phone sounded mechanical and distorted. It'd been half an hour since the attack, and she'd changed out of her wet pajamas, but chills still raced through her. She clasped her hands together to keep her fingers from trembling.

"The phone calls started shortly after I moved here. They weren't all like that one. In the beginning it was just hang-ups, sometimes heavy breathing. I brushed them off, but then things started happening on the property."

A muscle in Reed's jaw worked, and his shoulders were tight. He looked furious but when he spoke, his voice was calm. "What kinds of things?"

"Equipment was moved, flowerbeds destroyed. A couple of my patio chairs were broken. Small stuff. Annoying but not necessarily threatening."

He scrawled something in a small notebook.

Reed's chestnut-colored hair was darkened from the rain but still carried the faintest impression of a hat indention. A dusting of stubble hid the cleft in his chin.

She'd often thought of Reed over the years, but it'd been a surprise to discover he was the sheriff. Reed always talked about the day he'd leave Heyworth in his rearview mirror. It was one of the many things they'd fought over —her desire to return to the small town, his eagerness to never to see it again.

"You didn't report the phone calls or the things happening on the property?" he asked.

She bit her lip. "Not at first. It sounds foolish, I know, but I thought my cousin was doing it. Owen was dealing with a lot. First the death of his father, then the shock of learning about the inheritance."

"You felt bad for him." Reed's expression was sympathetic and nonjudgmental. "You were trying to give him the benefit of the doubt."

The understanding in his expression eased the guilt

and shame pressing down on her shoulders. "Yes. I figured if I ignored him, Owen would eventually tire of it and stop. But last week, things took a more serious turn. Someone left poisoned hamburger meat near the back patio."

"Why would Owen do that?"

"I think he was trying to kill Sadie."

At the sound of her name, the dog raised her head. Emma reached down and stroked her silky fur.

"He obviously didn't know Sadie has been trained not to eat food from anyone except me and Vivian. Unfortunately, an opossum found the untouched meat and died. That's how I knew it'd been poisoned."

Reed frowned, his glance flickering to the dog before settling back on Emma. "You trained Sadie to only take food from certain people?"

"It's a safety measure. She's a SAR dog." Short for Search and Rescue, Sadie was part of an elite class of canines trained to find missing people. "But that's not the reason why I filed a police report. Even if Sadie wasn't specially trained, she's my pet and my responsibility. Attempting to hurt her was crossing a line and not something I could ignore."

He nodded. "How many people know about Sadie's training?"

"It's not a secret." She smiled wryly. "Still not dialed into the town gossip, huh?"

"Not unless it pertains to a case." His mouth flattened. "I didn't know about Sadie, but your uncle told me about your husband. I'm very sorry, Emma."

"Thank you." A rush of unexpected tears caught her off guard. Emma blinked them back. Mark had been dead for almost two years, and still grief had a way of smacking her in the face. "While we're getting personal, Jeb also told me about your mom. And Bonnie."

Reed's mother had passed away from cancer. Shortly after that, his sister disappeared. The events had to be connected to his return home, but it didn't seem right to pry into his reasoning.

"Thank you." He cleared his throat before the corners of his mouth lifted. "Your uncle was a man of few words, but he had a way of sharing the most important ones."

"That he did." She paused, a sinking feeling settling in the pit of her stomach. "I was told by the desk clerk that you review every complaint but…you didn't know, did you?"

"No. If I had, something would've been done about it." Reed's words resonated with conviction.

She bit her lip. He'd saved her life, probably Lily's and Vivian's, too, and she'd thanked him with accusations and anger. "I'm so sorry—"

Reed held up a hand, cutting her off. "No, I'm the one who owes the apology. You were right to be angry. It's my job to protect you, and it didn't happen." He let out a breath. "I'm very grateful that you—that everyone—is okay."

Their eyes met. His were still the color of faded blue jeans. A flood of memories washed over her—church picnics, horseback rides and long talks by the lake. Emma felt a poignant stab at the loss of their friendship. But it hadn't escaped her notice that Reed had been avoiding her since she moved back to town. He'd nearly tripped over a paper towel rack in the grocery store trying to get away from her last week.

His behavior was the reason she believed her initial

complaint against Owen had gone uninvestigated. She'd been mistaken about that. But while she'd misjudged him as a sheriff, Emma wasn't wrong when it came to their relationship. It was obvious Reed didn't want to be friends. The knowledge hurt. She didn't want it to, but it did all the same.

"The latest threatening message…" he gestured to her cell phone still on the table between them "…when did you get it?"

"Sunday, the same day I filed the police report. I thought the bad thing he referred to in the message was the poisoned hamburger meat." She glanced toward the kitchen. "Clearly, I was wrong."

He frowned. "I'm not so sure you were. Come with me."

Reed led her into the living room. Sadie's nails tapped against the wooden floor as she trailed behind Emma.

The living room had been ransacked. Drawers hung open, books were thrown from the shelves and knick-knacks were knocked over. The little desk in the corner she used as an office had been torn apart. Paper littered the carpet.

She took a step farther inside, her legs trembling.

"Can you tell if anything is missing?" Reed asked.

She glanced around the room. "Without cleaning up, I can't be sure, but I do know my iPad is missing. It was sitting right there on my desk when I went to bed."

"And when you came downstairs, you didn't enter this room?"

"No, I went straight to the kitchen via the hallway."

She led him back to the banister and retraced her steps. Inside the kitchen, a deputy was dusting the doorknob for prints while another took photographs. Emma's gaze drifted over the broken bay window, the glass littering her kitchen floor and the shattered cookie jar. A coldness crept up her spine, stealing the breath from her lungs.

"Emma?" Reed stepped into her line of sight, dipping his head to catch her eyes. "We can stop for a minute if you need to."

"No. I'm fine." Emma realized she was absently rubbing her throat. She forced her hand down. "The attacker must have heard you or saw your flashlight, because he jumped off me and ran for the back door."

"Were you able to get a good look at him? Can you describe what he looks like?"

"No. It was dark, and he was wearing a ski mask. I didn't see anything." She scooted a leaf away with the edge of her tennis shoe. "I thought the branch had broken the window."

"He threw it inside to gain entry to the house." Reed glanced over his shoulder. "Then he went into the living room and started searching for stuff to steal. The noise from the thunderstorm would've covered his tracks."

"Except Sadie heard him moving around," she concluded.

"Yes. He probably saw you go right past the living room doorway to the kitchen. It spooked him, and he attacked."

"So you think it was a robbery then? Not something personal?"

His mouth tightened. "I don't know. I've got men out looking for Owen as we speak, but I don't want to jump to any conclusions. The threats could be connected to the break-in, or they could be two separate incidents. I'll know more once we're further into the investigation."

Vivian appeared in the doorway. She was dressed in jeans and a simple T-shirt, her hair piled on her head in a messy bun. On her hip, Lily bounced, stretching her arms toward her mother.

"She's tired, but I think she wants Mama," Vivian explained.

Emma took her daughter into her arms. She breathed in Lily's sweet smell, the familiar weight of her thirteen-month-old baby a reminder of her obligations and blessings.

Thank you, Lord, for protecting my family and for sending Reed in time.

The prayer soothed her, but it couldn't erase the dread as she surveyed the destruction in the kitchen. Could this have been a simple break-in gone terribly wrong? Or had Owen finally decided to take his opportunity to get rid of her once and for all?

THREE

Heyworth Sheriff's Department was a small red-bricked building tucked between the courthouse and a park. Midafternoon sunlight sparkled off the glass windows. Reed pulled into the parking lot and killed the engine. The scent of french fries from the diner across the street tickled his nose. His stomach growled. It was well past lunchtime and he hadn't eaten, but there wasn't time right now.

"Hey, Sheriff." Cathy, his daytime receptionist/dispatcher, handed him a stack of messages. "How's Owen?"

"Still in the hospital." It'd only taken an hour for Reed's deputies to locate Owen Tillman in the parking lot of a local bar. However, Owen was so inebriated, he had to be rushed to the hospital. Alcohol poisoning had nearly killed him. It had taken hours before Reed could question Emma's cousin about the break-in. "Is Deputy Shadwick here yet?"

She wrinkled her nose. "Waiting at his desk."

Reed went through the swinging half door separating the lobby from the rest of the department. "Shadwick," he called out. "My office. Now."

Reed ignored the attention from the others in the bull pen, his entire focus on the man marching to his office. Bald with a chubby face covered in a thick beard, Dean Shadwick was dressed in a vest covered with fishing lures and wading boots. His mouth was tight and his body vibrated with tension, like an angry hornet, but he did his best to plaster on a look of veiled concern.

"I'm not in uniform because Cathy told me to come right in," Dean said, once they were both inside Reed's office. His eyes narrowed. "I was fishing on the lake when she called."

"I'll get right to the point." Reed circled around the broad expanse of his desk and set the stack of messages down. He purposefully didn't sit. "Did Emma Pierce file a complaint with you last Sunday?"

"Is that why you called me in?" Dean took his time settling into the visitor's chair. He stretched out his legs and crossed his arms over his paunch. "She did come into the station. I listened to her story."

Reed clamped down on his rising temper. He'd inherited most of his deputies when he took over as sheriff nine months ago. Dean was one of them. "And?"

"The phone calls seemed like a prank to me. A couple of weird things happened on the property, but they could be explained a hundred different ways." Dean waved a hand as if flicking away an annoying pest. "She was making wild accusations. Mentioned someone might be involved in poisoning her dog. Ridiculous."

"Deputy, I can't help but wonder if this report disappeared because Emma mentioned her cousin Owen as a possible suspect. I've seen the two of you around town, and I know you go hunting together."

"That has nothing to do with it." Dean glared at him. "I made a judgment call—"

"Which wasn't yours to make. It was mine."

The idea that someone's complaint had gone uninvestigated and a person had almost *died* as a result pushed every one of Reed's hot buttons, as a lawman and a human being. He knew firsthand what lackadaisical police work could do to a case. If the former sheriff had taken Bonnie's disappearance more seriously in the beginning, Reed's sister might not still be missing. He wouldn't allow another case in Heyworth to fall through the cracks. Not on his watch.

"Due to your incompetence, Emma was attacked last night in her home and nearly killed."

"What?" Dean paled. He swallowed hard. "Is she… I mean, is she all right?"

His deputy's shock and concern seemed genuine, which tampered Reed's anger a touch. "Thankfully, no one was seriously hurt. This time. But if you'd filed the report and we had investigated properly, the attack on Emma might've been prevented. You are suspended, Deputy, without pay for two months. After that, you will be on probation for the next year. Desk duty with an overseeing deputy watching over you."

Dean shot to his feet. "That's insane!"

"Count your blessings. I could fire you."

Dean's mouth popped open as if he was going to say something, but Reed's glare stopped him. The deputy's lips flattened into a hard line and his nostrils flared.

"Let this be a lesson to you." Reed softened his tone. "Don't let your personal feelings cloud your professional duty."

"You can't seriously think Owen had anything to

do with the attack on Emma." Heat tinged the tips of Dean's ears bright red. "He's got a temper but he isn't stupid."

"It doesn't matter what I think. If Owen was innocent, an investigation would've proven it. You messed up, Deputy, by trying to protect your friend. You're dismissed."

Dean left his office with the flurry of a five-year-old in the midst of a temper tantrum. Reed watched through the blinds of his office window as Dean stormed out. Reed felt no guilt at the punishment he'd doled out, but neither did he take pleasure in it.

Austin Carter, his cousin and chief deputy, appeared in the doorway. His dark hair was cut military short. A faint scar, etched out by an errant bicycle handle when he was eight, marred his upper right cheek. "Hey, Emma's here. She came into the department while you were talking to Deputy Shadwick."

Reed's brow furrowed. "Is she okay?"

"Fine, but she wants to talk to you. She's waiting in the break room. I didn't think it would be a good idea for her and Dean to cross paths, all things considered."

"Thanks." Reed hesitated. "Did you tell her anything about Owen being in the hospital? Or the developments in the case?"

"No. I figured it would be easier coming from you."

Reed walked quickly down the hall. Emma was standing next to the window in the break room. She turned at the sound of his approach, her lips tipped up in a smile. Sunlight caressed the elegant curves of her face and brought out the red highlights in her dark hair. She was dressed simply, in jeans and a T-shirt, but it only made her beauty that much more striking. Reed's breath hitched.

"Hi," she said. "Sorry to barge in on you like this, but I cleaned up the mess from the break-in and discovered something else was stolen."

"Of course." His gaze dropped to her neck. Bruises marred the delicate skin, and his gut clenched. Emma was special, a piece of his childhood and his first love. But he needed to keep his emotions in check and his head in the game. Otherwise, he might make a mistake on the case. "What is it?"

She reached into her purse and pulled out a photograph. Her hands were slender, the tips of her fingers long and the nails unpainted. "Uncle Jeb's gold pen was taken. It's not extremely valuable, although I'm sure you could sell it to a pawn shop for several hundred dollars." She handed him the photograph. "He used it to sign the deed to the original property. This is a picture taken on that day. Sorry, I don't have a close up of the actual pen."

"That's okay. Was anything else taken besides the iPad and pen?"

"No, that's it. Were you able to find Owen and talk to him?"

"Yes." He hesitated. The last thing he wanted to do was worry Emma, but he had to tell her the truth. "There's a strong possibility Owen isn't behind the attack, Emma. The perpetrator might be someone else."

Emma blindly reached out and grabbed the back of a chair as the implication of Reed's words slammed into her with the force of a freight train. "Are you sure?"

"Owen has an alibi for last night. The bartender at

the Silver Spur said your cousin was there from six o'clock in the evening until closing time."

Her mind raced. As frightening as it was to have Owen stalking her, it was exponentially worse to have a stranger doing it. "My house is only five miles from the bar. Could Owen have slipped out without the bartender knowing?"

"I considered that, but the amount of alcohol Owen drank last night would make it nearly impossible for him to have the coordination and wherewithal to break in to your house." Reed took a deep breath. "My deputies discovered Owen in the parking lot of the Silver Spur this morning suffering from alcohol poisoning. He had to be rushed to the hospital."

She pulled the chair out and sank into it. "Is he okay?"

"Thankfully, yes. The doctor said there was a strong possibility he could've died if we hadn't been out looking for him and gotten him to the hospital in time."

Emma closed her eyes as a rush of pain radiated through her chest. Her relationship with Owen hadn't always been so rocky. They'd been close as children. "I'll contact my uncle's attorney and have him pay Owen a visit. I didn't get all of the inheritance. Uncle Jeb set up a trust for Owen. He'll receive it if he goes to rehab and remains sober for a year."

Maybe this time her cousin would take the help. She feared if he didn't, Owen's addiction would kill him.

Reed pulled out the chair across from her and sat down. "Did you know Jeb was going to name you in his will?"

"No, although he must've been thinking about it for a long time. We often talked about my hopes and dreams for the future, especially after Mark was killed in combat. It was in my plans to move to Heyworth before Lily started school, but I wanted to save up money to open Helping Paws first."

His brow furrowed. "Helping Paws? What's that?"

"It's the nonprofit organization I'm starting. Search-and-rescue dogs have been a passion of mine since vet school. I adopted Sadie five years ago and got my certification to be a trainer. It was always my dream to start a SAR canine-training facility. The goal is to train and provide SAR dogs to law enforcement and fire departments at no charge."

"That's amazing. The nearest SAR dog we have is more than three hours away. I haven't been able to convince the county to set aside the funds to purchase one."

"You aren't alone. There's a serious shortage of SAR dogs and most law enforcement departments in rural communities don't have the money to purchase them. Which is frustrating. Dogs like Sadie save lives. That's why I'm so passionate about this project. But a facility like the one I want to create takes a significant amount of income to get off the ground. You need the buildings and all of that, but the biggest expense is the land."

"You need a large area to do the training."

She nodded. "Uncle Jeb wrote me a personal letter, which he gave to the probate attorney. In it, he encouraged me to use his ranch to build Helping Paws."

She was deeply saddened by Uncle Jeb's death, but the opportunity he'd provided wasn't something she could pass up. It would've taken far longer to get her organization started without the inheritance.

Reed drummed his fingers on the table. "Can you think of anyone who might want to hurt you?"

"No." She bit her lip. "Everyone in Heyworth has been so welcoming, and other than Owen, I haven't had any altercations with anyone."

She got up from the table and went over to the window. In the park nearby, she spotted Vivian pushing Lily in the baby swing. Her daughter's chubby hands clung to the seat, and she kicked her legs in joy.

"What am I going to do, Reed? I have a child to protect and a criminal stalking me." She crossed her arms over her chest, hugging herself. "Vivian packed up her life to follow me to Heyworth, to help me raise Lily and get Helping Paws off the ground. I've already sunk most of my savings into making improvements on Uncle Jeb's land and getting the necessary equipment. God put this mission in my heart, and I want to see it through."

"And you will."

She turned. Reed came up close. His chin jutted out and his shoulders were squared. Emma knew that look. She'd seen it many times before, usually at the beginning of an argument. Reed was stubborn as a mule when he set his mind to something.

"I'm going to get to the bottom of this," he continued. "In the meantime, a deputy will be watching your property day and night. My top priority is keeping you and your family safe."

Some of the tightness left her chest. She took a deep breath. "Thank you, Reed. I can't tell you how much better it makes me feel to have you working on this."

"I'm glad. I want you to know you're safe. Heyworth is your home." He reached out and touched her arm. "This is where you belong."

Warmth spread though her. Emma's childhood had

been spent bouncing from place to place behind a mother who flitted through life like a hummingbird. She'd gone through thirty schools, dozens of friends and a handful of stepfathers. Coming to stay with Uncle Jeb the summer before her first year in college had been like a breath of fresh air. She'd fallen in love with Heyworth. The townsfolk all called each other by name, brought casseroles when a baby was born or a relative died, and told the same stories dozens of times.

Emma had vowed a long time ago to set her roots down in this town. There were only a handful of people who knew about her dream to live here. Reed was one of them. That he remembered touched her deeply.

It also set off alarm bells. Reed had made it clear he didn't want to be friends. The break-in had forced an interaction, but there was still an awkwardness to it, as if neither of them could navigate the new waters they found themselves in. She wasn't quite sure how to address it.

Will Norton stepped into the break room. Tall and handsome, with blond hair and the physique of a quarterback, Will was the golden boy of Heyworth. His uncle was a judge and he'd followed the family tradition by becoming the county's prosecutor.

Will paused midstep and his gaze flickered from Emma to Reed and back again. "Oh, uh, sorry to interrupt. Austin told me you guys were back here."

Emma's cheeks heated as she suddenly became aware of how closely she and Reed were standing to each other. She jumped back. "No, you aren't interrupting anything. How are you, Will?"

"Fine. Although I think I should be asking you that

question. I heard about the break-in at your place. Are you okay?"

"Yes. Thanks to Reed, no one was hurt."

"I heard. Nice job, Sheriff." Will ran a hand down his silk tie. He looked like he'd just come from court, dressed in a crisply pressed shirt and slacks. "Do you have any suspects?"

"We're taking a hard look at Owen, but he has an alibi." Reed gave a quick version of the information he'd uncovered during his investigation. "Emma's been receiving threats, and I suspect the break-in is connected to those."

"Hmm…" Will rocked back on his heels. "Did you consider any of the people who wanted to buy Jeb's property?"

Reed's eyebrows shot up. "You had offers to buy the land, Emma?"

"I did, but I never considered them seriously." She frowned. "You think someone might be trying to scare me into selling?"

"It's a possibility. Who made offers?"

"My uncle did," Will said. "That's what made me think of it."

Emma nodded. "There was only one other person. It was my other neighbor, the one on the south side. What's his name? Joshua something or other."

Reed stiffened. "Joshua Lowe."

"Yeah. That's it. Why, do you know him?"

Reed shared a look with Will. "You could say that."

FOUR

Reed knew Joshua Lowe well, but not because they were friends. Joshua was a small-time criminal and the town bad boy. He'd claimed to have changed his ways and was trying to be a respectable rancher, but reputations were hard to shake.

Joshua had also been secretly dating Bonnie at the time of her disappearance. Almost no one had known about the relationship, including Reed. That Bonnie kept it a secret wasn't surprising, considering Joshua's notoriety. But it hurt Reed all the same when he'd learned about it while retracing Bonnie's last steps on the night of her disappearance.

Bonnie and Joshua had made a plan to run away together. They were supposed to meet at a local park. Joshua claimed when he arrived, Bonnie wasn't there. He tried calling her, but she didn't answer.

Reed didn't believe him. Joshua refused to answer any questions about where he was in the hours prior to or directly after driving to the park. That fact, coupled with his criminal history, made Joshua the prime suspect in Bonnie's disappearance.

Given their history, it wasn't wise for Reed to interview Joshua by himself. He arranged for one of his best deputies to meet him on the ranch. Deputy Kyle Hendricks climbed out of his patrol car with a grunt.

"How ya doing, Sheriff?"

"Fine." Reed shook Kyle's hand. "Thanks for coming."

They located Joshua in the barn. He'd backed a dented farm truck up to the double doors and was loading hay bales into the bed. The thirty-year-old looked nothing like an all-American rancher. His long hair was pulled back into a man bun and tattoos covered his arms from shoulder to wrist.

"Joshua," Kyle called out as they approached.

Joshua turned and lifted a hand to block out the sun. His gaze settled on Kyle first, before jumping to Reed. Something flickered in the depths of his dark eyes but disappeared behind a shuttered expression of indifference.

He resumed loading his hay, tossing it with ease. "Deputy Hendricks. Sheriff. What can I do for you?"

Out of habit, Reed glanced in the cab of the truck. It was worn—the passenger seat ripped and the stereo missing—but there was no obvious contraband or drugs. "We need to talk with you about a recent attack."

Joshua stilled. "What kind of attack?"

"I'm surprised you haven't heard."

"I don't listen to gossip, Sheriff. I've been on the wrong end of it one too many times to pay it any mind."

There was a kernel of truth to the statement. Joshua had brought on his own troubles, but many of his exploits had been exaggerated by the townsfolk. Some were flat-out false. Reed suspected that if Joshua's mother wasn't still living in town, he would've left

Heyworth a long time ago. "Emma Pierce's home was broken into, and she was nearly killed."

Joshua met Reed's gaze. "And you think I had something to do with it?"

"Did you?"

Joshua's jaw tightened. "No." He threw another hay bale into the truck with more force than necessary. "Why would I?"

"You put in an offer to buy her property after Jeb died, son." Kyle plucked a piece of hay out of the nearest bale and placed it in between his teeth. "A sizeable one. I spoke to Emma's attorney. He said you upped it to nearly double what the land is worth. And since Emma moved in, she's been having trouble with a stalker."

Joshua snorted. "So what? You think I got mad she wouldn't sell to me, so I decided to terrorize her into it? And when that didn't work, I broke into her home and tried to kill her?"

"Your interest in the property gives you motive. Where were you last night?"

"Home." Joshua raised a gloved hand. "And before you ask, no one can confirm it. I was by myself." He leaned against the truck and muttered something about never being left alone, before taking a deep breath. "Yes, I did offer to purchase Jeb's property after he died. I'm trying to expand my cattle-rearing operation and I need land to do it. Judge Norton has already told me many times that he isn't willing to sell any more of his property."

The Norton family had sold Joshua a piece of their land, but he was boxed in on three sides by the rest of their ranch. His only other neighbor was Emma to the south.

"However, when Emma turned me down," Joshua continued, "I made inquiries into buying the property Old Man Franklin has for sale."

Reed's gaze narrowed. "When did you do that?"

"Last week."

That was convenient. Joshua was smart and this wasn't his first run-in with the law. Reed wasn't going to let him off the hook so easily. "If you were willing to buy another piece of land, then why offer so much for Emma's?"

"Because having the property next to mine would've been far better. Since Emma refused to sell, I didn't have many other options available. Old Man Franklin's land is three miles away, which makes it a nuisance, but the price is right."

"Has your offer been accepted?"

"We're still negotiating, but I figure things will be settled by the end of next week. I have absolutely no motive for wanting to run Emma off her land, nor would I ever hurt her."

Reed scoffed. "You'll have to excuse us if we don't take your word for it."

Joshua's cheeks, already flushed with exertion, darkened to a deep red. "I'm many things, Sheriff, but I'm not a liar."

"We both know that's a load of baloney. You refused to answer all of my questions about Bonnie's disappearance."

"Which is my right, under the law. That doesn't make me a liar. I've already told you everything I know. Bonnie and I were supposed to meet that night. I was running late. When I got to the park, she was gone." Joshua fished a set of keys from his pocket. "If you'll excuse me, I have cattle to feed."

He marched toward the driver's side of the truck but paused with his hand on the door. Without turning around, he said loud enough for Reed to hear, "No matter what you think, I loved Bonnie."

Joshua climbed into the old truck and the engine sputtered to life. Dust flew out behind the vehicle as he sped across the pasture.

Reed watched him go, uncertainty settling into his gut like a bad meal. "We need to follow up with Old Man Franklin."

"Agreed." Kyle unearthed a handkerchief and mopped his brow. "I'll stop by there on my way back to headquarters, although if what Joshua's saying checks out, he doesn't have a motive for wanting Emma off her land."

"Or he could be smart enough to make an offer on Franklin's property to make it *look* like he doesn't have a motive. Let's check with Old Man Franklin and take it from there."

Kyle and Reed walked back to their vehicles. Kyle drove off, but Reed slowed his SUV and pulled over to the side of the road. He took a deep breath to calm his rattled nerves. Joshua's words echoed in his mind.

I loved Bonnie.

Loved. Past tense. As if Joshua somehow knew she was dead.

Reed squeezed his eyes shut. He wouldn't go down that path until it was a certainty. Joshua's word choice cast doubt on his innocence, but that was nothing new.

As if of its own volition, Reed's hand reached for the cell phone hanging from his belt. He flipped through the messages to the right one and hit Play. His sister's voice came from the speaker.

"Hey, Reed. I was hoping you would be able to answer. You're probably working a big case or planning a stakeout or something. My big brother, the crime fighter. Listen, I really need to talk to you about something important. Can you call me back ASAP? It's urgent. Thanks. Love you."

Bonnie's tone was resigned, as if she'd somehow known he wouldn't return her call for hours. It reverberated inside him, mingling with the guilt and the frustration, until he wanted to exit his vehicle and punch a tree. Instead, he took a deep breath. Then another. His gaze drifted to the rearview mirror and the reflection of the ranch behind him.

Joshua had a motive for wanting Emma gone. Trying to scare her off the property so she would sell wasn't a far-fetched proposition. Still, Reed couldn't let his emotions get the better of him. Bonnie's case was separate from Emma's, and right now, Emma's had priority.

Two days after the break-in, Emma was trying to settle back into a normal routine. The attack and the threats kept crowding into her mind. True to his word, Reed had kept a deputy stationed at her house. There hadn't been any threatening phone calls and nothing on the ranch had been disturbed, which should have eased her worries but only put her on edge. She couldn't shake the feeling something bad was going to happen.

Emma threw a tennis ball and Sadie, nothing more than a flash of golden fur, streaked across the grass. She caught the ball midair. Her doggie grin was evident even across the distance separating them. They'd just finished a search-and-rescue training session. Another night of thunderstorms had left the ground muddy and Sadie would need a bath now, but Emma was grateful for the distraction.

Sadie dropped the ball at her feet. Emma picked it up. "One last throw and then it's bath time for you. Vivian and Lily are going to be back from the grocery store soon."

The dog pranced in anticipation. Emma hurled the ball and Sadie took off. The wind shifted, rustling the hair on the nape of Emma's neck. A creepy sensation of being watched flooded her.

She turned and peered into the trees, but nothing moved. She shook her head. Her imagination was running away with her.

"Ms. Pierce?"

Emma screamed and jumped, whirling around.

Deputy Jack Irving stood nearby. He lifted his hands. "Hey, hey. Are you okay?"

She closed her eyes, putting a hand on her chest. Her heart thundered against her palm. "I didn't hear you coming. Sorry for screaming. I've been a bit jumpy the last couple of days."

"After everything that's been going on, I don't blame you." He offered her a sympathetic smile. "I came out to tell you it's shift change now. Deputy Miller is taking over. He'll do a perimeter check first, so you won't see his car for a while. I didn't want you to worry."

"Thank you. That's very kind. Have a good night, Deputy."

He tipped his hat to her. "You, too, ma'am."

She watched him drive off and checked her watch. Reed should be arriving soon. He'd called earlier and asked if he could come by to give her an update on the case.

Sadie rolled around on the grass. Her paws, caked with dried mud, wriggled in the air. Emma chuckled. "Okay, you. Fun time's over."

She hooked a leash to Sadie's collar and brought her over to the hose. The dog's steps dragged as she realized what was about to happen. Emma dropped a kiss between her eyes. "It'll be quick. I promise." She tied Sadie to the porch post. "Stay right here and I'll run inside to grab the shampoo."

She retrieved it in a flash, pausing to make sure the new front door was closed securely behind her.

Sadie barked.

Emma spun and her heart stuttered.

Owen was standing on the bottom porch step. His face was mottled with rage, his eyes narrowed to tiny slits. "What exactly do you think you're doing, going to the sheriff and accusin' me of things?"

She took a step back, but there was nowhere to go. Owen had her trapped. She glanced around desperately but didn't see Deputy Miller's vehicle. He was probably still doing a perimeter check. Emma broke out into a sweat and the taste of her own fear, sharp and metallic, filled her mouth.

"I didn't say—"

"Liar!" Owen slammed his hand against the railing.

On the other side of the porch, Sadie went crazy. She barked, straining against the leash.

"You told them I was sending you threatening messages, that I tried to attack you."

Swallowing past the terror clogging her throat, Emma tried to keep her voice calm and authoritative.

"I told the sheriff you were angry with me over the inheritance. I didn't lie or accuse you of anything."

He came up the porch steps. Emma squeezed her hand around her house keys. They cut into her palm. Yes! She wasn't completely defenseless.

"This house, this land…" Owen gestured widely "… it's mine. It belongs to me."

She maneuvered a key in between her fingers. A makeshift weapon. Not great, but it could still do some damage. "How did you get past the deputy, Owen?"

He blinked, caught off guard by her question. "I cut through the woods."

The woods? The same place she'd felt someone watching her. It was also the same place the intruder had run to the other night. Owen had an alibi for the break-in, but that didn't clear him of the phone calls or the destruction around the property. Could more than one person be involved? A cold trickle of sweat dripped down her back.

"It's time for you to go, Owen. I don't want you here."

"You don't get to decide that."

He stepped closer. The scent of whiskey poured off his skin like a bad cologne. Emma fought the urge to gag.

"You're the thief here." He jabbed a finger at her. "You're the fraud. I'm not going to let you take what should be mine!"

He was so close she could see the individual threads of red in his bloodshot eyes. His breath was hot and rancid.

Emma tightened her grip on her keys. She didn't want to hurt him, but she would if she had to.

Jutting her chin, she looked him in the eye. "I said you need to go."

FIVE

Reed heard the barking first. It was insistent and alarming, growing louder as he took the turn into Emma's drive. Sadie was tied to the side of the porch. She strained against her leash. Reed quickly ascertained the dog's problem.

Owen.

The man had Emma cornered and was screaming in her face. The sight made Reed's blood run hot.

He radioed for the deputy patrolling Emma's property and slammed on his brakes. As he shoved the truck into Park, Sadie broke free of her collar. The dog bounded onto the porch and with a flying leap, tackled Owen. He let out a scream as Sadie's jaws clamped down on his arm and he stumbled backward down the stairs. Sadie didn't let go. The dog dragged Owen to the ground.

Reed raced across the yard, pulling out his handcuffs. "Call her off, Emma."

She gave a command, and Sadie immediately released Owen. Tears ran down the man's face as he cursed up a storm. Reed flipped him over and slapped the cuffs on him. "Owen Tillman, you are under arrest for trespassing, criminal threatening, public intoxication and anything else I can think to throw at you."

"What are you doing?" Owen screamed. "Her dog attacked me, and you're arresting me. I need to go to a hospital. Call an ambulance."

Emma appeared with a first aid kit in her hands. Reed shook his head. "We'll get the EMTs to do it. You don't have to."

"It'll take time for them to arrive. He's hurt. It might be his fault, but I'm not going to let him go untreated. He's bleeding pretty badly."

Owen glared at Emma. "Don't you dare touch me, you—"

Reed added some pressure to Owen's hurt arm and he cut off in a yelp.

A patrol car raced up the driveway. Deputy Miller clambered out. "I was on the far side of the ranch checking out the old barn for any recent activity. I'm so sorry."

"It's not your fault," Emma said, quickly reassuring him. "You can't be everywhere at once."

Reed hauled Owen to his feet. "Take this man to the hospital for treatment of his arm and to get him sobered up."

Owen screamed and cursed the entire way to the patrol car. The glare he shot Emma from the back of the vehicle iced Reed's blood. It also made him question everything he knew about this case.

Emma sat on the porch steps. The wind rustled her hair, blowing some strands across her forehead. Her face was pale and her body trembled. She stroked Sadie, who was tucked up next to her side.

"Are you okay?" Reed asked. "Did he hurt you?"

"No, he just scared me." She smiled weakly. "We have got to stop meeting like this."

"I couldn't agree more." He picked up the first aid kit from the step and fished out a cold pack. He activated it. "Put your head down to your knees."

She waved him off with a shaky hand. "I'm fine—"

"You're crashing from the adrenaline, Em." The old term of endearment slipped out of his mouth before he could catch it. He pushed Emma's head gently toward her knees and parted the silky strands of her hair, placing the cold pack on the back of her neck. "You pass out on the porch steps, and Vivian will read me the riot act for sure."

Sadie licked Reed's arm. He patted her on the head. "And you are such a good girl. What a hero. I'm buying you a box of doggie treats." He sat on the porch step on the other side of Emma. "Where is Vivian? And Lily?"

"They went to the grocery store. I messaged them while I was inside getting the first aid kit to make sure they were okay." She sucked in a deep breath, then another, before lowering the ice pack from her neck. "I feel better now. I don't know why that shook me so much."

"Owen is family. It's far more personal."

She nodded, twisting the ice pack in her hands. "Reed, Owen told me he cut through the woods to get onto the property. It's the same place the intruder escaped on the night I was attacked. Do you think it's possible Owen is working with someone?"

"It's something to consider. Owen doesn't hang out with a law-abiding crowd, and while he doesn't have the cash to hire someone to break into your house, your iPad and Uncle Jeb's pen may have been payment enough." His jaw tightened. "This little stunt he pulled gives me enough probable cause to get a search warrant for his phone records. I'm also going to question his friends again. If Owen did arrange for someone to break into your home, I'll find out."

He wasn't going to take Joshua off the suspect list either. Owen's attack just now was reckless and impulsive. It was in line with his personality and fit with a pattern of addiction. However, the stalking and break-in had been planned and well orchestrated. Reed wasn't sure Owen had the patience or discipline to pull off the criminal acts.

"How did your interview with Joshua go yesterday?" Emma asked, cutting into his thoughts.

"Joshua admitted he wanted to purchase the property, but when you refused to sell, he made an offer on another piece of land. Deputy Hendricks spoke to the other buyer—Old Man Franklin—and confirmed it."

"Well, that's a relief." Emma rose from the step and smiled down at Sadie. "You might be a hero, sweetie, but you're also still muddy."

"You aren't going to give this poor dog a bath after all her hard work."

"Afraid so." Her mouth twitched. "Wanna help?"

"Oh, no. She and I are working on becoming friends. I'm not about to mess that up by dousing her in soap and water. Besides, I have my own work to do."

Her brow crinkled. "You do?"

"I noticed you don't have floodlights on your house, so I went to the hardware store and picked some up."

Reed opened the rear of his SUV and pulled out a couple sacks from the local hardware store. He set them on the grass. "It's a bit presumptuous of me and I hope you don't mind, but the lights will make it easier for the deputies to see the yard."

"I don't mind at all. I appreciate you thinking of it." She smiled at him before patting Sadie on the head. "Come on, girl. Bath time for you." She started to turn away.

"Uh, wait." Reed reached out to stop her, his fingertips brushing along the soft skin of her arm. He jerked his hand back. Emma frowned, a flash of hurt crossing her pretty features.

Lord, I could really use some help here.

He didn't want to act on his attraction to Emma, but he didn't want an underlying tension between them either. Problem was, Reed wasn't great at dealing with the emotional baggage in his life. His sister had always been the one to steer him in the right direction. It was times like these he missed Bonnie's advice more than ever.

"Listen, Emma, I know things are a bit awkward between us and I don't want them to be." He shoved his hands in his pockets. "We're going to run into each other, not just in town, but also professionally. It's only a matter of time before we need you and Sadie to aid in a search. I hope...well, I hope we can be friends."

"Reed, you saved my life. I'm pretty sure that places you on the friend list permanently."

"Oh." The knot in his stomach loosened. "Good, cuz I could really use another set of hands to help me hang these lights."

She laughed. "Well, then you're going to have to help me bathe Sadie."

"Sorry, pup. She wrestled me into it." Sadie barked twice, and Reed nodded. "Right you are. Two boxes of cookies."

Emma laughed again. This time, Reed joined in, some of the weight pressing on his shoulders dropping away. He'd tackled one problem.

Now, he just needed to figure out who was stalking Emma and why.

Lily banged her tiny fists on her high chair tray and babbled.

"Hold on, little one." Emma snagged a slice of cornbread and broke it into pieces over the tray. Lily promptly fisted the crumbs and shoved them into her mouth. In the corner, Sadie snored on her bed.

Vivian handed Emma a set of plates for the table and some cutlery. "So what are you going to do about Owen?"

"Reed's going to continue his investigation, but he also recommends I take out a restraining order. Although Owen's been arrested for his actions today, it doesn't prevent him from making bail or being released from jail later. It's clear I have to do something."

"I'm glad he's taking these threats against you seriously."

"Me, too." Emma frowned. "You gave me one plate too many."

"No, I didn't. I invited Reed to dinner while you were giving Lily her bath." Vivian wiped her hands on her apron. "He ran home to clean up, but he should be here any minute."

Emma recognized the gleam in her sister-in-law's eyes. Heat crept into her cheeks. "Don't start matchmaking, Vivi."

"I have no idea what you're talking about. I merely invited the sheriff to dinner. It's the polite thing to do, considering he saved our lives." Vivian turned on the stove and picked up a spoon to stir the gravy. "But since you brought it up, I did recognize his name. He's *the* Reed. Your first love."

"That was a long time ago. A lot has changed since then."

"So what? A little romance never hurt anyone."

"Been there, Vivi, done that. And I have the broken heart to prove it."

"I know you do." Vivian sighed. "But Mark wouldn't want you to pine for him for the rest of your life. He's been gone two years. You've mourned him longer than you were married."

It was true. They'd dated, gotten engaged and were married all within eight months. Emma often wondered if the loss was more poignant because of the short time she'd had with Mark. She'd been robbed of lazy Sunday afternoons, the chance to see him go gray at the temples, the deepening of their blooming love into something as endless as the ocean. It all died with Mark, leaving her pregnant, with a chest of empty dreams.

Vivian removed the gravy from the stovetop. "I think you could do a lot worse than a handsome lawman. I mean, think of the stories you'll tell your grandchildren. He literally rescued you like a knight in shining armor."

Emma rolled her eyes. "You've been watching too many movies. Reed and I are just friends."

"Downplay it all you want, but I've seen the way Reed looks at you. Mark my words there's something there."

A knock came from the front door and Vivi waggled her eyebrows. "That's for you."

Emma pointed a finger at her sister-in-law as she moved toward the living room. "Behave."

Sadie trailed behind her to the door, tail wagging. Emma swiped her hands on her jeans as a few butterflies fluttered in her stomach. "Don't be silly," she muttered to the dog. "It's just Reed. We spent hours with him this afternoon hanging the lights and talking about the case."

Reed turned on the stoop when she opened the door, his lips tipped up into a smile, and those traitorous butterflies took flight. He'd changed out of his uniform into a denim button-down shirt the same shade as his eyes. It molded over his broad shoulders. "Hey."

Her throat tightened painfully, but she managed to choke out a greeting. His boots thumped on the tile entryway and the scent of his soap, warm and piney, wafted in her direction.

Sadie barked. Reed patted her on the head. "No treats yet, girl. I didn't have time to go to the store."

He lifted a mysterious tinfoil-covered object in his other hand. "I brought my Aunt Bessie's apple pie. She makes extras for me and I keep them in the freezer. If we pop it in the oven now, it'll be ready in time for dessert."

"That's perfect."

Emma escorted him into the kitchen. She busied herself with turning on the oven and setting the pie inside while Reed greeted Vivian and Lily. The next few minutes were a rush of final preparations, pouring iced tea into the glasses and grabbing extra napkins. Then they all gathered around the table and Emma said grace.

"Everything looks delicious." Reed picked up his fork. "Thank you for the invitation."

"After all you've done, I think we owe you a couple of home-cooked meals," Vivian said with a smile. "Emma tells me you're from Heyworth. How long—"

Sadie barked. Then she growled, the hair on the back of her neck standing on end.

Reed shot out of the chair. His hand flew to the gun holstered at his waist. "Stay here." Within three strides, he was at the back door. "Lock this behind me."

He disappeared into the night. Emma flicked the lock before grabbing a knife from a block on the counter. She ushered Vivian and Lily into the large walk-in pantry, shutting the door behind them and planting herself in front of it.

"Stay," she ordered Sadie. "Guard."

The dog stood next to Emma. Moments ticked by, the tension building with every passing breath. Where was Reed? Was he okay? Emma whispered out a prayer for his safety.

Sadie's ears perked as a scraping sound came from the back door. A shadowy figure appeared. The new motion detection spotlight they'd installed clicked on, but from this angle Emma couldn't see through the panes of glass in the door. She tightened her hold on the knife.

"Emma, it's me."

She let out a sigh of relief and hurried to unlock the back door for Reed.

"I checked around the house, but it's secure," he said. "None of the other motion detection lights went on." Reed's gaze dropped to Sadie. "Is it possible she was barking at an animal? I spotted some tracks that looked like opossums."

"It is. Sadie's well trained, but she's used to living in the city."

Then again, it could be more than that. Reed didn't say so, but he didn't have to. Emma instinctively understood that someone could've been out there, hidden in the woods just beyond the house.

The pantry door squeaked open and Vivian poked her head out. "Is it safe?"

"Yes." Emma took another breath to slow her racing heart. She set the knife down in the sink. "Turns out Sadie was probably scared of some opossums."

Vivian let out a bark of laughter. "Well...nothing like a little excitement to go with dinner."

Lily gave a screech of displeasure and leaned toward the table.

"Right, you are, Lily," Reed said. "I'm starving, too. Let's eat."

Emma didn't think she could stand to put a bite of food in her mouth. Her stomach was aching. But she joined them at the table anyway.

"Vivian, did Emma ever tell you about the time she attempted to make Uncle Jeb some eggs?" Reed's mouth curled up and he made a point to stare at the kitchen ceiling. "I'm certain they're still baked into the paint."

They all laughed, the tension easing. From there, dinner was a series of stories punctuated by Lily banging on her high chair for more food.

When they were all stuffed, Vivian rose from her chair and started to clear the table. Emma got up to help her, waving Reed back down into his seat. "It'll only take a few minutes. Rest."

Emma rinsed off the dishes and stuck them into the

dishwasher before pulling the pie out of the oven. She carried it to the table, her footsteps faltering.

Reed had removed Lily from her high chair. Her head rested against Reed's chest and her tiny hand played with a button on his shirt. He was murmuring something to her, his deep voice soothing but too low to hear the actual words. Sadie lay at his feet.

Something inside Emma's chest twisted, perilously close to her heart. Lily had never known her father. Seeing the little girl cuddled up to Reed sent a wave of mixed emotions churning through Emma.

Vivian came up behind her, gently squeezing her arm, before taking the pie from her hands. "This is beautiful but looks too hot to eat at the moment." She set it on the table. "And Ms. Lily is looking tired. I'll take her to bed while we wait for the pie to cool." She lifted Lily from Reed's arms and bustled out of the room.

Emma backed toward the kitchen. "I'm gonna wash the pots while we wait."

"I'll help you by drying." Reed rose and joined her at the sink. He picked up a dish towel. "I noticed the construction you're doing on the north side of the property. Is that going to be the training facility?"

"Yep. I'll do the initial training with the dogs, but once they're ready to be paired with a handler, there has to be additional training with them together. The handler will have to stay for a few weeks. I want to make that process as easy as possible, so I'm building small homes for them on the property."

"How far along are you?"

A strand of hair fell into her face. She pushed it back with her shoulder since her hands were covered in suds. "I'm about half done. Another month or so and we should be in operation." She scrubbed the pot and the hair fell in her face again. This time she attempted to blow it out of the way. "It helps that Uncle Jeb didn't clear huge swatches of the woods on the property. They'll be useful for the initial training. Once the dogs are more advanced, we'll use the nearby national park."

Reed's fingers skimmed the side of her face as he tucked the annoying strand behind her ear. Her breath hitched. "Thanks."

"Sure." He took the clean pot from her. "Will you breed the dogs yourself or buy them?"

"Actually, we're going to take dogs from the animal shelter. Most people aren't aware that SAR canines don't have to be purebreds. Sadie isn't." At the sound of her name, the dog raised her head. Emma smiled at her. "SAR dogs need specific traits like agility and a good nose. The pups that don't make it through the training program, we'll adopt out to loving homes. Vivian's good with accounting and fund-raising. She wants to handle the paperwork, which will free me up to do the training."

"It sounds amazing, Emma."

"It's a lot of work, but like I said before, God put this mission in my heart." She peeled off the kitchen gloves. She hated to ruin their easy conversation by bringing up a tough subject, but there would never be a great time to ask. "Reed, what happened to Bonnie?"

He let out a sigh, long and low. "She—"

Reed's phone trilled. He glanced at the screen and stiffened. "I have to take this. It's Dispatch."

He answered, walking to the other side of the kitchen. There were a few tense moments of silence. Emma sent up a prayer that whatever had happened God would watch over the innocent.

Reed hung up and turned to her. "I need you and Sadie to come with me. We've got a missing girl in Fairhill National Park."

SIX

In a missing person case, every second counted.

Reed's SUV bumped over the dirt road heading deeper into Fairhill National Park. Dusk was shifting into twilight and fireflies flickered in the trees on either side of the road. He ached to push down on the gas pedal, but the vehicle's suspension wouldn't survive.

"I've never been to this park," Emma said. She gripped the handle of the passenger seat as Reed swerved around a divot in the road. "Does this road lead to the main camping area?"

"No. Camping is allowed anywhere in the park, not just the designated areas. Molly—that's the missing girl—her dad is something of an outdoorsman. He likes to rough it."

She slanted a look his way. "You know the family?"

"Not well, but Derrick owns the hardware store in town. His wife is a teacher at the elementary school."

"How long has Molly been missing?"

Reed glanced at the clock, the knot in his stomach tightening. "About two hours. Derrick was smart to call us in early."

They rounded the bend and a campsite came into

view with a family-size tent, fishing poles and a fire pit. One deputy was off to the side with two young children. Austin was near the tree line talking with Molly's parents. He broke off when he spotted Reed's vehicle.

Emma hopped out and opened the back seat to release Sadie from her specialized belt.

"We've got a missing eleven-year-old female, Molly Hanks." His chief deputy skipped the pleasantries and jumped straight into a report. "Last seen wearing black jeans, a gray T-shirt and purple sneakers. She disappeared while her parents were making dinner. They did a quick search of the nearby area and didn't find her. The park rangers were called in and they did a more extensive search but haven't located her yet."

"Where was she last seen?"

"She was reading over there." Austin gestured toward the far side of the clearing. A novel, split open to save the page, rested on a fallen tree trunk. "I've called in for assistance from the state troopers, as well as the Texas Rangers. The nearest SAR team has also been alerted, although they're a couple of hours away."

"Emma and Sadie are trained in Search and Rescue. They're going to give us a head start."

Austin tossed her a brief smile. "Good to see you again, Emma. Appreciate your help." He turned back to Reed. "This could be more than Molly simply wandering off and getting lost. We could be dealing with a possible abduction."

Reed shoulders stiffened. "How so?"

"Derrick isn't Molly's biological father. He's her stepdad. Apparently, the family has had issues with Molly's father in the past. He's a drug user and recently lost his visitation. According to the mom, he didn't handle it well."

"Got a description on Dad?"

"Name's Vernon Hanks. Last known address is in Willowbend." Austin pulled up a photograph on his phone—a copy of a driver's license photo. Vernon had a gaunt face with a handlebar mustache. "Molly and her father still communicate on the phone. She told him about this trip during their last conversation."

Reed's gaze jumped back to the book resting on the log. "Let's reach out to our counterparts in Willowbend, see if they can locate Mr. Hanks. I also want a BOLO out on any vehicle registered to him."

With a Be On The Lookout alert, every law enforcement officer in the state would be watching for the vehicle. If Vernon had managed to abduct his daughter, Reed didn't want him getting too far.

Reed reached into his trunk and pulled out a spare bulletproof vest. He handed it to Emma. "Put this on."

Her eyes widened slightly but she put it on before grabbing a backpack and slipping it over her shoulders. Sadie was already outfitted in a reflective vest. "I'm ready when you are."

Reed grabbed his own backpack with food, water and equipment. He had no intention of getting stuck out in the woods, but it was prudent to take precautions.

Another couple of squad cars drove up. Detective Kyle Hendricks got out.

"Hand over the scene to Hendricks. I want you with us," Reed said to Austin. "I've got enough supplies in my pack for two. Just grab an extra flashlight."

He spared a few more moments to speak to Molly's parents and explain what they were doing before joining Emma at the fallen log. "Do you need an article of clothing?"

"No. Sadie's an air-scenting dog. She'll find any person in the area."

Emma unhooked the dog's leash and gave a command. Sadie lifted her nose and headed into the woods. The bells attached to her vest jingled, making it easier to follow her, even in the dark.

Reed followed behind, urgency fueling him. Somewhere an owl hooted above them. Emma's ponytail bobbed with every step. She kept right on Sadie, increasing her stride as the dog went faster. Her brow was drawn down, her focus entirely on the mission at hand. Reed stayed next to her, close enough to reach out and touch her, even as he continuously scanned the trees and brush with his flashlight.

Austin called out for Molly, his voice carrying through the woods. The ground sloped upward in a steady incline. Reed's heart thumped with exertion and his feet slid slightly on the pine needles coating the forest floor. Sweat dripped down his back, causing his shirt to stick to his skin.

Sadie sped up, breaking into a run, and disappeared around a bend. She barked. Reed held Emma back with his hand.

"Stay behind me," he whispered. It was likely Molly was on her own, but he wouldn't take chances. Not with anyone, but especially not with Emma.

Austin palmed his weapon, and Reed did the same. They separated slightly, using the trees as cover. Emma followed closely behind Reed, matching him step for step as they made their way down the other side of the slope to the small valley below. Darkness surrounded them, making it impossible to see any danger lying around the next bend. Sadie's barking grew louder.

Reed's flashlight lit up a purple tennis shoe. Molly lay crumpled on the ground, tears streaking her face. Sadie stood next to her. He scanned the immediate area, but there wasn't anything suspicious.

"Molly, don't be alarmed." Reed smiled and bent down next to the girl. "I'm Sheriff Atkinson. This is Lieutenant Carter and Mrs. Pierce." He pulled a bottle of water from his bag and unscrewed it. Molly took a long drink.

Austin pulled out his radio and attempted to call in.

Emma moved around to the other side of the girl. She praised and patted Sadie before slipping off her pack. "You're hurt. I have some first aid supplies in my pack. Can you tell me what happened?"

"I fell." Molly lifted a hand to her head. Her eyes were dazed, and she was shaking. "I rolled down the hill. My head… There's a lot of blood. And my ankle. I shouldn't have followed my dad out here."

Reed scanned the nearby trees. No movement. He yanked out an emergency blanket and opened it. "Where's your dad now?"

"I don't know. He left me here."

Emma placed gauze on Molly's head. "Reed, can you shine your flashlight over here for me so I can see better?"

The wound on Molly's head was huge. Reed wasn't a doctor, but he knew enough first aid to understand the child could be suffering from a concussion. In the background, Austin was still trying to get someone on the radio.

Reed scanned the trees again. Something about this

didn't feel right. Why would Molly's dad go to all the effort to kidnap her only to leave her in the woods? His gaze fell on Sadie and then shifted to Emma. Unless…was it possible this was some kind of trap? To lure them out here?

Something whistled. Bark on the tree behind Austin exploded as the sound of a gunshot carried through the night. Austin dove for Molly as Reed threw himself over Emma. She yelled a command to Sadie. The dog bolted into the trees for cover as ordered.

Gunshots rained down, pelting the ground and the trees nearby. Reed widened his body, cradling Emma's head against his chest to protect her. His heart thundered, even as his brain calculated their next move.

A bullet slammed into his back.

Emma's pulse pounded so loudly in her ear, she almost missed Reed's sharp intake of breath. Alarm ricocheted through her. Had he been shot? She tried to lift her head from his chest to ask, but he held her tighter. Emma could do nothing but pray he was okay.

The gunshots stopped; the sound of the last one seemed to echo through the night. Emma drew a ragged breath. Her body trembled.

"We need to move while he's reloading," Reed whispered in her ear. "There's a cave a short distance away. Follow Austin."

Before she could formulate a thought, Reed sprang to his feet, bringing her with him. Austin scooped up Molly and took off.

"Run!" Reed pushed her forward. Emma ran, doing her best to keep Austin's dark, shifting form in sight.

Her feet pounded against the forest floor. Sadie appeared at Emma's side, keeping pace.

A gunshot rang out. Dirt sprayed, pebbles hitting against her jeans. She urged more power into her legs.

Lord, please, keep us safe.

The dark cave beckoned, and Emma flew into its embrace. Chest heaving, she turned in time to see Reed join them. He dropped her backpack on the cave floor. Sadie crowded next to Emma, seeking comfort. Reed and Austin both pulled their weapons.

"I want my daughter!" The voice carried across the forest. Molly's face paled, and she shook.

Emma put her arms around the girl. "Your dad?"

She nodded, tears streaming down her face. "I tried to tell him I couldn't go with him but he wouldn't listen. We had an argument, and he pushed me. I fell down the hill." Molly gripped Emma's arms. "Please don't let them shoot him. My dad does drugs and—"

"It's going to be okay." She couldn't do anything about the shooter outside, but she could comfort a frightened child. Molly was only eleven years old. Smart enough to understand the bad decisions her father had made, too young to emotionally cope with the consequences.

Reed and Austin were talking quickly. Making a plan, maybe? Austin again tried to radio in.

Emma moved Sadie next to Molly. "This is my dog. She's pretty scared, too. Hold on to her."

Molly dipped her hands into Sadie's soft fur and a sob rose in her throat. Emma fished out an emergency blanket from her backpack and tucked it around the young girl.

Reed looked at his phone and shook his head. He and

Austin shared a tense few words. Emma joined them, keeping her voice hushed. "What is it?"

"Austin's radio was damaged, and mine isn't getting through," Reed said. "We also don't have reception on our cells. We can't call for help. Molly's dad was shooting from the ridge but he's on the move."

Reed winced as he lifted his arm attempting to get some reception. Emma grabbed his elbow. "Are you hurt?"

"He took a bullet to the vest," Austin said, without turning his head from where he was standing guard.

Emma's mouth went dry as irrational fear gripped her. She ran her hands along Reed's back. Her fingers brushed against the hole in his lightweight sheriff's jacket.

He grabbed her hand and squeezed it. "I'm fine and—"

"And we're sitting ducks," Austin said. "Give me your radio. I'll head for higher ground to see if I can get some reception and call for help."

"I'll go."

"Not with your injury. The bulletproof vest saved your life, but we both know getting shot isn't painless." Austin put his hands on his hips. "You're going to move slower than I will due to the bruising on your back."

Reed's jaw tightened, but he nodded. "Be careful."

"Always." Austin slipped out of the cave and disappeared into the shadows. The dark would help him stay unseen. It could also make it easier for someone else to sneak up on him.

Emma bit her lip and sent up another prayer for his safety.

"We need to move," Reed said.

"Molly's hurt. And so are you."

"There isn't a choice." he whispered. "Vernon saw us go into the cave, and it's the first place he'll come looking. There's no way out of here. Austin and I used to hike up here as kids. There's another cave close by with an exit in the back. It'll give us an escape route."

Emma crouched down and fished the Taser out of her backpack. It wouldn't help much in a gunfight, but it was something.

"Molly, I'm going to carry you over my shoulders," Reed explained softly. "Please stay very quiet."

The little girl nodded, and he lifted her into a fireman's carry. His mouth hardened, the only indication the extra weight hurt his back. Holding Molly in that manner left his weapon hand free.

They eased into the dark forest. Cicadas sang. Sweat trailed down Emma's back as she strained to listen for anything out of the ordinary. A branch snapped. She froze. Reed lifted a finger to his lips. The silence stretched out so long Emma wanted to scream from the weight of it.

Finally, Reed glanced at her and shook his head. He waved her forward. Together, they slipped into the next cave.

How long had Austin been gone? Ten minutes? If he wasn't able to get reception, how long would it be before Reed's men came looking for them? A thousand questions and possibilities rolled through Emma's mind as she arranged the blanket back over Molly. Sadie took her position next to the little girl.

Reed disappeared into the back of the cave and returned. "The exit is clear. Right down that pathway."

Gunfire erupted, breaking the stillness of the night.

Austin shouted. There was the distinct sound of an object—or a person—crashing down the embankment.

Reed took a few steps forward toward the mouth of the cave. He stopped.

"Go," Emma whispered. She lifted the Taser. "I've got this and Sadie for protection. Go help Austin."

"No."

"You can't leave him out there by himself." Emma wouldn't forgive herself if they didn't try to help. She was almost certain Reed wouldn't either. "You've seen Sadie in action. You know she's capable of taking some-one down. I'm not defenseless, but Austin might be. Go!"

He looked past her to the dog and Molly huddled to-gether. "Get farther into the cave, hide in the shadows." Reed touched her cheek, his fingers as light as a but-terfly wing. "Don't come out no matter what you hear."

Her throat tightened as the magnitude of his words sank into her skin with sharp claws. Only two hours ago, he'd been holding Lily. Now he was walking into a possible shoot-out with a criminal.

He turned and, on silent footsteps, slipped into the forest.

A breeze blew, whistling through the cave. Goose bumps rose on Emma's arms. A sense of foreboding washed over her. She'd prayed for Mark every day, but that hadn't prevented his plane from crashing in the middle of a war zone.

She gave herself a mental shake. There wasn't time to ruminate about her heartbreak. There wasn't any-thing she could do to help Reed beyond pray. Right now, her focus needed to be on keeping Molly safe and that started with moving the girl farther into the cave.

Using a flashlight wasn't an option. She didn't want to alert the shooter to their new hiding spot. Without it, however, she couldn't see well. Emma had a momentary fear of disturbing a bear or some other animal. That would be just the icing on the cake. But of course, Reed had gone in and come back out just fine.

"Molly, how are you doing?" Emma asked, keeping one eye on the cave's entrance as she bent down next to the girl. Sadie greeted her with a small lick to the shoulder. "How's your head?"

"It hurts."

The wound had stopped bleeding, but a large lump had formed next to her temple. Emma touched Molly's hands and found them ice-cold. Shock? She wouldn't be surprised. It only made their situation more dire. The need for medical attention was increasing with every minute.

"Let's move back a little." Emma helped the girl up and together they maneuvered farther into the shadows. Molly was already covered with one blanket, but Emma pulled out a second one. She wrapped Molly in it. "Keep your hands on Sadie. She's as good as a furnace."

The dog settled between them, her ears perked. Sadie seemed to sense Emma's tension and unease. She was guarding without being told.

"I'm sorry. I didn't know my dad was going to shoot at you." Molly's voice was slightly slurred. It only ratcheted up Emma's anxiety.

"Don't worry, honey. This isn't your fault."

"No, it is. It is." She took a shuddering breath. "I told him I was mad at my mom… I shouldn't have… And he made a deal with someone. He said it was the only way we could be together…"

An icy chill raced down her spine. Emma bent down and held the girl's chin in her hand. Her eyes were nothing but deep shadows in her face. "Molly, is your dad out there with someone else?"

A twig snapped. Sadie stood, her body leaning forward.

Emma whirled. She peered through the darkness but saw nothing except shadows and shifting branches.

There. A flashlight moving through the forest.

Heading in their direction.

SEVEN

Reed moved through the forest like a shadow. Every step made his back ache, but he smothered the pain behind a wall of steel, along with the self doubt about his decision to leave Molly and Emma behind in the cave. He'd mitigated the danger by hiding them in a second location, but still, it was risky. The deciding factor hadn't been just about helping Austin—although that was huge—it was getting in contact with Dispatch. Reed couldn't protect them all on his own. He needed help.

Wind rustled the leaves. Reed paused, holding his breath. A sliver of moonlight slipped out from behind a cloud, catching on the edge of a black boot. His heart skittered. He lifted his weapon and edged closer.

The boot turned into a shape. The moonlight glinted off the barrel of a gun.

"Police. Don't take one more step."

Reed sucked in a breath and lowered his weapon. "Austin, it's me."

He stepped out of the shadows and his cousin's eyes widened. Austin was sprawled across the forest floor.

Leaves and pine needles covered his clothes. Reed crouched down next to him. "Where are you hurt?"

"Forget about me." Austin gripped his arm. "Your instincts were right, Reed. Emma's the target. Molly was just an excuse to get her out here. Backup is on the way, but you need to get back to Emma. Hurry!"

Reed took off. His boots skidded against the pine needles and branches tugged at his clothes as he raced through the woods. The mouth of the cave came into view. Reed tightened his hold on his weapon and whispered Emma's name.

The cave was empty.

The muzzle of a gun touched the back of his head. Reed froze.

"Got ya." A pair of night vision goggles landed on the ground. "Okay, Sheriff, this is how it's going to be. Put your gun on the ground real slow and no one will get hurt."

Was it Molly's dad, Vernon? Had to be. Reed twisted his head, catching a glimpse of the handlebar mustache out of the corner of his eye.

"No one has gotten hurt so far, Vernon." Reed kept his voice even, no hint of his inner turmoil bleeding through. "Let's keep it that way. Why don't you put the gun down and we can talk?"

"We are way beyond talking, but I could be persuaded to let you live. Where is Emma?"

Thank you, Lord. Vernon didn't have her. "Why?"

"What do you care?" He applied more pressure to the rifle, the cold steel digging into Reed's skin. "You're going to put your gun down and you're going to show me where she's hiding. Along with my daughter."

Not a chance. "Okay, sure, Vernon. I'm going to put the gun down now."

"Yeah. Nice and slow."

Reed started lowering himself down to one knee. *One...two...*

He whirled up, grabbing the muzzle of the rifle.

Vernon stumbled. The gun went off, the sound like an explosion in the close confines of the cave. Reed kneed Vernon in the stomach and wrenched the weapon out of his hands.

A furry object flew past him and slammed right into Vernon. Sadie. Together the dog and criminal toppled over. Something whacked against the side of the cave, and Vernon yelped. Sadie held him trapped, snarling and barking.

Emma emerged from the rear of the cave. Breathing heavy, his back aching, Reed handed the rifle to her. He pulled out his handcuffs. "Call her off."

Once the dog backed away, Reed flipped Vernon around. He slapped the handcuffs on him and quickly read him his rights.

Outside, voices called out their names. Emma ran to the mouth of the cave, flipping on her flashlight and escorting the first responders to the rear of the cave. Probably where she'd hidden Molly. Reed patted Vernon down. He found a bag of drugs in his front pocket. "Why are you trying to kill Emma?"

Vernon glared at him. "I want a lawyer."

"I'm sure you do."

Reed picked up the cup of freshly brewed coffee from the vending machine. He took a long sip, letting the warmth and caffeine surge through him, before dropping in more coins for a second cup.

The hospital's emergency waiting room was mostly empty. Austin was still being examined by doctors. Emma sat in a plastic chair, talking on her cell phone. Her clothes were covered in mud and grass stains. Sadie sat at her feet, still wearing her SAR vest, allowed in the hospital because of her specialized training.

Reed's chest tightened. He didn't want to think about the number of ways tonight could've gone terribly wrong.

He took the second cup of coffee from the machine and crossed the room just as Emma hung up. He handed her the drink. "Everything okay with Vivian and Lily?"

"Yes." She sighed. "Vivian's more worried about me than herself. She says it's like a fort at the house. Deputy Irving is inside and there's another deputy on patrol around the property. Thank you, Reed, for arranging it."

"I told you, keeping you and your family safe is my first priority."

Not that he was doing a great job. Within the course of a couple of days, Emma had been threatened, choked and shot at.

Her hair had fallen loose from its ponytail. The strands curved around her face. A pine needle was tangled in them. Without a thought, Reed reached up and pulled it out. His fingers brushed across the silky threads of her hair.

Emma laughed lightly and took the pine needle from him. "I must look a fright."

"You look like someone who saved the day. Having Sadie take down Vernon probably saved my life."

It was a strange fact to acknowledge. Not that Emma

had put herself on the line for him or Molly. That wasn't surprising given her character. But still, she was a civilian. Reed was used to relying on his men. Law enforcement was a brotherhood and there was an understanding each would give his life for another. Emma had no training in that regard, or any obligation. It made her bravery even more outstanding.

He locked eyes with her. "If I haven't said it yet, thank you."

"We make a good team, Reed." She frowned, her gaze scanning his face. "Are you sure you're okay? Shouldn't you be checked out by a doctor?"

"I'm fine. Just bruised." His lips quirked. "I'm a lot tougher than I look."

"No one would think you weren't tough. Not for a moment."

The doors leading from the emergency room swung open and Austin walked out. His arm was in a sling and he favored his right leg.

Emma hopped up and gently hugged him. "What did the doctor say?"

Austin blushed as he pulled back. "It's nothing. My shoulder was dislocated, and I have a sprained ankle." His gaze jumped from Emma to Reed. "Molly?"

"She's going to make a full recovery, according to the doctors."

Austin let out a breath. "I'm glad. I saw Will going into Vernon's room with a defense attorney. Why aren't you in there interviewing him?"

"I decided it would be best to let Cooper take the lead on the case." Cooper Jackson was their local Texas Ranger. "It'll bump the case to a higher priority. Cooper can get the state lab to process the evidence quickly.

Plus, he has the additional manpower to question witnesses faster than we can."

It would also free Reed up to personally guard Emma. The danger to her was growing exponentially.

Austin nodded. "Good idea. Cooper is an excellent investigator."

"What happened out there in the woods?" Reed asked.

"I went to the ridge to call in to headquarters when I overheard Vernon talking to someone. He didn't give a name, but he explicitly said the plan worked. He told the other person on the phone to hurry up."

Emma gasped. "I saw someone in the woods with a flashlight coming toward the cave. That's why I moved Molly closer to the rear entrance, out of sight. I assumed it was Vernon, but maybe I was wrong."

"Two criminals…" Reed rocked back on his heels. "On the night of the break-in at Emma's house, a truck nearly ran me off the road. It wasn't the man who actually attacked Emma because he was still in the house, but it could've been a getaway driver."

If there were two men working together all this time, that meant any alibis they'd collected were worthless. It put the case back at square one.

"There's more." Austin hesitated. "Vernon specifically said he didn't sign up for the murder part. If the other guy wanted you dead, he needed to move it."

Reed was standing close enough to feel the small tremor shake Emma's body. He slipped his hand into hers.

Austin grimaced. "I must've stepped on a branch or somehow given away my presence, because Vernon started shooting at me. I ended up rolling down the embankment."

The hospital doors swung open again. Will Norton, the county prosecutor, emerged. He was followed by Cooper. The Texas Ranger was scowling.

"I take it the questioning didn't go well," Reed said once the men were close enough.

Cooper snorted, running a hand through his shaggy hair. "Vernon isn't as stupid as his crimes might suggest."

"He pled the fifth and refused to answer any questions," Will said. "I've spoken with the defense attorney. I'll throw every charge I can at Vernon and ask for the maximum sentence for each one if he doesn't agree to cooperate. Murder-for-hire alone is a capital crime. He's going to discuss it with his client, but I'm not holding my breath."

Emma's shoulders sagged and Reed squeezed her hand. "What about his phone? Since Austin heard him talking to someone—"

"We've recovered the cell phone, but it's locked." Cooper placed his hands on his hips, parting his sports jacket, revealing an oversize turquoise belt buckle. "Of course, Vernon refuses to unlock it for us or provide the password."

"We'll have to subpoena the records to see who he was talking to," Will said. "I've already had someone in my office start the paperwork. We should have it signed by a judge within the next couple of hours."

Reed let out a breath. Things were moving, but not fast enough. Whoever hired Vernon was still out there and free. What was to prevent him from trying to kill Emma a second time?

* * *

Emma sank into the seat of Reed's SUV. Exhaustion seeped into her muscles. She wanted a shower, some apple pie and a cuddle with her daughter. Sadie let out a sigh as she settled into the back seat.

The dome light didn't come on when Reed opened the driver's side door and climbed in. The engine rumbled to life. His strong hands held the wheel firmly, and his gaze flicked to the mirrors every so often as the hospital faded in the distance.

"You okay?" he asked.

"Emotionally drained, but otherwise I'm fine." She bit her lip. "Actually, I'm not fine. It was bad enough someone was stalking and trying to hurt me, but tonight Molly got caught in the cross fire. Vernon used his own daughter to set a trap for me."

"Which isn't your fault. You're not responsible for Vernon's actions."

"I know. Mentally, I get it. But I can't turn off my feelings so easily. I'm furious and I feel guilty. Molly's just a child, Reed. She didn't deserve what happened to her tonight."

He reached across the seat and took her hand. His palm was warm, the calluses rubbing lightly against the ridges of her knuckles. "You aren't the only one feeling that. I carry it, too. Maybe it's natural because of who we are."

Maybe it was. Reed's childhood had been marred by his father's abandonment and his mother's depression. Hers had been one of constant motion and chaos with new people and frequent moves. Circumstances had forced both of them into accepting responsibility for things outside of their control. It was a bond they'd shared as teenagers and, it seemed, now, as well.

"You did a good job tonight, Emma. You're tough." His mouth quirked up. "You'd make a fantastic law enforcement officer."

She laughed and wiped a stray tear from her cheek. "No, thank you. I'm much better at Search and Rescue."

"Don't tell Sadie, but I'm sure I owe her three boxes of biscuits now."

"You don't have to tell her. She's keeping score, I guarantee it."

He squeezed her hand. "I promise, Emma, we will get to the bottom of this."

"I know you will."

But what would be the cost until then? She trusted Reed to protect her and her family, but he wasn't invincible. He couldn't prevent everything or be everywhere at once. Tonight had been a close call. If Reed hadn't been wearing his bulletproof vest, things would've ended very differently. Just the thought of it sent her heart into overdrive.

Beyond the windshield, Emma could see the lights of her home winking through the trees. Her daughter would be asleep now, nestled in her bed, along with her stuffed lamb. Should they leave town? Abandon Helping Paws? The idea was gut-wrenching but there was more to consider than just herself. She had a daughter to protect.

Lord, please give me strength and guidance. Tell me what I'm supposed to do.

Reed squeezed her hand and she interlocked her fingers with his. A simple gesture and yet it brought her comfort. She wasn't in this alone.

Have faith. It was easy during good times. So much harder in the darker ones. Life was testing her, throwing curveballs she hadn't expected, but Emma had moved to Heyworth for a reason. She believed God was leading her. Maybe, just maybe, He'd sent Reed to help her through it.

The headlights picked up an object sailing through the night. It landed on the road in front of them. Emma blinked. Was that…a grenade?

"Reed!" she shouted.

He swerved. Emma's head slammed into the side of the SUV. A bright light preceded the sound of exploding glass. Then they were tumbling over and over.

Everything went black.

EIGHT

Awareness came slowly, like moving through a soupy fog. Reed smelled smoke and pine. His chest hurt. Something warm and wet swiped across his face.

He forced his eyes open. A tree branch was shoved through the shattered windshield. It took him far too long to realize he was upside down, his shoulder caught in the seat belt. The memories flashed like light bulbs. The grenade rolling into the road. His attempt to miss it. The explosion and the SUV rolling over. Emma's screams.

Emma. He twisted his head and was looking at a wall of fur. Sadie, freed from her seat belt in the collision, was blocking his view. "Emma, are you okay?"

She didn't respond. Reed fumbled for the seat belt release. For some mysterious reason, one of his headlights still functioned. The other was buried in the pine tree the vehicle had crashed into. Sadie licked the side of his face, her tongue leaving a wet trail. She had woken him. "Emma! Answer me!"

His fingers found the button and Reed pressed down. The seat belt gave way. He crashed in a heap onto the roof of the destroyed SUV. Glass shards cut into his pants and the palms of his hands.

He pushed Sadie out of the way. His breath caught. Emma was unconscious. The side of her face was covered in blood. "Please, Lord, no."

Sadie whined. Deeply embedded training cut through the shock caused by the accident. With a shaking hand, he reached out and touched Emma's neck. The thump of her pulse was strong.

"Thank you, Lord."

His fingers searched and located a large gash hidden in her hair. Emma moaned. She needed help. She needed a hospital.

The extent of their problem wasn't just her injury. Whoever had thrown the grenade out into the road could still be nearby. Was he close enough to come after them? Reed wasn't willing to wait to find out.

Unfortunately his phone had been charging, tucked into the cup holder. Where was it?

Headlights lit up the car from behind. Reed froze. A car stopped on the side of the road. Friend or foe? He wasn't going to take any chances. Not with Emma. His heartbeat quickened and his fingers flew to his weapon, still holstered at his side. He maneuvered his body out of the broken window. Pain screamed from his ribs. Reed ignored it.

Footsteps crunched over the gravel shoulder. He circled to meet them, his gun leading the way.

"Police! Freeze, right there!" He ordered the figure shadowed by the headlights. "Not one more step."

The man immediately put his hands up to his shoulders. "Sheriff? It's me. Dean Shadwick. Don't shoot. I'm trying to help you."

Reed hesitated. "What are you doing here, Dean?"

"I… I was on my way home from town. I saw your vehicle on the side of the road."

"At two in the morning?"

"My mom lost her cat. She was in a panic, and I went to help her search for it."

Dean's ranch was two miles away, but this road was a shortcut from town. Reed lowered his weapon. "Did you see anyone else on the road?"

"No." His deputy took a deep breath. "What happened?"

"Someone attacked us. We need an ambulance and backup, now."

Hospitals were no place to get rest. Or decent food.

Emma poked her fork at the lump of mystery meat on her tray. They'd taken her vitals all night, the doctor keeping her for observation after the car accident. Her ribs were bruised, and she'd needed several stitches in her scalp. All in all, things could have been a whole lot worse.

She sampled the white glop masquerading as mashed potatoes. It tasted like ground plaster. Emma winced and pushed the food tray away.

"I'm pretty sure you're supposed to eat that," Vivian scolded. Dark circles marred the delicate skin under her sister-in-law's eyes, a testament to her own lack of sleep, and her blond hair was tucked into a sloppy ponytail. Lily bounced on her hip.

"It's not meant for human consumption." Emma lifted her daughter from Vivian's arms. Lily patted her cheek with a chubby hand. Emma grabbed it, planting a kiss on the soft palm. "Were you keeping your aunt up last night?"

"A bit. I think she's teething." Vivian held up the torn and bloody shirt Emma had been wearing yesterday— was it only just yesterday?—and blanched. "Of course, I wouldn't have gotten much sleep last night anyway."

The explosion had been close enough to the house, Vivian had heard it. Guilt pinched Emma. Vivian hadn't taken her brother's death well, and like Emma, she had very little extended family. As horrible as the situation was for Emma, it had to be worse for Vivian. She was left worrying. If the shoe was on the other foot—and Vivian was the one in danger—Emma would be frantic.

"You're a trooper, Vivi. Thank you for bringing new clothes and taking care of Lily. This would be so much worse if I didn't have you."

"Flattery will get you everywhere." Vivian grinned and tossed the destroyed shirt in the trash. "Of course, it would help me sleep better at night if we caught the guys doing this. Or even understood why they were after you. These attacks are extreme, and I can't believe it's simply to scare you off the property."

"I agree. Maybe Austin and Reed will have some news once they come back from the conference call with the Texas Ranger."

Vivian folded the pants Emma had been wearing last night before placing them in an overnight bag. "As crazy as it sounds, if a grenade had to be thrown at you, I'm glad Reed was there. The doctor said things would've been worse if Reed hadn't provided first aid and stopped the bleeding."

"I know." She'd regained consciousness as the EMTs were pulling her from the car. Reed stayed by her side the entire time, holding her hand. The first thing he did was assure Emma that Sadie was uninjured. "How was Sadie this morning?"

"Completely fine. The vet at the emergency clinic said to give her a couple of days rest. Deputy Irving walked her on a leash instead of letting her run loose in the yard this morning."

Lily bounced in Emma's arms and she winced. Vivian held out her hands. "Let me take her."

"No, I'm fine. Just a bit sore."

She was grateful to be alive. Grenades. Someone had actually thrown a grenade at their car. This situation had spiraled out of control so quickly, it made Emma's head spin. What had once been a couple of irritating incidents and creepy phone calls was turning into murder attempts and bombs.

The door to her room swung open. Reed strolled in. He'd showered and changed his clothes since the accident but hadn't shaved. The dark bristles on his jaw turned his eyes a deeper blue.

Austin followed his cousin into the room. His arm was still in a sling, but his gait was even, the sprained ankle clearly not bothering him anymore. His expression was as grim as Reed's. Emma chewed on the inside of her cheek. Whatever they'd found out from Cooper, the Texas Ranger, hadn't been good.

Reed spotted her full food tray and frowned. "Didn't the doctor say it was important for you to eat?"

"I tried to tell her the same." Vivian put her hands on her hips. "Maybe you can talk some sense into her."

"Don't start, either of you. The doctor has already cleared me to go home and that—" Emma waved a hand toward the offensive tray "—is not what I would call food."

Austin picked up the unused knife and dipped it in the mashed potatoes. He grimaced. "Prisoners get better grub than this."

Emma shot a triumphant look at her sister-in-law. "See. I told you."

Reed laughed. "It must be bad if Austin isn't willing to eat it. I've never seen him turn down a meal."

Lily bounced again in Emma's arms and lifted her hands toward Reed. He obliged, swinging her up high. She giggled. Everyone in the room chuckled.

"Watch out, Reed, or she'll have you wrapped around her little finger," Austin said.

"Something tells me your warning is too late." Vivian picked up her purse from a chair. "I'm hungry, and I'm sure Emma is, too. Why don't I go across the street to the diner and pick us up something for lunch while we wait for the discharge paperwork?"

"I don't think it's a good idea for you to go outside the hospital," Emma said. The memory of the grenade rolling out into the road made a shiver run down her spine.

"I have to eat sometime. And so do you. We can't stay in here forever. Besides, the attacks have been solely focused on you."

"I know, but it doesn't hurt to take precautions."

"There's a café in the lower level of the hospital," Reed said. "They make the best roast beef sandwiches. I'll stay here with Emma, and Austin can escort Vivian."

Vivian shot a glance at the chief deputy. A blush

stained her cheeks. "I'm sure Austin has better things to do than babysit me."

"I'm not babysitting you. I'm protecting you. There's a difference." Austin winked. "And if you'll buy me a cup of potato soup to go with my sandwich, then we'll consider it a good trade."

Vivian's blush deepened, and Emma smothered a smile. It seemed she wasn't the only one struggling to resist a handsome lawman. They all placed an order for food and Vivian and Austin left.

"How are you feeling?" Reed asked, his gaze scanning her head.

"I'm fine. A bit anxious to hear what you found out from Cooper."

He shifted Lily in his arms and picked up the baby's favorite stuffed lamb from the bed. "He was able to confirm Vernon was hired to target you."

"How?"

"They located his girlfriend at a local bar, and she spilled the beans. She also confirmed that he wasn't working alone, although she doesn't know who hired him or who his partners are."

"Partners? More than one person was hired to kill me?" She wrapped her arms around herself. "The man in the woods holding the flashlight wasn't the killer after all. He was another hired gun."

Reed nodded. "That's my guess. But there's more, Emma. It wasn't an accident that Vernon waited for me to come back to the cave. Or that the grenade was launched at my vehicle. Vernon's girlfriend said he would get a bonus if he took me out as well as you."

She sucked in a sharp breath. "But…that doesn't make any sense. Why would anyone target you and me?"

"There's only one reason I can think of. This is about Bonnie, Emma. This is all about my sister."

Reed grabbed Emma's arm. She'd gone pale, and he silently berated himself for the blunt delivery of his theory. She'd survived a grenade and shooting attack only yesterday.

Emma's long hair hung down her back, hiding the lump and stitches he knew were there. The silky strands brushed against his skin. "Maybe you should sit down."

She backed up until her knees hit the bed. "I don't understand. How is Bonnie's disappearance linked to these attacks?"

"This is going to sound far-fetched, but I think she's alive and being held captive somewhere. It's common knowledge in town that I've never given up on finding my sister."

Her eyes widened. "Sadie and I are a threat because we could make it possible to find Bonnie."

"Before you moved to Heyworth, the closest SAR canine was three hours away. It's the only thing that makes sense and explains why both you and I are being targeted."

His shoulders tensed as the silence stretched out between them. Reed half expected her to say he'd lost his mind, that grief was causing him to wish for things that weren't true. After all, he didn't have evidence proving Bonnie was the link. Nor could he prove she was alive. Not yet, anyway.

Emma lifted her gaze to meet his. The color had returned to her cheeks and there was a determined tilt to her chin. "I think it's time you tell me what happened to Bonnie."

He let out the breath he was holding. "When my sister initially went missing, the former sheriff believed she'd merely left town for a while. He had good reason to. A suitcase and clothes were missing from her apartment. Her purse and cell phone were gone, and so was her car. Our mom had died six months before. My sister's best friend, Margaret, confirmed Bonnie wasn't taking it well."

"But you didn't believe she'd run off?"

"No. The day she went missing, Bonnie called me and left a message. She wanted to talk about something important."

"Did she say what?"

"No, and when I tried to call her back hours later, she didn't answer."

Bonnie had already gone missing by then. Reed's stomach twisted painfully. He would give anything to go back to that moment and answer his phone when she called, but he'd been questioning the suspect of a double homicide at the time.

"Twenty-four hours went by and she still wasn't answering. I knew immediately something wasn't right. Bonnie would never ignore me. Especially after leaving a voice mail that asked me to call her back ASAP. I came straight to Heyworth and started digging into the case myself."

Lily stuck her thumb in her mouth and rested her head against Reed's shoulder. He ran a hand down her back and swayed. "I questioned several of her friends and found out Bonnie had been having a secret relationship with Joshua."

Emma's eyes widened. "Joshua Lowe? My neighbor?"

He nodded. "Bonnie hadn't told me about it. Probably because my sister knew I wouldn't approve. Joshua is bad news. He's done time for theft. Supposedly, he cleaned up his act and is on the straight and narrow path, but that's a recent turn around. Still too early in my opinion to know whether it's true or not."

"Do you think he had something to do with Bonnie's disappearance?"

"I think it's a strong possibility. On the night Bonnie went missing, she and Joshua were running away to elope."

Emma frowned. "That's why she packed a suitcase."

"Exactly. Joshua claims he arrived at the meeting place late and she wasn't there. But he can't provide me with an alibi." Reed shifted his hold on Lily, careful not to wake the sleeping baby. "To complicate matters, Bonnie worked as a paralegal for Judge Norton. She and Will had been dating but broke up shortly before she got involved with Joshua."

Emma's head was spinning with all of the information. Will Norton was the county prosecutor. He was also Judge Norton's nephew.

"Hold on, let me make sure I understand everything," she said. "Will Norton and Bonnie were dating. They broke up. After that, Bonnie and Joshua started dating."

"Right."

"Bonnie and Joshua got serious and were planning to elope. They set up a meeting and, according to Joshua, Bonnie never showed."

"Yes. Will told me that he and Bonnie met for lunch on the day of her disappearance. They were talking about getting back together."

"If that's true, why did she pack a suitcase?"

"My guess is Bonnie didn't know what to do. That could be why she called me. Bonnie and I often gave each other advice."

"I remember you were very close." Emma tapped her fingers against her lips. "Okay, so Bonnie packs a bag, goes to the meeting place and...what? She tells Joshua she can't go through with marrying him?"

"Or Bonnie told him she still had feelings for Will. Either way, I don't think the meeting went the way Joshua wanted it to and there was an altercation between them."

"Where were they supposed to meet?" she asked.

"At Franklin Park on the edge of town. Her cell phone was recovered from the park, smashed into pieces. Her car, purse and suitcase are still missing."

"What about Bonnie's phone records?"

"They show Joshua tried calling her several times on the night she disappeared, but that doesn't prove anything. He's had run-ins with the law in the past. He knew we'd check her phone. It's possible he called Bonnie to bolster his own story."

"But you can't prove it."

"No." He drew in a deep breath. "While Joshua doesn't have an alibi, there's no physical evidence linking him to the crime. The former sheriff never took the case seriously. Leads weren't tracked down. By the time I was elected to take his place, the trail had gone cold."

She rose from the bed and placed a hand on his arm. "Reed, that's awful. I'm so sorry. I can't imagine how painful this has been for you."

Emma's touch was comforting, but it was the warmth and understanding in the depths of her gorgeous eyes that was Reed's undoing. Time had changed them both, given them pain and edges. But it hadn't shifted Emma's bravery or kindness. Standing there, with Lily in his arms, he felt the wall closing off his heart cracking.

"I always took my cases seriously, Emma. Always. But being on the other side…it changes everything."

"Of course it does." She met his gaze. "It seems I'm not the only one God gave a mission to."

"No, although it's difficult to understand why Bonnie had to go missing to make it happen."

She touched Lily's back. "I don't know why Mark had to die either, but there are some things at work bigger than us. We need to have faith, as hard as it is."

"You don't think I'm crazy to believe Bonnie might be alive?"

"There is nothing wrong with holding out hope, Reed. I've worked search-and-rescue cases when things looked bleak. Either the person had been missing for a long time or the weather was terrible. Wonderful things happen. I've seen it, and if there's a chance Bonnie is alive, then we have to try to find her." She leaned closer. "You said yesterday I wasn't in this by myself. Well, you aren't either. If there's any way Sadie and I can help, then we will."

He reached out and cupped Emma's face with his hand. Her skin was soft. Reed ran his thumb over the crest of her cheek. His breath caught as Emma's gaze drifted to his mouth and lingered.

He wanted to kiss her. Desperately. The spark created when they were eighteen still lingered, their connection unchanged by time or distance.

He was a fool. Reed knew that now. He'd tried to avoid it, tried to keep her squarely in the friend zone, but his heart didn't know how to resist her special brand of compassion and strength. She was his own personal kryptonite.

His thumb swept across the line of her lower lip. Emma inhaled. Their eyes locked in and time stood still. She edged closer.

The ground shook under their feet as a blast of light blinded them. The explosion rattled the windowpane with the force of an earthquake. Reed grabbed Emma. Tucking Lily between them, he used his body to block them from the glass.

The lights in the hospital went out.

NINE

"Reed, that was some kind of explosion." There was a faint tremble in Emma's voice, so soft, anyone else would've missed it. "Could it have been a transformer? Is that why the lights went out?"

"Possibly." Reed didn't say it, but he didn't have to. Emma was smart enough to realize it could also be the second attacker, Grenade Man. "Any moment, the backup generators should kick on. Here, take Lily."

Reed transferred the baby to her arms. Thankfully, the explosion hadn't woken Lily, and he was careful not to either. Whatever was happening, it would be better if the baby slept through it. "Hold on to the back of my shirt, Emma."

His mind was racing but he kept his voice calm and controlled. He turned. Emma grabbed the fabric of his shirt with a tight hold. Reed pulled his weapon. "Vernon is still here in the hospital. He's under guard, but he's one floor above us."

"If that was a bomb, he didn't plant it. But his partner may be trying to break him out."

The room was pitch-black except for a faint light

coming in from the window. It appeared the entire hospital had lost power.

He waited a moment. Two. The hospital's backup generator didn't kick in. Probably because the explosion had taken it out. There was no way this was a coincidence. Grenade Man was back and either desperate or determined enough to make an attack on the hospital. Who was this guy?

He pulled out his cell and shot off a text to Austin and Deputy Kyle Hendricks. Both were in this hospital somewhere—Austin with Vivian, Kyle with Vernon—and Reed had to be sure they reacted accordingly. He also sent a text to his dispatch operator, asking for backup, before pocketing his phone.

Behind him, Emma's breathing was rapid and shaky. She was whispering something. A prayer.

"Emma, listen to me, I'm taking you and Lily out of here." He reached behind him with his free hand and squeezed her arm. "Follow closely behind me, keeping your hand on my shirt and Lily in between us. You got that?"

"But what about Vivian?" Her voice rose an octave. "She's—"

"Austin will get her to safety. Don't worry about Vivian right now. Your job is to stay safe for Lily."

"Got it." The words were followed by another quick prayer. It touched him to hear her whisper his name. He found himself sending up a prayer of his own.

Lord, please, help me protect this woman and her young child. I care about them. I don't want them hurt.

He did care about them. More than he wanted to admit. Yet, those emotions were also dangerous. If he didn't give the case everything he had, mistakes would be made. People could be killed.

His job was to protect Emma and Lily. He had every intention of doing just that.

Behind him, Emma's breathing slowed slightly as she shored up her courage. Reed let go of her arm and eased forward. He reached for the door handle. It was cool to the touch. He swung it open, leading with his weapon.

The hall was in a state of pandemonium. Doctors and nurses scrambled while machines in various rooms beeped and a cacophony of voices came from patients and family members. Emergency lights glowed from the ceiling. The coverage was spotty and created long shadows big enough to hide an elephant in.

Reed didn't like this. He didn't like it at all. Leaving the room exposed them but staying was worse. Without knowing how many hitmen were on the killer's payroll, Reed couldn't be sure of their plan. No, it was better to get Emma and Lily to a secure location.

He scanned the hallway, but no one was focused on them. Reed lowered his gun slightly—no sense in terrifying people more than they already were—and moved toward the stairway at the end of the hall. It was the farthest away, but his vehicle was parked in the garage right next to it, making for a quicker escape.

Emma did as he asked. She was close enough he could feel Lily's small body pressed against his back.

Faint pops echoed from somewhere in the building. Reed paused.

"Are those gunshots?" Emma breathed out.

"Yes." Vernon was on the floor above him. Either he was making an escape attempt or he was being rescued. *Lord, if you're listening, please also watch over my men. Help them do their jobs and give us the strength and courage to protect the innocent civilians depending on us.*

Reed stopped a nurse passing by them, pointing to his sheriff's badge. "Grab your staff and initiate the protocol for a shooter in the building."

Her eyes widened for a moment and then she rushed to a nearby doctor. Reed stayed underneath an emergency light so he was visible. The doctor glanced at him, took in his badge and the gun in his hand, before quickly picking up a nearby phone.

An emergency code sounded over the PA system, alerting the rest of the hospital. The flurry of activity increased as staff started gathering patients and family members into rooms. Protocol was to lock them in.

More faint pops sounded. He needed to get Emma out of here. Now.

"Come on." He quickened his steps toward the staircase. The door swung into the cavernous space. Empty. Reed tried to keep his footsteps soft, but the sound echoed off the concrete floor and walls. Five floors. That's how far they had to go to access the parking lot.

He activated the light on his weapon. "Stay close."

Emma gave a sharp nod. Her jaw was tight with fear, but her eyes reflected determination. Lily, thankfully, stayed sleeping against her mother's shoulder. Reed steadied his breath and locked down his worry about them. It wouldn't serve him. He moved as quickly as he could without tripping Emma. One floor down.

Faster. Faster.

The urgency in his gut was matched only by Emma's breathing. Another floor down.

Below them, a door opened. Reed froze.

* * *

Emma's heart leaped as the door slammed shut in the stairwell below them. Reed's back went rigid before immediately relaxing. Not because the threat had passed. No, because danger was coming straight for them, and he wanted to be ready.

As if echoing her thoughts, Reed maneuvered her and Lily between him and the wall. The cool banister bit into her back. Reed's wide shoulders cut off her view. The light from his gun allowed her only the faintest glimpse of his shirt.

He wasn't wearing a vest.

The thought sliced through her. Panic threatened to well up and choke her. Only moments ago she'd nearly kissed this man. Now they were under attack. Reed might die protecting her and her daughter. She'd already lost her husband. Would she lose another man she was growing to care about? It seemed impossible but Emma tightened her hold on Reed's shirt. The fabric cut into her fingers.

Please, Lord, keep us safe.

Silence echoed in the stairwell. The only sound was Emma's heartbeat pounding in her ears. Where was the person who'd entered the stairwell? With every ticking moment, the intensity of their situation pulled her muscles tighter. Maybe it was another patient? Or family member? The hospital was on lockdown but that didn't necessarily mean someone hadn't wanted to leave instead. But then, why wasn't the person moving?

Lily wriggled slightly in her arms. Her lashes fluttered open. No, no, no.

Baby girl, don't wake up.

If Lily started crying or talking, it would attract attention. Emma gently rocked her and the baby's eyes closed again. She sighed back into sleep.

Reed jerked his head to the side and gently tugged on Emma with his free hand. He wanted her to move toward the door right above them. She eased out from between Reed and the wall, careful to keep her footsteps light.

Something whistled past her ear. Concrete exploded behind her. Someone was shooting at them! Fear drove Emma to quicken her steps, no longer concerned with staying quiet. All she wanted was safety.

"I know you're there." A man's voice from below echoed through the stairwell. "Don't make this harder than it has to be."

Another shot whizzed past her. Emma nearly screamed.

"Go, Emma," Reed encouraged. "Faster."

She increased her pace up the stairs. Reed was right behind her, keeping her body covered with his own. Emma shoved open the door and launched herself into the hospital hallway. Pounding footsteps were coming up the stairwell. Reed slammed the door shut. It provided some protection from the shooter and bought them precious seconds.

Emma ran down the hall. Her chest was tight and her head throbbed. There was no way they could outrun this guy. The hospital was devoid of people. The minute he came up the stairs, he would spot them. Reed grabbed her arm, stopping her momentum. "In here."

He pushed Emma and Lily inside an open supply closet before shutting the door behind them. Racks of medical supplies towered above her. It smelled of bleach and laundry detergent. She turned, the metallic taste of fear filling her mouth when she realized Reed wasn't with them. He'd stayed in the hall to confront the shooter.

A man shouted, voice muffled through the door, "Where is she? The dog lady?"

Dog lady. There was no doubt these guys were looking for her. And anyone around her was immediately put at risk. The patients and their families. Reed.

Lily.

Fresh adrenaline raced through her veins. Lily couldn't be found with her. Emma searched for a place to stash her daughter. She scrambled to the back of the closet, grabbing some towels along the way. The bottom rack held rolls of toilet paper. She shoved them out of the way and spread the towels on the shelf like a make-shift bed. She quickly pressed a kiss to her daughter's face before laying her down.

"Stay sleeping, pretty girl. Mommy will be right back."

She rapidly restacked the toilet paper in front of the baby to hide her. Emma scanned the room again, this time looking for any kind of weapon. Not that much could be used against a gun. Still, something had to be better than nothing.

A mop caught her eye. She removed the stick. Keeping it gripped in her hands, she moved back to the door.

"I'm with the Heyworth County Sheriff's Department. Put your gun on the ground and your hands in the air."

Reed's tone was authoritative and strong. For the second time in two days, he was negotiating with a man holding a gun while innocent civilians were within range.

"Where is she?" the other man screamed. "I will tear this floor apart looking for her, shooting everyone along the way, Sheriff. Have no doubt. You have thirty seconds to produce her. Now!"

No. Emma wouldn't allow that to happen. She couldn't. Her hand reached for the door handle. It was cold against her skin. She paused. Waiting.

Please, Lord. Have him put down the gun.

Shots rang out. Emma jumped.

Had Reed been shot? Her breath caught in her throat and she strained to hear something beyond the door. Nothing. Tears pricked her eyes. She forced them back. It wasn't time to fall apart. Not yet—

The doorknob rattled under her hand and she shrieked.

"Emma, open up. It's Reed."

She flung the door open. He stood in front of her, whole and unharmed. Her relief and panic must've shown in her expression because Reed gathered her into his arms.

"It's over. The man who attacked us is dead."

Her body shook as tears swept over her cheeks. She couldn't bring herself to pull it together. Voices rose up behind Reed. A radio crackled.

"Building secure…"

His hand rubbed up and down on her back. When her sobs subsided, she pulled back a bit. "I'm always crying on you."

"I don't mind." His thumb wiped away a straggling tear. "Where's Lily?"

"I hid her behind the toilet paper." Emma realized she was still holding the mop stick. "I didn't want him to find her..." Her voice trailed off. She couldn't finish the thought.

"Good thinking, Em." Reed passed her and crouched down. He uncovered Lily in record time. The baby giggled when he lifted her. It nearly set off Emma's tears again.

She swallowed hard. "Vivian?"

"She's safe. They'll meet us at the car."

Emma let out a whoosh of air. "What happened?"

"The attacker wanted to find you," Reed said. "He needed me to tell him where you were. When I didn't, he shot toward the nursing station. There were some people hiding there. I had to shoot him."

His words were flat. Harsh even. But Emma didn't have to be told why. He was keeping his own emotions bottled up tight. He'd saved lives, but Emma was under no illusions that it didn't come at a cost.

"The man who attacked us wasn't alone," Reed continued. "Someone else was helping Vernon escape."

Two men. Just like in the woods. Emma's throat tightened. "Did they get away? Was anyone hurt?"

"Vernon was shot, but his accomplice escaped." Reed held her daughter tenderly and took Emma's hand. "The building's secure, but we need to get you out of here. We're going back down the stairs, this time escorted by some of my men."

She nodded, and they stepped out. The hospital floor was crawling with deputies. Emma focused on the feel of Reed's hand in her own to calm her nerves. His grip was strong but also gentle. This time they traversed the stairs without a problem. The parking garage was full of vehicles. Reed had procured a new official vehicle from the department's spares. It sat in the fire lane next to another patrol car. Vivian popped out, running toward them.

Emma embraced her sister-in-law. Vivian gripped her tight enough to cut off her breathing.

"Ladies, let's get into the car," Reed said. "Now."

The tone of his voice alerted Emma to the fact that while the immediate threat was over, the danger wasn't. There was an attacker still out there. Somewhere. She climbed into the back seat. Reed deposited Lily into a car seat he'd obviously put in to bring the baby and Vivian to the hospital earlier. Emma busied her hands by strapping her daughter in good and tight.

Reed drove out of the parking garage. Lily pointed at something outside of the window and babbled. Desperate for normalcy, Emma tweaked her nose. "What are you looking at? What do you see?"

Emma glanced out the window. A flash of fabric caught her eye. A man with blond hair; a familiar gait.

Her cousin, Owen.

Running from the direction of the hospital.

TEN

Hours after the attack at the hospital, Reed's heartbeat was still working on settling itself into a normal rhythm. He'd driven Emma and her family to the only place he could guarantee they were safe—his own sheriff's department. Encasing them behind a wall of deputies allowed him to focus on the threats against them.

The bull pen was like a humming beehive. Deputies flowed in and out, phones rang, and keyboards clattered as Reed walked through. He entered the break room and went straight for the coffeepot. Several boxes from a local pizzeria were stacked on the table. Reed's stomach rumbled, and he snagged a slice to have with his coffee.

The blinds in his office were open. Vivian played on the floor with Lily using some blocks and foam cups she'd unearthed from somewhere. Emma spotted him through the glass and joined him in the break room. Sadie followed her mistress.

"Are you okay?" Reed asked. He took a new cup and poured some coffee for her.

"As good as can be expected." She rubbed her forehead. "But between you and me, I'm still shaken. This attack was a close call for Lily and Vivian."

His jaw tightened. "Too close. Not just for them, but for you, as well."

Thankfully, no innocent people had been hurt. Still, the weight of taking another man's life weighed heavily on Reed's shoulders. He didn't regret it. His decision had saved innocent lives. He just wished it hadn't come to that.

Emma took the coffee from him and their fingers brushed. A jolt of electricity arced through the air. His gaze dropped to her lips, remembering the moments before the explosion. Would they have kissed? Most likely.

Reed gave himself a mental shake. His train of thought was completely ill timed and inappropriate considering everything going on.

"Is there anything new?" She stirred some milk into her coffee. "Or some way I can help? I'm going a bit stir-crazy."

He didn't blame her. If he'd been sitting in a room for the last several hours, he'd be itching to do something, too. "I'm about to have a meeting with Austin and Cooper to go over what we know so far. Why don't you join us?"

Having another set of eyes wouldn't hurt. Emma had proven herself to be more than capable of handling tense situations. Besides, it was her life being threatened and her family caught in the cross fire. Reed didn't see any point in holding back information from her.

"Okay," Emma said. "Let me just tell Vivi where I'll be."

He took his coffee and went into the conference room. Austin and Cooper were already waiting inside. So was Will Norton. As the county prosecutor, it made sense for him to stay up to date on their investigation.

A whiteboard stretched along one wall, various photographs and notes arranged in an organized fashion.

Reed greeted the men and took a chair on the far side so he had a clear view of the board. "Let's go over what we do know, from the beginning."

The conference room door opened. Emma and her dog slipped inside the room. She took the chair next to him. Her vanilla scent tickled his nose and soothed something inside him. He liked having her close.

Austin stood up. "We've officially identified two of the suspects from the hospital. Vernon Hanks, you know. He was killed outside the hospital while trying to escape."

Reed's heart twisted. Not for Vernon but for his daughter. To lose a father under any circumstances was hard, but this was so much worse. Molly deserved better. Thankfully, she had her mother and stepfather to rely on.

"The man you shot…" Austin took a photo down off the board and slid it across the table to Reed "…was Vernon's cousin, Charlie Young."

Reed frowned. "That name sounds familiar."

"It should." Will smoothed a hand down his tie. This one was dark blue and matched his pinstriped suit. "He lives in Heyworth and has a rap sheet a mile long. Started out in petty theft and minor drug dealing, but over the years, he's worked himself up to aggravated assault. Got out of jail a few months ago."

The man at the hospital had been wearing a ski mask, so Reed hadn't gotten a good look at him. Charlie's mug shot showed a thin-faced individual with stringy hair. Reed remembered the same image had crossed his desk a few weeks ago. "Wasn't there an arrest warrant issued for him last month for skipping parole?"

Will nodded. "Yep. He'd gone underground, and supposedly, no one's heard from him. But you know how that is."

Deputies would've gone to Charlie's last known address, talked to his family and friends regarding his whereabouts. But with career criminals, police often got the runaround. Reed pushed the photo over to Emma so she could get a better look. "Ever seen this guy before?"

She studied it for a long moment before shaking her head. "No. Not that I recall."

Austin slid over another photograph. "This is Vernon's other cousin. Mike Young. The younger brother of Charlie."

Reed could easily see the family resemblance. Same beady eyes, same greasy hair.

"I've never seen this guy either." Emma leaned over to see the photograph better. "You think this is the other guy from the hospital? The one that got away?"

"It's impossible to know for sure until we find and question him. But my guess would be yes. Mike did a stint in the military for a while. He specialized in explosives."

Beside him, Emma inhaled sharply. Reed eyed the photograph with renewed interest. There was little doubt Mike Young was Grenade Man. "That bumps him to the top of our suspect list."

"We've got every officer in the state looking for him." Cooper rested his arms on the table. The Texas Ranger had shed his sports jacket and rolled up the sleeves of his white button-down. "He won't be free for long."

"Any idea who hired them?"

Austin shook his head. "We're still working on that. We do know Charlie was the primary contact. We recovered his cell phone, and we were able to open it. There are text messages between Charlie and Mike talking about a $15,000 payment. Charlie was probably the one who broke into Emma's house. We conducted a search of his apartment and found both the missing tablet and the gold pen."

Reed mulled that over for a moment. "Okay, so someone tries to scare Emma off the property, and when that doesn't work, he hires Charlie to break in. The initial plan was to make it appear as a home robbery that went wrong. Except I showed up."

"Agreed. When that failed, Charlie pulled in his brother and Vernon to help out."

Emma was pale, and her fingers trembled. She was keeping it together, but Reed knew inside she was freaking out. Finding out you were the victim of a murder-for-hire wasn't easy for anyone, but it was far worse for a woman who'd already lost a husband and had a baby depending on her.

Reed placed a hand on her arm. "You okay?"

She took a deep breath. "It's okay. I want to hear everything."

Reed gestured for Austin to continue, but it was Cooper who spoke. "We found evidence confirming what Vernon's girlfriend told us. The burner phone Charlie had on him contained clear instructions. Emma was to be killed. The fee was double if you were taken out, as well."

"Do we know when that decision was made?"

"After the break-in at Emma's house failed. Essentially, when you took over the case."

Reed sat back in his chair. "The only connection I can think of is Bonnie."

"Hold on." Cooper held up a hand. "We don't have a shred of physical evidence indicating these recent attacks are connected to your sister's disappearance."

"What else could it be?" Emma asked.

"Well, Reed has a reputation for being thorough and determined. Once he was involved, the perpetrator likely knew he wouldn't let it go. Especially if you were murdered. Taking him out along with you does two things. It muddies the investigation and removes, at least in the perpetrator's mind, the one person who would go to the ends of the earth to get justice."

Reed hated to admit it, but Cooper's logic made sense. "So you're suggesting we focus on Emma. We need to uncover why someone would want her out of the way."

"Precisely. Since this entire thing started with someone trying to run Emma out of town, I'm inclined to believe this has less to do with her and more to do with her land." Cooper leaned forward. "Emma, you're building a search-and-rescue canine training facility. Maybe there's something on your property the perpetrator is trying to prevent you from finding."

Her eyes widened. "Something we might stumble on by accident while training the dogs or while making improvements to the land."

"Exactly. It has to be big enough it can't be moved or it has to be something that couldn't be moved without people noticing."

Reed's stomach sank. There was only one person

he could think of who had a vested interest in hiding something on Emma's property. "We haven't located Owen yet, have we?"

Owen had been in the hospital because of an adverse reaction to some medication he'd been given for treatment of Sadie's bite. He'd been under guard, but the ensuing confusion during the attack had enabled him to escape.

"Not yet," Cooper said. "We need to consider that Owen may be the one who hired the hitmen. While we're looking for him, I recommend we conduct a search of Emma's property. Uncovering what's hidden there may be the best way to keep everyone safe."

Reed nodded, squeezing Emma's arm. Her face was pale, worry lines etched in the curve of her brow. She'd never been very good at hiding her emotions. The same concerns running through his mind were written in her expression.

When they conducted a search of Emma's property, what would they find?

By dinnertime, Emma's body ached and her head was pounding. The pain was exacerbated by the swirling emotions inside her. Could Owen really have hired hitmen to kill her? Where would he have gotten the money? A small part of her clung to the notion that there was no way her cousin was behind this. It seemed ridiculous, given his actions, but she couldn't quite let herself believe Owen wanted her dead.

The search of her property would start tomorrow morning. Until they uncovered what was hidden, she was a target. The first order of business was getting her family out of harm's way.

Reed punched a code into his phone, and the gates to his aunt's ranch opened. The SUV bounced over the cattle guard.

"Gorgeous sunset," Vivian remarked from the back seat. Deep purples and streaks of pink played across the wide-open sky. The driveway curved and the house came into view. It was two stories with a large wrap-around porch. "And a lovely house."

"You'll like Aunt Bessie," Emma said. "She's one of the sweetest people I've ever met."

Emma lifted Lily out of her car seat. Lily waved at Reed's aunt as she hurried down the porch steps to greet them. Everything about Aunt Bessie was soft, from the pale peach dress fluttering around her calves to the silver hair swept back in a bun at the nape of her neck.

"Welcome, welcome." Bessie introduced herself to Vivian before patting Reed's cheek. "Take the suitcases to the blue room, dear."

Bessie hugged Austin, careful to avoid jostling her son's shoulder, before turning her attention to Emma and Lily. "Emma, your daughter is beautiful. She looks just like you."

"Until she scowls. Then she looks like her daddy."

Bessie laughed. "Well, we are gonna do our best to prevent any scowls, aren't we, sweet Lily?"

Lily grinned and babbled in response. Sadie, freed from the car, bounded over. Reed's aunt greeted her with a pat to the head. "Hello, sweetness."

Emma bent down to kiss the older woman's cheek. "Thank you for letting Vivian and Lily stay here."

"Nonsense." Bessie wrapped an arm around Emma's waist, steering her toward the house. "Y'all are doing me a favor. It gets lonely knocking around this old house by myself."

Crossing the threshold was like stepping back in time. The leather recliner, its color worn away in places, still sat in the living room next to the L-shaped sofa. The wood cabinet holding the television gleamed in the waning sunlight. It smelled of yeasty bread and cinnamon. Emma's stomach growled.

"I hope y'all brought your appetites with you," Bessie declared. "I've made fried chicken and all the sides, including buttermilk biscuits. Dinner will be ready in fifteen. Emma, love, you remember where the blue room is, don't you?" She waited for Emma's nod. "Go on and show Vivian where she and Lily will be staying. Reed, I need your help digging the high chair out of the garage."

Emma waved for Vivian to follow her down the hall. From the kitchen Bessie's voice bellowed, "Austin Joseph Carter, get your grubby mitts away from my biscuits and start setting the table."

Emma and Vivian burst out laughing at the way Bessie scolded her grown son. There weren't many who probably spoke to the chief deputy that way. Lily also laughed. Some of the weight on Emma's shoulders seemed to dissipate. Aunt Bessie's house was like a bubble of warmth.

"You're right," Vivian whispered between chuckles. "I love her already."

"I knew you would."

Her sister-in-law paused by a photograph hanging in the hall. "That's you with Reed."

Emma backed up a few steps. Sure enough, a younger version of herself and Reed were sitting on Aunt Bessie's porch. Bonnie, her short hair tousled by the wind, was pointing to the checkerboard between them, probably giving advice. Austin stood behind Reed, his arms crossed over his chest.

"I remember this," Emma said. "We were having a checkers competition."

"Did you spend a lot of time here?"

"Not a lot, but some." Reed and Bonnie would spend days with Aunt Bessie when their mother's depression got to be too much. Emma tagged along, happy to be anywhere Reed was. "We always had a good time. Uncle Jeb and Aunt Bessie's late husband were good friends, so it was a natural fit."

They stepped into the blue room, aptly named for the bluebonnet wallpaper. There was a sitting area with a television, an attached bathroom, and gorgeous floor-to-ceiling windows overlooking the backside of the ranch. Bessie had even set up a crib for Lily.

"This is beautiful." Vivian walked over to the window. "And peaceful. I can see why you spoke so highly of it."

"It's a good place to stay under any circumstance, but it's a real blessing now. A state trooper will be assigned to watch the house. You and Lily will be safe here."

Vivian took a deep breath. "I wish you were staying, too. Please promise me you'll be careful."

"Of course. Reed's already said he's going to be glued to my side."

Lily fussed, so Emma placed the baby on the carpet. Sadie sniffed her and Lily laughed before crawling away to explore the room. Emma kept one eye on her.

"Glued to your side, huh?" Vivian's eyes twinkled. "Any chance the sparks I've noticed between the two of you will develop into something more?"

"Vivian!"

"What? It's a nice break from all this murder and mayhem. So, spill the beans."

Emma's cheeks heated. "We… Well, I think Reed was about to kiss me."

Vivian's face broke out into a grin. "Oh, really? When did this happen?"

"At the hospital. Before the attack." Emma picked at an invisible piece of lint before straightening her shirt.

Her sister-in-law's gleeful expression faded into something more serious. "What's the problem, Emma? I know you like him."

"Yes, but with all of this murder and mayhem, as you put it, I don't think now is the best time to complicate the relationship."

"Oh, hon, it's the only way you would've broken out of your shell. Don't get me wrong. I'm not wishing for your life to be in danger, but you were in a rut and determined to stay there. It was clear to me from the beginning there was something between you and Reed. If this brings the two of you closer together, then I'm glad some good came out of all of this ugliness."

"I hadn't thought of it that way." Emma paused. "But to be honest, we agreed to be friends. Maybe it's a good thing the kiss didn't happen. He might've regretted it."

"Or he might not have. You won't know until you talk to him about it. Something tells me that Reed doesn't act without thinking and my guess is, he's just as worried about rocking the boat as you are."

Vivian had a point. Still, things were a mess at the moment. Emma didn't want to say it, but she wasn't entirely sure she wanted to risk her heart again. Reed had a dangerous job. She'd already lost her husband. Could she fall in love again knowing the pain that would come if tragedy struck? Emma wasn't sure she had it in her.

A knock came from the doorway. Reed stuck his head in. "Hey, ladies, dinner is ready."

"Great. I'm starving." Vivian scooped up Lily. The little girl protested, and she bounced her a bit. "Let's go see what Aunt Bessie has for us."

Emma followed behind a bit slower. Reed greeted her with a smile that warmed the depths of his blue eyes. Her steps faltered. She mentally shook herself. Now was not the time to be gooey over Reed. Even if the man had saved her life and that of her daughter's. Several times.

"Thanks for arranging this," Emma said. "I think Vivian and Lily are going to have a good time with your aunt."

"So do I. And it'll make me feel better to know they're out of harm's way."

"Me, too."

He placed a hand on the small of her back as they walked down the hall toward the dining room. The warmth of his touch spread through her and reinforced Vivian's words. Eventually, Emma and Reed would have to discuss their relationship.

But now wasn't the time.

ELEVEN

The next morning, Reed rose at daybreak. His house was quiet. The doors to both his spare bedrooms were still closed. Emma was in one, Austin in the other. A deputy was patrolling Emma's property, but Reed didn't feel comfortable staying in her home given the circumstances. His house had a security system including an alarm and cameras. It would be a lot harder for anyone to sneak up on them.

He started the coffee and breakfast. Twenty minutes later, Austin joined him in the kitchen.

"Smells good." Austin said a quick prayer before snagging a piece of toast. "If I'd known breakfast was part of the bargain, I would've been a houseguest a long time ago."

Reed snorted. "Don't get used to it. How's your shoulder?"

"Better. Still a bit sore, but at least I can lose the sling now." Austin glanced at his watch. "You got a to-go cup for the coffee? I want to get over to Emma's property before the rest of the troops show up. It'll give me time to organize the search."

"Sure thing. Emma and I will be over soon."

"Take your time. After all she's been through, I'm sure she needs the sleep."

Austin ate quickly and left. The click of Sadie's nails on the tile flooring preceded the dog's appearance in the kitchen. Emma followed. Her hair was pulled into a simple braid. She hadn't put on any makeup and was dressed for hiking in jeans along with a lightweight long-sleeve shirt. "Morning."

Reed momentarily lost his words. Emma's beauty was striking, but it was nothing compared to the warmth and kindness shining in her eyes. "Uhhh, morning. Coffee?"

"Yes, please. Is the alarm off? I have to let Sadie out for a potty break and some exercise."

He poured a cup of coffee for her before topping off his own. "I'll come with you."

Outside, dew coated the grass in the yard. Reed took a deep breath of the fresh air and scanned the immediate area for any danger. Nothing stirred, except for a few birds flying overhead. Sadie trotted over to some bushes.

"Did you sleep well?" he asked Emma.

She took a sip of her coffee. "Better than well. I feel like a new person. I'm sure having two lawmen around, plus a full-scale security system had a lot to do with it. Has Austin already left?"

"Yes, he wanted to get a jump start on the search."

The sound of a car caught Reed's attention and he turned. A sedan pulled to a stop in his driveway, a young woman behind the wheel. Reed recognized her instantly. Margaret Carpenter was the local veterinarian. She'd also been Bonnie's best friend.

"Is that Margaret?" Emma asked.

"Yep. Maybe she wants to check in on Sadie," Reed said, as he and Emma crossed the yard toward the driveway. "She was out of town when Deputy Irving called to have Sadie checked out after the grenade attack. Her answering service referred us to the vet in the next town. Have you ever met Margaret?"

"Briefly, when I first moved to town. I wanted to talk with her about providing care for the dogs at my training facility. She seemed really nice."

Margaret climbed out of the vehicle, dressed in scrubs. When he got close enough, Reed lifted the cup in his hand. "Hey, Margaret. Would you like to come in for some coffee?"

"No, thanks. I have to run to work, but I'm glad I caught you. I was away on a cruise with some girlfriends until last night. Will gave me an update on what's been going on and the possible connection to Bonnie's disappearance."

Reed's hand tightened on his coffee mug. Will shouldn't have shared that information with anyone. "I'm sorry, Margaret. I can't discuss an ongoing investigation." He was, however, going to have a long conversation with the county prosecutor. Will knew better.

"Don't be mad at Will, Reed. I heard rumors going around at the diner when I stopped in to grab a quick dinner and confronted him. He knew Bonnie and I were very close. It was only a matter of time before I got the information from the rumor mill anyway. Besides, I may have information that pertains to the case." Margaret's gaze darted toward Emma before settling back on Reed. "It's about Owen."

"Okay."

Margaret opened her mouth but hesitated. Emma gave her a reassuring smile. "It's all right. Tell us."

The other woman nodded. "Bonnie and Owen had an altercation a few months before she went missing."

Reed reared back. "What kind of altercation?"

"Owen had a case in front of Judge Norton. A DUI, I think. Anyway, there was some kind of interaction between Owen and Bonnie outside the courtroom."

Judge Norton was only one of a handful of judges for the county, so it wasn't unusual for him to hear many of the cases from Heyworth. Bonnie had worked as Judge Norton's paralegal.

"Bonnie didn't get into specifics, but she made it sound like a normal, friendly conversation," Margaret continued. "Owen had gone to our high school and, although he was there as defendant, it wasn't in Bonnie's nature to be ugly to anyone."

"No, it wasn't. She always had a kind word for everyone," Reed said. A sharp ache settled in his chest, but he refused to acknowledge it. Instead, he focused on the conversation at hand. "What happened next?"

Margaret crossed her arms over her chest. "Owen waited for Bonnie to get off work and approached her in the parking lot of the courthouse. He repeatedly asked her out. When she refused, Owen became enraged. He called her a flirt or some other kind of nonsense. She managed to get to her car and leave, but the incident left Bonnie shaken enough to tell me about it."

"Did anything else happen?"

"No. As far as I know, Owen never bothered her again."

Reed's jaw clenched. "Why didn't you tell me about this earlier?"

Margaret bit her lip. "I'm sorry, Reed. To be honest, it slipped my mind until Will mentioned that Owen might be a suspect. The argument between Bonnie and Owen happened at least six months before she disappeared."

Reed wrestled back his frustration. Cold case investigations often got new information this way. Something that seemed benign long ago suddenly took on new meaning.

"Margaret, do you believe Bonnie ran off?" Emma asked.

She shifted in her soft-soled shoes and hugged herself tighter. "Frankly, I never did."

Reed sucked in a sharp breath. "But…you told me differently."

"I know. I didn't want to get your hopes up if I was wrong. The former sheriff was so certain Bonnie had taken off. He made it seem like I couldn't trust my own insights about my friend. After all, I hadn't known about her relationship with Joshua."

Reed pinched the bridge of his nose and fought back his frustration. The former sheriff had done a lot of damage to the investigation.

"We need to call Austin right now and tell him to stop the search immediately," Emma said. She started for the house. "Don't let them step into the woods on my property."

"What?" Reed chased after her. "Why?"

"Because I have an idea."

Emma refused to explain her plan until Cooper and Austin arrived. Reed wasn't going to like it, and she needed reinforcements. Once they were all settled at the kitchen table, each with a fresh cup of coffee, she displayed an aerial view of her property on a tablet.

"Let's do a quick review of what we know," she said. "I inherit my uncle's property and move to Heyworth. Shortly thereafter, someone starts breaking things on my property and making scary phone calls telling me to leave town. Then poisoned meat is left out for Sadie to eat. As a result, I file a police report. A week goes by and nothing else happens on the property. We now know that's because my stalker was looking for and arranging to hire Charlie."

She paused and Cooper nodded for her to go on.

"Charlie breaks into my house and attacks me," Emma continued. "Subsequently, Reed launches an investigation. Charlie is instructed to get rid of me and Reed. He calls in reinforcements—his brother, Mike, and his cousin, Vernon. They hatch a scheme to kidnap Vernon's daughter while she's on a camping trip with her mother and stepfather. As the nearest SAR team, it's almost guaranteed Sadie and I will be called out to aid in the search. The basic idea is to kill us once we locate Molly, but Vernon has poor aim and—based on the conversation Austin overheard Vernon having—probably didn't want to be responsible for the actual murders. He calls one of his cousins, most likely Charlie, and tells him to hurry up and get there so he can finish the job."

"Fortunately for us, he was late," Austin muttered.

"Agreed. When the attack falls apart and Vernon is arrested, a new plan is made. Charlie and Mike storm the hospital to rescue their cousin and kill me. Two of the hired hitmen are killed in the process—Vernon and Charlie—but Mike escapes. That's what we know and what we can prove."

"Right." Cooper drained the last of his coffee.

"The ultimate question is why would anyone want to kill both Reed and I?" Emma rose from her chair and grabbed the carafe of coffee, refilling each man's cup before her own. "Reed believes his sister's disappearance may have something to do with it. Cooper, you think someone—probably my cousin Owen—has hidden something on the property he doesn't want us to uncover." She took a deep breath. "I think you both may be right."

Reed's eyes widened as he followed her chain of thought. Austin, midsip of his coffee, choked and started coughing.

Cooper frowned. "What are you suggesting? That Bonnie's body is somewhere on your property?"

"No, that Bonnie is alive and being held captive somewhere on my property."

All of the men stared at her in disbelief. Emma pointed to the tablet, showing the aerial view of her property. "I have large swatches of wooded areas on my land. That was perfect for me because I intended to use it as a training area for the canines, but it also means it would be easy for someone to slip on and off the property without me knowing."

"Hold on, hold on." Cooper put up a hand. "If Bonnie was alive on your property, then wouldn't you have found her by now? I mean the kidnapper has to keep her in some kind of structure."

"But it could be an underground bunker. There have been cases like that."

"Even if that's true, the kidnapper would just move Bonnie."

"But he couldn't get rid of the structure," Emma

said. "Bonnie's scent would linger long enough the dogs might pick up on it. Or improvements to the land could uncover the bunker. DNA, fingerprints... It would be nearly impossible to get rid of all the evidence inside, right? Especially if Bonnie has been there for a long time."

Cooper nodded slowly. "That's true. It would be hard to clean away all the evidence."

"Which leaves the kidnapper at risk. Plus, he would have to arrange for a new hiding place for Bonnie. It would be far easier to keep her where she is and gain control of the property. Owen has been desperate to get his hands on this land from day one."

Reed inhaled sharply. His gaze dropped to the map before rising to meet hers. "Margaret said Owen was angry with Bonnie for refusing to go out with him."

Emma nodded. "Owen's interactions with me prove he holds on to grudges. Bonnie and Owen went to high school together. Who knows how long he's been interested in her."

"And interest can turn to obsession."

She snapped her fingers. "Like that."

Emma could've kicked herself for not putting two and two together faster. The conversation with Margaret was the missing link they needed.

Cooper's gaze jumped back and forth between her and Reed. "That's a lot of conjecture."

"But it makes sense," Emma continued. "Sadie is an air-scenting dog as opposed to a tracking dog. A tracking dog takes a specific person's scent and follows it to locate only that person. Sadie, however, will find any person lost in a given area. So, let's say I'm running a training exercise and I sent someone into my woods to be the lost person—" she put air quotes around lost person "—Sadie is sent into the woods to find the person. She doesn't know which specific person I'm looking for. She just knows to find someone."

"She could stumble across Bonnie by accident," Reed finished.

"Exactly. That's why I told you to stop the search and not let anyone in the woods on my property. I need to split the acres into sizable chunks and have Sadie search them. My hope is she'll find Bonnie."

"Absolutely not." Reed sliced a hand through the air. "It's too dangerous. Mike is still on the loose. We'll get another team to do the search."

She opened her mouth to object, but Cooper cut her off. "There is no other team available. We've got several missing hikers two counties over. They're aiding in that search."

"So ask one team to come here."

"Based on what, Reed?" Cooper asked. "A theory? Right now, we have no physical evidence indicating Bonnie is anywhere near here. Those missing hikers are a certainty and their lives are on the line."

"He's right," Emma said. She crossed her arms over her chest and reminded herself to stay calm. She couldn't be angry with Reed for wanting to protect her. The last few days had been harrowing. At the same time, if she was right, time was of the essence. There was no way to know what kind of rations Bonnie had. She wouldn't survive long without food or water. "Sadie and I are available, and we can do it."

"What if we do a thorough foot search?" Reed asked. "We've got enough law enforcement."

"There's nothing better for these kinds of searches

than a canine. Sadie can cover a larger area faster and her nose won't miss Bonnie, even if she's hidden underground."

"There are things we can do to lessen the risk." Austin pointed at the map. "We can set up patrols along the main road and assign deputies and troopers to keep an eye on the back roads, too. If there's a clear law enforcement presence, it should dissuade Mike from attempting anything."

"*Should* is the operative word in that sentence," Reed argued. "There's no guarantee."

"I'm willing to accept the risk." Emma jutted up her chin. "This is my job, and I'm going to do it."

Reed sighed and his shoulders dropped. "Fine. You win." He met her gaze. "But I'm going with you and Sadie. You have your job, and I have mine. I have every intention of keeping you safe during the search."

TWELVE

By noon, the coolness of the morning had morphed into a warm spring day. Reed rested on a rock under the shade of an oak tree. The radio on his hip crackled and various voices and codes filtered out. Shifts were changing among the deputies and troopers assigned around the property.

Sadie had cleared almost half of the wooded acreage. There was no sign of Bonnie.

Emma threw a ball, and Sadie streaked after it. Reed's gaze scanned the field, lake and tree line. Nothing moved. He was probably being overly cautious. After all, Sadie was likely to be the first one to let them know if a stranger was nearby. He reached inside his backpack and pulled out a bottle of water.

"Let's take a break for lunch." Emma dropped down next to him. Her cheeks were flushed with exertion, and the color brought out the gold flecks in her eyes. "Sadie needs a rest."

The dog joined them. She collapsed in the grass, panting, her fur shining in the sunlight.

"It looks like she's smiling," Reed remarked.

Emma laughed, pulling a small cooler out of her

backpack. "She is. Sadie loves to work. The playtime afterward doesn't hurt."

Reed's cell phone beeped, and he checked the message. "I got an email from your uncle's attorney, Emma. Owen wouldn't have received any money under Jeb's will unless he'd been sober for a year. But there's another trust."

Her forehead wrinkled as she waved a hand to shoo away a fly. "From Aunt Rachel?"

"Yep. Apparently, she inherited some money from her parents and set it aside for Owen. He gained access to it when he turned thirty-five. His birthday was four days before Charlie was hired."

"Well, I guess that explains where he got the money." She took a long drink of water, her gaze drifting over the field. In the distance, the lake sparkled in the sunlight. "You know Owen taught me to fish right over there."

"I remember. I'm sorry, Emma."

She let out a breath and tilted her head. "I'm not the only one with a connection to this place. Bonnie loved to fish here, too."

"Yes, she did. Bonnie convinced Judge Norton to let us cut through his property from ours to get here."

The large clearing and the lake sat on the border of intersecting properties. Joshua was to the north and Judge Norton was to the east. Jeb's land extended to the south and west. Back when Reed was a teenager, everything bordering Jeb's land had belonged to the judge.

Emma removed her sandwich from the plastic bag. "Cookies."

"What?"

"Bonnie used my grandmother's recipe and baked

Judge Norton a batch of chocolate chip cookies. Judge Norton was hooked on them. He agreed to let her cut across the property, as long as she would keep baking them for him."

Reed laughed. "I should've known he wrangled some kind of bargain out of it."

"Judge Norton's the one who inspired Bonnie to become a paralegal, isn't he?"

"Yes, he did. But her ultimate dream was to be an attorney."

Bonnie had been working and saving money for law school. Her bank account had a hefty sum of cash in it. She'd been halfway to her dream before she disappeared.

Emma let out a long breath. "I'm sorry, Reed. I shouldn't have brought it up."

"No." He glanced at the lake again. "Actually, it's nice to remember the good times. I spend so much of my time thinking about her case. But that's not Bonnie, you know?"

His sister was warm and loving, quick to laugh and always there to help a friend. Reed had a mountain of childhood memories about her he never discussed.

"Yeah, I know what you mean." Emma met his gaze, understanding etched in the curve of her brow and the tilt of her lips. "Bonnie is so much more than the moment of her disappearance."

His breath caught. He'd forgotten how easily Emma saw straight into his heart. Reed dropped his gaze under the pretense of grabbing a banana from his lunch sack. Their near kiss in the hospital lingered in his mind, but he did his best to snuff out the memory. They'd agreed to be friends and Emma had been under a lot of stress.

It wouldn't be smart to assume one small moment between them meant anything.

"Is it hard being in Heyworth?" she asked. "You always talked about never coming back. Returning under these circumstances can't be easy."

"Well, I did return because Bonnie disappeared, but I was already making plans to move home anyway."

"You were?"

He nodded. "My mom's depression was hard on me. I didn't understand it and I spent a lot of time angry with her. When she didn't get out of bed for weeks, taking care of Bonnie fell on my shoulders. Making the meals, getting ready for school, all of it. I wanted to escape and never look back."

Remembering his immaturity and lack of compassion shamed him. His mother had been struggling. Reed knew that now.

"College opened my eyes a bit," he continued. "I found a deeper connection with the Lord. Then I joined the Austin police academy. Living in a big city set me straight. Yes, my mom's depression created obstacles in my life, but I still had family—Aunt Bessie and Uncle Ray—plus the whole town. Neighbors would bring casseroles and cheer me on at track meets. Your uncle gave me work. Jeb paid far more than he should have so I could make the bills. That kind of community doesn't happen everywhere and there a lot of kids out there who never get to experience it."

Emma sighed. "Like me."

"Yeah. I remembered everything you said, and I started to look at things very differently. I wanted to give back to Heyworth. I applied to work in the sheriff's department and was on the waiting list to become a deputy. Then Bonnie disappeared. Everything changed. The sheriff wasn't as careful with cases as he should've been. I set out to run against him and won the election."

Her lips turned up into a beautiful smile. "Heyworth is fortunate to have you."

"It's home. It took me a long time to realize it, but I'm glad I did. My mom and I healed our relationship before she passed away, too." He blinked at the sudden rush of emotions washing over him. "I'm very grateful for that."

"So am I."

She shifted and leaned her head against his shoulder. Reed took her hand, interlacing their fingers together. The wind ruffled his hair, and for a brief moment, he allowed himself to simply be present with her.

Something moving across the field caught his attention. He frowned. "What's Sadie doing?"

The dog was sniffing around a small shack that used to contain fishing tackle.

"She's exploring." Emma sat up and squinted. "Although I think something in the shack has caught her attention. There's not much in there, aside from Jeb's fishing gear and some tools. I padlocked it once stuff started happening around the property."

He stood. "Do you have the key on you?"

"Yep. I grabbed it when I knew we would be doing a search of the property." She opened a zipper on her backpack and pulled out a ring of keys. "Reed, Bonnie can't be in there. I've checked it out already."

"Still worth taking a look at what has Sadie's interest." Reed scanned the tree line again. Everything was clear. He stepped out of the shadows and into the sunlight. "Stay with me."

They crossed the field. As they drew closer to the shack, the wind shifted. A rotten smell drifted over them. Emma gagged. "Oh, no."

Reed's gut twisted. He'd know that scent anywhere. It was decomposition.

He paused at the shack door. The lock was closed and appeared undamaged. Still, he pulled a set of gloves out of his pocket and put them on. "Stay outside, Emma. And keep Sadie back, too."

She ordered the dog to sit and Sadie promptly did. Reed twisted the key in the lock. The door swung open and the smell become overpowering. He made a conscious effort to breathe through his mouth.

The inside of the shack was dim. A small table covered in fishing lures sat on one side. Poles and nets were stacked against the far wall. The only light came from the open doorway.

Reed's boots made no sound against the cement as he edged farther inside. He blinked, giving his eyes time to adjust. A clump of fur in the corner caught his attention. The knot in his stomach loosened.

"It's clear." He grimaced. "It's a raccoon."

Emma appeared in the doorway, Sadie by her side. "Oh, no. Maybe I locked the poor thing in."

He turned, his gaze sweeping the shack. Emma moved and the sunlight shifted. Something winked on the cement floor. Reed bent down. With a gloved hand, he reached under the table and pulled out a bracelet.

"What is it?" Emma edged closer. She had a hand over her nose. "Where did that come from?"

Reed couldn't look away. The silver infinity band was dusty, but the diamond cross in the center still held some of its shine. His hand trembled.

"Reed? Are you okay?"

He blinked at Emma. His mouth opened, but he couldn't quite form the words on his lips. "This…this… It's my sister's bracelet. This belongs to Bonnie."

Sadie growled.

The distinctive sound of a shotgun being pumped cut it off.

Before Emma could blink, Reed positioned himself between her and the doorway. He pulled his weapon. She gave a hand signal to Sadie to keep her quiet. The scent inside the shed turned her stomach but was far less terrifying than the unknown individual outside with a shotgun.

"You there in the shed," a man bellowed. "I've got my weapon pointed right at ya. Come out with your hands up."

Emma let out the breath she was holding. She stood up on her tiptoes to whisper in Reed's ear. "It's Wayne Johnson."

Wayne was a jack-of-all-trades. He was hired by many of the farms and ranches when they needed an extra hand. She'd recently employed him herself.

Reed's stance relaxed. "Wayne, it's Sheriff Atkinson and Emma Pierce."

"Sheriff?" Wayne's voice wobbled. If Emma's heart wasn't still racing from fear, she would've felt sorry for the man. No doubt the last thing he wanted to do was pull a weapon on a lawman.

"Put your shotgun on the ground and step away from it," Reed ordered.

"Yes, sir."

There was movement outside the shed. Reed held

a hand up, indicating Emma should stay behind him. They edged to the doorway.

Wayne came into view. Midsixties and toothpick lean, he was dressed in faded overalls and a straw hat. A tool belt hung from his narrow hips. Wayne's shotgun rested in the grass several yards away.

Reed lowered his weapon and holstered it. Emma came around from behind him, taking her first deep breath of clean air. It took two more to clear the scent of the dead raccoon from her nose.

Wayne shifted in his worn boots. "I'm really sorry, Sheriff. I didn't know it was y'all in there. I've heard around town that Emma's been having some problems on the property. When I saw the shed was open, I figured there might be trouble." His gaze drifted to Emma. "Sorry to frighten you, ma'am."

"That's quite all right, Wayne." She mustered up a reassuring smile. "I appreciate you keeping an eye out."

"Where did you come from?" Reed asked.

Wayne waved a gnarled hand toward the far side of the clearing. "I was doing some fence repairs for Judge Norton."

"Why are you carrying a shotgun?"

"Cuz of all the stuff happening on Emma's land. Folks ain't sure who's behind it, and I'm working on a remote part of the ranch. Don't want to get caught off guard."

His explanation made sense, and in Texas, it was legal to openly carry a firearm. Wayne hadn't done anything wrong.

"Excuse me a moment." Reed jogged over to the tree line where they'd had lunch and retrieved an evidence bag. He dropped Bonnie's bracelet inside.

Emma glanced at the shed. A thousand questions ran through her mind. If Bonnie had been wearing the bracelet on the day she disappeared, then logic dictated she'd been on the property. "Wayne, you do a lot of work for Judge Norton, right?"

Wayne nodded. "From time to time when he needs me."

"Have you ever heard anything strange while in this area? Or seen something that didn't sit right with you?"

Reed returned, catching the tail end of her question. Wayne shifted in his boots again and tugged on his tool belt. "Whatta ya mean by strange?"

Right. She should be more specific. "Have you seen a woman on the property?"

Another long pause. His forehead wrinkled. "Only you and the lady you live with."

"Have you ever heard a woman crying or calling for help in this area?"

He squinted at her, probably because the question was an odd one. Wayne shook his head. "No, ma'am. If I'd heard somethin' like that, I would've told ya."

Emma chewed on the inside of her cheek. It'd been a long shot, but worth trying. She decided to change tactics. "Have you seen Owen coming and going from the property since I moved here?"

There was another long pause. Wayne rubbed the back of his neck. "Listen, I don't wanna get anyone in trouble—"

"This is a police investigation," Reed interrupted. "If you know something, you need to tell me."

"I did see him the other day talkin' to Joshua. Actually, they weren't so much talkin' as they were arguin'."

"What day was this?"

"Uhhh, musta been on Tuesday. That's the day I was doing a check on the fences to see which ones needed work. I heard some yellin' and came to check it out. When I saw it was just Owen and Joshua, I left."

Emma passed a glance to Reed. The argument happened on the same day Owen had attacked Emma on her porch.

"Did you hear what they were arguing about?" Reed asked.

"No, but it seemed pretty heated from what I saw. Owen was makin' a big old ruckus. You know that boy has a fiery temper, especially when he's had a few beers."

"Have you seen him around the property any other time?"

"Naw, just that once." Wayne adjusted his tool belt. "If y'all don't mind, I'd better get back to mendin' the fences."

"Sure, but if you think of anything else, give me a call."

"Will do, Sheriff." Wayne tipped his hat toward Emma before collecting his shotgun and ambling back to the property line.

Emma waited until he was out of hearing range. "I don't get it. None of this is making any sense. It's like one of those jigsaw puzzles you liked to do. I have a piece here and a piece there, but getting the whole picture is impossible. How did Bonnie's bracelet get inside the shed? And what does Owen and Joshua's fight have to do with anything?"

"One may have nothing to do with the other. Owen and Joshua used to run in the same crowd. The argument could be about any number of things."

"Okay." Emma took a deep breath. "Then we'll deal with just the bracelet. Is it possible Bonnie lost it in there before she went missing?"

"I don't think so. This bracelet originally belonged to my mother. Bonnie never took it off. I think it's safe to assume she was wearing it the day she disappeared."

"Then she was held in the shed."

"Yes, but there's no indication someone has been held there for an extended period of time."

"So Bonnie was there, but only for a short while. Long enough to lose her bracelet."

Reed's gaze went from the shed to the lake. His jaw tightened. "There may be another explanation for why we can't find Bonnie, her car or her suitcase."

The water sparkled in the sunlight, but a cold finger of dread coursed down Emma's spine as she followed his logic.

Everything they were looking for could be underwater.

THIRTEEN

The next several days melded into each other. Reed's emotions vacillated between relief, frustration and a renewed sense of urgency. The lake was dredged, but nothing more sinister than an old kitchen sink lay at the bottom. Emma's property was thoroughly searched—first by her and Sadie, then by cadaver dogs and law enforcement. Nothing new was uncovered.

Cases went like this. Reed had been in law enforcement long enough to know it was sometimes three steps forward and two back. Still, it was hard to be patient.

The front door to his house opened, and Emma stepped onto the porch. His breath hitched in his throat. She'd traded her normal jeans and T-shirt for a beautiful sundress. It swirled around her shapely legs and brought out the red highlights in her hair.

"Sorry," she said breathlessly. "It's so warm out, I almost forgot my sweater. The air-conditioning can be a bit cold."

"No worries. Church service doesn't start for another forty-five minutes. We have plenty of time."

He held open the passenger side door to the SUV. Emma breezed by him, the scent of vanilla lingering even after she'd lifted herself into the seat. Reed's hand tightened on the handle. Days of being together were adding up. Dinners at Aunt Bessie's with Vivian and Lily, time spent searching Emma's property, hours spent poring over every police report in Bonnie's case.

Each moment had deepened Reed's feelings for Emma, and it was becoming increasingly harder to ignore them.

"Thanks for arranging this," Emma said, once they were on the road. "Church sets my whole week up right. I don't feel the same when I miss it."

"I know. It's important to me, too." Reed had debated the risk until this morning. Mike, it seemed, had gone underground. There hadn't been any additional threats toward Emma. While Reed wasn't convinced things were over, he felt comfortable enough to attend Sunday morning service.

Emma cast a glance at him from the corner of her eye. "You've changed. You always attended church, but it seems your faith has grown deeper."

"I've gotten some bumps and bruises along the way. Hard times can push you toward your faith, if you let it."

"I know what you mean. When Mark died, I was lost." She smoothed a hand down her skirt. "He never even knew I was pregnant. I didn't get the chance to tell him."

"Ah, Em. I'm so sorry."

"I was heartbroken and terrified. In an instant, I became a widow with a baby on the way. I'd just graduated from vet school but didn't have job. We were living on a military base, so I had to move. Prayer helped pull me through."

"Where did you go after you moved off base?"

"To live with Vivi. She had her own grief—Mark was her only sibling—and we didn't know each other well, but Vivian jumped right in to help out. She changed her whole life for us."

His respect for Emma's sister-in-law deepened. The choices Vivian had made weren't easy, and he'd seen lots of families that didn't weather the storm together. "I'm glad you had her."

"Me, too. She even supported the move to Heyworth. Vivian understood the need for community and family. I want Lily to have connections she can rely on for her whole life. Church is a big part of it, too."

"There's something special about worshiping together."

"Yes." She smiled, her entire face lighting up. "Exactly."

The church was cool when they stepped inside. Aunt Bessie caught sight of them and waved. Vivian was holding Lily. The little girl bounced on her aunt's hip and squealed for joy when she spotted her mom.

Emma scooped her up into her arms, planting several kisses on her face. "Good morning, baby girl."

Reed kissed his aunt's cheek and greeted Vivian. Austin said in a low voice, "No one followed us here. Deputy Irving reported everything has been quiet at Emma's house, as well. I suspect Mike is sitting on a beach in Mexico somewhere."

"Could be. Still, we don't know who hired him." Owen was still missing, and they hadn't been able to link either him or Joshua to any of the hitmen. "If the person stalking Emma was willing to hire someone once, there's no saying he won't do it again. We have to stay vigilant."

Austin nodded. His gaze flickered to Vivian before returning to Reed. "Agreed."

They all settled into their seats. Lily crawled over to Reed's lap halfway through the service and flashed him an adorable smile. He planted a kiss on her sweet head. Having Emma at his side and Lily in his arms was a double whammy on his heart. The intervening days had been stressful and emotionally draining, but spending time with them renewed him in a way he hadn't thought was possible.

Reed had closed himself off from the possibility of having a wife and children because being sheriff required all of his energy. He never wanted another family to go through what he had with Bonnie. What he hadn't considered, until now, was that having Emma and Lily in his life actually made him better at his job. Like prayer and attending church service, their presence and affection centered him.

After the final hymn, parishioners beelined in small groups to the fellowship room for coffee and donuts. Aunt Bessie picked up her purse from the chair and slung it over her shoulder. "Service was lovely, wasn't it?"

"It was." Vivian brushed a slim hand through her honey-colored locks. "I wish we could stay for the fellowship."

A twinge of guilt prickled Reed. Vivian had been trapped at Aunt Bessie's house for days. A crease formed between Emma's brows and he knew she was thinking the same thing. They were surrounded by half of the town and escorted by two law enforcement officers. It would safe enough.

"Ten minutes of fellowship can't hurt," he said. Reed spotted Harry Norton standing off to the side. The tall, slender widower was chatting with the mayor and his wife. Will was with them, too. "Austin, do you mind keeping an eye out for them? I want to talk to Judge Norton."

"Sure thing."

Emma handed Lily to her sister-in-law. "I'll stay with Reed and meet you back at the house."

"Don't be late, dear." Aunt Bessie grinned. "I have homemade cinnamon rolls rising as we speak. Once we get home, I'll pop them in the oven."

"Is there cream cheese frosting involved?" Emma asked.

Aunt Bessie winked. "Of course."

Reed chuckled. "Then we'll definitely be on time. Otherwise, Austin will eat them all."

His cousin shot him a mock glare. "I take offense to that. Last time you were thirty minutes late. What's a man to do?"

The whole group laughed. They separated, but the judge was still speaking with the mayor. Reed caught Will's eye and the prosecutor nodded discreetly. Reed and Emma hung back to wait for a chance to speak to Harry.

"Do you really think it's possible Joshua and Owen are working together?" she asked Reed quietly.

"At this point, I'm checking out every avenue. The argument between the two men could be nothing, but since we didn't find anything else on your property, it puts Joshua higher on my suspect list. Maybe he's involved. Or maybe he knows something but won't tell us."

"Why not question Joshua about the fight?"

"I don't want to tip him off that I know about it yet. It's better to gather as much information as I can."

Emma's gaze drifted back to Will and Judge Norton. "Joshua wasn't the only man Bonnie dated. Will was a former boyfriend. Have you considered him as a suspect?"

"Early on I did, but Will was very cooperative. He allowed me to search his home, answered all my questions, and the information he gave me checked out. Plus, he has an alibi for the time of my sister's disappearance. At least, he sort of does. He ran a red light on Main Street, and the camera caught it. He got an automatic ticket. The timing made it impossible for Will to be on Main Street and in Franklin Park where Bonnie disappeared from at the same time."

Emma jerked her chin. "They're done and coming this way."

Emma's nerves jittered as she watched Will and his uncle approach. Side by side, the two men shared a striking resemblance. They had the same stature, the same patrician nose. Judge Norton's silver hair was slicked back from his face, drawing attention to his striking eyes and high forehead. Now in his late sixties, Harry had worked as a county judge for the last twenty years after a successful career as a prosecutor. There wasn't a person in town he didn't know.

"Sheriff, it's good to see you." Harry shook Reed's hand, his dark brown eyes crinkling at the corners.

"You, too, sir. Allow me to introduce Emma Pierce."

"Ms. Pierce, it's lovely to meet you." The judge shook her hand, as well. His grip was firm but not bruising. The slight smile dropped from his lips and his expression turned grave. "I'm so sorry to hear about the trouble you've been having."

"Thank you, sir."

Harry clapped Will on the back. "My nephew says you're building a canine SAR training facility."

Emma nodded. "It's a big project, but I'm excited about the opportunity."

"I'm so pleased. Your uncle was a cherished member of our community and I know he'd be proud to have his land used in such an important manner."

It wasn't the first time she'd heard the sentiment. Several members of Heyworth had told her the same. Still, it never failed to reinforce her decision. Honoring her uncle's wishes was a blessing she gratefully accepted.

"Judge Norton, I'd like to ask you a few questions about the land sale you made to Joshua Lowe last year," Reed said.

The older man's brow wrinkled. "What about it?"

"As I remember, that piece of property wasn't for sale at the time. What made you sell it?"

"Joshua came to my office and specifically asked for it."

Emma rocked back on her heels. "He did?"

"Well, it's not a surprise." Harry ran a hand down his tie in a gesture very similar to his nephew's classic move. "Joshua had saved up some money. He was looking to get a fresh start in life. I was under the impression he'd tried to buy from some others in the county, but they'd refused to sell on account of his reputation.

I, however, had grown to know and like Joshua over the years."

Harry's reasoning wasn't a shock. Uncle Jeb had spoken highly of Judge Norton to Emma many times. The two men had liked and respected each other. Judge Norton believed strongly in the power of redemption. He often encouraged those who appeared in front of his bench to improve their lives.

Will rolled his eyes. Clearly, he didn't share his uncle's opinion.

"Joshua figured I would be willing to give him a helping hand," Judge Norton continued. "That particular section of my land had the old foreman house on it, so it was a logical choice."

"When did he first contact you to purchase it?" Reed asked.

"Hmm, I would say about a week before we finalized the deal."

Will's gaze narrowed. "So he asked to purchase the property a week before Bonnie disappeared, and the actual sale went through the day before she supposedly left town. That's interesting."

Judge Norton frowned. "I don't think I like your tone or what you're implying."

Will's cheeks heated at the reprimand. "You sold that property to a criminal. I know you like to think of Joshua as your pet project, but a leopard doesn't change its spots."

"Will, I know you had feelings for Bonnie—"

"Don't you dare, Uncle Harry." The color spread to the tops of his ears. "It wasn't a fleeting relationship. I cared deeply about her."

Emma blinked, her gaze shifting back and forth be-

tween the two men. She'd known Bonnie and Will had
dated, but she hadn't realized they were serious. From
the way Reed's brows drew down, the news was a surprise to him, as well.

"Why did the two of you break up?" Emma asked.

"I was stupid." Will pressed two fingers against
the bridge of his nose. "A long-distance relationship
seemed too hard, and I didn't want to hold her back from
law school. But breaking up was a terrible mistake. I
thought I was setting Bonnie free to pursue her dreams.
Instead, I hurt her. If I hadn't broken up with Bonnie,
she never would've started dating Joshua."

Guilt laced every word. It seemed Reed wasn't the
only one carrying around a boatload of regrets. Will
dropped his hand. Tears shimmered in his eyes. "Excuse me. I think I need some fresh air."

He marched out.

Judge Norton watched his nephew go and gave a
deep sigh, before turning back to Reed. "Sheriff, I genuinely don't believe Joshua had anything to do with
Bonnie's disappearance. Maybe you'll chalk me up as
being an optimistic fool, but I'm proud of Joshua. He
had a rough time growing up. His father was a horrible man with a long criminal record. His mother was
strung out on drugs much of the time. All he needed
was someone to believe in him. When I offered Joshua
the option to go into a work program instead of jail, he
took it. They told me he was one of the hardest working ranch hands they'd ever seen. Two years later, he
had saved up enough to purchase the land from me."

Joshua's apparent turnaround didn't mean he couldn't
have hurt Bonnie. Sometimes things happened in the
heat of the moment. Although, Emma could see Judge

Norton's point. There was nothing in Joshua's criminal record to indicate he was violent, and he'd stayed out of trouble for years.

"Your opinion means a lot to me, Judge," Reed said. "I'll keep it in mind."

They said their goodbyes. Reed placed a hand on the small of Emma's back as they left the church and walked across the parking lot. Her gaze swept across the vehicles. Sunshine bounced off the windshields, making it impossible to see inside them.

"Well, Judge Norton muddied the waters." Emma bit her lip. "What do you think?"

"I'm not sure…" His voice trailed off. He pulled Emma closer. "I think someone's watching us."

She stiffened. Reed scanned the lot. Nothing moved, but a knot in Emma's stomach tightened. Was Mike close by? Reed wasn't one to create drama, and she trusted his instincts.

Reed picked up the pace, hitting the fob on his SUV. He ushered Emma inside and closed the door. They pulled out of the church parking lot onto Main Street. Traffic was light at this hour. Emma kept alert, watching the street for any potential danger, but nothing seemed out of the ordinary.

Suddenly, a beat-up Ford shot out of the parking lot of a local fast-food restaurant. Mud obscured the license plates. Emma's heart jumped into her throat. The truck was heading straight for them, and she tensed for impact.

Reed swerved. The truck narrowly missed sideswiping them. It clipped the bumper before tearing off down the street. Through the roar in her ears, Emma heard Reed calling for backup.

"It was Mike," she said. For one brief moment, right before Reed swerved, she'd been face-to-face with the driver.

With the man who wanted to kill her.

FOURTEEN

Emma sighed. The bed was comfortable and the house was quiet, but she couldn't sleep. The ceiling fan whirled above her, running at the same speed as her thoughts. How long could they keep going like this? Spending time with Lily in short bursts did nothing to ease the ache in her heart. She missed her little girl more and more every day.

At the same time, Mike was still out there. Not to mention the man who'd hired him. Despite everyone's best efforts, they were no closer to solving the case than they had been a few days ago. They still weren't entirely sure why Emma was a target in the first place.

Lord, I know You're guiding me, but I don't know where to. This is so hard.

The prayer gave her a measure of comfort. Fluffing her pillow, Emma rolled over and snuggled into the soft bedding.

Sleep eluded her. She tossed off the comforter. Sadie raised her head from her place at the foot of the bed.

"Stay here, girl." Emma ran a hand over her soft fur. "I'll go get some tea."

Emma eased out of the bedroom. Austin's door was

open, his bed unmade. He'd gone to headquarters to work after lunch at Aunt Bessie's. Chances were he was still there.

The light in the kitchen was on. She rounded the corner to find Reed sitting at the table. His hair was mussed, as if his fingers had run through it dozens of times, and bristles darkened his strong jaw. A laptop was perched at his elbow. The table's surface was covered with papers.

He glanced up. In all the time she'd known him, Reed had never appeared tired. Until now. Shadows rested under his gorgeous eyes, and the faint lines around his mouth had deepened. Emma mentally berated herself. She'd spent her time worrying about how this was affecting her, but what about Reed? This had to be torturous for him.

"Are you okay?" he asked.

"I couldn't sleep and thought some tea might help. Would you like some?"

"That's a good idea. I need something other than all the coffee I've had today. By the way, deputies located the truck Mike used to nearly run us off the road. It'd been reported stolen earlier in the day."

Another dead end. Emma grabbed the electric kettle and filled it with water. "What are you working on?"

"I'm trying to find some connection between Owen and the hitmen or Joshua and the hitmen. There's nothing though. They haven't been in jail together. They didn't go to the same school or frequent the same places. We interviewed friends and family, not that it helped a lot. No one seems to know much of anything."

"Maybe neither of them are involved. We could be moving in the wrong direction."

He rubbed his eyes. "I know, but my gut says otherwise. There has to be something I'm missing."

"The local bar seems like a place all of them would hang out."

"I thought the same, but Charlie and Mike liked to hang with their cousin Vernon for the most part. They always went over to the next town."

Emma poured hot water into two mugs and left the tea to steep on the counter. She took a closer look at the papers. There were printouts of criminal records. One caught her eye.

"Joshua looks so young here." His cheeks were plump, his skin mottled with acne. "How old was he when he started getting into trouble?"

"Twelve. His juvie record is spotty. That photograph was taken when he was seventeen. He'd been arrested for breaking and entering. Stole some electronic equipment from a home while the owners were on vacation."

She scanned his criminal record. "Looks like he had a habit of breaking into houses. It's a shame Joshua didn't have parents who taught him the right path…" Her voice trailed off and she stiffened. "Reed, what if you're looking at the wrong Lowe?"

"What do you mean?"

"Joshua's father was a criminal. Maybe he and one of the Young brothers crossed paths a long time ago."

His fingers flew over the keyboard. Moments later, he gave an excited yelp. "That's it! I can't believe I missed this. Joshua's dad and Charlie Young were arrested for a string of robberies in nearby Glatten. We never went back into Joshua's childhood. If we interview neighbors, we might be able to prove Joshua knew

Charlie and maybe even Mike. It's a tenuous link, but it's a place to start."

Reed got up from the chair and hugged her. "You're a genius."

"I don't know about genius, but I'll take the compliment all the same." She laughed and pulled back slightly. "I'm glad I could help."

"You do help. More than you realize."

Reed's gaze dropped to her mouth. He hesitated and she could see the questions in his eyes. In an instant, Emma realized Vivian had been right. Reed was holding back, not because he didn't want this, but because he wasn't sure about her feelings.

"I haven't dated since Mark died." The words burst from her like a dam cracked open. "My goal was to start fresh in Heyworth. To start Helping Paws and raise Lily. Everything is a mess right now because of the case." She didn't want to think about what would happen if they didn't find the person after her. One thing at a time. Emma took a deep breath. "And I don't know if I have it in me to fall in love again. Especially given your job. I know that's not fair, but losing Mark was awful. I don't want to go through it again."

He lifted a hand to cup her face and butterflies erupted in her stomach. "Emma…"

"At the same time, I care about you, Reed. Beyond just friendship. And I don't know what to do about it."

"That makes two of us. I don't know what the future holds, Em, but I'm thankful to have this moment with you."

Reed bent his head and kissed her. The warmth of his touch spread through her like molten lava. She lost herself in it. Everything about this man called to her. His bravery, his honesty, his goodness. In Reed's arms, she was protected and cared for. Nothing else existed except for the feel of his lips against hers, the gentle caress of his hand on her face, and the feelings they shared.

Reed's phone rang. He broke the kiss. "Sorry, Em. I have to grab that. It could be headquarters."

He scooped up the phone from the table and answered.

"Sheriff, there's been an explosion on Emma's property." Deputy Irving's tone was rushed and loud enough Emma could hear every word. "I've called for backup and the fire department—"

His voice cut off as a boom echoed over the speaker.

"Deputy Irving," Reed yelled into the phone. "Jack, answer me!"

Silence followed. He checked his phone to ensure the line was still open, but they'd been cut off. His fingers shook slightly as he dialed his deputy's number. *Lord, please. The man has a wife and children.* The phone rang and rang, but Jack didn't answer.

Reed called into Dispatch. "Mona, we may have an officer down. Send every available patrol to Emma's property. Deputy Irving isn't answering my phone call. Radio him now."

"Hold on, sir."

Reed paced the length of the kitchen. For days Emma's property had been crawling with law enforcement due to the search for Bonnie. Tonight was the first time only one deputy was left standing guard. Jack had specifically said there was an explosion and it sounded like there'd been another one right before they'd been cut off.

Mike must be following up his attempt to run them off the road with a new attack.

"I can't get him on the radio," Mona said. Her voice shook. "Backup is on the way, but the closest unit is at least twenty minutes out. Austin was working here at headquarters and he's also heading your direction."

Reed's hand tightened on the phone. He was trying to cover as many people as possible with the staff he had, plus keeping a lookout for Mike and Owen. It was a lot of ground to cover and not enough manpower to do it. "Radio the other units and tell them to approach with extreme caution. If this is Mike, he's probably armed and dangerous. He also has knowledge of explosives."

He hung up. Emma grabbed his sleeve. "We're the closest to him. We have to go."

"That might be exactly the reaction Mike is looking for. He's trying to flush you out."

He scraped a hand through his hair. "The safest thing to do is to stay here."

"Or he could be creating a diversion to draw all the officers to my property so he can attack your house. There's no way to read his mind, Reed, and I'm not leaving Deputy Irving out there for the next twenty minutes by himself."

He wrestled with the decision. There wasn't a good choice either way, and Emma was right. Trying to guess Mike's next move was a futile game. If there was a chance to save his deputy, they had to take it. "You need to do exactly as I say."

"Absolutely."

She hollered for Sadie, who came shooting down the hall. Emma snapped on the dog's leash. Reed grabbed his keys. Together, the dog between them, they hustled to the SUV.

Wind scattered pine needles and brought with it the scent of smoke. The tension in Reed's muscles ratcheted up a notch. If he could smell the fire from his property, it was big.

He paused at the SUV long enough to put on a bulletproof vest and fish out a spare. He handed it to Emma. "Put this on."

She nodded. He hit the gas, blasting out of the driveway and onto the back road leading to Emma's property. The SUV bounced over the ruts. He listened to the radio as his team communicated with each other. The closest unit was still twelve minutes out. Far too long.

He rounded a bend in the road and a brilliant glow glimmered beyond the trees. Reed's hands tightened on the steering wheel.

Emma gasped. "That's my canine facility. All of the handlers' houses are on fire."

They weren't just on fire. They'd been destroyed. Reed's anger burned as bright as the flames, but there was no time for it. He needed to stay focused on finding his deputy while keeping Emma safe. "Get down into the wheel well. If Mike starts shooting, I don't want you to be visible."

Emma unbuckled her seat belt and slipped down. Heat from the blaze washed over them. Sweat beaded on his forehead. Reed scanned for his deputy's patrol car.

"Do you see him?" Emma asked.

"No, but he might be parked in front of your house." He hit the gas, taking them farther from the flames. A flash of red and blue lights caught his attention. As he suspected, Jack's patrol car was parked in Emma's driveway. Reed slammed on the brakes and shoved the SUV into Park. He didn't bother to remove the keys from the ignition. "Stay here."

He eased out of his vehicle, using it as cover. A pair of feet stuck out from the back of the patrol car. The driver's side door was open, but the interior light wasn't on. Reed paused, straining to hear any movement. Nothing. If Mike was out there, he wasn't moving.

Reed quickly closed the distance between him and his deputy, running at a crouch. His breath caught. Jack's face was covered in blood. It looked like he'd been pistol-whipped. Reed grabbed Jack's wrist. A pulse thumped against his fingers.

Thank you, Lord.

For the second time in less than two weeks, he was standing over one of his men nearly killed in the line of duty. No matter what precautions he put in place to protect others, it seemed Mike and whoever had hired him were one step ahead.

A shot split the night air followed by glass shattering. Emma!

No longer worried about staying in a crouch, Reed raced back to his vehicle. Several shots thudded in the dirt at his feet.

That's right, buddy. Leave her alone. Come and get me.

"Emma." He took shelter at the rear of his vehicle. "Emma, answer me."

"I'm okay, Reed. He missed me." Her voice shook. "Deputy Irving?"

"He's alive."

A motorcycle roared to life in the woods. Reed peeked around his SUV and caught sight of a taillight winking in the distance. The passenger side door to the SUV swung open. The window was missing.

"Reed, get in. Hurry!"

He raced up the side and climbed in. Emma was already in the driver's seat. He didn't have time to close the door before she hit the gas pedal. Wind rushed in through the shot-out window.

"Emma, what are you doing?"

"I'm going after him." She leaned into the steering wheel. "It's enough. If we don't stop him now, how many other people is he going to hurt?"

"No, we aren't chasing him."

"I didn't ask you." Her teeth gritted. She turned onto the main road and the SUV picked up speed. "I've had enough."

The motorcycle's taillight appeared in front of them. Emma sped up even more. The man on the bike passed a glance over his shoulder. The headlights illuminated his face for only half a second, but it was enough to confirm his identity. Mike Young.

Reed radioed in their location, relayed the license plate of the motorcycle and ordered units to intervene. A curve appeared in the road. Emma never slowed down. She took it at a high rate of speed, the back of the vehicle fishtailing. She fought for control of the wheel. Mike shot ahead.

"Emma, we need to stop."

She pounded the steering wheel. "He's getting away."

Reed placed a hand on her arm. "It's too dangerous. Think of Lily."

His words had the desired effect. She slowed to a stop. The motorcycle's taillight disappeared.

"My guys are en route. They'll catch him."

He hoped. Still, chasing Mike down with Emma in the vehicle wasn't just dangerous. It was reckless.

She put the SUV in Park.

"You're right. I'm sorry. I just… He destroyed my facility. He attacked Deputy Irving." She stared out the windshield. Reed's heart cracked at the pain in her voice. "He shot at me. He isn't going to stop."

"I know, but we'll find him."

She nodded and turned the vehicle around. "We should go back and give first aid to your deputy. How badly was he hurt?"

"He was knocked out, but I think he's going to be okay."

They rounded the curve of the driveway. A figure appeared in the headlights. Emma screamed and slammed on the brakes.

Deputy Irving staggered toward them. Blood ran down his face from the injury to his head. Reed opened his door. He looped an arm around Jack's waist.

"We need to go," Jack said. Even injured, he propelled Reed toward the vehicle. "We need to move. Can't find my keys…can't drive."

"Help is on the way. Let's get you to a hospital."

"No…" He shook his head. Blood spattered on Reed's shoulder. "Went inside for phone… Bomb… House."

Reed glanced behind him. The front door to Emma's house was standing open. It took a second to register what his deputy was trying to tell him. His heart rate skyrocketed. He shoved Jack into the back seat of the SUV and slammed the door.

"Out of the driver's seat, Emma! Fast!"

She didn't ask questions. She scrambled to the passenger side. Reed tossed himself in the driver's seat, did a U-turn and hit the gas.

"Get down," he ordered her.

Reed glanced behind him. One breath. Two.

An explosion rocked the vehicle. Heat rushed over them in a wave. From the back seat, Sadie whined. In the rearview mirror, a huge fireball and thick clouds of smoke rose in the air.

FIFTEEN

The next afternoon, Emma surveyed what was left of her home. The porch her uncle had lovingly made was nothing but a pile of broken wood. Bricks had been blown off the foundation and scattered across the yard like discarded Legos. The chimney towered over a sagged-in, blackened roof.

Tears pricked her eyes. There was nothing left to save. The house would have to be demolished and rebuilt from scratch. Her canine training facility was in worse shape. The handlers' homes had burned to the ground. The fire had spread to the obstacle course and it was gone, as well.

Next to her, Reed let out a low sigh. "Emma, I'm so sorry."

"It's not your fault." She closed her eyes and took a deep breath. A pity party wasn't possible now, and no matter how bad things were, they could've been a whole lot worse. "I'm just glad Deputy Irving is okay, and no one was seriously hurt."

According to the bomb squad, the explosion would've likely killed the deputy if Reed and Emma hadn't driven him away in time. As it was, all he had was a concussion. Deputy Irving had already been released from the hospital and was recuperating at home with his family.

Heavy thunderclouds hung on the horizon. Emma hugged herself against the chill in the air. "Has there been any news from Cooper?"

She hoped this latest attack would provide some key piece of information. They had to find Mike. Soon. Before someone else got hurt.

"Not yet. Austin is personally communicating with every law enforcement agency within a hundred-mile radius. We're also putting out a reward for any information about his whereabouts." Reed's jaw tightened. "Part of me regrets telling you to back off following him."

"No, you were right. I was more likely to get us injured than to catch him. Besides, if we hadn't come back to get Deputy Irving…" She didn't want to consider the alternative. Instead she turned and rested her head on Reed's broad chest. The scent of his aftershave—warm and piney—mingled with the fresh smell of his laundry detergent. She breathed it in, letting it erase the stink of the smoke. "You're doing the best you can. We all are."

He wrapped his arms around her. "It doesn't feel like my best is good enough."

"It is." She pulled him closer. "We just have to keep holding on. Keep working hard, keep praying and lean on our faith."

"I will, but I'd love a break in the case, too."

She chuckled. "I think we all would."

Reed's phone rang and he released her to answer it. Cool air rushed in, replacing the warmth of his body, and Emma shivered.

She stared at the rubble. The loss was crippling. This

was supposed to be her fresh start, the beginning of a genuine home living in a town of wonderful people and training dogs in Search and Rescue. It was all slipping away.

Sadie lay in the grass, her head on her paws, a mournful look in her eyes. It wasn't the first time her dog seemed to sense Emma's emotions and share them. Emma bent down to stroke her. "It'll be okay, girl. We'll figure it out."

She didn't know how, but they would. One step at a time.

Reed joined them. "That was Cooper. He's got an update for us and asked to meet at headquarters."

"Let's go then."

The drive to town was quick. Emma stared out the window at the buildings on Main Street. Several ladies sat outside the Clip 'n' Curl with rollers and tinfoil in their hair. The diner was packed for lunch and two men loaded hay into the back of a pickup at the feedstore. Children ran through the park next to the Heyworth Sheriff's Department. Their cries of laughter sent a pang of longing in her heart. She'd visited with Lily this morning, but they hadn't been able to stay for very long. She missed her little girl fiercely.

Cathy, the daytime receptionist, greeted them when they walked inside. Her earrings swayed as she rose from her chair to give Emma a hug. "I'm so sorry about what happened, honey."

"Thank you, Cathy."

"The prayer circle is hard at work and we've already taken up a collection of items at the diner. Clothes, household supplies, toys for Lily. It's not much yet, but it's something to get you started." She stroked Sadie on the head. "I think there's even a doggie bed."

New tears pricked Emma's eyes. She blinked them back. "Thank you so much."

"It's nothing, honey. We take care of our own." The older woman patted Reed on the arm. "I'm so glad you're all okay. Deputy Irving has already called in. I told him to focus on recuperating and we'll call if we need something."

"You did exactly right," Reed said. "Is Cooper here?"

"In the conference room, waiting for y'all. Have you had lunch yet? Should I order something?"

"No, thank you. We were at my aunt's earlier, and she fed us until we nearly exploded."

They all laughed. Emma gave Cathy one more hug and said another thank-you before following Reed to the conference room.

The Texas Ranger looked up when they entered. Cooper was sporting a three-day-old beard and his complexion was pale. At his elbow rested several discarded to-go cups from a local coffee shop. He'd been working the case nonstop, and Emma was certain that, like them, he was running on very little sleep.

Will sat in one of the chairs, typing on a laptop. He barely looked up to greet them. His fingers flew over the keyboard. Sadie walked around him and settled down for a nap in the corner of the room.

"What's going on?" Reed asked.

"We've had a breakthrough in the case," Cooper said. "Will's working on getting us a search warrant."

Emma gripped the back of a chair. "Have you found Mike?"

"Not yet, but we did find where he was staying,

thanks to you." Cooper opened a file folder and pulled out several photographs, sliding them across the table. "Since you followed Mike and were able to give a description of the motorcycle as well as the license plate, we put out a BOLO on it. A police officer from nearby Harrisburg spotted the bike sitting at a motel off the highway."

Reed flipped through the photographs before handing them to Emma. The motel was run-down, with chipped paint and slanted numbers on the doors. Mike's motorcycle sat in the parking spot for room 103.

"Mike wasn't in the hotel room, and as often happens in these kinds of places, the front desk clerk didn't know anything about anyone."

"What about security cameras?" Emma asked.

Cooper snorted. "In our dreams. We did obtain a search warrant for the room, however, and found two things of interest."

"What?"

He pushed another photograph across the table. "Two glasses partially filled with beer were on the table. One had Mike's fingerprints. The other had Joshua Lowe's."

Emma sucked in a breath. "So they *do* know each other."

Cooper nodded. "We located a neighbor who was living near the Lowes when Joshua was a kid. She told us Mike and his brother, Charlie, were regular visitors. Joshua's dad and Mike were especially close."

"What else did you find?" Reed asked. "You said there were two things of interest."

Cooper's mouth drew down. Will stopped typing on the laptop. The stillness in the room was unnerving. Emma shifted closer to Reed.

"We found a ton of cash, along with a pile of jewelry," Cooper said, flipping to a new photograph. "Among the items were a set of etched gold hoops."

Emma glanced down at the earrings before focusing on Reed. Recognition flashed across his features. "Are these what I think they are?"

"What?" Emma asked. A sinking feeling settled in the pit of her stomach. "What are they?"

Will cleared his throat. "We have one photograph of Bonnie taken on the day she disappeared by an ATM camera. She was wearing a set of earrings exactly like those."

Cooper ran a hand over his beard. "I had them compared by my analysts at the state lab. The earrings we found and the ones in the photograph from the ATM are consistent."

"So…" Emma picked up the photograph. "These are Bonnie's earrings?"

"Yes. We're getting a search warrant for Joshua's property."

"I want to search it first with Sadie."

"Emma's right," Reed said, before turning to her. "Maybe your theory about my sister being alive was right. We were just looking for her on the wrong property."

She nodded. "That's how her bracelet ended up in my shed. She escaped from Joshua's and made it as far as Uncle Jeb's shed before she was caught again."

Cooper held up a hand. "Guys—"

"You don't have to say it, Cooper." Reed rocked back on his heels. "I know it's a long shot, but it won't harm anything to try. I need to do this."

The Texas Ranger glanced at her. Emma straightened to her full height.

"Sadie and I are ready. Get the search warrant and we'll look for Bonnie."

The wait for the search warrant didn't take long but for Reed, it might as well have been an eternity. He didn't want to get his hopes up. The possibility of Bonnie being alive was slim, but a part of him wouldn't let go of the idea. Only when he had definitive proof would he accept she wasn't coming home again.

Emma sat in the passenger seat, staring out the window.

"You don't have to do this," Reed said as they pulled off the highway and onto the country road leading to Joshua's property. "We can get another team to search."

"No. I wouldn't have agreed if Sadie and I couldn't do it. We want to help, if we can."

Joshua's ranch came into view. The driveway was filled with law enforcement vehicles and several deputies and troopers lingered outside. Reed and Emma had stayed behind, allowing the initial search of the house to take place before they arrived on the premises. It was safer for Emma and Sadie that way.

The carport next to the house was empty. The rain had washed everything clean, and heavy thunderclouds loomed in the distance. The reprieve from the storm was a short one. Cooper stood on the front porch.

"Wait here for a second, Emma," Reed said. "I want to make sure everything is clear with Cooper before we start the search."

She eyed the sky. "Sadie and I can work in the rain, but I'd rather not be out with lightning."

"Understood. I'll be quick."

He left the engine running, so she and Sadie would have cool air. Cooper saw him coming and met him halfway.

"Looks like Joshua isn't home," he said in lieu of a greeting. "According to a ranch hand who works for him here and there, Joshua has had a trip planned for months to attend the cattle auction in Dallas."

"Convenient."

"The timing is suspicious. We still haven't located Mike, so we need to take precautions. There's a possibility he's on the property. Everyone's been instructed to assume Mike is armed and dangerous."

"Emma's wearing protection." Reed glanced back at his vehicle. "I'd try to talk her out of searching again, but I already know she won't listen."

Austin came out of Joshua's house. His expression was stern, but Reed saw the worry hidden in the depths of his cousin's eyes. "Y'all should come inside. There's something you need to see."

The two men joined him inside the house. The living room was rustic, with mismatched furniture and wood paneling on the walls, but it was tidy. The kitchen had crooked wood cabinets and a scratched linoleum floor. The ancient fridge hummed. A mug sat in the sink. Several crime scene technicians were dusting for fingerprints.

Austin led them down a long hallway and they stepped into what Reed surmised was the master bedroom. His eyes widened. Unlike the rest of the house, this room was a wreck. The comforter was piled in a heap on the floor. A lamp, probably from the bedside table, was shattered into pieces. Blood covered some of the shards.

"It appears there was some kind of struggle," Austin said. With a gloved hand, he pointed to the nightstand's half-open drawer. "There's a handgun inside."

Cooper rocked back on his heels. "If Joshua was sleeping in bed, and an intruder startled him, he would go for the gun."

"But the attacker beat him to it, smashing the lamp over his head, possibly knocking him out," Reed finished. "But for what purpose? It doesn't make any sense."

Reed rested his hands on his belt. He wasn't wearing gloves and didn't want to touch anything. Through an opposite doorway, the bathroom was visible. He stepped inside, eyeing the sink and bathtub. "When did Joshua supposedly leave for Dallas?"

"This morning," Cooper replied.

"The sink and bathtub are dry." He eyed the towel hanging on the back of the door. "So is the towel. It doesn't look like he used them."

"But there are empty hangers in the closet. It appears a suitcase is missing. And his car is gone."

Reed stepped back into the bedroom. A photograph overturned from the nightstand lay on the floor. Bonnie stood in a field of bluebonnets. One hand held a wide brimmed hat and the other was outstretched. She was caught mid-laugh, her eyes crinkled with happiness. The echo of Joshua's words swirled in Reed's mind. *I loved her.*

"Maybe Mike attacked him," Cooper suggested.

"And what? Dragged Joshua out to his own vehicle,

taking his suitcase for good measure? That makes no sense."

"Criminals do weird stuff."

Reed couldn't argue with that. Sometimes people didn't always react logically.

Austin frowned. "There could be another explanation. I've got an empty bottle of whiskey on this side of the bed. Maybe Joshua got drunk and knocked over the lamp, cutting himself in the process. He got up this morning and ran out of the house to get to the auction without cleaning up."

Reed arched his brows. "That seems more reasonable. Is there a BOLO out for Joshua?"

Cooper nodded. "Yep, and I've got state troopers heading to the cattle auction to ask around for him."

Thunder rolled. Reed glanced at the window. "The storm is coming in. If Emma and Sadie are going to search the property, we need to do it now."

"I'll come with you," Austin said.

"Take a deputy with you," Cooper added. "And be careful. Mike is still out there somewhere."

Emma's fingers shook slightly as she strapped on Sadie's vest. The wind was picking up, adding to her anxiety. Every second counted. If Bonnie was somewhere on the property, Emma wanted to find her now.

"Are you okay?"

Reed's question was low enough only Emma could hear. Concern darkened the blue of his eyes, and his mouth was set in a grim line. He had to be scared about what they would find on the property, as much as she was, yet he took the time to comfort her.

God, why did you bring him back into my life and

then make things so hard? The kiss in Reed's kitchen had been wonderful. It also scared her. She didn't want to end up brokenhearted.

She squared her shoulders. "I'm fine. Let's get started."

She took Sadie to the outer edge of the woods, far away from any deputies searching the house, and gave the command. Her dog headed into the woods.

Emma followed, keeping Sadie in sight. Austin and Reed flanked her, and another deputy she didn't recognize took the rear. The tall pine trees blocked out most of the late afternoon sunlight. Goose bumps broke out across her arms. They were heading toward the back road, the one separating Emma's property from Joshua's.

Sadie stopped and sniffed something. Hidden within the branches and bushes was a huge, lurking object.

"What is that?" Emma frowned. "Is that a car?"

"Yes," Austin answered, his foot crushing a branch. "And by the looks of it, it's been here a while."

It was covered in pine needles and dust. Dead branches obscured the windows and the tires were buried in the bushes. Reed bypassed them both, his long strides covering the distance easily. He bent down and separated some branches to reveal the license plate. "It's my sister's vehicle."

Reed and Austin shared a look. Emma's stomach ached. They pulled on gloves and started peering into the windows. Reed tried a door handle. It creaked open. The car had been left unlocked.

Sadie started barking. With lead feet, Emma circled around to her dog. Her heart stopped and then thundered. Sadie was signaling at the rear of the vehicle.

Emma gave the release command. Her dog immediately backed off. She whined, her ears down.

Oh, no. No.

Emma pulled a treat from the bag at her waist out of habit and tried to give it to Sadie. The dog wouldn't take it. Instead, she whined again. She backed up farther from the car as if wanting as much distance between her and the vehicle as possible. Emma couldn't blame her. She ran her hands over Sadie's soft fur. A prayer left her lips, as automatic as the comfort she gave her dog.

Feet crunched the ground behind her. "There's something in the trunk, isn't there?"

Reed's voice was hollow. Emma bit her lip and turned. Their eyes met. She would spare him this if she could but there was nothing she could do. "Sadie's trained to find live people, but there have been times she's located a recently deceased person."

Had Bonnie been alive until last night? It was possible. Bile rose in Emma's throat.

Reed's spine went rigid. He gestured to the deputy waiting at the driver's side door. "Find the latch to open it."

Austin placed a gloved hand on the trunk. "Reed, maybe you shouldn't be here—"

"Open it, Austin."

The order was sharp and caustic. Reed was holding it together but just barely. Emma reached out. She grasped Reed's hand. His posture didn't change but he interlocked their fingers, drawing her closer until she was at his side. She could feel the tension in his muscles. The pulse at his neck was racing.

Austin sighed and nodded to the deputy. He fumbled

before finding the release. The latch snicked and the trunk lid swung open.

Emma gasped.

Mike Young's body was stuffed inside, a bullet wound on his forehead.

SIXTEEN

The next morning, Reed guzzled his third cup of coffee as he paced Aunt Bessie's backyard. Last night's thunderstorms had given way to a beautiful spring day. Bees flitted in a nearby flowerbed. He shifted the cell phone against his ear. "What do we know so far?"

"Well, Mike was killed sometime in the early morning hours yesterday," Cooper said. His voice sounded weary. "Initial ballistics tests conclude the gun in Joshua's nightstand doesn't match the weapon used to kill Mike."

"Maybe Joshua took it with him."

"Possible, but we've got another problem. Joshua never made it to Dallas, and so far, both he and his truck are missing."

Reed's gaze shot to the enclosed porch. Emma was rocking on the swing with Lily in her lap. Vivian leaned on the railing. The two women were having what appeared to be a deep conversation.

"What about the blood on the lamp?" he asked.

"Same blood type as Joshua's, although DNA is going to take a bit longer." Cooper sighed. "I gotta tell you, Reed, something about this isn't sitting right with me. The whiskey bottle we recovered from Joshua's room didn't have any fingerprints on it. It'd been wiped clean. I think it was placed in his room to make us believe the mess was the result of a drinking binge."

Reed's steps faltered. The niggle of doubt he'd been feeling since yesterday in Joshua's house grew. "You think someone's trying to frame him?"

"I think it's something we should consider. Emma and Sadie went over all of Joshua's property yesterday and didn't find a trace of Bonnie other than the car. If that's what Joshua was hiding, why stick Mike in the trunk? It seems like a guaranteed way for us to locate the vehicle."

"He didn't know we'd get a search warrant. Besides, his fingerprints were on the glass in Mike's room."

"About that. We initially thought those glasses were from the hotel. They weren't. We recovered a matching set from Joshua's kitchen cabinet. Normally, that would indicate Joshua took them to Mike's room, but... the move is sloppy. Everything about this perpetrator has proven he's smart. It doesn't fit."

"Let me get this straight. You think someone broke into Joshua's house, attacked him, loaded him into his own truck and...then what? Took some glasses from his kitchen to place in Mike's hotel room?"

"Yes. If we assume for just a moment that Joshua isn't involved, then there's only one person who knew where Bonnie's car was. The person who took her."

Reed set his mug on the concrete sidewalk and rubbed his head. "Cooper, Bonnie's vehicle was parked on Joshua's land."

"We can't assume he knew it was there. That part of the property was overgrown. Without Emma and Sadie, it would've been difficult to find it." Cooper paused for a long beat. "Reed, Judge Norton was at the sheriff's department looking for you this morning."

"I know. He texted me this morning—" Reed cut off, his tired brain catching up to Cooper's insinuation. "No way."

"I don't like it any more than you do, but we need to keep an open mind. Joshua bought that property from Judge Norton. By all accounts, Bonnie and the judge were close."

"Which doesn't give him motive."

"No, but…"

"Just spit it out, Cooper."

"Will came to me after we located Bonnie's car. He remembered there was a strange incident between Bonnie and his uncle a month or so before her disappearance."

Reed stiffened. This was the first he was hearing about this. "What kind of incident?"

"An argument between Bonnie and the judge. Will wasn't sure what it was about—neither of them would tell him—but he had the vague impression Bonnie was very upset about it. She fled the office as soon as Will arrived."

"That's extremely vague."

"I know. Will was being careful with his wording, but finding Bonnie's car and bracelet in such close proximity to his uncle's land clearly got him thinking."

"We need to take what Will says with a grain of salt. He's had a problematic past with his uncle. Besides, Joshua's the one who asked to buy that piece of property from Judge Norton. Judge Norton wasn't even looking to sell it."

"You're saying Joshua bought it specifically to hide the car?"

"Yep. Ten to one, the technicians will find the car died and wasn't able to be moved without a tow truck. Bonnie's vehicle was a hunk of junk." Reed let out a breath. "There are some other loose threads. What about Bonnie's earrings in Mike's room? And the fact that Joshua couldn't provide an alibi for the time around my sister's disappearance?"

"Trust me, I'm not wiping Joshua off the suspect list. Not by a long shot. I'm just telling you there are inconsistencies in the evidence. He might not be our man."

Reed heard the frustrated note in Cooper's voice. He shared it. "Any news on Owen?"

"No. I've had troopers investigate all of his favorite drinking places. We've talked to his friends and his ex-girlfriends. No one has heard a word from him since he ran away from the hospital."

Another piece of the puzzle that didn't fit. Was Owen behind all of this? Or was Joshua? Or were they overlooking a vital suspect, like Judge Norton?

On the porch, Emma and Vivian's discussion was taking a turn for the worse. Reed was too far away to make out the words, but the stiffness in Emma's shoulders was enough to worry him.

"I'll go talk to Margaret Carpenter again," Reed said. "She was Bonnie's best friend. If there was a problem between Bonnie and Judge Norton, maybe she knows something about it."

"Keep me updated."

"Will do." Reed hung up. He strolled across the yard. Vivian slipped into the house just as he climbed the porch steps.

Emma glanced up as the screen door closed behind him. Lily was sitting in her lap.

"Hey," Reed said, gesturing to the space next to them. "This seat taken?"

"We were saving it for you. What did Cooper say?"

He repeated their conversation. About halfway through, Lily worked her way onto Reed's lap. He tucked the baby into the corner of his arm and rocked the swing. With Emma nestled on his other side, it felt right. A little whisper of worry told him not to get used to it. Emma was hesitant to give her heart to a man with a risky job. Not that he could blame her. Especially after she'd already lost one husband.

But what if he wasn't in law enforcement anymore? Could he live a happy life working his family's old ranch? He loved being sheriff, but his career had taken a toll on him. Maybe it was time for a change. A slower pace of life. A less dangerous profession. He wouldn't make any decisions until after Bonnie's disappearance was solved, but it was something to consider.

When he was done telling Emma about his conversation with Cooper, she shook her head. "Wow."

"Wow is right."

"I'd like to go with you to talk to Margaret. I know we stayed here last night, but it's probably better for me to stay away from Lily and Vivian until we know what's going on."

"I agree." He paused. "Everything okay with you and Vivian?"

"No." Emma's gaze slid away from his and she bit her lip. "We were talking about what's going to happen next for us."

"What does that mean?"

"We can't keep going like this, Reed. The case keeps stretching out and now my facility and house are gone. I have to start thinking about my family and creating a permanent place for Lily."

He stopped the swing. Lily dropped her toy on the floor. "You're leaving Heyworth?"

"I don't want to, but I may not have any other choice."

"Where will you go?"

The baby started to cry, and Emma handed Lily her favorite toy. The stuffed lamb was looking worn around the edges. "Vivian's house hasn't sold, so I think we'll go back to Boston."

Boston. It was thousands of miles away. With his sister's case unsolved, Reed couldn't leave town. The pain in the center of his chest radiated out. It hurt so bad, Reed actually looked down at his uniform to make sure he wasn't bleeding. "When?"

"Soon. I want to give it a bit more time, in the hope that the threat can be eliminated and we can stay. I love Heyworth, and as it turns out, Vivian doesn't want to leave either. She and your aunt have discovered a mutual love of cooking. They're talking about opening a restaurant together."

Her voice vibrated with pain. The interaction he'd witnessed between the two women suddenly made sense. "You've done more than your fair share," he said. "I know this hasn't been easy on any of you and the decision is a tough one. I know this isn't what you wanted."

"No, not at all—" Her voice choked off. Emma's gaze dropped to Lily in his arms. The baby hugged her lamb and babbled.

"This was supposed to be your home," he said.

A safe place to raise her daughter and build a life. Now it was a nightmare filled with dead bodies and threats.

"Yes," she whispered. "I thought God had brought me here to settle down and make my life. Now, I'm not sure. Maybe…maybe I was brought here to aid Bonnie's case. I pray finding the car will provide the necessary evidence to locate her."

"Emma…" A lump in his throat choked him. He wanted to ask her to stay. The words burned his tongue, but he swallowed them back. Lily's safety and happiness had to be first. "I hope we can stay in contact and remain friends."

Tears shimmered in her eyes. "Always."

Reed pulled Emma closer, until she was nestled up next to him, and pushed the swing. Her tears wet his shirt. There were no words to make it better. He knew that, but he also knew he had to hold on to this moment. This breath of time when his arms were full with a family he hadn't known until recently he wanted.

Reed didn't know when it happened, but it was as undeniable as the sun. He'd fallen in love. When Emma and Lily left town, they would be taking his heart with them.

Heyworth Veterinarian Clinic smelled like a mixture of wet dog and antiseptic. Sadie's tail went down as they crossed the threshold. The poor dog hated coming here. No amount of treats or reassurance seemed to ease her visits.

"Don't worry," Emma whispered. "No shots today."

Sadie gave her a baleful look. Reed chuckled. "I don't think she believes you."

"I know."

The office was empty. The receptionist's computer flashed with a screen saver. Margaret came around the corner, looking at her phone. Her hair was pulled back into a high ponytail and it bobbed as she drew up short. A hand fluttered to her throat. "Emma. Reed. You startled me."

"We're sorry," Reed said. "The bell rang over the door, and your receptionist is gone."

"All of my staff is at lunch. You didn't have an appointment, did you?" Margaret bent down to stroke Sadie. "Emma, I heard about what happened to your uncle's house. I'm so sorry. It's fortunate Reed was there to help."

"Thank you, Margaret."

Emma refused to allow herself to glance at Reed. If she did, she feared she might burst into tears. The entire car ride over had been painfully silent. She couldn't blame him for putting up a wall, but it stung all the same.

The memory of their conversation on Aunt Bessie's porch scraped at the raw edges of her heart. The loss of her uncle's home and Helping Paws was devastating. Salt on the wound was saying goodbye to Reed. But Emma didn't see any way around it. She had a daughter to think about, and Reed would never leave Heyworth. Not while his sister's case was still open.

Maybe it was better this way. Better to say goodbye before things got any more serious between them.

"Margaret, we need to ask you a few questions about Bonnie." Reed's tone was blunt. "We located her car."

The veterinarian shot up from her crouch. "Where?"

"Near the back road bordering Joshua's land with

Emma's. Can you think of any reason Bonnie would be out that way?"

Her brows drew down. "No. I mean, she used to fish at the lake sometimes. Jeb let her borrow poles from his shed. But I can't imagine she was there late at night."

Emma's hand tightened on Sadie's leash. "You mentioned the last time we talked that you hadn't been aware of Bonnie's relationship with Joshua. Do you know why she kept it secret from you?"

"She knew I wouldn't approve." Margaret's nose wrinkled. "Joshua had a criminal history and was known as something of a bad boy. Bonnie was a sweet girl. She had a soft spot for those with sad stories."

"You think he took advantage of her kindness?"

"I don't know. People often did."

Reed's expression never shifted, but Emma sensed his interest. "Like who?"

Margaret licked her lips. "I wasn't thinking of someone in particular. Just…people. Bonnie interacted with a lot of the townsfolk because of her work at the courthouse. She was a regular at the sheriff's department. People were always asking her to do favors and stuff like that. She never learned how to say no."

"What was Bonnie's relationship like with Judge Norton?" he asked.

Something flickered in Margaret's expression before she smoothed it out. "I assume it was fine. We didn't talk about it much."

Emma had the distinct sense she was lying. "If you know something, Margaret, you need to say so. We aren't gossiping. We're trying to get to the truth and help Bonnie."

"Of course you are. I'm sorry. This is a small town

and things have a way of getting around." Margaret fiddled with her scrub top. "Bonnie had some issues with Judge Norton. She felt he was interested in her… romantically."

Reed stiffened. Emma shifted in front of him. Margaret would have an easier time telling a woman. "Did she ever report it? Judge Norton was her boss."

"No. It was a tough situation. I mean, she'd been dating Will for a long time and she didn't want to hurt him. And the judge was discreet about it. He would massage her shoulders or stroke her hair. It was weird and made Bonnie uncomfortable, but it didn't quite rise to the level of sexual harassment."

Could that have been what the argument between Bonnie and Judge Norton been about? It was possible.

"Did Will know?" Emma asked.

"Bonnie certainty wouldn't have told him. Will is the jealous type and his relationship with his uncle is rocky. Like I said, it made her uncomfortable, but Judge Norton was careful not to cross the line."

"Do you think it's something she would've told Joshua?"

Margaret shrugged. "Honestly, I don't know. Maybe."

They talked for a few more minutes, but Margaret didn't have any other information. They said their goodbyes. Emma waited until they were in Reed's SUV before placing a hand on his arm. "Are you okay?"

He pounded the steering wheel. "There was so much about Bonnie's life I didn't know."

"She was protecting you."

"That wasn't her job." His jaw tightened. "It was mine. I'm her big brother."

"It doesn't work that way, Reed. We always protect

those we love. You and I both know, if Bonnie had told you about Judge Norton, you would've confronted him. It's who you are."

He closed his eyes and leaned his head back. "Judge Norton. If what Margaret says is true, Emma, he has motive. If he was interested romantically in Bonnie…"

"Then there's a chance he wanted to prevent her from marrying Joshua. Permanently."

SEVENTEEN

The lamp in the corner of the living room cast a soft glow over the room. Emma lay on the couch, covered in a throw, her dark hair spread across a pillow. She'd fallen asleep reading a book. Sadie lay on the carpet next to her.

Reed shifted the laptop on the rickety tray table. The recliner wasn't the best place to work, but he didn't consider moving. Silly perhaps, and more than a little sentimental, but he wanted to be near Emma.

His phone beeped with an alert from his security system, indicating activity near the house. Reed pulled up the camera and saw Austin getting out of his truck. His hand tightened on the phone. Austin had been in charge of coordinating the search of Joshua's property. Had the cadaver dogs found anything?

Reed disarmed the house alarm and met Austin at the door. "Shhh, Emma fell asleep on the couch."

Austin removed his cowboy hat and hung it on a hook next to the door. In his other hand was a takeout bag from a fast-food restaurant. The scent of fries tickled Reed's nose. He gave his cousin a questioning look.

Austin shook his head. "They didn't find anything," he whispered.

Reed let out a breath. The two men went into the kitchen. Austin opened the fridge and pulled out a soda. Sadie wandered in and beelined for the back door.

"You need to go out, girl?" Reed asked. He opened the screen door for her, and she dashed out. Reed's phone beeped with an alert. He ignored it. The cameras were picking up Sadie's jaunt through the yard.

"What's the latest, Austin?"

"There isn't much that's new. The cadaver team isn't finished. They've done about half the property. The rest will be done tomorrow." Austin unwrapped a burger and bit into it. "We did find several more handguns in the house. They were in the basement. Cooper has sent them to the lab to be tested."

Which meant Joshua could've shot Mike, they just didn't have the proof yet. "How soon before we get the results?"

He shrugged. "Tomorrow sometime. He's put a rush on it."

"Did Cooper tell you about his theory? That Judge Norton might be involved?"

"Yes. He also informed me about what Margaret told you."

"I've done some additional digging. Hold on." Reed retrieved a file folder from his home office. "All of them—Vernon, Mike and Charlie—appeared in Judge Norton's courtroom."

"So have most of the criminals in the county." Austin dunked several fries into some ketchup.

"Yes, but these men never were sentenced harshly.

They've committed crime after crime, but only received a slap on the wrist each time."

It didn't sit right with him. It was almost as if the men were being protected. Not all of the cases appeared before Judge Norton, but it would've have been difficult for him to put in a word with the other judges.

"Listen, Reed, we need to pursue every avenue, but I think you and Cooper are barking up the wrong tree with this one. Judge Norton doesn't have so much as a speeding ticket. I can't see him kidnapping Bonnie or killing her."

"You know as well as I do, sometimes evil resides in a place you would least expect."

Austin wiped his hands on a napkin and flipped through some of the records on the table. "Look at this. Deputy Hendricks arrested both Mike and Charlie at different points. Will was the prosecutor on several of these cases. If you're looking for connections, they're all over the place. We aren't that big of a department or a county. You'll need a lot more than this to accuse a sitting judge."

"We aren't looking to accuse him of anything," Reed corrected. "And no one knows we're looking into Judge Norton except for a small group of people. For obvious reasons."

Emma came into the kitchen, squinting at the light. "What's going on?"

"We're just discussing the case."

The fog in her expression lifted when her gaze fell on Austin. She stiffened. "Did—"

"No," he said quickly. "The cadaver dogs didn't find Bonnie."

"Well, that's a relief." She rubbed her face. "Is Sadie

in here with you guys? I woke up on the couch and she wasn't in the living room."

"I let her out," Reed said. He got up and opened the back door, but the dog wasn't in the yard. His phone beeped with a new notification. An unfamiliar truck was making its way up his driveway. "Someone's coming."

Austin stood and joined him at the front door. Sadie raced up the steps and Emma let her inside. The floodlights clicked on. Wayne Johnson dropped out of the cab. The ranch hand was wearing a dusty set of overalls and a bandanna around his neck. His shotgun was attached to a rack on his truck.

"Sorry to disturb you so late, Sheriff."

"That's all right. What's going on?"

Wayne settled his hands on his hips. "Well, now, after our discussion down by the lake the other day, I got to thinking you needed to talk to Owen. I remembered Jeb mentioned he had an aunt in Livingston. I gots to thinkin' maybe Owen was hiding out there."

The screen door creaked as Emma joined them on the porch. "I thought Mabel was dead."

"No, ma'am. She's over ninety, but she's still alive and well. Anyway, I ventured out there and talked with her."

Reed drew up to his full height. "Wayne, you shouldn't have done that."

He lifted a hand. Dirt was embedded in the skin of his fingers, staining them darker than his palm. "Don't be warmin' up for a lecture, Sheriff. I did what I thought was best. Owen is as jittery as an untrained coonhound. The last thing he needed was people showing up with guns blazing."

Reed wanted to tell the ranch hand they wouldn't have gone in guns blazing, but it would've fallen on deaf ears. Some of the citizens of Heyworth were used to taking matters into their own hands. Wayne was one of them. "Did you find Owen?"

"I did. He's in the truck."

Reed's hand immediately went to his weapon, although he left it in the holster. Wayne waved at the vehicle.

The rear door on the extended cab opened. Owen appeared. His hands were held up in a classic sign of surrender.

"It took a bit of talkin' but I convinced him you were good folks who would hear him out," Wayne said. "Don't make a liar out of me. And, Sheriff, trust me. You want to hear what he has to say."

Reed nodded. He went down the porch steps. Owen watched him approach with a wary expression, but his eyes were clear and focused. He appeared sober, which was a good start. Still, the man was criminal and had run away from the law. There was only so much leeway Reed would give him.

"Owen, I need to check you for weapons but then we'll all go inside and talk."

Owen nodded. Within a few minutes, they were settled around the kitchen table. The coffeepot gurgled. Emma bustled around pulling down mugs and plating some cookies.

"Where have you been?" Reed asked.

"A rehab facility in Houston." Owen shifted in the chair. "I was wrong to escape from the hospital, especially since I was under arrest, but Vernon and Mike were looking for me. They wanted to kill me."

Emma froze, before handing a mug of coffee to her cousin. "Why would they want you dead?"

"I'm Joshua's alibi for the night Bonnie disappeared."

Owen's words had the effect of a bomb going off. Everyone was still and quiet. Reed leaned in. "If that's so, why is this the first I'm hearing about it?"

"Because I made Joshua promise to keep it a secret. The night of Bonnie's disappearance, I was with Mike. We broke into a house on Franklin Street. The owners were supposed to be gone, but I guess the husband stayed behind for some reason. We got caught. Mike escaped, but the husband beat me pretty badly before I was able to get out of the house."

Reed glanced at Austin. His cousin nodded. "There was a robbery that night. The owner couldn't identify the two men, but he did mention beating one of them pretty good."

"I couldn't go to the hospital, for obvious reasons," Owen said. "Mike had taken the truck and disappeared. I was desperate and called the only person I could think of to help me. Joshua used to rob houses with us but he stopped a long time ago. Still, I figured he would give me a ride."

"And did he?"

Owen nodded. His shaggy hair fell into his eyes. "Although Joshua was upset about it. He warned me it was the last time he would help me. He advised me to straighten out my life. Anyway, I'm the reason Joshua was late to meet Bonnie at the park. We went there together but she was already gone. Joshua tried calling her a few times, but she didn't answer. He was worried she'd think he'd gotten cold feet."

Reed made a point to keep his expression impassive,

but if Owen was telling the truth, then Joshua couldn't have hurt Bonnie. And if Joshua wasn't behind his sister's disappearance, then someone else was.

Maybe Judge Norton's involvement wasn't such a stretch, after all.

Sadie nudged Emma's hand with her head, and she stroked her dog's soft fur. She took a sip of her coffee, but it swirled in her stomach like battery acid. Owen's delay in providing an alibi for Joshua may have caused serious harm. Joshua was missing, after all. She could only hope he was hiding out and not hurt or dead.

"What time did Joshua drop you off?" Reed asked.

"Late. I'm not sure. He was going to drive over to Bonnie's apartment to see if she was there. He was frantic. I was too messed up at the time, but in the morning, I felt really bad. Especially when I heard about her disappearance."

"Why didn't you come forward when she went missing?"

"Because I didn't want to be arrested for the robbery. Joshua and I had several arguments about it—the most recent one happened on the same day I confronted Emma on the porch."

Emma's gaze flickered to Wayne. It was the fight the ranch hand had observed and told them about.

"Joshua wanted me to come forward and explain he had an alibi," Owen continued. "He knew you wouldn't give up on finding Bonnie, Reed. But Joshua was worried time and energy was being wasted looking into him. I refused. I knew Joshua wouldn't say anything either because he'd given his word to me."

Emma pushed away her coffee. "Why come forward now?"

"Because Joshua was right. It's time I straighten out my life. Getting sober is the first step, but I also need to take responsibility for my actions."

Reed drummed his fingers on the table. "I heard you and Bonnie had an altercation a few months before her disappearance?"

Owen blanched. "We did. I was drunk and it shouldn't have happened. Drinking has gotten me into a lot of trouble." He took a deep breath. "I owe you a huge apology, Emma. I treated you badly. I was angry and hurt, but that's no excuse."

His voice rang with shame and regret. She closed her eyes. Holding on to her anger wouldn't get them anywhere. Owen's addiction had caused him to make choices she knew in her heart weren't true to who he was as a person. "Apology accepted. All I wanted—all Uncle Jeb wanted—was for you to be healthy."

"I know that now."

Wayne took a cookie from the plate in the center of the table. "Tell the sheriff what you told me, Owen. He needs to know the rest."

"There's more?" Reed asked.

Owen scratched his chin. "Being arrested for the robbery wasn't the only reason why I didn't want to come forward. Dean Shadwick is the other. He's a dirty cop."

Emma's posture went rigid. Dean was the deputy she'd filed a complaint with after someone tried to poison Sadie.

"How do you know this?" Reed demanded.

"Because he's the one who introduced me to Mike Young. Dean's been working with the Young brothers for a long time. Lately, they've been cooking meth and selling it in the next county."

Emma let out a breath. "That's why Dean was so protective of you when I initially reported the stalking on my property. You knew his secrets."

"Not all of them, but enough to count."

"Dean always was a sneaky one," Wayne said. "His daddy was a good man, but my wife used to teach in the high school and she never trusted Dean further than she could throw him. Many townsfolk didn't like it when the former sheriff hired him to be a deputy."

Austin was silent, but from the hard line of his mouth, Emma was sure he had a few choice words to share with them in private. He probably knew more since he'd worked with Dean for a longer period of time than Reed had.

"Deputy Shadwick did a lot of work on Bonnie's case." She frowned. "His name appeared on most of the reports."

"That's because he headed up the investigation," Austin said. "The former sheriff insisted on it. At the time, I thought it was odd. Dean had little to no experience investigating such a serious crime."

Owen cleared his throat. "There's something else. Dean bragged about working with someone higher up. Someone who would always protect them."

Reed's brows shot up. "Who?"

"I don't know. He never would say, but he made it clear they wouldn't be punished seriously if they ever got caught. It was how he convinced me to get in on some of the crimes."

Reed's phone trilled. He pulled it from his hip and answered the call. Aunt Bessie's voice spilled from the speaker. Emma couldn't make out the words, but they were rushed. Her spine stiffened. Nothing good could come from a call at nearly midnight.

She leaned closer to listen in. Reed took the hint and put the call on speaker. "Aunt Bessie, slow down and tell me exactly what's going on."

"I don't know what's going on." She sucked in a big breath. "I went to bed early and woke up to someone in my room. He attacked me."

Austin grabbed his phone. Within seconds he was snapping out orders in the corner of the kitchen.

"He must've hit me over the head because I don't remember a whole lot," Aunt Bessie continued. "I woke up locked in my closet. I managed to get out, but the trooper outside... He's unconscious and bleeding, Reed."

Emma's body went cold. "Bessie, where are Lily and Vivian?"

Reed placed a hand on Emma's arm, the warmth of his palm a stark contrast to the chills racing through her body.

The sound of running came over the line. Doors opened and closed as Aunt Bessie yelled their names. The panic in the woman's voice added to Emma's. She clamped her lips together to prevent the scream bubbling inside her from tearing loose.

Aunt Bessie started sobbing. "Reed, they aren't here. Lily and Vivian are gone. They've been kidnapped."

EIGHTEEN

Reed raced down the country road, lights flashing and siren blaring. After the phone call from his aunt, they'd received one from Deputy Kyle Hendricks. Aunt Bessie's car—stolen from her house—was spotted on a rarely used back road. It was four in the morning, but still pitch-black outside.

"Hold on," he said to Emma. She gripped the handle above the door as he took a right turn. His tires bounced over a pothole. Sadie, strapped in the back seat, swayed. Behind them, Austin followed in his patrol car.

"This is Old Man Franklin's land," Emma said. Her face was pale and her lips drawn tight. "Isn't that the property Joshua mentioned he bought when I wouldn't sell?"

"Yes."

Reed's hands tightened on the steering wheel until his knuckles were white. Someone had attacked his aunt. Assaulted a trooper. Taken Vivian and Lily. A blinding rage unlike any he'd ever experienced threatened to take hold, but he battled it back. There was no room for emotion. Right now, he needed to focus on getting Emma's family back.

The road curved and the trees parted. A patrol car sat behind Aunt Bessie's sedan. Kyle raised a hand to shield his eyes from the approaching headlights. Reed slammed on the brakes. He flipped off the engine but didn't bother to take the keys out of the vehicle. His boots hit the dirt with a thump.

"There's no one in the car," Kyle said. The deputy struggled to catch up to Reed's long strides. "I already looked."

He didn't care. At this moment, Reed wasn't sure he could trust anyone besides his cousin and Cooper. He quickly walked around his aunt's sedan. The outside appeared untouched. "How did you know the car was here?"

"I got a call from Dean Shadwick."

Emma ran up, catching the last bit of his deputy's answer. She inhaled sharply.

Kyle's brows clashed together. "What's going on?"

Reed had no intention of answering him. "When?" he barked. "When did Dean call you?"

"Right after the BOLO on your aunt's vehicle went out. He mentioned he'd heard about it on his scanner."

"He's suspended."

"He has a police scanner in his personal vehicle."

Reed yanked on a pair of gloves and opened the sedan's driver side door. The overhead light flickered on. Keys were in the ignition.

"I've got what looks like blood," Austin said quietly. Reed's gaze shot to the back seat. A dark stain spread across the leather, dripping down toward the carpet.

Emma cried out. Reed caught her as she rushed toward the vehicle. She wasn't wearing gloves. He couldn't let her accidentally disturb evidence they may need. She gripped his biceps, her fingers clawing into his skin through his shirt.

"Lily's lamb." Tears streamed down her face.

Austin reached in and pulled the familiar stuffed animal from the floorboard. Reed's own knees weakened but he forced himself to block it out. His gaze swung toward Kyle.

"Did you check the trunk?" he demanded.

Emma slapped a hand over her mouth. Reed kept an arm around her waist, holding her up.

Kyle's face was stark in the headlights. "Yes. It's clear."

Emma shuddered against Reed. He wanted to tell her to wait in his SUV, but there was no way she would listen. Not that he could blame her.

"What did Dean tell you specifically, from start to finish?" Reed asked his deputy.

Kyle straightened. "He called my personal phone and stated that he'd heard the BOLO on the scanner. Dean mentioned he was on his way back from a fishing trip and used this road to cut across town. He spotted the vehicle and said I should check it out because it matched the description."

There was no way Dean was simply coming back from a fishing trip. Reed hadn't been convinced of Owen's claim that Dean was a dirty cop until this moment. Reed had no doubt he'd driven the car here and called his friend to find it. "Did Dean say where he was going?"

"I assumed home." Kyle's gaze flickered to Emma before settling back on Reed. "I thought it was strange he was coming back so late from a fishing trip, but I didn't question it."

No, he wouldn't think to challenge his good friend and fellow deputy. Dean had been counting on that.

A state vehicle slid to a stop and Cooper got out. The Texas Ranger's stride was furious, his hands balled into fists. "What do we have?"

Reed got him up to speed. Cooper stepped over to look at the vehicle himself. Kyle followed. Their flashlights bounced off the chrome bumper of Aunt Bessie's car.

Emma shivered again. Her face was drained of all color and, when Reed touched her skin, she was frigid. He shrugged off his jacket and wrapped it around her before pulling her into his arms. Sirens wailed in the distance.

"Hold on, Em. We've got backup coming and every available unit working on this."

"I don't know if I can keep it together, Reed. My little girl—" Her voice choked off.

"Lily is in God's hands. He's watching over her. I know it's hard, but your faith has pulled you through so much. It will get you through this, too."

She took a deep breath. Then another. Reed rested his head against hers and closed his eyes. He quietly whispered a prayer. It was as much for him as it was for Emma. Lily had stolen his heart and the idea of anything happening to the little girl was enough to cripple him. But what he'd said to Emma came from the depths of his own faith. It was the mantra that got him through the long nights after Bonnie's disappearance. No matter where his sister was, Bonnie was in the Lord's hands and He would see her through.

Emma cupped his cheek with her hand. "Thank you, Reed. I needed the prayer."

"So did I."

A shout from Cooper drew his attention. Releasing Emma, Reed snapped back into professional mode. "What is it?"

"I've got drag marks." Cooper's flashlight drifted across the tall grass a short distance from Aunt Bessie's car. "They disappear into the woods."

Emma raced to Reed's SUV. She unhooked Sadie.

Reed studied the marks. "Those are obvious. The perpetrator wanted us to find them. He practically hung a sign."

"No kidding." Cooper frowned. "It could be a trap, a way to lure Emma and Sadie into the woods."

"It doesn't matter," Emma said. "We still have to go."

Sweat dripped down Emma's back despite the chill in the air. The Kevlar vest was heavy and more than uncomfortable. With every step, it pressed down on her shoulders. The woods were a tangle of limbs and bushes in the faint glow of the moonlight. Sadie's collar jangled.

Reed's flashlight led the way. He'd insisted on walking ahead of her for safety. Arguing would've eaten precious time, and Emma wasn't willing to waste a minute of it. She needed to keep moving. Each step brought her closer to Lily and Vivian. At least, she hoped so.

The sound of running water reached her ears.

"What is that?" she asked.

"There's a natural spring on the property. It feeds into a river," Austin answered. He was behind her, providing cover from any potential attack. "Teenagers often come here to tube down it when Old Man Franklin says it's okay."

Sadie barked.

Reed stopped short. Emma bumped into the back of him. His flashlight beam bounced off the dog's reflective vest.

"I don't see Vivian," Emma said.

Austin pointed. "There."

A tree curved at the water's edge. Some of the branches drifted into the water. Vivian was balanced precariously on the edge of one. She was unconscious, and when Reed's flashlight drew close to her face, Emma's throat clenched. Her sister-in-law had been beaten. Badly. Sadie barked again.

"Where's Lily?" Reed said.

They scanned the immediate area but saw no sign of the little girl. Emma refused to even consider her daughter had been out there on the branch with Vivian but had already fallen in the water. No, she had to focus on one thing at a time. Otherwise she would collapse and wail a mountain of grief.

They scrambled down the bank. Emma took a few precious moments to praise her dog. Reed had pulled his weapon and was keeping watch on their immediate area.

"There's no way to reach her without climbing out on the branch," Austin said. "I don't have rope in my bag. Anyone else?"

Reed shook his head. "We need to call for backup."

They'd purposefully refused to allow troopers and other deputies to traipse through the property since Sadie could search the area faster. Emma sent up a prayer of thanksgiving. It would've taken hours to find Vivian without the dog, and her sister-in-law would've probably died.

"We don't have time to wait for backup." She tore at

the straps of her bulletproof vest. "Reed, you hold on to me while I climb out to get her."

"No," Austin said. "I'll go."

"That branch looks ready to break off. It won't support your weight. Or Reed's. I'm the lightest one. I have to go."

Reed's mouth tightened. She felt he wanted to argue with her, but he couldn't deny physics. She dropped the Kevlar vest on the ground. Bark bit into her hand as she shimmed her way into position. Underneath her, the water in the river swirled. It was black as ink. Spring-fed meant it was cold, too.

"Slow and steady," she muttered to herself. "Okay, Reed, hold on to my feet."

His hands grasped her ankles. The grip was firm and steady. It grounded her. Emma eased out on the branch. It swayed closer to the water.

"Vivian, can you hear me? I'm coming to get you. Don't move."

Her sister-in-law stayed motionless. Only the faint movement of her chest indicated she was breathing and not dead. Emma clung on to that fact. She crept out farther. Her hand strained forward, but Vivian was just out of reach.

The branch creaked. Emma glanced behind her. "Reed, you have to back off. Your weight is too much."

"No. I'm not letting you go."

"There's no other choice. I need a few more inches and then I've got her."

A long pause followed. Reed's hand let go of her left ankle. He flattened himself out, spreading his weight as much as possible. "Try now."

Bark scraped against her stomach. Something tickled the back of her neck. A pine needle or a bug, she couldn't tell. Emma blocked it all out, focusing on reaching Vivian. Her fingertips brushed against her sister-in-law's.

Just a little more.

A resounding crack broke through her concentration. Vivian tumbled away and Reed's cry followed. Her ankle was ripped from his hand.

The world spun. A slap of cold water stole the breath from her lungs. Darkness covered her and, for a heart-stopping moment, she wasn't sure which way was up. Then she hit bottom.

Shoving against the mud, Emma shot herself upward. She surfaced, coughing, and dragged in a breath. The current pulled her downstream. Vivian. Where was Vivian? She twisted in the darkness, searching. Her tennis shoes and clothes dragged her down. She dunked under the cold water.

Lord, please, help me.

She kicked off her tennis shoes and resurfaced. Sucking in a breath, she yelled Reed's name, although it felt like the wind and the current stole it from her. Her fingers brushed against a tangle of something. Seaweed? No, hair. Emma grabbed a handful and yanked. Vivian popped up although her sister-in-law was deathly pale and still unconscious.

"Emma!" Reed yelled from the shoreline.

"I'm here," she cried. Her limbs were going numb, yet she fought to keep Vivian's head above water. Emma couldn't tell if Vivian was breathing. The current thrashed them. Lights to the left indicated Reed and Austin were running along the edge ahead of her.

Rocks. Huge lurking objects in their path. Emma

kicked but the river was too difficult to fight. She twisted, using her body to block Vivian from being battered against the stone. Her shoulder whammed against rock. Pain vibrated through her. She gritted her teeth and reached out blindly. Her fingers caught a groove. She held on.

The beam of a flashlight bounced toward her. Emma blinked rapidly to clear the water from her eyes. Reed balanced on a rock. His position was precarious. The surface was wet and smooth as glass.

"Take Vivian," she shouted. Emma struggled to keep her sister-in-law's head above water. Her arm trembled from the cold and exhaustion.

Reed bent down. Water stained his pants leg, turning the fabric dark. With one hand, he grasped Emma's wrist and leaned across to grab hold of Vivian.

"I can't…" His face reddened with the effort. Austin appeared behind him, but the rock wasn't large enough for both men to balance. He couldn't hold on to Emma and pull Vivian from the water. Not at the angle he was at.

"Take her first," she yelled. Vivian wouldn't survive if she was lost in the water. "I can't hold her much longer."

Reed nodded. He released her arm. "Don't you dare let go. Hang on for me, Em."

She was trying, but her fingers were already growing numb. Reed used both hands to yank Vivian from the water. He stood and handed her to Austin. The chief deputy cradled her as if she was more delicate than spun glass.

Emma's hand slipped. A fresh wave of adrenaline shot through her veins. Reed gave a shout. He lunged for her, slipping on the wet stone, and nearly fell into the water. His hand clasped over her wrist.

"I've got you, Em. I've got you."

Reed pulled her from the cold water. He swung an arm under her legs and delicately balanced along the rocks until they hit the shoreline. Emma collapsed on the bank, gasping for breath. Her heart thundered in her ears. She couldn't feel her toes. Austin immediately started CPR on Vivian.

Reed yanked the jacket off Emma's shoulders, replacing it with a blanket. "We need to get you warm, Em."

Her teeth chattered. Sadie licked her face. Someone coughed and vomited. It was the sweetest sound Emma had ever heard. She pushed the dog out of the way. "Vivian?"

Her sister-in-law was tucked against Austin's chest. Her blond hair clung to her face in strings. Somehow it made the bruising on her cheek and the black eye worse. Despite being tossed in the river, blood still stained her pajama top.

Reed pulled another blanket from his backpack and covered Vivian with it. Emma scooted across the distance between them.

"Li-Li-Lily?" Vivian gasped.

"We haven't found her." Emma took Vivian's hand. "What happened?"

"T-t-took her from me. Hurt me. Fight. Don't take the b-b-baby."

Emma's chin trembled. Of course Vivian would've fought fiercely to protect Lily. She'd nearly paid with her life.

"S-s-sorry."

"No. You have nothing to be sorry for. We'll find her, Vivian." Water dripped on their conjoined hands and it took Emma a moment to realize she was crying. "Just like we found you, we'll find Lily."

A phone trilled. Surprise flashed across Reed's face. "That sounds like it's coming from Vivian."

With trembling fingers, Emma lowered the blanket covering her sister-in-law. Vivian was wearing two shirts, a tank top under a pajama button-down. A dark string hung around her neck and disappeared into the button-down. Emma pulled on it. A cell phone came out, secured in a water-proof pouch.

Reed took over. He yanked the phone free of the pouch and answered the call, putting it on speaker so everyone could hear.

"Well, hello, Sheriff." The voice was mangled by a digital voice distorter, making it unrecognizable. "As nice as it is to hear your voice, you aren't the one I'm interested in talking to. Put Emma on the phone."

Reed's gaze shot to her and she grabbed the phone. Her daughter's life was on the line. Whatever the kidnapper wanted, she would give it to him.

"I'm here," Emma said.

"Good. How is your sister-in-law?"

"She's fine, no thanks to you. What do you want?"

"All in good time, Emma. All in good time. First, we need to make something clear. Vivian's bruises, along with her dip in the river, was a message. I'm capable of harming everything that is dear to you."

Goose bumps broke out across Emma's skin. This entire scenario was a setup, designed to terrify her into submission. "You didn't need to bother. I would do anything for my daughter. If you wanted me to follow orders, all you had to do was call."

He chuckled. It was cold and manic. The thought of sweet Lily being with this monster made bile rise in Emma's throat. Reed met her gaze. In the depths of his blue eyes, she saw the strength she needed to hold it together.

"I'm glad we understand each other," the voice said over the phone. "Now, listen closely. Something very important to me was found on your property and I want it returned."

She frowned. "Bonnie's bracelet?"

"That's right. I want it back."

He was crazy. Absolutely nuts. "I don't have it. The police—"

"Took it to the state lab. I know. That's why I need you to get it back for me."

Reed waved a hand, indicating she should stall. Emma swallowed. "That's difficult. I'm not allowed to handle evidence."

"Don't insult my intelligence," he snapped. "Reed can get it for you. And you better pray he does because your daughter's life depends on it."

Anger vibrated in his voice. Emma swallowed hard. "Okay. Okay. I'll get it. Just please don't hurt her."

"Don't make me. Do as I say and everything will be fine. Bring Bonnie's bracelet to the lake on your property in an hour. You will come alone. No bullet-proof vests and no tricks. If I see the sheriff or any of his men, there will be a penalty."

"I'm in the middle of the woods. I'll need more than an hour."

"One hour or else."

A click punctuated his words, followed by the sound of a dial tone.

NINETEEN

A soft pink glow from the rising sun shimmered along the trees. Emma parked her car along the back road separating her property from Joshua's. She glanced at her watch. Ten minutes until her hour grace period was up. She needed to move fast. It would take time to traverse the path through the woods to the lake.

Leaves crunched under Emma's ballerina flats. They were slippery and a poor choice for a hike, but she had little choice. Her tennis shoes were still floating down the river. Vivian had been taken by ambulance to the hospital. Emma wanted to be there with her, but she hadn't had an option about that either.

She gripped the burner phone provided by the killer in her left hand. It was untraceable. She knew. They'd already tried. Cooper was fit to be tied. Reed, too, for that matter. Neither one of them had been comfortable obeying the killer's orders. Emma knew the two men were trying to protect her, but nothing was more important than getting Lily into safe hands. She would not risk her daughter's life by having a SWAT team surrounding the lake.

Her gaze darted around. The hair on the back of her

neck rose. A nearby bush rustled. Emma spun in time to see a squirrel dart across the path. She closed her eyes and took a deep breath. Fear threatened to cloud her mind. She wrestled it back. Her jean pocket bulged with Bonnie's bracelet. It'd taken a trooper, even with lights and siren going, forty-five minutes to travel the distance between the state lab and Heyworth.

The trees thinned, revealing the clearing and the lake. Bird flittered above her. Emma hesitated. Once she stepped into the clearing, she'd be exposed. There was little doubt her stalker would be watching. A single shot was all it would take.

You can do this. You have to do this.

Her hand drifted to the zippered pocket of her light jacket and brushed against a familiar lump. Lily's lamb. She took another deep breath to settle her nerves. Saying a quick prayer for her daughter's safety, Emma stepped into the early morning sunshine.

The burner phone rang. She answered it, her voice cracking. "Yes."

"You're late." Same voice distorter, but Emma sensed a desperation in the man's voice that hadn't been there before. It fueled her anxiety. Desperation could cause him to make drastic decisions.

Keep calm. Keep him talking. Stall.

Reed's advice replayed in her mind. Thinking of the handsome sheriff threatened to shred the last of her frayed emotions. Emma wanted him with her. Right next to her, holding her hand. She hadn't realized until now how much comfort she drew from Reed's quiet strength. Emma was tough, she could stand on her own, but she didn't want to anymore.

She forced the thoughts back and cleared her throat. "Sorry for the delay. It took time to get the bracelet."

Could Cooper and his team in the van a mile away hear her through the listening device hidden under her shirt? She had no idea. Having an earpiece to hear them would've been nice. It was also too risky. They didn't know how close she would get to the killer.

"Where is it?" he demanded.

She tugged Bonnie's bracelet free from her pocket and held it up. The diamond cross winked in the sunlight.

A sigh came over the line. "Good. That's good."

He was definitely watching. She scanned the trees again but saw nothing out of the ordinary. "Why do you want it?"

"What difference does it make to you?"

"My daughter was kidnapped for it. Color me curious."

He chuckled. "I'm sure you are, but that's not part of our deal. Now, I want you to take the bracelet and put it back in the fishing shed."

Her gaze darted to the building across the clearing. Was this some kind of trap? Was the killer in the shed? She couldn't make heads or tails of this. "I want Lily back first."

"No. I told you. I get the bracelet, then you get your daughter. Don't make me angry, Emma."

The coldness in his tone sent a fresh wave of panic through her. She couldn't push him too hard. Getting the truth wasn't worth risking Lily's life.

The spring sunshine swept her shoulders as she crossed the field. Dandelion fluff danced in the air. Somewhere in the lake, a fish jumped. Was Lily nearby?

Was her baby hungry? Or hurt? The thoughts raced around inside her head and Emma was powerless to stop them.

She paused outside the shed door. It was cracked open. Although the raccoon had been removed, the scent of death still lingered. Emma's stomach churned. Her hand tightened even more on the burner phone. It was a wonder she didn't snap the thing in two.

"What are you waiting for?" he growled in her ear.

To be ambushed. The words caught in her throat and she swallowed them down. Emma raised a trembling hand. The wood of the shed door under her fingertips was cool to the touch. She shoved. Fishing poles clattered to the ground as the door banged against the opposite wall.

Emma blinked. The shed was empty.

In her ear, the killer chuckled. "Gotcha."

Emma gritted her teeth together. He was somewhere nearby, watching, relishing in her terror. No more. She wouldn't give him the pleasure. She threw the bracelet inside.

"There." She turned in the doorway and jutted up her chin. "It's done. Now give me my daughter."

"Very well."

"How—" She paused. What was that?

Faint crying came from around the corner. Lily! Emma raced behind the building. The sound grew louder, her daughter's cries coming from the trees on the edge of Judge Norton's property.

Emma's shoes slid on the dewy grass as she ran toward the sound. "I'm coming, Lily. I'm coming."

She got closer. Her gaze swept the ground, searching for her baby's small form. Was she okay? Was she crawling among the pine needles?

The cries grew louder. They tore at Emma. "No, baby, don't cry. Mommy's here. Everything's going to be okay—"

She drew up short. On the ground was a recorder. Lily's cries grew frantic, louder, before cutting off completely.

Emma stared in disbelief. "No, no, no."

A branch snapped behind her. Emma whirled but it was too late. Something slammed down on her head. She saw stars and her knees collapsed. A rock on the ground jabbed her in the ribs. Emma inhaled sharply.

She swung out with her fists, but the attacker yanked her by the hair. An arm wrapped around her chest, locking her arms next to her body. The breath was squeezed from her. Her back was slammed up against a man's hard form.

The unmistakable sensation of a gun's barrel pressed against her temple. "Don't move."

She froze. The sound of her own frantic heartbeat roared in her ears. It was so loud, she almost didn't hear the attacker's next words. His breath was hot against her face. "Sheriff! I will shoot her. It's time to come out now."

Quakes overtook Emma. She knew that voice. Recognized the distinctive and cultured Southern drawl immediately, even without seeing his face.

Will Norton.

"He's not here," Emma said. "You told me not to bring anyone."

Please, Lord, keep Reed away from here.

The lake was a huge area. It wasn't possible for one

man to cover all of it at once. Plus Emma had disappeared from sight by entering the woods.

Will yanked her free of the trees. "Look what I caught!"

"Let her go, Will." Reed roared from the tree line. "We've got you surrounded."

"Don't play me for a fool. Backup is nowhere close. I've made sure of that. Now come out where I can see you."

"No!" Emma yelled. "Don't."

She didn't need to be told what would happen next. Will had drawn them into a trap, just as Reed had suspected. There was little chance they would both walk out of this alive.

Reed ignored her. He appeared several meters away, his gun drawn. There was no fear in his expression. His mouth was hard, his stance confident. Sunlight played along the chiseled edges of his features and bounced off the sheriff's badge pinned to his chest.

He was a protector. Her protector. Reed couldn't hide in the woods, any more than he could stop breathing. It was who he was.

And she was in love with him.

It hit Emma with the force of a punch to the gut. The depth of her emotions had been lingering below the surface, but she'd refused to acknowledge them. Because she was scared. Because she'd walked through the pain of loss and wasn't sure she could do it again.

But it was there. She was in love with Reed.

And Will was going to kill him.

Things had unraveled within a blink of an eye. One minute Emma was crossing the field toward the shed, the next she was darting into a copse of trees. Reed had lost her in the woods and those precious seconds had given Will the opening he needed to attack.

Reed kept his gun trained on the county prosecutor. He stepped out farther into the clearing. It was risky. There was no way to know if Dean was hiding somewhere nearby with a rifle, just waiting to take him out. But he didn't think it was a strong possibility.

Will wouldn't have done his own dirty work unless he was out of options.

Reed spared one quick glance at Emma. Blood dripped from a wound on her head. She was pale, but her hands were fisted at her sides. That was his Em. Terrified but ready to fight. Will pressed the handgun harder against her temple. Rage raced through Reed's veins. His vision narrowed.

"Drop it, Will."

"Good try, Reed, but that's a no-go. Unless you want me to shoot Emma right here in front of you, you'll do everything I say. Put your gun down on the ground. Nice and slow."

Reed's hand tightened on his weapon. He couldn't put down his gun. Will would only shoot him and then Emma. "What are you doing, Will?"

"I said put your gun down!"

Reed shifted again. He didn't have a clear shot. Will was using Emma as a human shield. There was no way to take him down without hurting her in the process.

He needed to stall and give his backup time to arrive. Cooper had to be on his way. Emma was wearing a wire.

"I'm serious, Reed." Will said. "I'll kill her right here in front of you."

There was a wildness in his eyes that chilled Reed to the core. Will was a desperate man, and that also made him a dangerous one.

Emma swayed a bit. Blood dripped down her neck, disappearing into the collar of her shirt. It wasn't possible to tell how badly she'd been injured but it was enough to cause him serious concern. Reed met her gaze. With his eyes, he tried to say all the words he couldn't out loud.

I love you. Hold on. I'll get us out of this.

"We can put a stop to this now, Will. Things haven't gone too far yet. A man like you doesn't deserve to be in jail." It took every ounce of Reed's law enforcement training to keep his expression sympathetic, to have the lies fall from his lips without a hint of his true feelings. "Why don't you tell me what this is really about? We can fix it."

"It's too late for that now. Emma should've left when I told her to. None of this would've happened if she had."

Reed racked his brain, desperate to keep Will talking. "You were trying to prevent Bonnie's vehicle from being found."

"Duh." Will sneered. "I knew if Bonnie's car was uncovered, the investigation into her disappearance would be given a fresh look."

Reed desperately wanted to ask if his sister was alive but held back. Will was talking, but a move in the wrong direction could cause him to clam up. "When Emma wouldn't leave, you hired Charlie Young to kill her."

Will knew Charlie because he'd been the prosecutor on several of the man's criminal cases. Owen had mentioned someone high up was protecting them. It had to be Will.

"It was supposed to be a simple hit," Will said. "Instead, the idiot, along with his family, made a mess of everything."

Reed kept his gun locked on Will. If an opening presented itself, he wanted to be in a position to take it.

"When Bonnie's bracelet was found in Emma's shed, you changed tactics." Reed edged forward, making sure to time his movements to his words, so Will wouldn't notice. "You decided to frame Joshua for everything. You killed Mike Young and placed his body in Bonnie's truck."

Will tightened his hold on Emma. Her face paled even more and her mouth pinched with pain. The trip down the river must've injured her ribs. It took everything in Reed not to cross the distance between them and tackle Will. Where was his backup? They should've been here by now.

"Why Joshua?" Reed asked, although he already knew. The point was to keep Will talking.

Will glared at him. "Nice try, Sheriff. I'm not stupid enough to waste time explaining things to you."

"Come on. We both know I'm not getting out of this alive. You've got me in an impossible situation."

"Exactly, so put your gun down before I blow Emma's head off."

"Come on. You've had me spinning my wheels for weeks. Bonnie was my sister. At least, tell me how you outsmarted me."

Reed's skin crawled. He hated complimenting Will, but they needed time. Where was Cooper? SWAT should be in position by now. He glanced at Emma's shirt, where the wire was hidden, and his stomach sank. Will was blocking the listening device with his arm. Maybe the team had no idea they were in trouble.

Will was quiet for a moment, before a smirk played across his lips. "I did outsmart you, didn't I?"

"You've pulled off the perfect crime. No one suspected you. So, again, why Joshua?"

"I needed a scapegoat and you already suspected Joshua. I knew it would be easy to frame him for Bonnie's murder. Besides, he had it coming. That idiot actually thought he was good enough for Bonnie. I should've gotten rid of him a long time ago."

Will didn't know Owen had come forward to provide an alibi for Joshua. No doubt, he would tie up that loose end if given the chance.

"How long has Dean Shadwick been involved?" Reed asked.

"Oh, he's been my eyes and ears for a long time. There were rumors he could be bought for the right price." Will chuckled. "Surprise, it's true."

Reed's hand tightened on the weapon. He was going to find Dean and put him behind bars. There was nothing worse than a law enforcement officer who broke his oath to protect and serve. "You weren't driving your vehicle at the time of Bonnie's disappearance. Dean was, wasn't he? You told him to run a red light so you'd get a ticket and have an alibi."

"I knew I'd be a suspect since Bonnie and I had dated."

"Aren't you forgetting something?" Reed inched forward again. Time was running out. He was wearing a Kevlar vest. If he could convince Will to take a shot at him instead of Emma, they might have a chance. "Bonnie's car is going to be processed for forensic evidence. Removing all trace of DNA is difficult."

"I know." The smile turned hard, and his gaze went flat. "If you weren't such a Goody Two-shoes, I wouldn't have bothered worrying about it."

"I can't be bought," Reed said, as the final pieces of the puzzle snapped into place. "You knew I was a liability. I'd track down any piece of evidence, run down every lead, to find the truth. Kidnapping Lily and Vivian was your way of getting me alone."

"Don't be so prideful," Will said. "I needed to kill Emma, too."

Lily had to be close by. There was no other explanation. And based off the fact that Bonnie's bracelet was discovered in Emma's shed, chances were, if his sister was still alive, she was close, too.

"Time's up, Sheriff. Drop your weapon."

It was now or never. Reed said a quick prayer and leaned forward on the balls of his feet. "We can make a deal—"

"There are no deals," Will screamed. He jabbed the gun farther into Emma's skin. "Now drop your gun before I kill her."

A guttural growl came from the trees. Reed caught sight of a flash of brown as it leaped out of the woods and tackled Will. Emma went flying toward Reed and he caught her.

Sadie! The dog sank her teeth into Will's arm, and he screamed. The gun, held in his other hand, went off. A bullet flew wildly, whizzing past as Reed tugged Emma into the woods for safety. A flash of blue appeared in the distance.

Dean? Reed raised his weapon, but the gait of the

other man set his mind at ease. It was Austin. Backup had finally arrived. Sadie had been with his cousin, but the dog must've broken away when she heard the screaming. She'd rushed ahead to protect her mistress.

Sadie gave a yelp.

"No!" Emma screamed. "Sadie!"

Reed spun in time to see the dog fall back. Will sprang to his feet. Reed fired his weapon, but the other man was a moving target. He darted into the trees.

"Austin, he's on the move. I'm going after him."

Reed dashed after Will. They needed the man alive. He was the only one who knew where Lily was.

TWENTY

Emma rushed to Sadie's side. The dog was already on her feet. There wasn't any blood. Chances were Will had hit her with the butt of the gun. Sadie whimpered slightly when Emma touched her shoulder, confirming her suspicions.

Relief was short-lived. No other law enforcement stormed the clearing. Austin had disappeared with Reed after Will. The chief deputy had been alone. Will's iron clasp around Emma's chest must've interfered with the listening device. When things went silent, Cooper and the rest of the team hadn't known what was going on. Austin probably came quietly to investigate.

"Cooper, if you can hear me, Will Norton is the killer. He's escaped. Reed and Austin are in pursuit."

She reached into her pocket and pulled out Lily's lamb. She let Sadie sniff it. "We need to find Lily, girl. I know we've only done this in training, but I'm relying on you."

The dog's brown eyes seemed to mirror Emma's own worry. Based off Will's actions, there was no guarantee he wouldn't hold Lily hostage. She needed to find her little girl and she needed to do it now. There was no time to wait.

She gave Sadie the command to find. The dog took off into the woods. Emma bolted after her. "Cooper, I'm in the woods. I'm following Sadie in the hopes that she's tracking Lily."

She prayed they could hear her. Running through the woods while SWAT was storming the area was a bad idea. She could be accidentally shot by friendly fire. Still, it was a risk she had to take.

Sadie stopped, taking a moment to lift her nose to the air. Then she altered course slightly, taking them farther into Judge Norton's property. Sweat dripped down Emma's back. Her head ached. The wound in her scalp started bleeding again. Still, she pressed forward.

When her dog picked up the pace, Emma did, as well. Tree branches smacked her face. Her feet—clad in the stupid flats—slid along the pine needles. She tripped, flying forward. Her hands instinctively went out to brace herself. She hit the ground with a bone-jarring force. She sucked in a breath. Glancing up, she found herself face-to-face with a set of empty eyes.

Deputy Dean Shadwick. Dead.

Emma recoiled. Her stomach heaved. The man had been shot several times and left to rot half-hidden under a bush. From the looks of it, he'd been murdered recently. Maybe only hours before.

Will was cleaning house. Eliminating any threats against him. Emma staggered to her feet. A fresh sense of urgency fueled her steps. She feared her instincts were right and Will would use Lily as leverage to save his own skin.

In the distance, Sadie barked. The dog had passed

over Dean as if he didn't matter. Hopefully, that meant Sadie was only tracking Lily's scent.

Shots echoed in the woods. Emma's heart stopped. They hadn't been close, but there had been several. She sucked in a breath as a few more followed.

Were they from Reed? Or from the SWAT officers? Or was that Will shooting? He'd been out to kill Reed. He wasn't going to give up easily. The worst-case scenario played in her head like a horror movie on fast-forward. Emma said a quick and desperate prayer.

The forest was dead silent. She waited two more breaths. Then Sadie barked again. Emma ran toward the sound.

A break in the trees appeared. A rustic cabin sat among the towering pines. The windows were sealed with large boards. Heavy chains and locks kept them from being opened. Sadie sat next to the building and barked once more. When the dog spotted Emma, her tail thumped.

"Good girl, Sadie." She patted the dog's head before circling around the building, looking for a way inside. It didn't appear as if anyone had used this cabin for a long time. Some of the shingles were missing from the roof and the wood siding was rotting. Yet several cameras hung from the rafters.

She rounded the corner. The cabin had a broken front porch. The only door was closed off by a heavy wooden bar across the front. Emma swallowed. This didn't look like a simple attempt to keep people out of the cabin. No. These were the kind of measures taken to keep someone *in*.

She gripped the wooden bar across the door and shoved. It wouldn't budge. The thing had to weigh more than she did. The wood bit into the palms of her hands. Her muscles trembled. Still, it wouldn't move.

Sadie growled. Emma spun.

Will stood at the base of the porch. His arm was bleeding and scratches from running through the woods marred his face. His hair stood up on end. He looked wild and unhinged. Her gaze shot to the weapon pointed straight at her chest.

"It's no use, Emma. You can't move it. And no one's coming to save you. Reed's dead."

No! It couldn't be. A hot rush of tears stole the breath from Emma's lungs.

"Once I kill you, I can convince the rest of the police department Joshua was behind it all," Will continued, almost as if he was speaking to himself. "He'll shoot himself, of course. Leave a nice suicide note full of apologies. Everything will be fine."

Emma's gaze flickered around. There was nowhere to go. No place to hide. Will had her trapped against the cabin. Emma played the only card she had left. She lifted her shirt to reveal the listening device. "Cooper knows everything. You won't get away with it."

Will's eyes widened. He cursed. The hand holding the gun shook. For one moment, she thought he was going to back off. Then something in his eyes snapped. He raised the weapon and trained it on her. "Goodbye, Emma."

A shot rang out. Emma waited for the pain, but nothing happened. Will's mouth dropped open. Blood bloomed on his shirt. It spread like a rapidly growing flower. He glanced down at it, incredulous.

Someone stepped from the trees. Emma blinked, her heart not quite believing what her eyes were telling her.

It was Reed. He was limping, his shirt torn and bloody. But he was alive.

Will collapsed. His gun clattered against the rotten boards of the porch. Emma kicked it farther away.

Things happened in a blur. Reed quickly closed the distance between them and slapped handcuffs on Will. Austin appeared. He began rendering first aid. Once it was safe, Emma launched herself into Reed's arms. She started sobbing. "He told me you were dead."

"No, Em. Not a chance." Reed cupped her face in his hands, swiping away her tears with his thumbs. "He took a shot, but he missed."

She sucked in a gulp. "Reed, I think Lily might be inside the cabin. I can't lift the bar off the door."

"I'll help you."

As they moved toward the cabin, Will struggled against the handcuffs and cursed. Emma ignored him. She took one side of the wooden bar and Reed took the other. As one, they lifted it.

Emma reached for the door handle, but Reed pulled her back. "Let me go first. Just in case."

She nodded. He led with his weapon, pulling the door open. She heard his sharp intake of breath. Were they too late? Had Will already hurt Lily? Maybe he'd killed her immediately after the kidnapping because he had no intention of ever giving her back.

She darted around Reed and then drew up short.

The cabin was decorated like a small house. A kitchen with a small sink and a hot plate sat to her left. A sagging twin bed was pushed against the wall. In the center of the room was a large eye hook cemented into the floor. A heavy chain was linked to it. Emma followed the length of the tether across the room to the far side of the bed. A woman was hiding in the corner.

Emma inhaled. "Bonnie?"

"You…you're real?" Bonnie asked. Her gaze jumped from Emma to Reed and then back again, almost as if she couldn't trust her own vision.

Beside her, Reed trembled. "Yes, we're real. I've been looking for you, Bonnie. I've been searching for a long time."

Tears streamed down Bonnie's face. She struggled to her feet. Emma came closer to help her and discovered why Bonnie was having so much trouble. Her heart soared.

Nestled in Bonnie's arms, sleeping soundly, was Lily.

Emma cried out for joy. She took her little girl and hugged her close, showering kisses on the top of her head. Tears filled her eyes.

"Is this your daughter, Emma?" Bonnie asked.

"Yes, it is. Thank you, Bonnie. Thank you for keeping her safe."

A flurry of activity followed. Deputies and other law enforcement descended on the cabin. Bonnie was freed from her chains and Reed helped load her into an ambulance.

Emma tightened an emergency blanket around Lily before bending down to pet Sadie. The dog nudged the baby's leg. "She's okay, girl. You did a great job."

Lily appeared completely unharmed. She babbled and giggled, waving her hands.

"Excuse me, ma'am." A deputy approached her. "The ambulance is ready to take you and your daughter to the hospital now."

Emma held up a finger. "I need just a moment."

Reed came toward them. Emma met him halfway. Without a word, Reed hugged them. His touch was gentle, and Emma rested her head on his chest. His heartbeat, strong and sure, thumped a steady rhythm.

Reed pulled back. "Go in the ambulance, Emma. I'll take care of Sadie. I'll get to the vet and have her leg checked out."

"No, I can't. Not yet."

Lily reached for Reed and he lifted her into his arms. Seeing the two of them together only cemented Emma's feelings. The Lord had given her a second chance and she wasn't going to waste a moment longer on her fears.

Emma took a deep breath. "I love you, Reed."

He drew in a sharp breath and locked eyes with her. Lily patted his cheek with one plump hand.

"I know it's bad timing," she said. "Horrible timing, actually, but you nearly died today and all I could think about when Will had the gun pointed at you was that I loved you." A fresh wave of tears pricked her eyes. "I didn't think there was anything worse than losing someone I love, but there is. It's not sharing the love in the first place. It's not telling the truth about how I feel. So I'm saying it now. Before something else happens and I don't get another chance—"

Reed lifted his hand, cupping her face. "I love you, too, Emma."

Her heart stuttered. "You do?"

"Completely and utterly in love. With you and Lily." He glanced at the little girl in his arms before focusing back on Emma. "When you told me you were leaving town, I was devastated. But I didn't want to tell you because Lily's safety, along with yours, had to come first. And I don't want you to be scared every time I walk out the door. I'll quit my job as sheriff, if it'll make things easier for you."

"No. Please don't. It's a part of you." Reed was a good man. The very best kind of man. Someone who would put the needs of those he loved above his own. "I won't promise to not worry, but every time I do, I'll say a prayer. You reminded me at the car, when Lily was taken and I was terrified, that she was in the Lord's hands. And so are you. I need to rely on Him to see us through no matter what comes."

He searched her expression. "Are you sure?"

"More than sure." Emma stood on her tiptoes and brushed Reed's lips with her own. The kiss was gentle and light but filled with promise. "I love you."

"I love you, too." Reed's lips tipped up in a smile. "I hope that means I can convince you to stick around town."

"I don't need convincing." She touched Lily's back and returned Reed's smile. "I asked the Lord to help me make a home for Lily. He answered my prayers. Heyworth is where we belong."

EPILOGUE

Six months later

Reed tightened the last screw on the swing set. He placed his weight on the ladder leading to the slide, checking to make sure it would hold up. The screen door slapped against the house. Sadie barked and raced across the yard. Reed grinned and patted her on the head. "What do you think, girl?"

"She thinks it's a new obstacle course for her," Emma called out. A smile lit up her beautiful face. Reed's breath hitched. They'd seen each other almost every day since Will's attack, and still she had the power to make his knees weak.

"Sadie won't be too disappointed when she finds out it's for Lily, will she?"

Emma laughed and handed him a glass of sweet iced tea. "No. Not now that I've finished the big one over at the training center. We tried it out yesterday and she loves it."

"I'm glad." Reed wrapped an arm around Emma's waist and drew her closer.

"We have an audience," Emma murmured.

Reed glanced over his shoulder. Vivian, Bonnie and Aunt Bessie were sitting on the front porch with Lily. The women were laughing at a story Vivian was telling. "They're distracted."

Emma playfully smacked his chest. "Reed Atkinson. For shame."

He swept in for a light kiss before releasing her with a chuckle. Sadie nudged his leg and he patted her on the head again. "Yes, yes, I love you, too."

Bonnie's laughter carried across the distance between them. It brought a smile to Reed's face. His sister wasn't completely healed from the year she'd spent as Will's captive, but in the intervening months, she'd made huge strides. He thanked God every day for sparing her life and giving them a new start. "It's nice to see Bonnie so happy."

"It is. Family and prayer have seen her through." Emma winked. "I think Joshua has had something to do with it, too."

Joshua was found in Will's house, tied up and drugged. Will had intended to kill him after Reed and Emma were both dead. The thought sent a cold shiver down Reed's spine. "I'm glad the trial is over. Maybe now we can all have some peace."

Will had survived being shot, but he was never going to see the outside of a jail cell, something that brought comfort to them all. Most especially to Bonnie. When Will had found out Bonnie was going to marry Joshua, he'd kidnapped her. Taking Lily had been another layer to the plan. He'd had some sick delusions of them being a family together.

Emma rested her head against his chest. "Let's not ever be the target of a criminal again, okay?"

"Sounds like a good plan to me."

"Should I get Lily out here to try the swing set?" she asked.

"Yep. It's ready."

Reed took a long drink of his tea, relishing in the sweet refreshing taste, and watched Emma stroll back to the house. Sadie bounced at her side.

It'd taken some time to rebuild Jeb's house along with the canine training center, but he'd never seen Emma more happy. She loved her work. Already she was starting to train a new set of puppies. The first one would go to the Heyworth Sheriff's Department. Austin had agreed to be the handler.

Emma helped Lily toddle down the porch steps. Reed quickly drained his glass and set it on the ground. As he expected, Lily broke away from her mom. She raced toward him on chubby legs.

He bent down and swung her into his arms. She squealed with laughter. "Okay, kid, I'm not going to be your personal swing anymore. I've built you a new one."

Emma chuckled. "Now you know that's not going to work. She's going to keep you and use the swing set, too."

"Is that true, little girl?" Reed tickled Lily in the stomach. Her nose scrunched as she laughed.

Sadie ran up barking. Her tail wagged.

"Don't worry, Sadie. I didn't forget about you." Still carrying Lily, he reached into the treehouse attached to the swing set and pulled out a box of biscuits. "A lifetime supply, remember?"

The dog barked.

"You spoil her," Emma said.

"She saved our lives. I can't spoil her enough." Reed

handed the box to Emma. "Here, open that up for me while I put Lily in the swing."

His hands trembled as he slid Lily's legs through the holes on the swing's seat. Sweat beaded on his forehead. From the porch, Bonnie and Vivian's voices mingled with the music playing on the radio.

Emma opened the box and frowned. "What is this? That's not supposed..."

Her voice trailed off as she pulled out a diamond ring. Her gaze darted to him. Reed gently took the box, spreading the remaining few cookies on the ground for Sadie, before setting it aside.

He took Emma's hands and bent down on one knee. She inhaled sharply.

"Emma Pierce, I love you. I can't imagine my life without you or Lily in it. Will you marry me?"

Tears flooded her eyes. "Yes, yes. A thousand times, yes."

Reed let out the breath he was holding. He slid the ring on her finger before gathering her in his arms and kissing her. His heart soared. When they broke apart, he swiped the tears from her cheeks.

She laughed. "I'm always crying on you."

"Well, these are happy tears, and that makes a difference. But you go ahead and cry on me whenever you want. I've got you." He couldn't prevent every hurt from coming Emma's way, but he intended to be there to shoulder the burden alongside her. Without a doubt, he knew Emma would do exactly the same for him. "We make a great team, Emma."

She kissed him again. "Yes, we do."

From the porch a holler went up. Bonnie, Vivian and Aunt Bessie were jumping for joy and hugging each other. Lily clapped at their exuberance. Reed laughed as the women rushed down the yard to congratulate the couple.

His heart had never been so full. God had blessed him. Blessed all of them.

And he was thankful.

* * * * *

Heather Woodhaven earned her pilot's license, rode a hot-air balloon over the safari lands of Kenya, parasailed over Caribbean seas, lived through an accidental detour onto a black-diamond ski trail in Aspen, and snorkeled among stingrays before becoming a mother of three and wife of one. She channels her love for adventure into writing characters who find themselves in extraordinary circumstances.

TRACKING SECRETS

Heather Woodhaven

Being confident of this very thing,
that he which hath begun a good work in you
will perform it until the day of Jesus Christ.
—*Philippians* 1:6

To Heath, Christina, Justin and Kaitlin.
You know what you did.

ONE

Nick Kendrick lifted the edge of his shirt to wipe the sweat from his eyes. He needed to run only a little farther before starting his cooldown. A creek to his left rushed over boulders. The birds chirped and trees rustled in the breeze.

Despite his struggle to get started, the exertion loosened his neck and back muscles after a long day of treating animals and appeasing their owners. The trails south of Barings, Idaho, were a treat for the senses. He could leave all the stress behind.

A black Labrador rounded the corner, followed by a woman. Her brown hair, highlighted by the sun, blew back in waves. Unlike him in his sloppy basketball shorts and gray T-shirt, she looked as if she had just stepped out of a corporate meeting. A peach button-down blouse and matching pleated skirt ended just past her knees. Her sparkly sandals reflected the sunlight streaming through the trees.

While pretty, it wasn't exactly the most practical apparel for hiking the trail on the outskirts of town. The black Lab by her side looked to be a little over a year old, maybe two. If he had to guess, the dog still had to gain a good ten pounds before it'd be considered full-grown.

The lady's wide eyes regarded him. Perhaps she was a client, as he was the only veterinarian in the area. If he got closer, he might recognize the dog, which could jar his memory. He'd been so inundated with meeting new people the past several months that he was failing to recall their names.

She frowned and slid her hand into a pocket hidden by the folds in her skirt. If she carried pepper spray, or worse, he didn't want to do anything to startle her. He moved as far right as the trail would allow.

The dog stiffened, and the little hairs on the back of its neck sprung up like a Mohawk hairstyle. Nick followed the dog's gaze behind him but couldn't see anything past the barbed wire fence except aspens and cottonwood trees. He wasn't positive, but he thought the property bumped up against his own.

Was barbed wire really necessary around the residential property? The first wire started two feet off the ground—unless there was another hidden by the tall grass and weeds—followed by two more lines roughly a foot apart.

A rustle in the trees triggered an electric feeling in Nick's spine, and he came to an abrupt stop. A patch of brown moved. A squirrel camouflaged within the matted leaves between the trees wagged its tail.

The dog shot past him, darting underneath the fence. The woman cried out, holding a leash with a collar dangling from its clip. Nick narrowed his gaze and suppressed a groan. Didn't she know better than to walk a dog with a breakaway collar?

"Dog!" she hollered. "Come back!" She ran past him

toward the fence and placed a hand over her mouth at the sight of the barbed wire.

"I'll help you get him." The words were out of his mouth before he could process what that would mean. How would he get over the barbed wire?

"I think it's a her."

His jaw dropped. "You think? You aren't sure?" He cleared his throat and tried to focus on the task at hand. He couldn't afford to get a bad reputation in a small town, but people really shouldn't own dogs without at least some knowledge of how to take care of them properly.

Unless he was willing to slide through on his belly, which he wasn't, the options for getting past the fence were limited. He put one foot on the bottom line to lower it as far as possible. He slipped off the other sneaker and used it like a glove to lift the upper line.

The woman didn't hesitate and stepped through the space. The edge of her skirt caught on one of the barbs, forming a string that now hung down past the hem. She groaned. "I wore the wrong clothing for this. It was supposed to be a nice stroll. Dog!" she hollered again.

"It might help if you called her by her name."

She ignored him and gingerly took his sneaker from his hand so she could mirror his method of holding the barbed wire apart. "Your turn," she said. "Maybe we should call the police. I'm a little worried the owners won't take kindly to intruders if they have a barbed wire fence."

"I'm pretty certain they won't mind if we're merely trying to get a dog off their land." He bent over to step through the space then slipped his shoe back on. It would also give him an excuse to introduce himself to them. If his neighbors knew something he didn't, maybe he needed to invest in an upgrade of his own fence. He scanned the land and spotted movement ahead. The dog had slowed near a house barely visible through the thick grove of trees. He quickened his pace back to a jog.

"Speaking of names, I'm Nick Kendrick."

She raised her eyebrows and pumped her arms alongside him. "That rhymes. I'm Alexis."

Nick couldn't help but notice she didn't offer a last name. "And you don't know your dog's name?" He tried to keep the frustration from his voice.

"No, I do…" She inhaled but focused on her footing. The sandals were strapped on but couldn't be very comfortable for running through a forest. "I think it's… Raven. Yeah. I'm pretty sure that's her name. And it's not my dog. I'm temping for a pet-sitting service."

Her hands moved to emphasize each sentence. "I said I'd never pet sit, but I let my friend twist my arm since it's a holiday weekend. I'm worried the dog won't come back to me. She doesn't know me. I was supposed to take her for a forty-five minute walk. That's it."

Nick's indignation slipped away. It was the pet-sitting company's fault for not having enough staff on Labor Day weekend. They'd obviously sent her without training. The name Raven sounded familiar, though. He pointed at the leash in Alexis's hand and the empty collar hanging from it. "That's a safety collar. They're great for during the day in case they catch themselves on something but not so great for walking and squirrel-gazing."

She rolled her eyes. "Well, someone could've told me that."

They burst through the last row of trees into the

clearing. A Tudor-style house with a steeply pitched roof and a half-timbered frame sat in the center. Raven had lost the race with the squirrel and seemed intent on something else. The dog ran around the house, jumped up onto the gutter downspout at the corner and feverishly scratched at it.

"Oh, great. No! Dog, no," Alexis shouted. "That's the last thing I need. I'm not an official contractor with the company. If she damages the house, I'm probably liable. Why do I let myself get talked into these things?" She spoke at speeds that could rival auctioneers or impassioned lawyers.

The dog hopped down and shoved its nose as far as it could go inside the end of the gutter before it sat, almost as if at attention. Had the squirrel run up the gutter? Raven wagged her tail, looked back at them and then caught another sniff. She raced to the other end of the house and jumped on the corresponding downspout, repeating the entire routine. "An odd thing to do twice," he commented.

With Raven's full attention on the gutter, it was their best chance to get her. Nick sprinted ahead at top speed, hoping he wouldn't scare her away. The dog looked up but seemed to grin at his fast approach. Nick smiled back. "Good girl."

She wagged in response. Nick dropped to a knee and put one hand on the loose skin behind her ears so he could grab her if need be. "I'll take that leash now," he called out. The dog lurched forward, shoving her nose into the gutter again. A rustle of plastic caught Nick's attention. "What do you see, girl?" He bent over. A plastic package filled with white powder peeked out.

His stomach sank, and he prayed it wasn't what it appeared to be.

Raven sat, and Nick spotted a white patch on her chest that looked like a heart. It jogged his memory. Of course, she was the new drug dog in detection training. He'd performed a physical and administered vaccinations right after her owner—a name that escaped him—adopted her a few months ago. But that meant Raven thought she was working. His heart rate sped up.

Alexis slid a little on the leaves as she came to a stop. "Here's the collar." She dangled it, still attached to the leash, as he straightened. "Is there a problem?" she asked.

He didn't know how to answer that. He removed the breakaway collar and looped the leash around Raven's neck to make sure she couldn't escape again in the event she caught the scent of another squirrel. Nick stood, the end of the leash in hand. The dog took off in front of him, heading back for the first gutter.

Nick let her lead. Raven shoved her nose in the gutter before she sat, wagging her tail. He took a knee and bent over to see what was in there. The same telltale bag was squished inside. If it was what he thought it was, they needed to get off the property fast. He hoped this property had a better cell signal than his did. "We need to call the—"

Something crunched.

Brown work boots rounded the corner. Nick flung his hands to his own shoe closest to the gutter as if he were tying the shoelaces. He looked up into the eyes of a burly middle-aged man and attempted a smile. "Hi. Shoe untied."

The man's eyes narrowed, but he said nothing. It

didn't take a genius to realize this was not normal neighbor behavior.

Nick straightened to standing but didn't take his gaze off the man. He could hear Alexis approach, so he began walking backward in hopes she'd get the hint. "Sorry to intrude," he said. "As you can see, our dog took off after a squirrel, and we had to catch her. Had a collar issue, but it's fixed now. One-time issue. You won't be seeing us again. We'll be going."

Alexis entered his peripheral vision. She tilted her head and gave him an odd look. The man raised his phone to waist level. His right thumb was busy moving. Awareness hit Nick in the gut.

Either the guy thought they were trying to steal his drugs, or the man was a scout for the real traffickers. Both options meant they were in serious trouble.

"It's my fault we're on your property," Alexis said. She took a step forward with her hand outstretched. "I'm—"

"Honey," Nick blurted. He couldn't let her reveal her name and become marked.

She whirled around on the spot, her dark brown eyes wild with indignation. Her forehead creased and smoothed in an instant. She pursed her lips, tilted her head and studied his face as if searching for a reason for his sudden change in behavior.

He reached out with the hand that didn't have a leash and grabbed her wrist. She frowned but didn't try to pull away or argue.

"We've taken enough of this man's time," he said. "We need to finish our jog." Nick glanced at the way Alexis was dressed and knew that was the wrong thing to say. "More of a fast walk, really. Our friends are waiting back on the path." He chanced a glance at the man's hard eyes. "We're visiting, and they're eager to take us to the shooting range." Okay, the last part might've been a bit too much because it was obvious they didn't have guns on their persons. But he wanted to make it clear to the man they weren't going down without a fight.

The sound of tires spraying gravel echoed through the trees. A vehicle was approaching at high speed. Not good.

The man straightened his torso so he looked even taller. "How about you meet *my* friends first?"

The coldness of his voice chilled Nick's bones, and he knew the vehicle fast approaching wouldn't be filled with friendly neighbors. He lifted his chin to the right. "You mean them?"

The man turned his head. Nick didn't wait for him to realize the vehicle hadn't arrived yet. He pulled on Alexis's arm and yanked her around the corner of the house. She tugged her arm free but ran with him and Raven without any discussion.

A truck squealed to a stop. Nick picked a path around the thickest grouping of trees, choosing the biggest ones in hopes they'd obscure the view of the men who started yelling at each other behind them. The man's *friends* had arrived.

He couldn't make out much of what they said except two words: "Get them."

A gunshot rang out. Alexis ducked and put both hands over her head. A scream tore from her throat. The dog answered with a bark. The bullet snapped a branch, which spun and smacked the side of her neck.

She fought against confusion. For some reason men

were shooting at them and she'd just helped give away their location. She hadn't meant to scream, but she'd never been shot at before.

Nick grabbed her upper arm again and pulled her around another tree. He kept his fingers there, tugging, silently urging her to run faster, but her sandals didn't have much grip. It was all she could do to keep up without falling on her face.

Alexis fought a surge of nausea as several men's voices filtered through the trees. "Use the jammer," one shouted. They were trying to make sure she and Nick couldn't call for help.

"Shoot only on sight. We don't need the whole valley showing up!" It sounded like the voice of the man who had confronted them at the house, but she couldn't be sure. Why were these men so angry they'd stepped onto the property? It didn't make sense.

Maybe they'd recognized Nick and had a score to settle with him. What kind of man had she aligned herself with? Maybe Nick had seen something she hadn't. It seemed too late to point out to the men with guns that she wasn't a threat to them.

Tires squealed and covered up whatever else the man yelling had to say. She couldn't afford to slow down to dial 911 on her cell phone, but she had an uneasy feeling that it wouldn't work anyway.

She stumbled over a rock, and Nick's fingers slipped off her arm. She managed to fall forward in a sloppy run but regained her balance. Nick's golden eyes met hers for half a second before he motioned with his head which direction they needed to go. He took off without waiting for her agreement.

That was the opposite direction of where she wanted

to go. Instead of heading for the path near the river, he was taking her through the trees and, in a roundabout way, back toward the front of the house. Though if they could reach the road unseen, maybe they had a better chance of escape.

There were rarely cars on the outskirts of town, so she couldn't count on waving someone down for help. The area was mountainous, and the only reasons anyone would come out here were that they owned property or were heading for the trail.

Nick gave the leash a quick tug, and the dog stayed right at his side. She followed them around a full-grown blue spruce with spider webs running over sections of the branches. He held up a finger. Her bare calves brushed up against a prickly branch, and she cringed but didn't move.

Stepping past her, Nick peeked around the tree, and then pivoted back toward her. He grabbed her hand and shoved her farther into the prickly foliage. She resisted slightly, not so much because of the uncomfortable pine needles but more because of the potential of spiders.

For a second it looked as if Nick wanted to give her a high-five, but he swung his hand in an arc at his side. Raven flopped down as if she was bored, though she kept her eyes on Nick. Alexis was impressed at his use of the silent command, but the crunching sound of tires nearby flung the thoughts away.

She slipped her hand into her pocket and, using tiny movements, fished her phone out. The slash through the image of the cell tower on the screen confirmed her fear. No help would be coming. They were alone.

A motor roared. She turned her head slightly, hoping she wasn't drawing attention to herself. A white pickup truck vaulted through the trees, breaking branches left and right. Her breath hitched at the sight of men carrying assault rifles. They flanked the truck in a V shape as they marched south toward the trail and the river.

She remained frozen, her back protesting from the strain of a typical office workday. She was very aware of Nick pressed against her, especially after she lost sight of the men with guns. His face was a nice oval shape with kind eyes and a full mouth. His hair was a light brown, flared up at the crown, either from running in the wind or hair gel. He was slightly taller than she was, so probably close to five foot ten, and he obviously stayed fit.

It felt like hours passed, but the sun's blinding glare from the west never changed, so it had likely been mere minutes. The beams filtered through the tree branches, making it hard to see if the men were truly gone.

Her heart rate sped, and her stomach churned. Her breathing remained erratic, but Nick stood as still as a statue. Maybe he was used to running from guns.

"The scout is still at the house," Nick whispered into her ear. His breath smelled like Junior Mints, a fact she tried to ignore. "There might be others waiting there, as well. Stay quiet and follow me."

She wanted to ask what he meant by "the scout" but didn't trust herself to open her mouth without being too loud. Her mom had always told her she didn't know how to whisper properly. It's why she'd always chosen to pass notes rather than confer in law proceedings.

He seemed to be waiting for a response. She nodded her agreement. He squeezed her wrist in reply and gave it a small tug. They darted around the next tree. Nick froze again. Her ears strained to hear signs of someone close by before moving on.

The pattern continued until Alexis felt certain they must be nearing the road. Instead they came to a fence. Nick audibly sighed. He took off his shoe and handed it to her in a wordless request to hold the barbed wire fence the way she had when they'd followed Raven's dash for a squirrel.

This is what she got for not following her instincts. Theresa knew that she would temp anywhere except the pet-sitting company. But Alexis loved Theresa. The woman had become as close as any friend she'd had, despite technically being Alexis's boss. And when Theresa had called, her voice had sounded deliriously happy.

"Please, Alexis. You know I'd never ask you to do this if I wasn't in a bind. If you can't, I'll come back early, but the thing is…" Theresa's voice had dropped to a whisper. "I'm seeing someone. And we're already out of town on a weekend together. I know what you're going to say, and don't worry. We're in separate rooms, but honey, I've known him all my life, and I think he could be the one."

"Who?" Alexis had pressed.

"I can't tell you yet. I promised him we'd keep it hush-hush. He doesn't want us to have the pressure of being under a microscope. You know how small towns can be."

She *did* know how small towns could be, but in the last year she'd heard no evidence of the rumor mill. Perhaps because she kept to herself since she'd moved back.

Nick stepped through the barbed wire fence first. Alexis looked over her shoulder. Nick must have chosen this section of the fence to cross since the trees were especially thick here. Raven didn't seem so keen to slide underneath the fence this time.

"Hand her to me," he whispered.

Alexis cringed. If the dog so much as licked her, it would have to fend for itself. She exhaled and put her arms around the dog's torso. Her biceps and lower back strained with the effort. The dog had to be at least fifty pounds!

If she hadn't been such a pushover she would've told Theresa no. Then Theresa would've been forced to skip her weekend to walk the dog, probably on the sidewalks of downtown instead of the trail, and none of this would've ever happened.

Nick reached over the fence and took Raven from her. She'd never seen the man around town, which was unusual. He was either new in town or they ran in completely different circles. It made her question again whether she should've trusted him enough to follow him, but she didn't have much choice now. He had the dog.

He held the fence open for her, and she stepped through. Her outfit, now covered with black dog hair and smudges of nature, would never recover, but it was a small price to pay for getting back to safety. The list of charges she wanted to report against those men ran through her head on a loop.

Nick gathered the leash tightly and waved for her to follow him as he broke into a fast-paced jog. Her feet felt every rock and hard patch of uneven ground through the thin soles of her shoes. If she ever got home, she'd never wear the sandals again.

Five minutes later, the trees opened up into a pasture. The tall grass swayed with the breeze, and in the distance, a yellow house with white shutters looked welcoming. A red barn stood behind it. Two horses grazed nearby.

She marveled at the perfect picture of tranquility. It belonged on a postcard and made her long for her own pair of cowboy boots. "Do you know the owners?"

"The owner. Yes," he answered.

They approached another fence, this one made from wooden rails. The large spaces made it easy to slip through. Even though the wood couldn't protect her, the physical barrier made her heart slow ever so slightly. "I'll feel a lot safer once we're inside that house. I hope someone's home."

He pulled a phone out of his pocket and dialed. "We need to find a signal now. I don't think those jammers can cover that large a distance." He ran a few steps. "Weak," he muttered. His eyebrows rose. "Dial tone." He pressed a few numbers and held it up to his ear. "We need help."

Alexis put a hand on her racing heart and issued a silent prayer of thanks that he'd been able to reach the authorities. Their pace didn't slow as Nick spoke feverishly about men with guns and rattled off an address Alexis didn't recognize.

"Please hurry." Nick swiveled the cell phone so the microphone rested on his shoulder. "They want me to stay on the line until they get here."

He looked over her shoulder, and she followed his gaze. The property appeared to be roughly five acres until a line of trees obscured the rest. She imagined that just past it was the walking path and the river. "Is that them?"

The sound of cracking branches in the distance made her flinch.

"Follow me." They sprinted until they reached the porch of the house. He lifted the phone to his ear. "It sounds like they've made it to the trail behind my property. I have to put the phone down now. Please hurry."

His property? He pulled a set of keys out of his pocket and opened the navy blue door. Past the darkened hallway, bright sunshine streamed through a wall of windows. A rifle suddenly blocked her view, taking her breath away.

Nick held one in each hand. "I hope you know how to shoot a gun."

TWO

Nick reached back into the gun safe hidden within his front closet to grab ammunition. He had only a couple of guns just in case wolves attacked his horses. When he first acquired the property, the previous owner said it'd be a good precaution. So far, there hadn't been any need. "Ideally we won't have to use these."

"I've shot a handgun." She held the rifle gingerly with both hands. "Once. A cop I knew was showing me how. I decided it wasn't for me." Her hair looked wild and mussed, and one side of her blouse was no longer tucked into the skirt. "I'd rather hide than try to use this."

He glanced out the window and squinted. The white metal through the trees slowed. If the men in the truck didn't have binoculars, they wouldn't be able to see Alexis and him. But if they did…

"Step into the shadows." He waved at Raven to lie down again, and the dog complied.

The truck didn't make another appearance, but men spilled from the trees onto his property. Maybe barbed wire fences weren't overkill after all. He shoved the ammunition into the rifle and proceeded to load the second rifle for her. "Only as a precaution."

She nodded. "How many times have you shot a gun?"

It probably wouldn't help her anxiety to admit he was no sharpshooter. Sure, he practiced, but only enough to feel safe and competent. It wasn't a hobby or something he considered fun. He'd rather ride a horse or hike in his free time.

"Enough to know what I'm doing," he replied. The thought of having to shoot at a human being made his stomach turn. "You stay here and holler if they reach the wooden fence. I'm going to my office to see if they're approaching from the side."

For a second he thought she'd refuse, but she inhaled and took a knee at the corner of the hallway and the living room. Raven lay down and rested her head against Alexis, who flinched and stared at the dog warily but didn't move away.

He wondered what her story was, because there were few people in the world who could resist the charms of such a sweet Labrador. But then again, he couldn't judge her true personality when they'd just had to run away from gunmen.

He strode down the hall and lifted the window just enough that he could slip the barrel of the gun outside to aim. He closed his eyes a half second. "Please, Lord," he whispered, "defend us."

The dog howled, a mournful song with vibrato.

"Nick, how do I get her to stop?" Alexis cried out. "They're going to know we're here for sure if she keeps this up."

He ran back to them. Raven remained on the ground

but pointed her nose in the air as she released another song. Odd unless... He strained his ears. "Listen."

Alexis dropped the rifle and stood up, a gorgeous smile on her face. "The police. Help is coming." She looked over her shoulder to the window. Men were running back into the trees. "They hear it, too." She placed a hand on his arm. "Thank you for getting us somewhere safe."

The rifle rested at his side. He was relieved, as well, but the danger had been too close, too real. His chest hurt from either breathing too hard or the fight to keep his heart from jumping out of his chest.

His mom had already received one sorrowful call too many. It would've destroyed her to be told her remaining son was also killed by drug dealers.

His brother, an undercover federal agent, had been killed by the drug runners he had tried to expose. Nick wouldn't allow his brother's death to be in vain, and while it didn't make sense for him to abandon his veterinary training and take his brother's place in the DEA, he could step up and lead. The memory of his brother had driven Nick to develop an interest in politics.

In his opinion, the current elected officials weren't doing all they could to diminish the impact of living in what the government had deemed a High Intensity Drug Trafficking Area. No one wanted to acknowledge the label, but living right alongside a major interstate meant they needed to face facts. Which was why he was running for mayor in the upcoming election.

The sirens grew closer. Alexis glanced back and forth between the view of the backyard and the front window. Raven stopped her soulful song but looked at

Nick with expectation. He opened the front door in time to see two police cars pull to a stop in his circular drive.

He set the rifle against the doorway before he ran down the stairs to greet them. Four officers jumped out of the two vehicles. They all seemed to have eyes only for Alexis. Nick still hadn't gotten used to feeling like the outsider in the town where he'd lived for over a year now.

"They are driving on the hiking trail just past the trees," Alexis shouted as she stepped beside him. "If you hurry you can get them."

While he'd never seen vehicles on the trail before, it was wide enough to accommodate horses, bikes and runners, and if the cops didn't hurry, the men would be able to drive all the way to the parking lot at the trailhead. Once there, they could hit the road that went into town or take the interstate and disappear.

The older policeman who seemed to be in charge pointed a finger at the men in front of him. Two officers jumped into the first cruiser and took off. The remaining officer looked significantly younger, as if he was fresh out of high school.

"Chief Spencer," Alexis said, "I didn't get a chance to tell them it was a white pickup truck."

The chief frowned. "Is that all you can tell me?"

She crossed her arms. "I'm sorry I didn't get a better look while they were shooting at me." She emphasized the last three words. "It's something to go on, right?"

Nick racked his brain to think of another defining detail he could offer, but she had a point. They didn't take time to look as they focused on staying alive.

Chief Spencer shook his head. "Over half the town

owns pickup trucks, Lexi, and a quarter of those are white, including mine."

Nick couldn't help but notice Alexis's grimace when the chief called her Lexi. Her nickname? "He's right," Nick admitted. "I've got a white pickup, too."

The young cop nodded. "Easiest color to keep clean."

"You all have white trucks?" Alexis asked, sounding more incredulous. "Well, I think it was a Ford F-Series." She raised her eyebrows as if they should be impressed.

Nick didn't recall the make and model, so he acknowledged her keen observation with a slow nod.

"That narrows it down to maybe sixty percent of the white trucks," the chief said. Alexis seemed crestfallen, but the chief paid no attention. He looked at Nick. "You said the shooting started at the mayor's house?"

Nick frowned. "Mayor Simonds is my neighbor?" That seemed like a tidbit someone could've mentioned before now. The houses were several acres apart, but still. "I've tried to introduce myself a few times, but no one has ever been home."

The chief narrowed his eyes. "Yes, he is. And I believe you're his opponent, Dr. Kendrick, so if you don't mind, I'd like an impartial party to tell the story." He turned his gaze to Alexis.

Her mouth dropped open. "You're running for mayor? Have you even lived here long enough to be a resident?"

Her tone sounded almost accusatory, and he didn't really understand why. "I've met all the eligibility requirements, if that's what you're asking. Barings is my home."

"Everyone knows he's running, Lexi," the young officer said to Alexis. "Old news."

Her eyebrows shot up, and she eyed him a minute before turning to Chief Spencer. She relayed the events of the past hour without commentary, as if reporting for the six o'clock news. Nick did his best to keep his mouth shut until she reached the part about the man who'd walked around the corner. "Six feet tall, I'd guess," she said. "Late thirties or early forties. He wore a white polo shirt and carpenter jeans. No other identifying factors that I can remember."

"There were drugs," Nick interjected. "In the gutter downspouts. I can show you."

Alexis's jaw dropped. Chief noticed. "You didn't see these drugs?"

She cringed. "No, but it certainly explains a lot. I can't think of any other motivation they'd try to kill us just for getting a dog off the property."

Chief Spencer shook his head again. "I need a reason to get on that property. And frankly, having the mayor's opponent as the only witness doesn't do it."

"Forget that, then," Alexis said. "We're talking attempted murder. I was witness to that! Those men shot a branch that hit me." She lifted up her hair. An angry red line streaked across the side of her neck.

Nick flinched. He should've moved faster, gotten them out of the line of fire before that had happened. He turned to enter the house. "I'll grab my first aid kit."

Her hand blocked him. "I'm fine. It just stings a little." Her gaze swung to the chief. "My point is, I don't understand why you don't have enough to go on."

The younger officer picked up his radio and stepped away for a moment. "Chief, no sign of the vehicle or armed men. They confirmed tire tracks and a broken fence section on the mayor's property. Permission to proceed?"

Nick tensed. He wasn't used to having his word questioned. Was that how every officer would react if a challenging political opponent witnessed criminal activity? Or was it possible the chief was proving his alliance with the current mayor? Either way, Nick breathed easier knowing they couldn't avoid the proof that something had happened.

Chief Spencer pointed to the backseat of the vehicle. "Okay. Get in, you two."

Alexis couldn't believe they had to share the backseat of a police vehicle with a dog. Logically, she knew it wouldn't attack her, but the positive thoughts did nothing to stop her heart from racing. Why people liked to keep animals around for company was beyond the scope of her imagination. If they knew what it felt like to be attacked by one like she did, maybe they'd feel differently. The dog's breath alone was enough to make her want to go running. And yet, even though Alexis had shown her no signs of affection, Raven stared up at her, panting.

"She knows you don't like her," Nick said. "Animals can sense that, especially dogs. She's trying to win you over."

She eyed Nick. The chief had referred to him as Dr. Kendrick. Judging by his tan skin and athletic physique, he had to be active and a lover of the outdoors. And it seemed like those types often loved dogs just as much as nature, so maybe he knew something about animals. "So if I pet her, she'll leave me alone?"

He shrugged. "Wouldn't hurt to try."

She held back a sigh. She'd already touched the dog more than enough for her lifetime when she had to pick it up to get it over the fence, but she humored the both of them and reached out to touch the top of Raven's head. It was smooth yet wiry.

Raven stretched her neck at the touch so that Alexis's fingers brushed against her ears. They were soft and velvety like a fuzzy pillow. The dog shifted in the small space between her and Nick until its whole body leaned against Alexis.

Admittedly, the warmth and connection were nice for a second, but she still didn't trust the dog to keep its mouth to itself. She shot Nick a look.

He smirked. "Or petting her could just encourage her."

Her gut twisted. She knew he was teasing, but she didn't know him well enough to explain why it wasn't funny. Alexis pushed away from the dog, calmly, forcing it to snuggle with Nick instead.

How could he have lived here long enough to be running for mayor? She'd thought she knew the few doctors who lived in the area. She'd worked for almost all of them, subbing for their receptionists.

She'd kept to herself ever since she returned to town, but she must have been more antisocial than she'd thought if Jeremy, the young officer driving, was right and his candidacy was old news.

Nick patted the dog's head and her tail wagged, slapping Alexis's thigh. Nick's warm laugh soothed her nerves. "Sorry about that," he said.

She tried to smile in response.

Jeremy parked the cruiser in front of the mayor's house. She'd known Gerald Simonds lived out here somewhere but hadn't known which house until now. He was only a few years older. She'd never imagined him as rich or running their town, but he owned a successful mechanic shop and had made some smart investment moves. In fact, his brother, Barry, owned the financial firm responsible. Barry used to do only book-keeping, but everyone, it seemed, including her parents, had wanted to sign on with Barry as their financial advisor after seeing Gerald's success.

Officer Jeremy Wicks opened the door for her. She had over ten years on him. Most days, she still considered herself young. She'd crossed the thirty-year mark, but she could remember changing Jeremy's diapers when she worked as a mother's helper one summer. He'd been an officer for a little over a year, but it was still weird seeing him with a gun and handcuffs.

He nodded at her. "Ma'am."

She fought back a groan and hustled around the car. While she hated when people used her childhood nickname of Lexi, she hated even more when they called her *ma'am*. She was still a *Miss* until she got married, in her mind.

Some days she wondered if she had missed out on her chance for marriage by going after her career and law school with such singular focus. Her head had spent so much of the time stuck in the pages of law statutes that she'd forgotten how to flirt. Maybe she had never known how in the first place.

There weren't many attractive, employed, witty men in Barings. The few that existed had already been taken. She'd pegged Nick for a nice guy as soon as he'd offered to help her get Raven. That is, until she found out he had political ambitions. Now she realized he had to be either a naive idealist or power hungry. At least, that had been her experience with political science majors back in school.

Maybe she was wrong and Nick was the nice guy she'd first imagined. But if he was, she should keep her distance. Her past would prove a problem for his dreams.

Nick led the dog back around the gutters. Raven stuck her nose in both, but when Jeremy leaned down in front of each of them, he shook his head. "Nothing, sir," he said to the chief.

"Can't you do a drug residue test?" Nick asked.

"Here's the thing." The chief tilted his head to the side. "I can come on this property because I had reason to suspect I'd find some gunmen. We haven't. I can look at the gutters because they're on the outside of the house. If contraband is in plain sight, it's fair game, but I don't have enough probable cause to perform a residue test."

"But I saw the drugs," Nick said.

He nodded toward Alexis. "And if Lexi had seen them, too, then we'd be in business."

Alexis shifted her gaze away from Nick. She felt bad enough that she'd put him in the situation in the first place. He'd saved her life and the dog's, for that matter. She wished she had seen the drugs, but she couldn't bring herself to lie.

"What about the dog?" Nick's demeanor brightened. "I can't verify without my records, but I think this is the K9 detection dog I examined several months back."

"Wait," Alexis said. "You examined her? You're a veterinarian?" The questions came out accusatory. The information had just taken her by surprise. She hadn't imagined he would be a doctor of animals. Well, that ruled out another eligible bachelor. Even if he ended up losing the mayoral election, they could never have a future because as a vet, he probably wanted to own a dog, if he didn't already. And that was a deal breaker. Why did all the great guys love dogs?

Jeremy raised an eyebrow. "You need to get out more, Lexi." He stepped forward. "So is this Raven? Joe's dog?" He dropped to a knee and looked at Alexis. "They left you to take care of her?"

He could've skipped the incredulous tone. Though it was no secret in the town that she wasn't exactly fond of dogs. One notch short of terrified, really. "It was a favor for Theresa. Theresa said if she didn't get someone to take care of her right away, she'd have to come back tonight to do the job personally."

Jeremy took the leash from Nick and ruffled Raven's ears. The dog responded by nuzzling into him.

The chief folded his arms over his sizable chest and studied the dog. "This is Raven, huh? Joe's technically retired from the force but trains K9 dogs all over the country. You know, he was training this dog for us. She was going to be his last one. He planned to gift her to our department."

Jeremy shook his head but kept his gaze on the dog. "Last I heard he was in critical condition." He straightened and handed the leash to Alexis.

"Critical?" Alexis asked.

Chief nodded. "Hit-and-run just last night. Raven was in her harness and did fine, but Joe had to be air-lifted a few hours away to Boise."

That explained the sudden need for someone to watch the dog.

Nick's frown deepened. "Well, if she's a drug detection dog, you should have cause to test for residue."

Chief shook his head. "I know for a fact Raven's not certified yet. Last I knew, Joe said she had a heap of potential but some obedience issues. She hasn't been in the program long enough for testing. Takes a minimum of a year, from what I understand. Besides, didn't you say you were on this property because she broke off the leash in pursuit of a squirrel?"

Alexis felt her cheeks heat but knew that the chief was right. If Raven wasn't certified and court-qualified, her skills would be inadmissible in court. Not that they needed or wanted her opinion.

Chief sighed. "I'm sorry, but I can't hunt down a judge and an out-of-town mayor on a holiday weekend for this." He gestured to the downspouts. "Let's say you're right. For all we know, this was a dead drop gone wrong, so it doesn't do me any good to search the mayor's house. He's visiting family."

In other words, the chief didn't want to risk bad publicity. She'd read the news headlines. A mayor in Maine had been an unwitting victim of a dead drop. The drug runners would send packages of drugs to addresses that likely wouldn't answer the door. The mayor in Maine sued the police department after they'd raided his home, scaring his wife and children.

Nick's eyes implored Alexis. "Did you recognize any of the men?"

"From town? No, but I haven't been that observant lately. I didn't recognize you." She sighed. "I'd guess the man who talked to us was in his early forties. The men with guns…" She strained to remember any important details and failed. "Everything was a blur once shots were fired."

"I think the guy we talked to was a scout," Nick added.

"You said that before. What was he scouting for?" Alexis questioned.

Jeremy looked like he was struggling not to roll his eyes. "They serve as guides for drug shipments. They aren't the actual ones to pick them up. They go ahead and make sure the coast is clear. Oftentimes they don't have weapons or drugs on their person, so if they get picked up, we've got nothing on them."

"They serve as both spies and decoys?"

Nick looked at her, as if impressed. "Basically."

"If Lexi thinks they're not from here, it's unlikely they've made the two of you targets," the chief mused.

She wasn't so sure they should rely on her knowledge of residents. She hadn't recognized Nick as being from the area, either, though he claimed he'd been here the past year. He was running for mayor, after all. She knew she'd been closed off, but this seemed like a wakeup call. The past year she'd been downright antisocial with her head stuck in the sand.

"I made sure they didn't get our names," Nick added.

"That was quick thinking," she admitted. Her neck grew hot as she remembered how it felt to have him speak so tenderly when he called her *honey*. Now Nick smiled at her, which didn't help. She knew from experience that her neck probably was beet red at the moment.

Chief nodded. "Good. Here's what we're going to do. My boys are going to walk the property and see if we have anything to go on. I'll set up a patrol car to drive by your houses tonight. We'll keep a watch out for any trucks that look suspicious." His radio chirped. "We're going to be combing the area now. We'll give you a quick ride back to your place and take it from there."

"What about Nick? They know where he lives."

Chief shrugged. "Not necessarily. They just saw you run to the neighboring property."

Alexis tightened her hold on the leash. His words didn't comfort her.

She replayed the events of the evening on a loop, searching for something that could help. There'd been a click. She was sure of it. "What I don't understand is, if scouts are just making sure the coast is clear, then why did he take our picture?"

Nick spun around, a look of alarm on his face. "Are you sure?"

"I think…" She looked up at the clouds, trying to picture it. "He had his phone in his hand while you were talking to him." She nodded. "His thumb moved, and the phone clicked when I stepped toward him to introduce myself. That's when you stopped me. What else could the click have been?"

"Let's not jump to conclusions just yet," the chief said.

Nick's face took on an ashen tone as he closed his eyes. "We've been marked."

THREE

Only a few hours ago, Nick had been looking forward to a quiet long weekend at home. Now he was on a drug ring's most-wanted list.

"What do you mean marked?" Alexis stepped in front of him. Her intense gaze demanded his attention.

"It means they'll take us out if they think we are going to cause them problems." He gestured out at the town, north of them. "It means that every member in their cartel likely has our photo. It means we need to watch our backs."

Chief put his hand on Alexis's shoulder. "We don't know that for sure. Let's just take it one step at a time." He led her to the backseat of the cruiser, but not before he leveled a disapproving glare at Nick.

Nick didn't regret what he'd said, though. Not knowing the full truth wouldn't help Alexis stay safe. Ever since his brother had died, Nick had found out everything he could about drug trafficking, specifically in the Northwest. It wasn't something to be taken lightly. The cartels had sophisticated ways of communicating, and the intel they shared with each other rivaled that of most three-letter government agencies.

Nick called Raven into the car and took his seat. Alexis scrunched her nose. "Didn't you hear the click from his phone, too? Maybe I imagined it."

The hopefulness in her voice was difficult to ignore. "It was hard enough to think straight with blood rushing to my head. Don't second-guess yourself, even though we'd both love it if you were wrong."

She stared ahead, her face pale. It took only a minute to arrive back at his place.

"Where'd you park?" the young officer asked her.

"The lot at the trailhead. Could you take me there, Jeremy? I'd really rather not walk back alone, if that's okay."

"Understandable." Jeremy nodded. "You still driving that bucket of bolts you call a car?"

She lifted her chin. "Hey. A little respect. It's a classic."

"Dream on." Jeremy shook his head. "Never seen a lawyer drive such a crummy car before."

Nick's neck tingled, and he couldn't place his finger on why. If he hadn't known better, he'd have wondered if he was jealous that the young cop talked to Alexis in such a friendly manner. "You're a lawyer?" he asked her. "I'd tell you a lawyer joke, but—"

"—you're afraid you'd get sued," she said. Her face reddened, and she pressed her lips together in a firm line. "Trust me, I've heard them all. Besides, I wasn't that kind of lawyer."

A crackly voice came over the radio. "Possible domestic disturbance called in. Shouting heard next to the burned-out barn on Garrett property."

The dispatcher's description was yet another reminder that Nick wasn't in the big city anymore. The chief shook his head. "We need to get this."

The car pulled to a stop. "I'll take her to her car," Nick said. They hopped out and the cruiser sped away.

Alexis swung her chin from left to right, her eyes darting every which way.

"If they had come back here already, the cops would've seen them," Nick said gently.

Her shoulders sank. "I hope you're right."

Nick escorted her and the dog to the garage, where he entered the five-digit access code. The cab of his pickup truck had two rows, so he guided Raven into the back instead of next to Alexis. He pointed in the direction of the trail. "It would've taken you a good half hour to get back to the parking lot if you had walked."

"Theresa said the dog needed a forty-five minute walk. I rounded up." She flashed a sheepish grin, and they both got situated in the truck. "I hadn't reached my daily step goal yet, and I needed some time to clear my head."

He started the ignition and pulled out onto the county highway. "It seems common knowledge that you have a love for dogs." He hoped his teasing tone would get her to open up.

She groaned. "Why is it that when people say they don't like cats, it's okay, but disliking dogs is equivalent to hating babies?" Her eyes widened. "Which I don't!"

"Good to know." He smiled in the rearview mirror at Raven, who seemed to be enjoying the conversation. "Dogs make it pretty easy to love them."

"You mean aside from the presents they leave in the yard, the smell, the drool and the nice things they eat?"

He laughed. "Bad experience?" If she was a lawyer, maybe a dog ate a pair of her expensive shoes.

She stiffened and watched him for a moment, as if

considering whether to talk or not. She looked forward. "A rabid dog attacked me when I was little. The scar doesn't hurt, but when I think about the rabies shots..." She let her voice trail off.

The smile fell off his face at the thought. "That should've never happened," he said softly. "I'm sorry." It frustrated him to no end that some pet owners neglected treatment of their animals. A simple vaccine would've prevented the dog's disease and Alexis's pain.

"Not your fault. I'm not scared anymore. I got over it." She nodded with each phrase, as if reciting a script. "They just aren't my favorite."

She pulled her shoulders back and raised her chin. She might have told herself she wasn't scared anymore, but the way she'd flinched when Raven tried to snuggle proved otherwise. It wasn't that she disliked dogs, like she tried to infer, but that she was scared.

The mountains served as a backdrop to the rows of trees on either side of the road. If he kept going, the trees on the right side would be replaced by a rock wall. Just before town, all the trees disappeared and a sharp curve provided a gorgeous viewing point for the valley. An unbidden image of having a picnic there with Alexis while enjoying the scenery popped into his head. He'd been so focused on school and career the past several years that he'd saved relationships for later. He never wanted to start one that would only end up in the pain of a long-distance relationship. He'd done that once in college and vowed never to do it again.

"Later" had finally arrived, but he'd yet to find someone in the small town who he could imagine as more than a friend.

She pointed at the black medical bag in between their seats. "So you're really a vet?"

The question made him laugh. "Why is that so hard to believe?"

She smiled. "I guess it's not. I just didn't think our small town could support more than one."

He made the final turn toward the trailhead. "That's because it can't. I bought the practice from Doc Finn so he could retire. He moved to the Oregon coast when I came here."

Her mouth dropped. "He did? But his office is practically across the street from where I live."

"My office," he corrected her.

She pulled her head back in surprise. "But the logo hasn't changed! Your name isn't on the building."

He held back a laugh. She must have prided herself on keeping up to date with all new residents if this bothered her so much. "Barings Animal Hospital had a nicer ring to it than Dr. Nick Kendrick's Animal Hospital, so I kept it the same."

She shook her head. "I guess I've had tunnel vision."

"Your law practice staying busy?"

She squinted in confusion. "My what?" Her eyebrows rose and she leaned back. "No. I don't practice law anymore. I came back to spend some time with my parents. I've been working for Theresa's temp agency until I figure out my next step."

"Are they ill?"

"Who? My parents? No, they're doing great. They actually retired to Arizona last month. I'm sticking around until I sell their house. After that…" She looked down at her clasped hands. "Well, I guess time will tell."

In other words, she wouldn't be around much longer, so it'd probably be smart to forget the dinner invitation he wanted to extend to her. Now, if she was willing to open up a practice in town that would be another story. He was tempted to ask why she no longer practiced law, but it seemed too soon for what could be a personal question.

The box of Junior Mints he kept in the cup console rattled when he drove over a rock. He spotted her interest. "You want some? I like to have some after work, before I go on a run. It gives me a little extra burst of energy."

She smiled and almost seemed to be fighting a laugh. "What brought you to Barings? Are you from Idaho?"

"No. I was a city boy, but I wanted my practice to be more than just domestic pets. I like variety and enjoy making house calls for cattle and horses. Barings is a long way from Seattle, but I can make the trip home in one day."

It could've been his imagination, but it seemed she paled. "Seattle, huh?" She pointed to the left. "Turn here."

The small, dusty lot sat next to a brown outhouse and a bulletin board covered in trail maps. A beat-up, rusted, baby-blue Honda Accord that had to be circa 1980 sat by its lonesome. He gaped. "I see why your cop friend was surprised."

"Not you, too. The whole town gives me a hard time." She sighed. "No one sees what I see. This beauty has been faithful to me ever since I bought it cheap in high school. It helped me graduate from law school debt-free." She eyed him. "Not an easy feat."

"If it's anything like veterinary school, I agree." His current debt load wasn't as high as that of most members of his graduating class, but it would've taken a ridiculous amount of discipline, planning and an over-loaded work schedule to graduate without a bill. Her debt-free status only served to intrigue him more. He wondered if she'd be willing to have dinner together, just as friends. Though he'd have to make it clear he wasn't interested in a relationship. So it'd be wise to let the idea go, especially since she was moving on soon. Besides, she seemed like the type that took a long time to lower her guard.

He pulled to a stop and stared at the bucket of bolts. "Unfortunately your faithful beauty doesn't look like it's going to last much longer. Is it safe?"

"Absolutely!" Her grin faded. "Probably more than we are, if I understood what you said back there. I hate that it takes a court order to get full-time police protection."

"I didn't mean to scare you, but I believe a healthy dose of caution is necessary." He almost offered to give her one of his rifles but stopped short. She'd made it clear she wasn't comfortable with guns. "Keep your eyes open and don't go places alone."

"That's good advice for any woman on any day." She stepped out of the truck. "I guess I need to get the dog back home." She tugged on the leash, and Raven followed her out of the truck.

The dog turned her head around and flashed Nick a look so pathetic he almost laughed. "Let me know if you need any help with her."

"I think I've asked enough of you today." She gave him an awkward wave. "Sorry I got you into this mess in the first place, Nick. Thanks for helping me."

"My pleasure, Alexis."

"Thompson," she replied. "Alexis Thompson."

Her eyes narrowed as she said it, as if watching him for a reaction. "Nice to meet you, Alexis."

She nodded. "I'll see you around."

He searched for the right words to say more, to ease the fear he saw in her eyes. She moved to close the passenger door, and he leaned over to stop her. "The more I think about it, the more I realize they have no reason to go after us. We aren't going to be any problem to them. It's going to be fine."

The creases in her forehead disappeared as an authentic smile transformed her face. She looked young and energetic and downright beautiful. She closed the door and walked away. As he waited for her to start her car, Nick hoped he had told her the truth. At the very least, he'd drive behind her until she got home, if only to make sure danger didn't follow.

Alexis placed Raven in the backseat of her car before she got herself situated in the driver's seat. She refused to look, but she felt Nick's gaze on her. From what little she'd observed, he seemed like the type of guy who would wait to make sure she got on the road safely.

Her hands shook as she inserted her keys into the ignition. What a day. If she stopped and reflected on it now, she might never get home. Death was something far in the future. When she read her Bible and spent time in prayer, she had peace that when it was her time, she'd be ready. Her throat tightened. But she wasn't ready for it to be time yet. There was so much more in her life she wanted to do, wanted to be.

Fear must have had an unusual effect on her, since she'd practically gushed her life story to Nick in the course of five minutes. Thankfully she hadn't had much experience with being scared to death before, but she was still surprised at her reaction to Nick.

It would be interesting to see if their dangerous game of hide-and-seek would make the *Barings Herald*. She didn't want to tell her parents and cause them worry if it wasn't absolutely necessary. Her mom had struggled with insomnia enough as it was since Alexis had left Seattle.

The engine struggled to turn over. She groaned, and her cheeks heated. She resisted the urge to look at Nick's reaction. The motor gave another hearty try and hummed to life. She let out a breath, shifted into Reverse and drove out of the lot. Her finances couldn't support a car payment at the moment.

While she was grateful that eight years of ramen noodles, part-time jobs, thrift-store clothes and little sleep had allowed her to graduate debt-free, there weren't too many well-paid jobs available for a disbarred lawyer.

Her stomach turned at the thought. It'd been almost a year, and the shame still washed over her like it was yesterday.

She'd chosen patent law as her specialty because she'd known that she couldn't compartmentalize enough to be a defense lawyer. Never in her wildest dreams had she suspected her client would want to unburden himself and tell her the story of how he murdered his partner. He'd practically gloated over the fact no one had found out. Everyone had assumed the partner had taken some money and left the country.

After two weeks of sleepless nights, she thought she'd found a loophole for attorney-client privilege and submitted to the police what he'd told her. The Washington State Bar Association didn't agree with her conclusions. The confession her client had made to her was inadmissible, and the state of Washington issued the verdict that she would no longer be practicing there.

But it did no good to rehash the past continually.

Alexis clicked on the radio to drown out her thoughts. There would be no more processing of the day, or the past, or even Nick until she reached the safety of her bathtub. And she'd most definitely earned scented bubbles. Lots of them.

She focused on the road. The sun dipped below the horizon and outlined the mountains and trees with pastel colors. She pressed the brakes at the stop sign, but it took some extra force on the pedal to get it to slow down. Her car really was on its last leg. The pedal had never felt this mushy before.

She took the left turn to head back into town. Her rearview mirror showed Nick right behind her. Either he had business in town that he hadn't mentioned, or he was following her all the way home. She smiled into the rearview mirror and hated to admit that it felt good to have someone care like that.

Relationship goals had never been part of her five-year plan, but chatting with Nick had unleashed a sudden, intense longing to have someone to share her life. It was probably past time. But what did a disbarred lawyer have to offer?

The terrain began to change. On the right, the road butted against a foothill. The side was covered with chains to help prevent rockslides. To the left, the evergreens blocked a lot of the light. The road changed into curves, taking her down to the heart of Barings.

In a short while, there would be the sharpest curve, a breathtaking viewpoint where you could look over the cliff at the entire valley. If it weren't for Raven, she'd be tempted to pull into the small parking lot to sit and process the last few hours. The downgrade steepened, and she pressed her brakes on the curve.

The car slowed slightly before it lurched forward. Her head flew backward at the sudden momentum. The resistance on the brake pedal had completely disappeared. She shoved her foot hard on the brake three times. "Come on!"

Her grasp on the steering wheel tightened as she fought to stay within her lane and lost. Thankfully no one else was on the road. The needle on the speedometer rose to fifty. The speed limit on the curves was thirty-five. The bend straightened a bit, but the downgrade would continue for the next three miles.

In roughly two miles, the viewpoint would appear. The trees would disappear, but the rock wall and a ninety-degree turn would mean that if she couldn't slow the car down, she would likely get the best view of all before plunging to her death.

She stomped on the brake pedal over and over. Her stomach threatened to lose her lunch. "What do I do? What do I do?" Her mind raced, frantic to find a solution.

Raven whimpered in the backseat and stuck her nose over the console between the seats. "Oh, not now, dog, please," Alexis cried. "I'm trying to save our lives!" She needed to get her head on straight. "Lord, we need help!"

The parking brake line was separate from the other brakes. She gasped. Yes, that would stop them. She'd walk home after that, never to drive the bucket of bolts again. She shoved the car into Neutral.

The speedometer rose to sixty, matching the pace of her heart.

She yanked on the parking brake, but it flung upward without resistance. Useless. Her breathing grew erratic. It should've worked.

The likelihood of all the brakes going out at once was…

Her insides shook. At this rate, she'd hyperventilate. Her car had been the only one in the trail parking lot. Everyone in town knew she drove it.

This was no accident.

Another curve approached fast. Too fast. She could drive into the trees, but the only way that would slow her down was if she steered directly into a tree trunk. It'd have been a worthwhile option if the car weren't traveling over sixty miles per hour. Her 1982 beauty didn't come equipped with airbags, so the outcome of that scenario was certain death.

She abandoned the pedals on the floor and placed her feet on either side to use as leverage while she took the second curve. She released a guttural cry as she did so.

Please let Nick see what's going on, Lord. She didn't know how he could possibly help, but she didn't think she could take even one hand off the steering wheel to reach for her cell phone.

The moment the road straightened, she looked in the rearview mirror and then ahead. Nothing in either direction but a sheer rock wall, trees and an upcoming deadly curve.

FOUR

Nick cringed at the sound of branches hitting the side of his truck. He'd jogged through this area of the forest before so he could sit at his favorite bench overlooking the farmlands in the valley, but driving through the forest was another matter. He swerved and barely missed a thin aspen that seemed to come out of nowhere.

It was hard enough to motor through the foliage without the additional challenge of doing it at high speeds, downhill, as the sun dipped below the horizon. The perspiration dripped down his neck as he second-guessed the possibility his plan would work.

The stakes were high, though. At first he'd laughed when he realized how fast Alexis was going. Maybe she was an adrenaline junkie out to prove that her bucket of bolts had plenty of life left in it. But when her car swerved wildly and barely made it past the last curve, he knew she had to be in trouble.

He could've tried to overtake her on the road, but he was so far behind it seemed unlikely. The curve would take her far to the right before bringing her back to the left, while the forest next to the road was on a separate sharp incline. It seemed like the only way to catch up to her.

Another tree seemingly jumped out of nowhere into his path. He missed it, but an outstretched branch made contact. A sickening crack of metal preceded the side mirror flying off into the distance. Something in his peripheral vision begged his attention. He couldn't afford to take the time to look, but if he was right, he'd caught up to Alexis. In an instant, the car was gone again which likely meant she'd had to take another curve.

He was running out of forest. The curve she was on would buy him some time, but if he didn't beat her to the drop-off, it would be too late. He stomped the pedal to the floor. His truck bounced over a fallen log. The terrain dipped. His torso lurched forward as he fought gravity to remain upright.

A crunch echoed through the forest. He didn't even want to think about the condition of his axles after this.

A strong beam of light illuminated the trees a mere hundred feet ahead. He veered to the right as far as he could manage. Fifty feet later, he spotted the edge of the road. He just needed enough space between the trees to sneak through.

The truck nose pitched, and his head bounced off the steering wheel. The ground was about to disappear. The throbbing in his head threatened to slow him down. He squinted through the pain and yanked the wheel to the right. Another screech of metal confirmed his fears: he'd lost the left side mirror as well.

He couldn't think about anything but keeping his speed high. He was running out of time to save her.

The truck bounced as he bounded over the rough rock bordering the road. Except the road ended in just a few feet. Nick slammed on his brakes. He fought back nausea as he stared at the open sky. If he'd waited thirty seconds more before turning onto the road, he'd have driven off the cliff. Some hero he would've been.

He turned his head in the direction she'd be coming. A flash of light reflecting off metal came from just past the rock wall. Alexis would fly around that curve any second and face the ninety-degree turn. He shoved the truck into Park and looked out the passenger window to see the baby-blue Honda barreling toward him at an unimaginable speed.

If she didn't make the sharp curve, the mass of his truck would slow her down for about ten—maybe fifteen—feet, if he chose to be optimistic. He pulled up the parking brake and braced for impact.

The Honda hugged the rock wall. She was trying her best to make the turn, but the laws of physics would work against her. His heart pumped fast against his rib cage. Instead of seeming like the wisest move to help her, he found himself in a one-sided game of chicken. He couldn't take the chance that the truck would succeed and keep him on solid ground.

He flung off his seat belt, hopped out and sprinted toward the front of the truck as he heard the screech of her tires skidding out of control. The shriek of metal against metal filled the valley.

He pressed off the balls of his feet, diving to get out of the way, and strained his arms forward while airborne. A searing pain ripped through his hip as the corner of her car's front bumper scraped past him. The force of it twisted his body so that he was facing the sky as his back hit the ground and he slid toward the cliff.

Dirt and gravel flew up around him, pressing

through his clothes, poking every inch of his back. He reached his hands out blindly. His fingertips found a branch, and as he slid past, he tightened his grip until he came to a stop.

He panted, trying to catch his breath while ignoring the pain in every part of his body. His elbows had escaped unscathed thanks to his flailing arms. Alexis! Had it worked?

He propped himself up on his elbows as he watched the Honda come to a standstill. His truck had moved to the very edge of the cliff. Maybe he could've remained inside after all and avoided the massive amounts of pain currently begging for his attention.

The truck groaned, teetered, tipped…and fell.

An unearthly groan escaped his lips. Crunching metal and booms rivaling thunder echoed throughout the valley. His mouth went dry.

The Honda door flung open, and a cry reached his ears before he could utter one himself. She was safe… unlike his gorgeous truck, but she was more important. Obviously. His head fell backward, his body and emotional energy utterly spent.

Moisture and soft fur brushed against his cheek.

"Nick. Nick!"

He opened his eyes to find Raven kissing his cheek. "I'm alive." He held up a hand to reassure the dog, and the dog licked it instead. His brain told his body to move, to get up, but his sore backside didn't respond. "Are you okay?" he asked instead.

Alexis's tear-filled eyes met his gaze. She nodded. "My brakes wouldn't work." Her voice shook and her shoulders began to follow suit. "And…and I thought you were still in the car."

"It was a truck." Calling it a car would insult its memory, but in the back of his mind, he knew now wasn't the time to argue the point. "Do you think it was because your car was old or…"

Alexis held out her hands and helped pull him up to standing. If not for the stinging sensation in his palms, he would've enjoyed how soft her hands felt. She looked into his eyes as he fought against the discomfort in his back and straightened.

"It wasn't an accident," she said. She let go of him and pulled her phone out. "I'm calling the police." She frowned at the screen and jumped up, straining her arm, most likely in an effort to find a signal. On her tiptoes, she held the phone to her ear.

Light from above hit his eyes, which didn't make sense as the sun was setting. He turned his gaze ever so slightly to the top of the ridge above them. For a brief second he thought for sure he'd seen a man watching them.

It seemed possible, in his state of mind, that his eyes were playing tricks on him. Maybe it'd just been a flash of reflection from her shiny sandals.

The sun continued its rapid descent, but the colors in the sky illuminated the tower of rock above him enough for him to see a shadowed form kneel. It was almost as if someone was holding a…

"Gun." His insides seized up. No more time to lick his wounds. In one motion, he curled into a crouched position. His spine and muscles objected to the fast movement, but he fought through it. "Alexis, take cover! Gunman!"

The sound of tires fast approaching from the direction of town barely registered before a truck pulled up in front of him. Alexis lunged toward Nick, staying low enough that she was also underneath the cover of the silver truck. The passenger window rolled down and the man leaned toward them from the driver's side. "Everything okay?"

"Stay down, Gerald. Nick said there was a gunman."

The man in a ball cap flinched and looked around.

"On top of the ridge." Nick pointed upward.

Gerald stuck his head out of the driver's window. His shoulders relaxed, and he huffed. "There's nothing but a lone tree and a bird circling up there. Eyes can play tricks on you when the sun is setting."

Nick had never met the man, but Alexis seemed to know him, so maybe he was credible. He straightened to look for himself. Sure enough, there was nothing but pink and orange streaks in the sky.

He wasn't crazy, though. He'd seen someone, and the silver truck had apparently scared the person off. Odd. If the gunman had been part of the drug ring, Nick would've thought that knocking off another witness would have been nothing to them.

"You guys look a little rough for wear. Everything okay?" Gerald gestured at Alexis.

She looked down at her stained shirt and skirt, and then glanced at Nick, uncertainty crossing her face. "It's fair to say we've had a bad evening."

Nick remained silent. If she knew the man in the truck and wasn't gushing about what had happened to him, perhaps he'd be wise not to say anything, either. But if the man drove off, there was a chance the gunman would return. They needed him to stay until the police arrived. If Nick had to, he'd talk to the man until he was blue in the face.

"We had a little accident," Alexis said.

That was the understatement of the year.

Gerald leaned forward, straining his neck to see over the cliff from the comfort of his vehicle. "You certainly did. It's a good thing your truck went down in the river instead of causing a fire. Otherwise you really wouldn't have a chance with the voters, Mr. Kendrick." He winked and chuckled. "Not that you have any chance against me in the first place."

Nick flinched as he connected the dots. He leaned forward to see the face underneath the ball cap. This man was his neighbor and opponent?

Alexis kept her eyes on the ridge above them. While Nick could have a motive to lie about drugs being stashed on Gerald's property, he'd had to run away from the gunmen the same as she did. Besides, someone had messed with her brakes. If it hadn't been for Nick, it would've worked. So she couldn't fathom what reason he'd have to lie about a gunman on the ridge. Whoever had been there would've had the perfect view if she'd wrecked.

She shivered involuntarily. What was taking the police so long? While she had no doubt that Gerald would hear about the incident on his land eventually, she didn't want to be the one who told him.

"Did this out-of-towner make you crash?" Gerald asked Alexis, a teasing lilt to his voice. Despite his smile, his eyes looked a little red, as if he'd either suffered an allergy attack or heard some upsetting news.

Nick's jaw tensed. "I think I've earned resident status if my name is on the ballot."

After the day she'd had, the last thing Alexis needed

was to be the only audience member for an impromptu political debate. "Nick saved my life. My brakes stopped working."

Gerald shook his head. "I know you don't want to hear this, but take it from me. There's a point when it's time to put a car to rest, Alexis. I make more money keeping cars in business, so you know I'm not lying."

She didn't need a lecture. Her car's age hadn't been the problem. If Gerald had anything to do with the men on his property, then it followed that he would want her dead, as well.

Her parents had considered him their trusted mechanic for most of her life, so she wanted to think Chief Spencer had the right idea. The more likely scenario was that Gerald had been used as a pawn. She'd learned time and time again, though, that she wasn't the best judge of character.

She smiled and nodded as Gerald finished his speech on when a car wasn't worth repairing.

"Gerald, I promise I'll look for another vehicle soon. Word on the streets was you were out of town for the holiday weekend, visiting family."

Nick flashed her a knowing look. Judging by his posture, he didn't want to confront Gerald about the incident, either. Probably wise, as they were on a cliff without a vehicle or a place to hide.

Gerald shrugged. "You know how family can be. Visit got cut short." He looked forward at the road. "Do you need me to call you a tow truck?"

Raven nuzzled her nose against Nick.

Gerald paled. "Whose dog is that?"

"I'm pet-sitting," Alexis answered. "Client confidentiality." There probably wasn't such a thing in the pet-sitting business, but it rolled off her tongue so fast that she was shocked at how the words stung.

She hated the memory of those words as they'd been barked at her during the disbarment hearing. Thankfully no one in town, aside from her parents, knew of her shame, and she wanted to keep it that way. It'd made her nervous to find out that Nick had come from Seattle.

Her story had made *The Seattle Times*, but as far as she knew, her photograph hadn't been released. Alexis Thompson wasn't a rare name, so she hoped no one would ever find out.

A siren sounded once behind the truck. Gerald flinched and waved into the rearview mirror. "Looks like they'll take care of you. Have a safe weekend, Lexi."

Jeremy stepped out of the cruiser. "Now, didn't I just tell you that thing was an accident waiting to happen?" He flung his arm in the direction of the blue car. "You could have died!" He frowned at the sight of Nick's scraped up arms and ripped clothes. "What happened to you? I'll call for an ambulance."

Nick waved away his concern. "I'm beat up, but there's no need for emergency care." He pointed upward. "There was someone watching us from up there. Possibly a gunman. Can you send someone to check it out?"

Alexis stepped forward, not waiting for Jeremy to answer. "This wasn't my fault. The car was perfectly fine earlier. But when I picked it up from the parking lot, the brakes felt mushy, and then suddenly they went out."

Jeremy looked back and forth between the two of them. "That doesn't mean—"

"And the parking brake was out, too." She hadn't

meant to shout. She pulled her shoulders back. She couldn't handle it if one more person implied it was because of her poor judgment in driving a junker that this had happened. Yes, she drove an old car. Yes, it was hilarious for a lawyer to own a junker. It wasn't relevant. Someone had sabotaged her car.

Jeremy closed his mouth. He turned his gaze upward. "I don't see anyone now. And there's no one to send. I'm it. All our officers are on calls or on vacation. I've been told this is usually a quiet weekend for us."

He turned, and his eyebrows rose as he stared out into the valley, his focus on Nick's truck. "I'll admit, the parking brake not working makes it a little more suspicious. Everyone knows your car..." He let his words trail off as his brow furrowed. "It was sitting in the parking lot at the trailhead for quite a while after your interaction with suspected drug runners. That's if Nick was right about what he saw." He seemed to be talking to himself more than them.

She tilted her head. "Mine was the only vehicle at the trailhead, Jeremy. It wouldn't be hard to figure out I owned it."

Jeremy sucked in a breath through his nostrils and exhaled loudly. "I'll take your theory to the chief, but we're going to have to do an official investigation before I can confirm it's foul play, Alexis. If you're right, it should be obvious that someone tampered with the lines."

She placed her hands on her hips. "Okay. What now?"

"I'll see what Chief wants to do, but I can give you both a ride home, where you can wait to hear from us. I've already got a call in to a tow truck for your car."

It didn't seem wise to leave Nick at his house without a vehicle, especially since the gunmen probably knew that was where he lived now. "Take us both to my house."

Nick turned his head, his eyebrows high.

"I have an extra car." Alexis sighed. "It's my dad's. You can drive it until we get everything sorted out." She saw the objection in his expression. "I'm in town. Everywhere I need to go is in walking distance. You can use the car to go back and forth from your place to your practice until we take care of insurance. I insist. Besides, the rental place is already closed for the day. It's the least I can do for getting you in this mess. You saved my life." Her throat closed as the last few hours overwhelmed her. "Twice," she whispered.

"Okay, then. That's settled." Jeremy looked Nick up and down and pointed to his scrapes. "You sure you don't need medical treatment? You're not going to self-treat, are you, Doc?"

"Besides some bandages and ointment? No. I don't prescribe myself any pain medicine."

She gave the leash a tug to lead Raven to the squad car. "Vets can write themselves prescriptions?"

He shrugged. "It happens, but I think it's a potential gateway to drug abuse that I'm not willing to tempt. If I need anything, I'll go to Urgent Care."

He certainly seemed to know a lot about the illegal drug trade.

Jeremy opened the back door to the squad car. Alexis groaned. They would have to drive into town on the main drag. She didn't mind riding in a police cruiser when they were out on the edges of town where no one would see them, but if Jeremy drove into town with her in the backseat, the rumor mill would go into full effect.

Her parents would hear about it clear in Arizona by morning. They didn't need to add to their worries about her. "Um, maybe I could ride in the front?"

Nick swung his gaze to her so fast she worried about his neck. His look said it all. He wished he'd called shotgun first. She almost gloated until she remembered that his truck was at the bottom of the valley because of her. He sported injuries because of her. And, since he was running for town mayor, she could grudgingly admit he had more at stake if his reputation was ruined.

Jeremy shrugged. "Sure. It's open."

"You take the front," Alexis told Nick. "I'll—" she swallowed "—sit with the dog."

"You don't like dogs."

"We have the entire backseat. She can keep her distance."

Nick eyed her for a minute. Indecision played across his features. He seemed the type always to put a lady's needs first. Seemed? No, judging by his actions today, he was.

"I'm sure, Nick."

Jeremy put his fists on his waist. "I don't care who goes where, but if you don't decide, I'm going to drive off without either of you."

She slid into the backseat before Nick could argue. Raven followed without hesitation and tried to rest her head on Alexis's knee, but Alexis shooed her away.

Maybe she could lean her head down so her hair would cover most of her face when they entered town. Of course, that kind of posture would make her look guilty of something. She could lean back and bravely smile. Or would that make her look crazy and high on something?

Jeremy started the cruiser, and a sudden illogical need to get out of the car gripped her. No one could've messed with his brakes, though. She inhaled as the car took the sharp turn. Normally she enjoyed the curvy drive from the trail down to town as if it was a mild roller coaster that she controlled, but it was too soon after her brush with death to be in a car again.

Her right hand clung to the door's armrest. How often did they clean and sanitize the inside of police cruisers? She cringed and let go. A hot shower had never sounded so good.

The dog slid along the vinyl seat until its backside hit the opposite side of the car. Raven jumped up on all fours, seemingly alarmed as they approached another curve.

"Sit. Lie down." Alexis patted the spot next to her.

The dog obeyed. Alexis tensed as she allowed Raven's head to rest on her lap. She placed her other arm on top of the dog's torso to make sure it didn't slide around anymore. Oh, Theresa would be hearing about every single detail of this afternoon and evening over many dinners. Or chocolate bars. Or both.

The warmth from the dog slowed her own heart rate slightly. She looked down to see Raven gazing up at her. It was hard not to smile in response. She cleared her throat and stared ahead.

Jeremy glanced at Nick. "I hope you have good insurance. I don't envy you trying to get money out of a lawyer." He winked at Alexis in the rearview mirror.

Alexis fought the instinct to roll her eyes, but the dread at having to swap insurance information and the interrogation the claim adjusters would run her through made her limbs heavy. "What are we going to do to make sure something like this doesn't happen anymore? How do we know they won't target us again? Jeremy, what are you guys going to do about it?"

Jeremy shook his head. "I can't comment on that, Alexis. It's on the chief's radar, and we'll be investigating. It's a high priority."

Nick huffed. "I think it's in our best interest to be proactive."

"Well, Alexis knows everyone in town. If she didn't know—"

"Not everyone," she objected. "I'd never met Nick, and I certainly didn't recognize the guy—the scout—who took a pic of us. I didn't see the faces of any of the men who had guns, but I would've thought their outlines, their backs, would've sparked some guess as to who they were. I've got nothing. So, not likely."

Nick sagged against his headrest. "Ever dealt with something like this before?"

Jeremy shook his head. "No. We don't have too many drug problems here."

"You are right off the interstate—The Corridor. It may not be openly a problem, but I guarantee it is. There's not a town, city or county that hasn't been touched, and ignorance is the greatest risk to this town."

His impassioned voice stirred her. He wasn't just a walking dictionary on the drug problem in their region. This seemed personal. Her curiosity almost got the better of her, but she fought it off. She'd asked enough of the man for one night.

Jeremy stiffened. "I'm not ignorant."

She could've cut the tension in the air with a knife.

"I didn't mean you personally," Nick said. "I apologize if it sounded that way."

Jeremy didn't respond, and they rode in silence. Stars began to twinkle in the sky. A few minutes later the decline and curves flattened out. They were about to enter town.

Alexis exhaled. She could move the dog away now but something kept her from doing so. The warmth wasn't unpleasant. She certainly wasn't a dog person yet, and probably never would be, but as long as Raven didn't start drooling on her skirt, she supposed the dog could stay put. Alexis straightened and pulled her hand back. She didn't need to hold the dog's torso anymore.

She let her hand rest on top of Raven's neck, just below the makeshift collar Nick had rigged from the leash. Something hot, wet and sticky met her skin.

Alexis yanked her hand back.

Blood.

FIVE

Nick kneeled in the driveway where Officer Jeremy had dropped them off. He pushed back Raven's fur to see the matted area of blood. The dim lighting didn't help him reach a confident diagnosis. "I can't be sure, but it might need stitches. If she breaks into a run anytime soon, it could gape open."

"How do you think it happened?" Her face looked pinched.

"There wasn't any glass in your car," he mused. Raven stayed still while he took a second look at the jagged cut. "The barbed wire fence had to be the culprit."

"But I lifted her over it. You took her from me."

"The second time, yes. The first time, she zipped underneath it in hot pursuit of that squirrel." Raven's ears perked at the last word, and she looked around hopefully.

"Oh." She worried her hands together. "I didn't know. She didn't whimper."

"Dogs don't openly express pain every time. And adrenaline might have played a part." He straightened to standing. "I'd like to take her to my office and examine her."

Alexis nodded rapidly. "Whatever you think is best."

She looked slightly pale, come to think of it.

"Are you okay?" He reached a steadying hand toward her arm. The softness of her skin jolted him, but she didn't seem too hot or too cold. He wasn't a physician, but he had spent a short amount of time in medical school before deciding it wasn't the right field for him. "Can you tell me how you're feeling? Do you have a problem with blood?"

"I'm fine." She shook her head. "I mean, I don't know. I feel horrible that she got hurt on my watch. It's my fault. I've done everything wrong. Theresa never should've entrusted me with the dog."

In his opinion, the blame rested with Theresa for asking so much of her friend. "There's no need to feel guilty. If you've never been a pet owner, there's no reason to think you'd know about breakaway collars."

Alexis sucked in a gasp. "I haven't reached Theresa. I need to let her know what's happened. That the dog is hurt." She pointed at Raven, but her eyes drifted to the dried blood on her hand, and her face lost what little color it had left.

"How about you wash up first?"

She nodded. "Okay." She turned to the house. "I'll get you the keys to my dad's sedan. I can join you at your office in a few minutes."

He hadn't argued with her earlier, but Nick would not leave a single woman alone without a vehicle all night when there was potential she was still in danger. Officer Jeremy had promised Alexis that an officer would make regular rounds past her house all night, but there was no mention of what "regular rounds" entailed. If they were short on officers, who knew how often someone would actually check up on her?

Nick was accustomed to making fast decisions. He had the impression that Alexis tended to do so, as well. So he'd argue over the car issue later, after he took care of Raven. Besides, he'd likely need complete focus when arguing with a lawyer.

"I'll walk. It's just across the street. See you in a few." He bent down and ignored the pinch in his back as he lifted Raven into his arms. For now, he wanted Raven immobile so the bleeding would continue to diminish.

"Um, okay."

He walked across the street. Not a block away, he punched in the pass code and unlocked the employee side door. The undeniable smell of animals combined with soft meows, chirps and barks greeted him. Raven shifted and shivered in his arms. "It's okay, girl. It's normal to be nervous, but there's no need."

He set her down to hang out alone in an exam room with a treat while he turned on lights, unlocked the front door for Alexis and gathered his supplies. Raven was so enamored with the brushing chew that Nick could trim the fur and clean the area around the wound without assistance. "That's going to help your breath, too, girl. Might help Alexis like you," he said in soothing tones.

"I've never heard of good dog breath winning a girl over." Alexis stood in the doorway. She'd replaced her skirt, blouse and sandals with jeans, a gray T-shirt and canvas shoes. Her hair was pulled back into a loose ponytail.

Nick's stomach heated. "Talking to animals while I work helps soothe them."

Alexis stepped closer. Raven wagged her tail at the sight. "I couldn't reach Theresa."

"Well, you tried." He pointed to the bench. "Please sit there and hold the leash for me." He lifted the prepared syringe and pulled up the loose skin above the wound to inject a painkiller. "It would help if you kept her head in your lap. I need her calm and still." He turned to prep the needle for sutures. She frowned with concern. "Don't worry. I'm fast," he added.

She bit her lower lip and nodded.

"If you stroke her head and talk to her, she won't feel anything but a bit of tugging." He told himself he wasn't trying to win her over to dogs. Keeping the dog motionless was in its best interest.

"I'm not talking to an animal." She bent her head and rested her hand on top of Raven. Raven pulled her ears back and looked up at Alexis in response.

She sighed. "How about I talk to you instead while I look at her?" Her voice took on a soothing quality.

The research on what dogs could understand was conflicted. Some estimated a Labrador could obtain the same level of vocabulary as a toddler, but other research pointed to the tone of voice as the method for understanding. "I'll take what I can get." He needed to keep her talking while he worked, then. Fortunately, he had a ton of questions about her. "Tell me what kind of law you used to practice." In his peripheral vision he could see her stiffen.

"Patent law."

Well, so far he wasn't getting her to talk much. Nick prepared the needle for sutures. "Was that your passion? Patent law?"

She laughed. "Uh, no. It made for a well-paying first job, though. My real hope was to get my feet wet, get some money saved up and then transition to elder law. There aren't enough people advocating for senior citizens."

He loved the lilt in her voice while she talked at the dog. A former lawyer who wanted to fight for the rights of senior citizens would be perfect to lead his team of volunteers. The cops seemed to think she knew most everyone in town. The combination could be the answer to his prayers about the campaign.

"So why didn't you?" he asked. They sounded ridiculous talking to each other in higher-pitched, soft voices, but Raven remained calm. Nick had three stitches done. Just a couple more and he would tie it off. Thankfully, there was no way Raven would be able to lick or chew on this part of her back. It should heal nicely.

Her eyes flicked upward before landing back on Raven. "Life happens. Plans change."

There was pain behind her eyes. He knew she was here to help her parents, but she said they weren't ill and had moved to Arizona. The chief and Officer Jeremy both seemed to respect her, so she couldn't have done something seedy. Maybe she'd stopped practicing law because a loved one had died, or she'd suffered a bad breakup with a coworker.

If any of those were the case, needing time to heal before going back into such a stressful career made sense. He certainly wouldn't be able to handle being a lawyer. "So you'll be here until you sell your parents' house?"

"Yes. That's the plan for now."

A lawyer who enjoyed her job would've outsourced the task to a real-estate agent and contractors, wouldn't she? So that couldn't be the real reason she was still in town. But it was yet another reminder that she had no interest in putting down roots in Barings.

"Houses don't seem to be selling very fast here," he finally said. He swirled the thread into a final knot. "It's something I hope to change if we can bring some new business into town. I imagine temp work isn't exactly challenging for someone with your experience. It's usually entry-level work. Am I right?"

She no longer looked at the dog but stared right at him. "I can see you have an excellent bedside manner, Nick. But I feel like you're trying to lead up to telling me something. Since this isn't my dog and she doesn't need some drastic treatment, give it to me straight. What are you getting at?" She raised her eyebrows. "I can tell you right now I won't be willing to temp as your vet tech or even as a receptionist." She scrunched her nose. "I couldn't handle being around dogs all day even if you doubled my pay."

He grinned. Yes. She was a straight shooter, which was exactly what he needed. "You're right, but I don't need another tech or receptionist. I've been running my mayoral campaign all by myself. I've got only a couple of months before the vote, and I've been praying to find someone who knows everyone in this town, who understands laws and policies. I thought it was a tall-order prayer, but here you are. I'm not flush with cash, but I imagine I can pay you as much as a temp job could in this town. Would you consider being my campaign manager?"

Her jaw dropped and eyes widened. "No. Absolutely not."

"Because you're voting for Gerald?"

She flinched. "Gerald? No."

"Is it the money? We haven't even talked numbers yet. I could settle for part-time and you wouldn't leave anyone in the lurch. What's her name—Theresa? I'm sure we could work something out."

She scrunched up her forehead. "It's not that." Raven seemed to realize he was done working on her and flopped down to the floor.

He raised his eyebrows. "Is it because I said I prayed? That I'm a Christian?"

She stood. "No." She walked toward the door, turned around to face him, opened her mouth and promptly shut it again. She looked like she was in a daze as she crossed the lobby and rested her hands on the door.

His heart raced as Raven stood by his side, watching Alexis leave with him. He'd known she might turn him down, but her reaction—almost as if he was too vile to consider—threw him for a loop. She could've at least let him down easy. He really was fun to work with, at least according to his employees.

Her shoulders sagged as she looked out into the street. "It's not you, Nick. It's nothing about you. I can see you are a good man, and you might even be what this town needs, for all I know. I just can't help you." She swallowed but still didn't make eye contact. "Thank you for asking."

She looked tired and wounded. He wanted to ask, to help, but it seemed clear he'd never be able to breach the invisible barrier surrounding her. In the end, it wasn't any of his business, though the mystery would drive him crazy. "Fair enough," he finally said. "End of discussion."

She nodded, relief evident as she sighed. "I forgot to bring the car keys with me."

"I'm not taking the car. I'm staying here tonight."

Her wide eyes swung to meet his. "Why?"

Several reasons came to mind. The practice had a good alarm system and would elicit a faster police response time than if he went home. The men knew where he lived, which probably meant it wasn't safe. The most important reason to him, though, was that she wouldn't have a reason to insist he take the car and she wouldn't be left without transportation, but he felt sure she'd object if he voiced it aloud. "I have a cot and a change of clothes here. And this way, my receptionist can give me a ride out to the car rental office in the morning."

She studied him for a moment. "Okay. Then I'm feeding you dinner. Come over as soon as you can."

It wasn't a question, and for a split second, he almost refused on reflex. People weren't in the habit of telling him what to do, and as a strong-willed man, he wasn't in the habit of taking orders...at least without being asked nicely. His stomach, however, rumbled at the thought of dinner, and it was nice of her to think of it. After the day they'd had, they both probably needed extra grace in how they addressed each other. "Okay. If I leave now, it'll give Keri—the teen who comes to take care of the animals during boarding—a chance to feed and play with them without feeling like she's being watched."

Suspecting that a photo of Alexis and him was out there, circling among drug runners, Nick wished he could say the same.

* * *

Alexis moved to open the front door. Why did she need a conscience? Most of her life would likely have been easier without one complicating matters. Being a lawyer certainly would've been easier.

Nick's supposed reason that he wanted to sleep in the veterinary hospital sounded weak to her. She could see right through him. He was doing it to make sure she had a car. He'd already saved her life…twice. As if that wasn't enough heroism for the day.

So, since saying thank you seemed like the understatement of the year, the least she could do was make sure he had more dinner options than wet or dry dog food. But in reality, the last thing she wanted was to spend more time with Nick.

"Wait up. It's dark out," Nick said. "Let me put Raven in a kennel with some food and water, and I'll walk you out."

She bristled. There he went again, making sure she'd stay safe. She wasn't going to argue, though, because he had a point, but she hated owing him so much. How could she repay a debt to him that kept growing? It had almost killed her to say no when he'd asked for help with the campaign, but she also wasn't ready to tell him why her help would effectively ruin his chances at the position.

"I'm going to try Theresa again," she said. She could hear the edge in her own voice. The Lord might have kept her conscience in good working condition, but He hadn't curbed her pride yet. Not that she was asking Him to help work on that. No, thank you. She'd already suffered enough humiliation to last a lifetime. Unfortu-

nately, instead of humility, she felt more insecure while
simultaneously defensive.

"Thanks for offering to walk me," she called out after
Nick and Raven. She looked through the glass door at
the stars, hoping the Lord could see she had acknowledged and, at least outwardly, amended her prideful at-
titude. It would be great if the Lord could round up the
drug runners who wanted her dead while He was at it.

A silver station wagon drove down the road. Alexis
pulled back from the glass door. The lone streetlight
at the corner had never bothered her before, but she'd
never felt in danger on her own street before, either.

The dogs in the back of Nick's practice sounded
happy to see him, assuming barking could sound happy.
If Theresa answered the call, she'd be shocked at the
background noise. Alexis held the phone up to her ear
as it started to ring. Three rings, four...and it connected
to voice mail. Alexis didn't want to leave a message.
She opted to text:

Need you to call. Urgent. Bad things happened today.
You need to come back home.

Alexis studied her own message before she pressed
Send. While she didn't begrudge Theresa a chance at
fun and time with her mysterious boyfriend, she really
needed to take over the care and decisions for Raven.

Once again, Alexis's mind drifted to who the potential boyfriend could be. If Theresa had known him
all her life, maybe it was the owner of Barings Heating
and Air. When Alexis had temped as a receptionist for
the guy, he'd been very eager to know how Theresa was
doing. And he was a recent widower, which would cause

tongues to wag around town that it was too soon for the man to date. So that would explain the secrecy. Alexis grinned at the thought. They would make a good couple. Theresa deserved a kind, thoughtful man in her life.

"Good news?" Nick asked. "Something must've made you smile."

She tried not to react at his appearance. He'd not only put Raven away but also taken the time to change into a light blue dress shirt and brown dress pants complete with a belt. Alexis knew that the clothes did not make the man, but they certainly didn't hurt. He must have kept extra clothes at the office. Smart, given his occupation.

"No news," she said. "Daydreaming about happier things."

He raised an eyebrow and placed a hand on his stomach. "Dinner, perhaps?"

A nervous laugh escaped, and Alexis realized with horror that she'd been twirling the end of her ponytail. While it was just an unconscious habit whenever she got flustered, she knew it looked flirtatious—her girlfriends had teased her about it mercilessly in college.

She dropped her hand to her side. "I'm afraid dinner is not likely to be dream-worthy." She pushed open the door, and he followed her to the street. "I'm still using up my mom's freezer meals and emptying her pantry. She has enough to last until Thanksgiving."

"I'm sure it'll be wonderful." His stomach growled as if in answer. "Raven is enjoying her food. Keri will be in there soon to give her more attention, as well."

They crossed the street to the driveway. In the distance, toward the end of the block, the silver car she'd seen pass earlier sat on the side of the road. She squinted. "Does it look like someone is in that car?"

"I can't tell." His eyes widened in the moonlight. "Should I be concerned?"

Across from the car were two houses, both rentals. She didn't know who'd moved into those particular ones since she'd been back, which proved that she didn't know every single person in the town, despite Jeremy's assumptions. "I think the events of the day have made me paranoid," she finally said.

Her statement wasn't entirely truthful. She'd been paranoid for months, ever since hearing a confession from a murderer, from someone she'd thought was a nice man.

Nick kept his gaze on the car. "Paranoid or not, caution should be the order of the day. Let's get inside and let your cop friend know. Silver Subaru Outback." He shook his head. "That model's popularity is basically tied with the pickup truck in Idaho."

"It makes sense. Everyone wants all-wheel drive around here. I imagine it'll be my next vehicle."

Her parents' living room's bay window faced the driveway and the street. She rounded the corner and pulled the keys out of her jeans to unlock the brown entry door, which faced the garage, making a corridor of sorts between the two unattached buildings.

Two pots of wilting geraniums sat on either side of the front door. She'd been so busy she hadn't noticed until now. She glanced up at Nick, hoping he didn't notice, but he still had his eyes on the street. If any prospective buyers actually came to look at the house, dying flowers probably wouldn't help win them over.

Nick crossed the threshold right behind her and

closed the door. He slipped off his shoes before following her onto the plush beige carpet. The house took on a new appearance before her eyes as she saw it in a new light, imagining she hadn't spent a lifetime in it.

The bookshelves and walls were covered in framed photographs. Her mother had never been fond of knick-knacks or artwork but loved to be surrounded by images of the people she loved. Fake potted flowers were in almost every corner of the living room, in addition to the two recliners and love seat. Maybe she could switch out the dying flowers for some of the fake ones. The spot where the television had resided was empty. The relatively new flat screen had taken the trip to Arizona with them.

Nick ignored it all, crossed the room and placed a knee on her favorite spot in the entire house, the cushioned ledge of the bay window. He leaned forward and peeked out the sheer curtains. "Car is still there, but I don't see anyone in the driver's seat."

"Then it's probably nothing. It is Labor Day weekend. Families like to come visit." Or so she'd been told. She didn't have many extended relatives closer than Texas, and she'd never visited there.

Nick's face looked pinched. Either he was really hungry or something she'd said had sparked pain.

"I have Jeremy's number, though. I'll let him know, to be safe." She sent him a quick text. The phone vibrated in response. "He says someone will drive by soon." Knowing an officer would check out the car, she felt the tension in her back loosen a little.

She hustled to preheat the oven before she grabbed a bag of premade burritos out of the freezer. Sweet potato fries didn't really complement the dish, but they were the only vegetable she could find.

Nick put his hands behind his back and perused the photographs on the shelves. "Wait a second." He turned to look at her, his finger pointing at the photo of her father receiving an award for public service from the governor. "Was your dad the mayor at one point?"

She dumped all of the food onto a cookie sheet and shoved it into the oven, not bothering to wait for it to preheat. She'd never claimed to be a good cook. She got too impatient. "Yes. He served for most of my childhood and adulthood, until Gerald took his spot last term."

Nick's pensive nod said it all. He was making the assumption that her dad's political history was the reason she'd said no to his campaign manager job. There was a grain of truth to it. Her dad had hoped to move on from being a mayor to campaigning for senator. He'd held off during her rebellious teen years but thought maybe enough time had passed for him to run. When her little "hiccup," as her dad called her disbarment, happened, he decided maybe it would be best to retire early, for her sake.

Heat flooded her chest. She wished she'd never opened up to Nick. He made it way too easy, though, as he had such a kind face and demeanor. His silent smile practically begged her to say more. It's why she'd admitted to him that her passion was elder law when she could count on one hand how many people she'd told.

She knew what he was thinking, what the whole town was probably thinking. It didn't make sense for a lawyer to take so long prepping a house for sale. She could've flown out for a weekend or hired people to do it. Good lawyers had money. They had luxury vehicles.

They weren't wasting their skills working entry-level jobs at a temp agency.

If she was honest with herself, she still wanted to go into elder law, but she hadn't gotten up enough nerve to plead her case to the Idaho State Bar. Her license was revoked in Washington, but there was a slim-to-none chance she could be allowed to serve in her home state.

Once she built up enough courage to do that, her past would no longer be a secret. The entire town would hear about it. She'd have to travel to Boise to appear before the Bar. Boise wasn't too far away, and plenty of people from Barings had relatives there. Someone would find out, she just knew it. And if she lost, her last hope of moving on would be dashed. She wasn't ready to face it. Not yet.

Nick stepped into the kitchen and nodded at the office nook nestled between the counter and the dining table. "Would it be okay to borrow a piece of paper and pencil?"

"Of course. Dinner won't be long now."

"Proverbs 31." He pointed at the Bible she'd left open on the counter. "Good stuff."

She blushed. Had it really been just this morning she'd been rereading that? "Most people think of the wife of noble character." She tried to ignore the approving look in his eyes. "But there are two verses in there that I clung to as a lawyer, which, come to think of it, you might appreciate. My dad pointed them out to me many years ago."

His eyebrows rose. "Oh?"

"Verses 8 and 9 basically say we should speak up for those who don't have a voice, for those who need defending, for justice…" She let her voice trail off when she realized how passionate she sounded. Her neck heated again. She grabbed some glasses and filled them with iced tea.

"I appreciate you sharing that with me," he said, his voice soft. "Is that why you wanted to practice elder law?"

"Partly." She'd gone and gotten personal again. She focused on the food. The house was devoid of every other Labor Day weekend staple. Her menu was as weird as her life lately.

Nick had taken a spot at the dining table and appeared to be sketching something. Maybe he was one of those people who liked to color to relax. Personally, she couldn't understand the compulsion. The only thing that could relax her was jotting down every single thing on her mind, like an epic to-do list, and then following it up with an engrossing book to forget it all until she could start crossing things off. Maybe that's why she made a good lawyer. *Had* made a good lawyer.

She peeked over his shoulder. Rough short lines formed a misshapen circle. "Are you drawing a turtle?" Did he treat turtles? "One of your patients?"

He twisted his torso to look at her, an amused smile on his face. She smiled in response, not even knowing why and fighting the urge to twirl her hair again. "No," he said slowly. "I was trying to be proactive and draw the scout's face as best as I could remember. I know I'm not the best artist in the wor—"

"Clearly." She laughed at his facial expression and held up both hands. "Sorry. I'm no artist, either, but it's not a bad idea. We both saw him." She pulled out the chair beside him and took a seat.

"Exactly. If we could agree on what he looked like,

then maybe the authorities would have a better shot at getting him."

"Yes, but how much good would that do us? He still sent our picture out to the drug network or whatever they call themselves."

"We don't know he did that for sure, but even if that's the case, at least we've started somewhere." He tapped the sketch. "Maybe the authorities could get this guy to talk. At the very least, it should help in getting the runners to back off. Awareness is our greatest weapon. The more people who know what we're dealing with here, the better."

An annoying repetitive noise interrupted her next thought. It sounded like a faraway car alarm. She stood and crossed to the bay window. "The Outback is gone." She shifted her view to the right. A flicker of light from what looked like the back of his practice made her pause.

A dark figure could be seen running toward the building. The orange light grew. "Nick—" Her throat closed. The animals…

Nick rushed forward and put a hand on her back as he peered forward. "What is it?"

Her hands shook as she pulled out her phone. "Fire."

SIX

Nick barely had the presence of mind to shove on his shoes before sprinting across the street. He passed Alexis, but his legs and arms felt weighted. He couldn't run as fast as he wanted. The shrill pitch of the fire alarm grew louder as he got closer. Flames licked the back of the building and could be seen on the roof.

"Keri," he screamed, scanning the sides of the property. The sixteen-year-old girl should've been tending to the boarded animals by now. What if she was trapped inside with them? He couldn't imagine the sprinkler system he'd installed in the boarding area would be a match against the vicious blaze for very long. The smoke alone...

"They're coming," Alexis yelled, mere steps behind him. She panted. "Fire trucks are coming."

He didn't bother to reply. Emergency personnel should've already been on the way if the alarm system was working properly. He attempted to slow down, but his knee hit the front door as he tried to pull it open. Locked. He keyed in the code to unlock it. The second it took for the little light to turn green seemed like an eternity.

He swung the door open. The smoke dimmed the lights in the lobby, and the acrid smell almost bowled him over. The deafening beeping of the alarm was accompanied by at least one howling dog. "Stay back." He waved Alexis away as he charged forward and hunkered down.

The strobes from the firelights illuminated the door he wanted. He yanked it open and Keri, drenched from the sprinklers and holding a carrier, almost barreled into him. She screamed. Then her eyes widened. "Oh, Dr. Kendrick." She burst into tears. "The back door. Someone blocked it. Most of the dogs are out—" Keri launched into a fit of coughing.

"Go!" They could figure out what had happened after everyone was safe. He stepped aside. Alexis had ignored his plea to stay out of the way. She grabbed the cat carrier from Keri and ran her toward the front door.

Nick put his arm over his mouth and tried to squint through the smoke. The left wall had flames licking it, but the sprinkler system on that side was squirting out a steady stream. Not enough to put the fire completely out, but to keep it from spreading.

He followed the howling until he reached the kennel. Raven sat shivering and shaking, wet and clearly scared. His heart twisted as he unlatched the kennel and picked up the dog. The second half of the sprinklers sprayed down on them. The blaze licked the surrounding walls now. He needed to make sure there were no more animals in danger.

Alexis appeared at his side. He startled. He didn't risk opening his mouth, but he wanted to scream at her to get out. She threw her arms around Raven, pulled her from him and darted out the door.

Nick ran throughout the small area, flinging doors open. Daisy, the golden retriever with a wounded paw, remained. Otherwise the boarding area was empty. He lifted the seventy-pound, full-grown animal and struggled to keep her still as he ran with her into the lobby.

Alexis and Raven cowered against the side wall. A ceiling beam had fallen, flames devouring it. They were trapped.

Nick stepped up onto the receptionist's office chair, stood on the desk and fumbled to open the window with one arm. He shoved the pane upward and felt before he heard the whoosh of flames coming his way.

He jumped off the desk with Daisy in his arms. The flames on the ceiling hungrily headed for the side window. Alexis touched the handle to the exam room door hesitantly before she opened it. It was smart thinking. There was a large front window in there, but as it was for decorative purposes, there was no way to open it. He grabbed the large glass jar of treats sitting next to the exam station and waved Alexis back. He pitched the jar at the center of the window. The glass cracked, then shattered into a million little pieces.

Alexis didn't wait for his instructions. She stepped onto the bench she'd sat on a mere hour ago and launched forward, with Raven in her arms, out the ground floor window. Nick joined her a second later with the wriggling Daisy. He gulped the air greedily, too greedily, as he began coughing.

Flashing lights sped down the street and pulled into his empty parking lot. The volunteer firefighters poured out of the red truck and set to work as EMTs rushed at him and pulled him to safety.

Daisy began shaking in his arms. "She needs oxygen."

"Sir, I need to take care of you first."

"Give her oxygen," Nick repeated. He spun frantically until he spotted Alexis and Keri being treated by another EMT. "If they're okay, give the black dog and the cat oxygen, too."

"Sir…"

Nick saw the uncertainty in the young man's eyes. He knew some states had passed laws allowing emergency personnel to treat animals, but he wasn't sure if Idaho was one of them. If it turned out to be a liability issue, he'd take responsibility. "I'm a veterinarian. Let me."

The EMT didn't say a word as Nick gently set Daisy down. The flames overtaking his practice barely registered until the dog stopped shivering. He pointed at a policeman. "You. Come watch this dog for me."

The policeman frowned but didn't argue, compassion in his eyes as the dog's front paw bandages registered. Nick hustled over to Raven and administered the oxygen. Alexis met his eyes, soot covering her cheeks and nose. "You were brilliant," he said. He turned to Keri. "I can't thank you enough. The other dogs we were boarding weren't in there. Are all the other dogs in the pen?"

She nodded, tears still streaming down her cheeks. "I had taken them out for playtime before bed. But when I looked back, I saw flames. I ran inside—" she coughed for a minute "—but after I grabbed the kitty," she sobbed, "the back door wouldn't open."

The chief stood behind her. He had heard the whole thing. His face turned a purplish hue as he took a knee and pulled her into a hug. "You were a hero, Keri. A hero."

Tears filled Nick's eyes. Alexis sniffed beside him. "Keri is Chief Spencer's niece."

The chief's hard eyes met Nick's. "I will make sure

to take down whoever is responsible." His chilled voice seemed to be implying it was Nick's fault somehow. He wouldn't even dignify the threat with a response.

The cat was the hardest to treat. Nick's arms took the brunt of the scratches as he tried to make sure the cat wasn't suffering from smoke inhalation.

Alexis wiped the tears from under her eyes. "What do you need me to do, Doc?"

He didn't know where to begin. The practice…the… He took a deep breath. The animals came first, and he needed more hands. He passed her his phone. "Could you call my staff? Abigail and Marla? They're in my contacts. Ask them to get in touch with any owners who are still in town, then get down here and help me find places for these animals tonight."

Her eyes widened. "On it."

Nick went on autopilot. Alexis wordlessly followed him as he guided Daisy and Raven behind the building and into the pen with the six other dogs that had been boarded. The fenced-off area was a few hundred feet behind the building.

The floodlights that normally illuminated the grassy area were off. Whether from sabotage or fire, he couldn't be certain. The breeze carried the smells of wet dog, smoke and burning lumber. A few houses' worth of people came their way, forming a crowd on the sidewalks.

When he shifted to check on each animal, Alexis moved directly behind him, rapidly talking into the phone. The dogs in the pen had to be scaring her. "You don't have to stay here," he said softly.

She put one hand over the receiver. "Oh yes, I do. I tried to go out the gate, and two dogs almost managed to get past me." She shivered. "Marla says she's on her way. She wants to know if she should bring anything."

He shook his head. What they really needed were volunteers to bathe the dogs to get any potential soot out of their fur, house them and provide humidifiers to decrease the chance of suffering from the effects of smoke inhalation.

Thanks to Keri and Alexis, no animals had been harmed tonight. His heart sped up at the thought. It was too close, just as Alexis's brush with death on that cliff had been.

The fire was dying fast, thanks to the work of the firefighters behind them, but the remaining flames illuminated the approach of the chief and Jeremy. "Doc," the chief called out. "Need to ask some questions."

Alexis stiffened.

Nick regarded her. "Do I need a lawyer?"

"They probably just want to ask questions to start the investigation, but I'll be the first to tell you to get one."

For some reason the response hurt. "You wouldn't be my lawyer?"

"Not my field, remember?" She worried her lip. "Trust me. You wouldn't want me."

"Pretty sure I made the opposite point an hour ago." He realized it was the worst time to discuss it, but there was something about having his life's work go up in flames that put him in an argumentative mood.

"Nick, that was a completely different matt—"

"What can you tell us?" the chief interrupted. He stood just outside the pen.

Alexis spoke before Nick had a chance, relaying the details of what they'd seen and done.

Jeremy threw a thumb over his shoulder. "We found

cement blocks up against the back door." He sent a tentative glance to Chief. "That's why Keri had to come out the front."

"Why would someone do that?" Chief asked.

"I was hoping you could tell me." Nick's voice raised an octave.

Alexis rested her hand on his forearm. Her touch simultaneously calmed and invigorated him. He took a deep breath and consciously relaxed his muscles.

"You have all the facts," Alexis told the chief, her voice steely. "I imagine you should be looking for the same person who cut my brakes."

Chief exchanged a glance with Jeremy. "Lexi, we can't jump to conclusions until we—"

"Investigate. Yes, I know. Surely you see this is arson." She gestured wildly to the burning building behind them. Unfortunately one of the dogs, Sugar, took the arm motion to mean *jump* and did so right in her face. Alexis squealed and spun, shoving her face into Nick's chest.

He wrapped his arms around her and pointed his finger down. "It's okay," he whispered. Sugar plopped on the ground, looking up, pleased she'd obeyed the command, and waiting for a treat. She wasn't the only one. Raven followed her example.

Nick tried not to enjoy the sensation of Alexis in his arms, especially as both Jeremy and the chief were glaring at him. He tried not to sigh aloud, but the burden of what lay before him in the days to come felt heavy enough to bury him alive. Was anyone on his side?

Alexis stiffened. Nick Kendrick's arms were around her, and her hands and face were pressed against his chest. She pulled away, her face hotter than the remaining blaze behind her. "Sorry." Her eyes searched for the dogs. The offending black Lab that had jumped in her face lay on the ground like nothing had ever happened.

Someone cleared his throat and coughed behind her. She whirled around to see the chief behind the gate, arms crossed over his chest. "I think it's time someone helped me out of here," she said.

Jeremy opened the gate and blocked the animals from escaping as she slipped out.

"You have an alarm system," the chief said to Nick. "I'm told Doc Finn never had one. Why did you feel the need to install it?"

"Doc Finn never had a sprinkler system, either," Nick answered coolly. "If I didn't have that, there would have been a lot of sorrow in this town. The practice needed some upgrades."

Alexis looked between the chief and Nick. It seemed like an odd thing to ask. Doc Finn had been in practice for over forty years. Nick adding such features was reasonable.

"Since I store pharmaceuticals, I need to take precautions, so I got the alarm system."

"Which pharmaceuticals were you worried about?" the chief volleyed.

Nick raised an eyebrow. "Tramadol, for one."

"What's that?" Jeremy asked.

"A pain reliever. It's narcotic-like but it isn't monitored like opiates, which can make it a target for some addicts."

Jeremy and the chief shared a knowing look. Alexis couldn't figure out why, though. It wasn't as if Nick was a drug dealer.

"Do you stock something called carfentanil?" Chief asked.

Nick's eyes went wide. "Elephant tranquilizer? No. I would have no need for that. I work with horses and cattle occasionally, but not anything of the size and weight to justify that."

Alexis studied the stances of the men. "What's going on? Why are you following this line of questioning?"

Jeremy's young face looked like he'd aged several years in the last day. "There was an overdose a couple days ago. Our EMTs gave three doses of Narcan." He turned to Alexis. "It's like an antidote for opioids, only it didn't work. We just got confirmation that the death was due to elephant tranquilizer."

Nick leaned forward. "Was it mixed with heroin?"

Chief lifted his head in surprise. "How did you know that?"

"My brother worked for the DEA. That combination of drugs seems to be one of the latest highs sought after and also one of the more dangerous. Even in school, when we had to handle carfentanil, we needed to wear protective gear. In its pure form, it can be absorbed through the skin or by inhalation." He shook his head. "It's ten thousand times more potent than morphine. They put a miniscule amount in the heroin. But even then, the risk of overdosing, of having a bad reaction…" His voice trailed off, laced with concern.

The chief's stance relaxed. "The DEA? Where's your brother stationed?"

"He's not. Drug runners killed him a couple years ago."

Alexis barely registered the noises in the background. Even the dogs seemed to know to quiet down and give Nick his space. So his brother had died trying to get lethal drugs off the street.

A loud crash shook the ground. The back half of the veterinary hospital's roof had collapsed. She wanted to cry for Nick. The strain on his face suggested that if one more thing went wrong, he would break.

"Doc Kendrick!" Marla, a woman Alexis recognized from church, rushed up in a rain jacket, baseball cap, T-shirt and polka-dot pajama pants. "We've got volunteers coming to take care of the animals. What else do you need me to do?"

Nick's eyes hardened. He pointed at the barely smoldering fire behind them. "Our main concern is smoke inhalation. Ask the volunteers to give the dogs baths and let them sleep inside, preferably with a humidifier." Marla's scrunched up face matched Alexis's confusion. "It'll help them cough up anything in their lungs," Nick added. "After that…well, we'll take it a day at a time."

The chief waved Nick to come out of the pen. Marla took his place as four more women and three men rushed to the scene. Nick gave them a small wave of thanks, then stepped aside to let them take it from there.

"Doc, hold up." Marla spun around. "I found volunteers for all the animals we've boarded, but I didn't know anything about this young Lab. Any medical considerations before I find her a place to stay?"

"She comes with me," Nick said. Marla led Raven out of the pen with a leash someone had brought over. He accepted the leash and led her closer to the cops.

Alexis didn't understand why he wouldn't want to let a volunteer take care of her. Didn't he have enough to deal with as it was? Or did he think she wanted to take care of the dog? He would be sorely mistaken. "Is this because I haven't reached Theresa yet? I've left messages."

"Raven's a detection canine. Her nasal care will be a priority so her sniffing ability isn't hindered. Until we get word from Theresa, I'd prefer to keep an eye on her myself."

Nick joined the officers, but before the chief could say another word, Alexis rushed in. "Wait a second. Jeremy, why'd you even bring up elephant tranquilizers? Where is the silver Outback? I called you about the suspicious car, and you said you'd send someone. What happened?"

"Officer Sanders did a drive-by, Lexi. He didn't—"

"It's Alexis," she interjected.

The chief and Jeremy shared a conspiratorial look as if she was overreacting. Well, she'd tried to get people to call her by her real name since she'd been back. And after the night she'd had, it was the least they could do to acknowledge her by her legal, adult name instead of the nickname she'd had as a child.

"Okay, Alexis," Chief said slowly. "None of my men saw a silver Outback at the scene. We need to ask about the tranquilizer since Nick is a veterinarian and the only witness to the alleged drugs on—" he looked around for eavesdroppers "—the mayor's property."

"I don't see how that's relevant," Alexis said.

The chief leaned backward and swung forward as if gearing up to tell her off. Instead he just blew out a breath of frustration. "I'm not accusing the man of anything, Lex—Alexis. I'm just gathering information."

She would've taken a deep breath herself, but the wind had shifted and smoke tendrils were heading their way. "Well, how about gathering more information on the fire, then?"

Her mother had always told her she would make the perfect lawyer because the instinct to argue came to the surface in a heartbeat, but Alexis thought there was more to it than that. She gave in to the impulse when she advocated for someone, not only for the sake of debating. Nick tilted his head, studying her, but with no obvious emotion other than curiosity.

Chief raised an eyebrow. "Do you have more to tell me?"

"Yes. I saw a figure—a shadow running to the build…" She faltered. "Never mind. It was probably Keri running back inside to get the animals before someone blocked her in. And even if it was the person who barred the door and set the fire, I didn't see any identifying characteristics."

Though it did mean that whoever started the fire saw Keri run back into the building before blocking her in. On purpose. Why would someone do that? Surely whoever did this didn't mistake Keri for Nick. While it was possible they thought Nick was still inside the animal hospital, why not wait for the girl to leave? Unless… Nick wasn't the target.

"What is it?" Nick put a hand on her shoulder. "You look as if you've figured something out."

"Chief, you said that there was a hit-and-run. Both Joe and Raven were inside that car, right? Raven was also inside my car when the brakes went out, and she was inside the animal hospital when the fire started. Maybe the arsonist wasn't trying to kill Keri or Nick. Maybe they were out for Raven."

Chief raised an eyebrow. "That's an awful lot of speculation without any facts."

Nick's face became animated. "Chief, you said yourself that Raven was going to be a gift that the town could never afford in the budget. In the next county alone, drug detection dogs sniffed out almost five million dollars in drugs within eight years. I know we're a small town, but we're also next to the interstate—The Corridor."

Jeremy's eyes widened. "We haven't looked at it from that angle."

Chief flashed an aggravated expression at Jeremy and shook his head. "That doesn't seem plausible to me. You're trying to give yourself hope that you're not in danger, which is understandable. But I think we're dealing with more than someone who has it out for a dog. I hate to break it to you, Lexi, but in the dark, you and Keri have the same build and hair length. No one has any reason to want to harm Keri. But if we assume you and Nick are targets and they thought you were heading into the vet hospital, it stands to reason they would think Nick was already inside."

Nick took a step to the side and looked at her profile. He sighed. "I'm afraid he's right."

Dread weighed down her bones. She looked into Nick's eyes but addressed Chief. "You're saying we're still in danger."

The chief rubbed his forehead. "Do you two have somewhere you could go for the night? Somewhere in town most people wouldn't assume you'd be staying?"

In other words, they needed to hide.

SEVEN

Nick waited in the car as Alexis had suggested. He struggled to stay awake and probably wouldn't have succeeded if not for being keenly aware of how bad he smelled. Even his skin had the putrid scent of burnt plastic combined with wood and wet dog. Of course the last smell might have been due to the dog pressed up against his side in the backseat. At least she seemed to be breathing well.

Alexis opened the door at the back of the hotel. She leaned forward, a backpack looped over her shoulder, and looked both ways before she waved him to come toward her. He stepped out of her dad's car before grabbing the duffel bag of clothes and toiletries she had gathered for him at her parents' house before they'd left. By the time the firefighters and police were done with them, it'd been well past midnight.

Nick stepped through the entrance with Raven right by his side. He questioned whether he had the energy to make it through a shower before his head hit the pillow.

"I know the hotel receptionist from high school." She hustled him into an elevator and rapidly pressed the button to make the doors close. "She was willing to put our rooms under fake names."

"I'm pretty sure the button doesn't respond faster the more you press it."

She rolled her eyes. "But it makes me feel better."

Far be it from him to argue with that. He would do anything to feel better at the moment, but his problem was more physical than emotional. His entire body hurt from the cliff incident as well as the fire. He reckoned his emotions were too worn out to make themselves known.

Alexis's clothes and face showed the telltale signs of soot, the same as his, but somehow she still looked beautiful. "There's something I've been wondering about," he said.

She raised an eyebrow. "If after today you're wondering about only one thing, then something is wrong with you."

"No denying that." He smiled as the elevator jolted to a stop. "It's about you."

The doors opened and she stepped out into the hallway. "Oh?" She didn't slow her pace as she strode, glancing down at the numbers on the packet of keys she held and back up at the numbers listed on the doors.

"At the fire, you were quick to advocate for me." In his opinion, it hadn't gotten to the point of needing a defender, but he still appreciated the way she passionately took up his cause with the police. "It just made me wonder if you were reconsidering—"

Alexis stiffened and looked over her shoulder at him. "No." She shoved the key in the slot and waited for the light to switch to green. She turned the handle and opened the door. "I haven't changed my mind. I'm sorry I'm not up for going into more detail, but it's personal."

"I can honestly say that's the first time I've received the 'It's not you, it's me' line."

"You're welcome." She flashed a tired smile. "Everyone should hear that at least once in their lives. It's part of getting old."

"So you've experienced it?"

She looked at her shoes for a moment. "I plan on staying forever young." She kept her head down, but her eyelashes rose slowly until she met his gaze and smiled. She turned her hand over so he could take his keycard. "Good night, Nick."

He remained rooted to the floor as she gently closed the door. If he weren't in such an exhaustion-induced fog, he'd almost have believed she had flirted with him. Raven shook, her entire body resembling a giant spinning brush. What remaining droplets she had on her fur flung onto his exposed forearm, as if she was trying to tell him he was way off base.

It was enough to snap him out of his stupor. "Let's get both of us cleaned up and pass out." First order of business was to take his clothes and tie them up in a hotel laundry bag. He couldn't wait to smell something other than fire-tainted clothes and hair.

By the time he'd separately bathed and dried off himself and Raven, it was almost two in the morning. Raven had a short sneezing fit after her shower, which was probably the best thing for her after the smoke exposure. Nick examined her once more, struggling to keep his eyes open. Confident she didn't need any more treatment, he passed out the moment his head hit the pillow.

Sleep came in fitful bursts as he woke up multiple

times after experiencing the horror of his business going up in flames all over again. He'd close his eyes and try to picture something nice, like the river flowing over rocks, but those dreams quickly morphed into a repeat performance of running with Alexis and Raven away from gunmen.

The moment six in the morning came, he gave up on trying to rest. He wouldn't get any answers about insurance until the holiday weekend was over. He wondered if there was an abandoned storefront that would serve as a makeshift practice. There would be so much to do next week. He needed a walk to clear his head.

Raven probably needed a break outside anyway. At least she seemed to have slept peacefully. Her breathing sounded normal, which was a relief.

He took the stairs to avoid other early risers. Using a back alley—the town seemed to have more alleys than streets—they walked to a drive-up coffee booth. The barista didn't mind and even gave Raven a dog treat. He was glad Raven had enjoyed a full meal before the fire.

He loved the small, laid-back town, and such a small gesture was an example of why. There would be a long journey ahead to rebuild his practice at the same time he was campaigning for mayor. The thought overwhelmed him enough that he put it out of his mind. With two lattes and breakfast sandwiches in his hands, he returned the way he'd traveled, on high alert for anyone who might be watching him. The dog seemed relaxed, though, all the way to the room.

Only when he felt certain he heard Alexis moving around did he knock on the connecting door. She wrenched it open. She was dressed in sweats herself, and her hair stuck up and out in every direction. Her wide eyes gazed at Raven. "Everybody okay?" She noticed the two cups in his hands. "My hero." She grabbed one and greedily sipped it before her face flushed. "I'm sorry. Did it matter which one I took?"

He'd yet to meet someone who needed coffee in the morning as badly as he did. All those late nights studying in veterinary school had conditioned him to need it before functioning, even before getting dressed in the morning. He supposed law school had a similar effect on her. "Either one." He grinned. "You can go back to sleep."

"No." She shook her head. "I was having a nightmare when you knocked."

Nick sobered. The noise he'd heard had been her thrashing in a nightmare? It served as a reminder that they needed to be proactive to get their lives back. He waved his hand at the breakfast sandwiches on the table in his room. "Since we both can't sleep…"

She left the connecting door open and eagerly sat down to eat.

He took a seat at the small desk on the opposite side of the room and pointed to the paper and pen. In small towns, sometimes an officer who had a knack for drawing would volunteer in a dual role as forensic artist, but to his knowledge, the Barings police wasn't that fortunate. "How about we try again to sketch the drug scout? Tell me everything you remember."

She swallowed and stared up at the ceiling. "He looked like an out-of-work cowboy."

Maybe this wasn't going to be as useful as he'd hoped. "I don't remember cowboy boots."

"No. They were brown work boots. But his stance, the faded jeans plus the green-and-brown flannel shirt made me think of it. Thin brown hair that was starting to recede emphasized his round face. No five-o'clock shadow, but he had stubble over his upper lip. I don't remember the color of his eyes, just that they were a little too close together and had nothing in them but coldness." Her voice shook slightly. She stared at the curtains but seemed lost in her memories.

If she thought about it anymore her fear might increase, so Nick broke in, "I think we remember him the same way. I can take it from here."

She stood and shook her head. "No. I think it would help if I could get him out of my mind. We should both try to draw our own versions, then compare notes. If we are in agreement, we can take it to the chief, they can put out an alert and maybe this whole thing will finally be over."

It wasn't a bad idea. "Only if you let me be the one to sign it."

"You want to take credit for my artwork?"

He ignored her attempt at a joke. "I don't want you to be a target anymore."

She shook her head. "Like it or not, we were both on that property. We are in this together. It's my fault you're even in this mess."

"I was the one who peeked in the gutters," he argued. As far as he could tell, no good would come if they focused on fault-finding.

She pointed at Raven. "You can thank her for the gutters tip." She held up the cup of coffee. "But I thank you for this." She shuffled to her side of the door but didn't close it.

Nick shut his eyes, trying to recreate fully his memory of the scout who'd started this whole mess. He sketched, erased and tried again. Minutes turned into hours. Raven's soft snores and the sound of the pen strokes were the only noises except for distant vacuuming down the hallway.

"Nick," Alexis cried. "This is horrible." She ran into the room and held up her phone. "Theresa called in the middle of the night. My Do Not Disturb setting automatically comes on at night, and I missed it!" She shivered. "Listen." She pressed the speaker button on her phone's voice mail feature.

Nick jumped up and went to her side, wondering how to comfort her as he listened.

"Alexis, something's happened." The woman hiccupped and sniffed. "We need to talk immediately. In person. I got your message. I think you might be in danger, honey." The crashing of small items and a shuffling of papers could be heard in the background. "Where are my stupid time cards?" The sound of glass smashing blasted through the phone speaker. Alexis flinched, even though it had to be the second time she'd heard it. The message abruptly ended.

Alexis bit her lip. "I'm worried something's happened to her."

Nick barely registered her words. The only thing that stuck in his mind was what Theresa had said on the message: *I think you might be in danger.*

"Let's go. You can call the police on our way." He grabbed the dog and ushered Alexis out the door.

Alexis shoved the keys at Nick as her other hand held the phone to her ear. "She's still not answering." She looked at her phone and pulled up the number Theresa had called from. "She used her office landline, not her cell, so we know she came back into town. Let's start there." She dialed the police, rattled off the address of the office and repeated the information to the dispatcher.

She directed him as he slowed at the front of the storefront of the employment office. "Park in the back." The side mirror showed an empty street behind them, but she didn't want to risk leading the drug runners to Theresa's place.

Nick pulled into one of the spaces behind the strip of local businesses. One building down, a sprinkling of shattered glass from Theresa's employee entrance was spread across the pavement. Alexis's heart jolted. "Theresa." She shoved open the passenger car door before Nick had shifted into Park.

"Alexis, wait!"

She couldn't wait. Theresa had called her. She'd needed help, and Alexis had slept through it. She had the good sense to pull her sweatshirt sleeve down over her hand as she wrenched open the door. Unlocked. Of course.

"Someone could still be in there," Nick hollered as he caught up.

"Don't touch anything. If someone stole Theresa's stuff—" Her feet crunched on the broken glass on the tile floor.

Straight ahead, Theresa's broken body lay in the middle of the floor on the cheap gray commercial carpet.

Alexis's throat closed, so tight and painful she could hardly breathe. Her legs refused to move forward.

"I'm calling for an ambulance." Nick passed her and crouched down at Theresa's side.

"Is she…?" Alexis couldn't speak her fear aloud.

He stood up, his face pinched. She knew the truth as he approached. She understood, but she couldn't believe it until he said it. Nick put his hand on her shoulder and turned her around.

"She wouldn't have wanted you to see her like that," he whispered.

Alexis choked on a sob as Nick led her outside the building and back to the car. "We need to wait for the police," he said softly. She left the car door open, her feet on the ground, as she sank onto the car seat and fought to hold the tears back. Raven climbed over the console and tried to rest her head on Alexis's shoulder.

The caring that came from an animal, of all things, was her undoing. The warmth helped the tears break. Nick reached around her to open the glove box and found a box of tissues. Her mom had always kept Dad's car well stocked.

Nick remained standing but put a hand on her shoulder. He opened his mouth as if to say something when sirens approached. Two officers she recognized from the mayor's property and one of the EMTs from last night barely gave them a second glance as they charged inside.

"H-how did…?"

Nick swallowed. "I'm not a—"

"Then give me your best guess. Please." She knew he wasn't a doctor, but he had eyes.

He avoided her gaze and crouched down. His hand moved to her wrist. "Did she have any medical problems?"

"Asthma."

He frowned. "Any legitimate medical reason to use a syringe?"

"No." Her breathing grew ragged. She shook her head. "No. Theresa was a health nut. What are you not telling me?"

One officer came out of the office and approached. "Were you the ones who called it in?"

Nick stood. "Yes, Officer." He explained about the voice mail Alexis had received, presumably so she wouldn't have to talk.

The officer looked over Nick's shoulder. "Could you save a copy of the message and send it to our main email address?"

"Of course." Alexis pulled her phone out and went through the motions as the officer rattled off the address. She blinked rapidly as the message sent, trying to force her mind to work properly. "What do you think happened to her?" she asked.

The officer shuffled his feet and looked out into the trees behind the parking spaces. "I can't say. There will be an investigation and a toxicology report. But, unofficially, it looks just like an overdose we had the other day."

Alexis hopped to her feet. Her heart jumped to her throat. "No. Theresa would never use drugs." She sought out Nick's gaze. "She wouldn't." She pointed at the door. "What about the broken window?"

"Like I said, there will be an investigation."

A cherry-red BMW pulled into the lot and parked roughly ten spaces down. Dr. Bill Tindale worked in the small clinic inside the final building at the end.

He got out of the car, frown lines etched on his otherwise handsome face. He spotted Alexis, and his eyes widened. A familiar face served as a balm at the moment. She waved at him, and he strode over. "Alexis, what happened?"

"It's Theresa." She poured out the story again. "Please tell them this wasn't an accident. Can you go in and tell—"

The officer held up a hand. "I'm sorry, Doctor. I can't let you—"

"I understand," Dr. Tindale said. He put an arm around Alexis's shoulders. "I'm afraid this isn't my area of expertise. But if there is anything I can do to help—"

It might've been her imagination or the grief, but it looked like Nick tensed. She didn't take time to analyze it, though. "Were you about to go into the clinic?"

He nodded and removed his arm. "Yes. I just wanted to catch up on some charts and paperwork."

She pointed over his shoulder in the direction of the dermatology clinic's employee entrance. "You have a security system. A security camera?"

"Yes, we do," he said eagerly as if just remembering it himself. He gestured toward the officer. "You're welcome to look through our footage." The officer seemed relieved and pulled out a notebook to write something down. Dr. Tindale reached for Alexis's hand and gave it a gentle squeeze. "You have my number, Alexis. Don't hesitate to use it, okay?"

Her cheeks heated under the intense scrutiny. "Thank you... Bill." She'd never called him by his first name before, despite the many times he'd asked, but he was going to be the answer to catching Theresa's killer. He beamed and gave a gentlemanly nod before he walked back to his clinic.

"Okay, so we'll get the tape," the officer said, almost

as if he was hinting for them to leave. Why wouldn't anyone acknowledge that this wasn't an overdose?

"Tell me this," Alexis said. "Why would a woman who drinks kale smoothies instead of coffee, eats carob instead of chocolate, and runs an air purifier in both her workplace and home ever choose to put drugs in her body?" She held up a hand and swallowed another sob threatening to overtake her. "No. If she died from an overdose, it was by force."

Nick put a hand on her back. "Maybe we should let them work." He said the words softly. "I'm sure Jeremy would be willing to give you updates if you asked him."

She whirled to Nick. "We're on the same page, though, right? This was murder. You heard the glass breaking at the end of the message."

"We can't offer any statements, ma'am." The officer looked as if he'd rather go back inside to the murder scene.

"Listen. She'd left on a romantic weekend with someone from town. The man, whoever she was dating, he might know something."

"You don't know who this man is?"

She deflated. "No. They were keeping their relationship discreet."

The officer didn't look convinced. The second officer stepped outside. "We found her landline and identification but no cell phone." He pointed at them. "Did you see a cell phone when you found the deceased?"

Alexis sucked in a sharp breath. The deceased? She had a name. Her hands fisted. This was her boss, her friend…

"No," Nick answered. "Other than the landline on her desk, I didn't see any phones." He pressed his hand at the small of Alexis's back and gently guided her to the car. "You have our phone numbers and names if you need us. Can we go?"

The first officer nodded and joined the second in conversation. How could they stand there as if nothing had happened? Nick closed the door once she was seated and walked around to the driver's side. As soon as he started the car, her stomach tightened, not appreciating that breakfast sandwich after all. "You didn't answer the question. Do you agree with me?"

"After the last twenty-four hours, I don't claim to know anything, but—" he turned the car in the direction of the hotel "—someone with asthma would've been at increased risk of overdose. I didn't know her, but I trust your opinion of her."

She pressed her back against the seat. His trust should've soothed her in some way. Instead, it just reminded her that her opinion of people couldn't be trusted. Could Theresa have been into drugs? No. Although Theresa had admitted to loneliness in the past. Maybe the new mystery man led her down the wrong path. The heart could be deceitful.

"So, are you and the doctor…?"

"Uh, no."

"Sorry. He just seemed…extra friendly."

"Well, it wasn't your imagination. He has been, and I've turned him down flat. Many times. I have no intention of dating anyone in town when I don't plan to be here permanently." Besides, she sometimes temped in his practice, and it seemed weird.

"Makes sense," he said drily.

"But Theresa was dating someone in town, and we need to find the guy. We need to get answers."

She watched Nick's profile. He remained stoic, without a nod of agreement. Why was she trying to include him? Theresa's death might not have anything to do with what happened to them yesterday, but it did involve drugs. "Is your number one agenda as mayor to pull drugs off the street?"

He blinked in surprise as he turned into the hotel parking lot. "Won't do any good if we're not helping people at the same time. At the bare minimum, I want a resource officer at the schools and some kind of community program to help users get the rehab and counseling they need."

Right now she wanted only justice. She wanted the dealers and runners to pay, to be punished. Nick said dealers had killed his brother. "Are you running for mayor for yourself or your brother?" The question slipped out before she could filter it.

He shrugged. "Does it matter?"

"Don't you want revenge?" She blinked rapidly, hot tears trying to escape.

A heavy sigh escaped him as he sagged and closed his eyes. "Not on good days."

"Is today a good day?" She hated the way these antagonistic questions slipped out. She wanted to chase this horrible sorrow and helpless feeling away. She wanted him to get angry, be angry, with her so it would hurt less.

He opened his brown eyes and looked at her with compassion. Her bottom lip trembled. She couldn't handle sympathy right now or she'd fall apart, without any hope of pulling herself back together again.

He laid a hand on her wrist. "No. It's not a good day." His touch eased her swirling emotions just enough that she could blink back the tears. He was struggling, too, and didn't offer platitudes to gloss over it. She should've felt guilty that she'd likely pulled him down to her emotional level, but instead she felt exceedingly grateful.

"The only thing I know to do," he said, "is to put one foot in front of the other and do the next right thing." He turned to stare into her eyes. "I don't go a day without thinking of it."

A shiver went down her spine. Her hand twitched. She was tempted to flip her palm over and hold hands with him.

He removed his touch and leaned back in his seat. "Doing something productive usually helps," he said. "I would like to spend some more time trying to sketch out what I remember about that scout guy, but I don't want to ask that of you right now."

"No, that'd be good." He was right. They stepped out of the car. She needed something constructive to do, or she was going to go mad.

Nick walked Raven to a small grassy area while Alexis waited at the hotel door. She needed to shower and get dressed for the day. The temperatures were climbing fast, and the sweats were beginning to add to her discomfort. Every time she thought her life couldn't get worse…

"Did you want to call anyone?" Nick asked. "You can take the car and go to a friend's house while I stay at the hotel."

She shook her head. Because the truth was, she had no one. Not anymore. She'd been shunned by most of her lawyer friends back in Seattle, and she'd alienated everyone but Theresa when she'd come back to town.

Even Theresa didn't know how she'd lost her job. She hadn't even asked.

The elevator opened on the second floor. Raven lifted her head and touched her snout to Alexis's hand. Normally she would have flinched and been annoyed at a dog's touch, but she didn't mind at the moment. Raven seemed to understand her emotions. It was probably a rare trait in a dog.

Shuffling behind Nick down the hall, she saw his spine stiffen. Raven made a guttural sound.

"What is it?"

"Call the police," he whispered.

She peeked around him. Her hotel door was slightly ajar. "Maybe it's housekeeping, or I didn't close it fully."

Nick tugged on the leash so Raven would step closer to him. "There's no housekeeping cart, and we both left the hotel through my door, not yours."

The moment he said it, she knew he was right. She dialed the number right away as they walked in the opposite direction of their rooms. "I think someone might be in my hotel room."

"Address?" the dispatcher asked.

Was she joking? There was only one hotel in their small town. She rattled off the name and cross streets.

"What's your room number? We've already received a call about two hotel rooms. A unit is already en route," the dispatcher said.

Alexis frowned. Two other hotel rooms? Her heart sped up. What was the likelihood after everything happening in the past twenty-four hours that two other rooms had been robbed? She looked up and down the hallway. All the other doors were closed. She clicked the phone off. Someone had called in their rooms, but only one of their hotel doors was ajar, which meant...

Nick's forehead wrinkled. "What?"

She strode back toward her room. "Something doesn't seem right." Her mind was so jumbled she couldn't put it into words. At the moment, she felt like she had nothing to lose.

"Alexis!" Nick warned her.

She ignored him and shoved past him.

"At least let me peek first."

"I have a weapon," he called out. Of course he didn't, but if people were in the room, it might make them think twice and leave from the other room.

She peeked around his shoulder from the doorway. The sunlight streamed through the gap in the heavy curtains, and the three lamps in the room were all on.

But not a single person was in the room.

She strode past him. The bed sheets were in disarray, exactly as she'd left them. Her backpack sat on the couch, open. The clothes inside looked jumbled, not folded as she remembered. She strode to the desk. The drawing she'd started to sketch was missing.

Clarity hit her over the head. She spun around to tell Nick to check his room, but he was too busy being led by Raven, who was sniffing frantically at the dresser. Raven barked and sat down.

As a drug-sniffing K9 in training, it could mean only one thing. "We've been set up."

EIGHT

Nick grabbed a couple of tissues and used them to prevent leaving fingerprints as he pulled the drawer open. Two small bags of white powder and two syringes sat neatly inside. He suspected it was several hundred dollars' worth of heroin. He stepped backward. "I can't believe this."

"Please don't tell me it's what I think it is." Alexis ran to his side and put a hand over her mouth.

Raven put her nose to the carpet and pulled him through the connecting door into his own hotel room. He let her lead until she sniffed near the refrigerator and stood on her hind legs, her nose up in the air. She sat down and sneezed.

Odd. He opened the minifridge. Nothing.

"We need to get out of here, Nick." Alexis stood in the doorway with her backpack slung over her shoulder. She looked past him to his desk and strode across the room. "Your sketch is gone, too."

Great. Hours of work, stolen. Nick pulled open the microwave. Nothing there. Maybe Raven had lost her touch, but she lifted her head again as if pointing. "If someone is framing me, I'd like to know exactly what I supposedly did."

On the countertop, he used the tissues again as he opened the lid of the coffeemaker where the water was to be poured. A clear glass vial about three inches long was propped up on its side. He reached for it and stopped. He leaned forward and squinted at the printed label. "Carfentanil." A wave of nausea rushed through him at the sight. He blew out a breath and closed the lid softly. "We need to go into the hall."

In veterinary school, he'd handled the drug only once. And even then, they wore protective outer coverings, masks and goggles. One drop of pure, undiluted carfentanil, either inhaled or touched had the potential to kill multiple people. He'd heard that there was a new trend for drug dealers to lace heroin with fentanyl, another dangerous and potentially deadly opioid, but carfentanil was an entirely differently matter. "Call the police."

"I did, remember? They're already on their way, but they're not coming to help us, Nick. I have a feeling all these little presents we're finding are connected to Theres—" Emotion overtook her voice. She shook her head. "Let's go." She picked up the duffel bag of her dad's clothes, zipped it and threw it at him.

He lunged for it and caught one of the handles with his left hand. "Careful! If that had hit the coffeemaker, we'd have much bigger problems. At least the vial is closed. We should just tell the police what happened."

She raised an eyebrow. "Do you think you're going to have a chance at winning the mayor's office if you've been arrested for drug possession?"

"But I'm not possessing it! And I think it'll hurt my campaign if I leave."

She flicked her index finger at him. "You have the means and the opportunity."

"No motive!"

"No? Seems to me you tried to pin this on our current mayor?"

"I did no such thing."

"I believe you, but I'm trying to show you what could happen." She shoved her index finger toward her collarbone. "And I'm a lawyer who has been working entry-level jobs and probably needs to sell this heroin for the money. See? I'm telling you, they've got enough to hold us. I say we be proactive and clear our names. Let's at least go somewhere we can sketch out this scout picture and then regroup. I'm not waiting around for them to decide we should be arrested. If they come to that conclusion, hopefully I'll have found something to clear our names by then."

Her reasoning was attacking his first instinct to stay and reasonably plead his case to the local authorities. She strode past him and opened the door. "I'm going with or without you. I need to know who is behind this, for Theresa's sake."

He followed her to the stairway. "At the very least, will you call the police and be up front about what we found? Pass on the strict instructions on how to handle the carfentanil. They could die packaging the evidence if they decide to open it and take a sniff."

She eyed him for a second. "You can talk to them in the car."

They raced downstairs and out the back door. "What I don't understand is how someone found us," he said.

"We were very careful to make sure no one followed us here." He barely made it inside the vehicle before she turned the key in the ignition. She sped through the parking lot and turned into a back alley.

Gravel pummeled the bottom of the car, making rattling noises as she drove. "Two thoughts come to mind," she said. "Someone might've recognized my parents' sedan in the parking lot." She shook her head. "But that seems very unlikely to me. It's been in the garage for months, and they don't so much as have an air freshener hanging from the mirror. No identifying factors unless someone has the resources to look up license plates easily."

"The mayor makes that a possibility."

"Nick, you're starting to sound like a broken record. The chief isn't the mayor's puppet. More likely, my high school reunion in the lobby was cause for gossip, despite asking my so-called friend to keep it quiet. In this town, it's hard to keep a secret." She inhaled and shook her head. "I should've known."

Nick wondered if she'd had secrets of her own spread through town before. He didn't come from a small town, but he knew the same could be true of the little communities within cities, especially in a college setting.

He knew from experience, and he never wanted to be the source of that kind of gossip again.

She took a sudden turn, and her eyes focused on the rearview mirror. The force of her turn sent Raven into his lap. He barely kept his head from hitting the side window. "Do you know where you're going?"

"The only place where no one would think to look."

"And that is?"

"Raven's home."

That would mean going to the handler's house. "The police said Joe's in intensive care in Boise."

She nodded. "I still have the key from when I picked up Raven."

"That's probably a good idea. I imagine Raven is pretty hungry by now."

Alexis paled. "I hadn't thought of that. I'm such a horrible dog sitter."

She turned into another alley and barreled past trash cans and bushes until she turned into a small carport and slammed on the brakes. The moment the car was still, Nick moved to check on Raven's stitches. "Good," he murmured.

She opened the door for him. "Come on. I don't want to be out in the open long. I'm sure no one is looking for us yet, but neighbors will take notice if we're not careful. If the rumor mill starts operating, we'll be in trouble."

"I have nothing to hide." He stood up straight. "And I'm not going to start acting like I do."

Alexis stepped up to the back door and unlocked it. Raven tugged on the leash, and Nick let her lead the way. Sure enough, she ran for the full food dish set beside the washing machine.

He closed the door behind him. In the modest but clean home, the room adjoining the laundry room was filled with dog toys and training tools. Alexis made a beeline to the living room, where she found a desk and pulled out papers and pens. "We might not have much time."

"We haven't called the police yet," Nick said.

She took out her phone and pulled up Jeremy's contact information. "I think I'd rather text him right now than give him a chance to tell me to come in."

Nick looked over her shoulder as she typed:

I called the police when I saw my hotel room was broken into. We spotted planted drug paraphernalia in our hotel rooms and got out of there to let police handle it.

"Only a lawyer would type out *paraphernalia* in a text."

She eyed him. "Do you want to do this?"

Nick tried not to smile at her response. The day had been filled with sorrow and stress. He needed to control his coping instincts to deflect and joke around. Especially since he enjoyed teasing her entirely too much. He dictated the important pieces of information as she texted:

Check the coffeemaker but wear protective goggles and gloves. We haven't touched any of it.

Her phone buzzed right after she pressed Send.

Where are you now?

She clicked the phone off. "I'm not going to give him a chance to tell me something I don't want to hear."

His gut turned to stone. She'd shut the phone off on a cop.

She gestured to the dining room table. "I think we should get drawing."

His nerves were shot. He rummaged in the cabinets until he found a drinking glass and got himself some water. Surely Raven's handler wouldn't mind if he did that. When this was all done, he might even go down and visit the guy in the hospital.

At the moment, it felt like this nightmare would never be finished. He turned around to face Alexis and leaned against the sink. Maybe if they understood why someone would murder her boss, then they would have a clue who planted evidence in their rooms. "Why would someone want to hurt Theresa?"

Alexis let her head drop so that her hair covered her face. At the sound of a sniff, he filled another glass of water and brought it to her. She drank greedily and wiped the gathering tears from her eyes. "I have no idea why anyone would want to."

She looked on the edge of collapse, but her determined glare made it clear she wouldn't be taking a rest. He picked up the pen and began sketching again. She followed his example. He took extra care to make it look more like the beady-eyed man who had started this mess and less like a turtle.

Minutes passed with only the sounds of swiping pens on the paper. Alexis straightened and flicked her hair back over her shoulder. Her drawing captured the essence of the man they'd seen. He pushed his paper closer so that they were side by side.

"You got his nose and face shape better," she remarked.

"But you got the eyes and mouth exactly right." He passed over his sketch, and they worked for another hour, combining their two sketches and making small changes until they both agreed they had it right.

He stood up, his back tight, and stretched his arms

toward the ceiling. "I think that's the best we're going to do."

"Agreed. I'll send it in." She turned her phone's power back on, and it vibrated like crazy. Notifications of text messages and voice mails flashed on her screen. "I'm going to ignore those for a moment." She aimed the camera's phone at their artwork and snapped a photo. "Sending this to Jeremy."

The phone buzzed again. She stared at it. "He's calling. Should I answer it?"

It'd been only a couple of hours, but Nick was ready to stop hiding. The lack of sleep from the night before was catching up with him. He desperately wanted a nap, and the couch in the living room looked inviting, especially with Raven asleep on the rug in front of it. Sleep often helped him process things, and after the past couple of days, he needed a whole lot of processing. "Yes. Take the call."

She nodded and pressed the speakerphone.

"Alexis, where'd you get this photo?" An older man's voice came through loud and clear.

"Chief?" Her eyebrows rose. Apparently the chief had used Jeremy's phone. "Are you referring to the sketch of the drug scout I sent in?"

"I'm referring to the man I found dead from an apparent overdose twenty minutes ago. They appear to be one and the same."

Nick grabbed the edge of the chair to steady himself. The scout was dead? It seemed highly unlikely that the scout would die from an overdose. Usually those guys didn't touch the merchandise so they could be used as chase bait without charges worse than a traffic violation.

Nick leaned over and spoke into the phone. "Did

you get the scout's phone? Could you tell us if he sent our photograph to anyone else? You could figure that out, right?"

The hope that the danger might all be over, that he could begin to rebuild his practice without having to look over his shoulder, filled him with hope.

"Mr. Kendrick is with you, then." Chief Spencer sighed. "Why don't you come in, Lexi, and I'd be glad to discuss everything with both of you."

Alexis pursed her lips and frowned. "Okay." She hit the End Call button. "Soon," she added. Her eyes steeled. "If the scout is dead, then why would they plant those drugs in our room? We can't identify anyone else."

"Maybe because we spotted the drugs at the mayor's house? We're still a threat."

She worried her lip. "Perhaps…but no, that still doesn't make sense to me. The mayor isn't going to get charged with anything. The drugs weren't there when the police arrived."

Nick stared at the ceiling. "Maybe Theresa's killer knew that once an investigation happened, it would become clear that it was murder and not an overdose."

"Then they would want to misdirect the police. Frame someone." She leaned forward. "What if the scout didn't willingly overdose? What if he was killed by the same thing that was sitting in our hotel room?"

He groaned. "Carfentanil."

She began pacing the room. "Why would the killer want to take out the scout in the first place?"

"Easy. We spotted him, which made him a risk to their operation and expendable. Plus, the killer could've seen the sketches in our room when he planted the drugs. Maybe he realized we were getting close."

She pivoted on her foot and faced him. "So why frame us?"

"Somehow they think we're still a risk. Maybe we've seen something else or—"

"—or might figure something out that they don't want us to know. I think we need to start by finding Theresa's mystery man."

"Won't the police do that?" Nick asked.

"Not if they take the easy way out and focus on the overdose theory. You said yourself that it looks like an overdose. They won't act on anything else until an autopsy. It'll take time for them to figure out it was murder. Thankfully, we're not waiting in a prison cell on possession charges while they puzzle through it." She crossed her arms over her chest. "The only way they know there is a mystery man is that I told them. Are they going to believe me after I had drugs in my hotel room?" She shook her head. "Theresa didn't want the whole town to know she was involved with someone local."

"It sounds like you knew her well. You must have some idea who she was seeing."

She shook her head mournfully. "No, but I have an idea of where to start looking."

Alexis reached for the leash but didn't see Nick's outstretched hand until their fingers bumped over the nylon. Heat rushed up her arm, and she yanked it back. "Probably a better idea for you to take her." The view from the window showed nothing but bushes, trees and houses. "It's clear. I'll drive."

She drove in silence, taking a roundabout way to Theresa's house to make sure they weren't being followed. It was pretty easy as there weren't many cars on the road. Anyone who hadn't traveled for the holiday weekend was probably at the End of Summer celebration happening at the park on the outskirts of town.

She took the closest alley to get to the backside of Theresa's house without using the street. Like many of the older houses in town, Theresa had a carport instead of a garage. The house next door belonged to a family Alexis knew went out of town for every holiday weekend. She parked the car in their carport just in case the police drove by and wondered why there was a car at Theresa's house.

Nick clicked his tongue and Raven stayed close as they walked together. Nick's stomach growled so loudly that Alexis flinched. His sheepish grin almost gave her the giggles.

"Sorry," he said. "We missed lunch."

Judging by the colors in the sky and her hunger pangs, they were getting close to missing dinner, as well. They reached Theresa's back door, and Alexis stuck her hand into the flowerpot to retrieve the extra key, but her fingertips found only loose soil. She took a knee to make sure she was looking in the right place.

Nick touched her shoulder. "Alexis," he whispered. "I think someone is already in there."

"What? Who?"

He shrugged and shook his head.

Her skin electrified as all her senses heightened. Who, other than the police, would be in Theresa's house? She straightened and tiptoed to the side window. A lone lamp was on, and a shadow crossed the room. "Not the cops," she whispered.

A guttural sob seeped through the thin windowpane. She met Nick's alarmed expression. "Someone is hurting in there." Nick grabbed the doorknob, and it turned easily.

"Wait," she cried. Raven and Nick rushed ahead of her.

She followed him inside, several paces back. Nick's spine stiffened as he reached the entrance to the living room. Alexis quickened her pace until she could look around him.

There, in the middle of Theresa's faded navy couch, Mayor Gerald's shoulders shook over the teddy bear clutched in his hands as he cried.

"You?" The word slipped out of her mouth before she could stop herself.

Gerald startled. His mouth hung open as tears ran down his cheeks. Confusion clouded his features. "Lexi?"

She pushed past Nick and Raven to face him. "You were her mystery guy?" She tried to recall everything Theresa had said about him. "You?" she said again. He was the last person she could imagine with Theresa.

Gerald leaned forward and pulled out a tissue from the box on the coffee table. He wiped his eyes. "I've known her forever. I've always—" He choked on his words and took several deep breaths. "She was the love of my life."

"Do the police know?" Nick spoke up behind her.

Gerald shook his head. "They can't help. I never should've taken—I—" His bottom lip wavered.

The renewed sorrow of losing Theresa washed over Alexis. She fought the tears back. "She didn't die of an overdose." She steeled her voice.

Gerald's head dropped. "I know."

"You had heroin on your property," Nick said.

Gerald raised an eyebrow but didn't make eye contact. He closed his lips and shook his head. "You should go," he whispered.

Fury swirled in her gut and threatened to be unleashed. This man knew Theresa hadn't died of an overdose but admitted it in such a nonchalant way? She wouldn't stand for it. "She was my friend. I want answers!"

"Well, you can't have them," Gerald shouted back.

Raven growled and appeared at her side. Nick put a hand on her arm. "Maybe we should have the police ask the questions, Alexis."

"That's a bad idea," Gerald said. He leaned back into the couch cushions, staring at the teddy bear still in his hands. "We were perfect for each other. I got her this in Boise before…" His voice trailed off, but he smiled sadly at Alexis. "We felt like kids again. She loved it."

In the distance, slamming doors could be heard. Gerald frowned. "She should've never died." His eyes lifted to meet Alexis's. "She wouldn't want you to be hurt, too. Go," he said.

Alexis turned to Nick in confusion. Nick's forehead scrunched, and he rushed to the front window. "Call the police. We've got men with guns."

"The cops won't make it in time." Gerald pointed to the left. "Go out the old back door. The one in the guest room."

"But our car is—"

"They'll have already seen it. Go. It opens right into the bushes. Most people don't even know it's there."

The house used to be smaller before she renovated it,

but Alexis didn't remember an old back door in there. "But you—"

"They won't hurt me, but I can't protect you. Go. For Theresa's sake, just go."

"Oh, is that so? Why won't they hurt you?" Her veins grew hot as her heart rate sped up. "Maybe because you're the ring leader of the drug operation?"

"Where's your truck?" Nick pressed. He had a phone pressed to his ear.

"Too far away for you to reach," Gerald responded with an eerie calm.

Nick spoke into the phone. "There are gunmen roaming the neighborhood." He listed the two closest cross streets and hung up.

"We don't have enough answers to go to the police yet," she told Nick.

"If they arrest these guys, maybe we don't need them." He tugged on her arm. "I have a feeling we should listen to Gerald, though, and get out of here while we have a chance. Come on."

She heard shouts outside and through one of the windows could see men approaching the car in the neighbor's carport, rifles in hand. The mayor didn't even move a muscle. "Just tell me this," she said. "If you loved her, why'd you give Theresa heroin? Even if I believed she wanted to get hit up—which I don't— you would've had to have known she had asthma. You meant to kill her." They couldn't leave without a single answer. They'd be back to square one.

"I didn't. It wasn't me." The mayor closed his eyes and leaned his head back. "Right now, keeping her friends alive is all that matters. Just leave."

She gritted her teeth. She wanted to grab him by the

shoulders and shake him until he told her who was behind Theresa's death.

Raven whined, and Nick grabbed Alexis's hand. His touch grounded her, and she knew she had to press past the swirling emotions and just stay alive. *For Theresa's sake.* Her tears threatened to escape. She focused on Nick's hand holding hers, reminding her to stay in the present moment.

He pulled her through the hallway and ran toward the first bedroom.

"No." She led him in the opposite direction. "That's her room." She couldn't bear to see Theresa's room without her in there. She pulled him to the guest room that she had stayed in once.

Nick ran for the first door he saw. It turned out to be a closet. "She's moved the bed," Alexis said. She pointed to where the bed used to be. The floral canvas that had hung above it was no longer there, either. The wall was covered with the same white vertical paneling as the rest of the room, but she realized she could see the outline of a very low door. It would have been covered by the canvas and headboard that had once been there.

Nick twisted the knob and had to push with some force before the door shoved open directly into hedges. No wonder Theresa kept it covered up. It wasn't a very practical place to have a door. Gerald had probably used it to visit Theresa while keeping their relationship a secret.

Nick couldn't open the door all the way, but Gerald had been right. It left them about one foot of space to squeeze outside. Nick took a step down onto the ground. Raven and Alexis quickly followed. She heard men running but could see no one. The foliage was too thick for them to hide inside the bushes, but if they were willing to endure some prickly branches, they could slide in between a set of them into the neighbor's yard. It was their only chance.

A man rounded the corner holding a rifle. Nick launched himself at the man, shoving the barrel up into the air. Raven's leash fell from his hand, but the dog stayed put.

The sound of a gunshot filled the air. A screech wrenched from her throat as she flinched, her hands over her head. Nick punched the man in the chin. The guy swung the barrel toward Nick's head. He evaded just enough that the rifle swished through the air half an inch over his forehead. Nick used the advantage to jab a fist into the guy's stomach and shove him backward.

Alexis didn't stand around and wait for the gunman to get back up. She dove through the bushes with Nick and Raven on her heels as the sound of another gunshot filled the air.

The sting from the scratching branches was hard to ignore, but she pumped her arms harder as she ran through the next backyard. Another gunshot sent her ducking. So far the only thing they'd accomplished was letting the rest of the drug ring know their location.

Within seconds, more gunmen would be on their way. Her first instinct was to hide behind the gas grill on the neighbor's patio and wait, but she knew if they did that, they would be dead meat. On either side of the yard was a hedge, but a five-foot-high cedar fence outlined the back border.

The men shouted at each other to surround the area.

Her breathing escalated. They were trapped.

NINE

Nick grabbed her hand and pulled her around the corner of the house and into a tight space between the wall and a freestanding shed. Raven stayed close to Alexis, despite the leash dragging on the ground. He picked it up and they all hid in the tiny, dim spot.

"So, what's the plan?" she whispered.

"What do you mean?" He spoke into her hair. It smelled like the hotel shampoo, with the faint scent of vanilla and sugar cookies. It was enough to make his stomach roil with hunger again. "This is the only idea I've got. I'm hoping they think we went through the other hedge and kept running."

"How is this any different than when we started? At this rate they can find us in ten seconds."

"We're outnumbered with nowhere to go," Nick said. "Do you have any better ideas?" Raven sat on her haunches and stuck her nose in the air. Her ears twitched and her hackles rose. "See that? It means help is on the way."

She squinted. "What?"

A half second later, sirens could be heard. Alexis looked momentarily impressed until she saw the smug grin Nick knew he sported. "Let's hope the gunmen hear it, too, and start running before you get all smug."

The sound of panting and quick footsteps approached. Whoever they were, they had to be on the other side of the bushes. He held up a finger for a moment until he felt certain they'd kept running.

"Attack," Alexis whispered to Raven.

Raven tilted her head.

"Go get 'em, girl." She shoved her finger in the direction they'd come.

The dog scratched her ear with her back paw.

Alexis huffed. "Shouldn't she attack?"

He shrugged. "It's possible she hasn't or won't be trained to do that. I only knew about her health." Their shoulders touched as they leaned against the side of the house. Tight spaces made his skin crawl. Raven sat on his shoes and leaned her body into his legs as if she was prepared to take a nap. He gave her leash a small tug to keep her upright in case they needed to run. The sirens grew closer.

Alexis shook her head. "I'm not ready to go into police custody. I'll talk to them on the phone, but once I step into the station, I won't get a chance to find out who killed Theresa. Besides, Gerald is clearly involved in this. Who's to say we won't be in more danger once we're at the station?"

She had a point. "You're the one that thought the mayor wasn't in the pocket of the police. I agree with you now."

"After it's clear he's involved? What's your proof they're not?"

He shrugged. "No proof, just a feeling."

"Feelings are misleading."

That was also true, but he didn't want to dissect or think about it any longer. They needed a plan. In his mind, it was more important to focus on proving their innocence. "Do you know how long it takes them to run things for fingerprints?"

"I'm a lawyer, not a cop."

Someone yelled over a megaphone, "Put your hands up or you risk being shot." A gunshot sounded and Alexis flinched. It seemed to have come from the opposite direction of the police car. "I hope Jeremy is okay."

An unbidden spark of jealousy flew through Nick at the caring tone she used for the officer. He wouldn't let himself think about it now.

"We have to get out of here." She scooted past him and chanced a look around the corner of the shed. "How high do you think that back fence is?"

Gunshots in the distance accompanied her question.

He grimaced. Scaling fences wasn't exactly on his wish list for the day. Every muscle in his body still hurt from yesterday's events. He fought against rolling his eyes or arguing and peeked around the shed to see for himself. "Guessing five feet. At least it's cedar. Won't be as slippery or flimsy as vinyl."

She nodded. "If you can help me and Raven get over that back fence, I think I can get us somewhere safe."

Getting Raven over could be a problem. It would take all of his strength to lift the dog to that height to help her clear the fence. "It'll work only if you go over the fence first, and you'll have to get the dog down on the other side."

He was a grown man, a professional and a potential mayor who had been driven into hiding behind sheds and jumping fences. If he could have convinced Alexis to turn herself in to the police and trust God to be their defender, then he would have. But it was obvious she'd made up her mind, and he wouldn't let her go off on her own when he knew the drug trafficking ring was out to kill her. And the current mayor was…well, Nick wasn't sure what the man was doing, but he couldn't deny the possibility that Gerald was the one who had tried to frame them.

Gunshots sounded again. Obviously the gunmen weren't going to surrender to the police without a fight. Unless there were more police officers in the vicinity than usual, he felt certain that the gunmen would outnumber them.

The sky had turned a dark blue-gray and the stars were just starting to become visible. Day was turning into evening before his eyes. How could that be possible? Alexis's stomach growled as if in proof.

Alexis eyed him. "What? It's past my dinnertime, too." She blew out a breath.

A loud bang erupted, and sparks of blue and red filled the dark sky in the distance. It must be the practice set of fireworks before the End of Summer show that would start in a few minutes. He hoped the entire town was there and safe from the gunfight erupting behind them.

"When you hit the fence, jump vertically. Grab the top, but use your legs to climb the fence. All you need is one heel or knee to get over. Then you can twist and roll the rest of the way."

She blinked. "Okay." She pointed at Raven. "Do that 'stay' command thing with her." She noticed the hesitation that must've been evident on his face. "When I make it over, run. I promise I'll be waiting to catch her on the other side. Let's go."

He nodded. He didn't feel ready. He held his hand out and firmly spoke. "Stay."

Alexis peeked around the shed and took off running. Raven's foot shoved off Nick's shoe as she launched after Alexis like a rocket. Nick groaned and charged after them both.

A gunman stepped out of the shadows on the other side of the house and aimed what looked like a sawed-off shotgun at her. The moon reflected off something near the grill. Nick grabbed what turned out to be the grill brush and flung it at the gunman. The metal edge hit the man's temple, but the gun still went off.

A bullet splintered the top of the fence right next to where Alexis had been half a second ago. She shrieked but managed to fling herself over the fence. Raven jumped over in a beautiful arc, the leash sailing behind her, proving she didn't need anyone to hoist her up.

Nick sucked in a sharp breath. That had been too close. They couldn't back down now.

Hearing the gunman behind him reloading, he vaulted across the yard before the man could take aim again. He launched himself sideways through the other bordering bushes. The branches slashed against his face and arms, much more painful than the first set of hedges, but he managed to get through. The yard resembled Theresa's except there was more furniture.

"Nick!" Alexis screamed from somewhere over the fence.

Nick didn't take time to answer. He didn't want the gunman to be able to zero in on his voice. Another gunshot and a scream told him the man had tried to aim at the sound of Alexis's voice instead.

Nick jumped, placed his hands on top of the fence, swung himself over and barely missed landing on Raven.

Alexis stood next to her. "Follow me."

Nick pumped his arms, careful not to pass her because she seemed to know where she was going. He leaned down and scooped up the middle of Raven's leash, picking up a handful of gravel with it. The grit stung underneath his fingernails, but he couldn't afford to slow down.

Alexis glanced down at Raven. "So she didn't want to obey and stay. I can see why she's still in training."

"Or maybe she just figured out who was really the boss," he said. Alexis might not want to admit it, but Raven acted as if she'd decided Alexis was her owner.

Fireworks hit the night sky, causing Alexis to flinch and shriek a little each time. Raven lifted her head up with each gallop but didn't bark or shake at the blasts and booms. It was becoming hard to recognize which booms came from guns and which from pyrotechnics. "Try not to make noise," he said, huffing his words.

Her eyes seemed to light up, reflecting another set of bursts in the sky. "I'm not doing it on purpose." She pointed to the left. "I know that home. I used to babysit for them. They never miss a fireworks show. It'll be empty." They ran to the porch, and she kicked back the mat to reveal a key. He looked over his shoulder to make sure the coast was clear as she opened the door and they slipped into the darkened house.

A hiss sounded and Raven responded with a bark. "Shh," Alexis responded. "It's just their cat. It's old.

It won't hurt you, dog. We'll be right out of your hair, Snookums. Just passing through." She spoke in such soft, soothing tones, Nick felt his own spine relax a little.

He remained still until his eyes adjusted. Her footsteps echoed throughout the house, but he worried that if he tried to follow, he'd smash into something valuable. A moment later he could see her form down the hallway. She stood next to the back door, where a sliver of light came through the curtain.

"I don't know about you," she said, "but I'd rather avoid jumping a fence again. Follow me, but don't let the cat out."

He reached her at the door. "You sure it wouldn't be better to stay indoors for a bit?"

"Trust me. Come on." They slipped back outside as the fireworks increased in frequency in the fully darkened sky. In the distance, they could hear whoops and hollers.

Alexis closed the door behind him. He couldn't see details, but judging by the trellises and inverted cone shapes in long rectangular boxes in front of him, he imagined the owners gardened a lot. Alexis walked down a set of cement stairs to what looked like a cellar door.

"They told me I could come by anytime to pick up some of their produce." She used the same key from the front and shoved the heavy door open. "I never intended to take them up on it until today."

She waited until they were inside before she pulled a string. A lone lightbulb illuminated the shelves filled with glass jars. In the middle, a long countertop held baskets of fresh veggies awaiting a rinse from the industrial-sized sink sticking out of the right wall.

Alexis took a lone sugar snap pea out of a basket and shoved it toward him. "Am I wrong or did you think that Gerald was telling the truth about Theresa?" She put one hand on her hip as she waved the vegetable at him. "Because it seemed to me that you could've helped me press him until he told us what we needed. It's obvious that he's behind the entire thing. The drugs on his property had to be his."

Nick shrugged. "I'm not so sure."

"Why is that?" Her eyes narrowed.

He searched through the basket for snap peas without any indentions. "I didn't think we were going to get any more out of him. He seemed truly sorrowful." Nick strode to the sink to rinse the veggies, and Alexis followed close behind him.

"Yeah. From guilt. He shouldn't be able to live with himself." She scrunched up her face.

"I don't believe he killed her." Nick turned around and chewed on a pea. The taste just made him wish he had hummus nearby, but his stomach was happy to have any food.

"I'll ask you again. What makes you so sure?"

He couldn't help but smile. "I know I get argumentative when I'm hungry, but you…"

Her shoulders dropped a bit. "I admit I can get carried away."

"It's what makes you a good lawyer."

Her eyes lifted to meet his. "*Made* me a good lawyer."

He tilted his head. "There has to be a story behind that." He'd learned over the years that if he waited long enough, both people and animals would show him what they were hiding. Judging by her stance, Alexis was hiding something.

She pursed her lips. "Back to Gerald."

Clearly he hadn't earned her trust yet. He sighed. "Gerald struck me as a man who was genuinely in love."

Her eyes widened, and she took a step back. "Have you ever been in love?"

Alexis fought the urge to cover her mouth with her hand. The question came out before she could stop it. She'd lost control. Her emotions were more wild and rampant than they'd ever been, even when she'd been disbarred.

She wanted justice. She wanted truth. And she couldn't make herself take back the question to Nick, for some reason.

His raised eyebrows dropped and his lips formed a slanted smile. "Seems like kind of a personal question."

"We're on the run together. I don't see how you can get any more personal."

He nodded. "Fair enough. There have been plenty of times I wondered if I was falling in love, but in the end…no. I don't think I've ever been in love. Romantic love, anyway." He held out his hands. "So, I guess you're right not to trust my opinion of Gerald." His smile warmed her core, and she wished they'd stayed outside in the cool air. He stepped closer. "So now that I've answered your question, I would like you to answer mine."

She'd walked right into that one. It's what happened when she let emotions rule her mind instead of pure logic. "You want to know why I haven't been practicing law."

He shrugged. "When you're ready to tell me."

Oh, he was good. She found herself really wanting to open up at that very moment.

"Right now," he said, "I want to know if you have a history with Jeremy."

A snort threatened to escape. That was the last thing she ever expected him to ask. "I guess you could say we have a history. I changed his diapers when I was eight years old. I was a mother's helper. I worked for a couple dollars an hour and the occasional basket of free homemade cookies. Jeremy comes from a big family."

Nick looked pleased. "Just like you," he said.

She blinked, unable to process her feelings because she was too busy having to correct him. "I'm an only child."

"Seems like most of this town is your family."

At one time, she would've heartily agreed and been proud of it. Now she felt like an outsider. It was her own doing, but she couldn't focus on that. She looked toward the door. "I think we have a couple of hours before they'll be back from the festival. We could wait here to make sure the police caught the gunmen."

"Then what?" He stepped closer. His hand rested on the countertop, near hers.

Her index finger twitched. It'd helped when he had grabbed her hand back at Theresa's house. It'd grounded her emotions and kept her mind on the present. But most of all, it had comforted her. She closed her eyes. "I need time to process, to focus, to pray." While it was true, wasn't that what she'd been saying the entire past year about the Seattle incident?

Before she could change the subject, Nick's hand slid on top of hers, his fingertips squeezing ever so slightly. "Lord, we need Your wisdom. Help us see and find the truth and comfort Alexis while—"

"In Jesus's name, Amen." She finished for him before he could pray any more. She opened her eyes. "I love that you prayed, but if I think any more about Theresa—" Her voice broke.

He rubbed the outside of her arms as if she was cold. "You're trying to keep it together," he said softly. "I understand."

Raven pressed her warm torso against the back of Alexis's legs. She reached down to pat the dog's head. "I think she's having a hard time keeping it together, too."

Nick released Alexis. "Are you up for calling the chief again, or would you like me to? He needs to know about the mayor."

"No, I know him. I will. His reaction when I tell him about Gerald will help me figure out the next step."

"Us." He winked. "Help *us* figure out the next step."

He said it so softly she almost missed the inflection. She'd been so used to navigating life and her problems alone lately that she had a hard time accepting that someone else was in this with her. She didn't know what to say, so she merely nodded and picked up the phone.

The chief answered on the third ring. "You'd better be calling to tell me you are on the way over to my station."

She cringed. Chief had been a presence in her life since she was a little girl, when her dad had been the mayor. It went against every fiber of her being to disappoint him, but she didn't see any way around it. "You need to bring Gerald in for questioning," she said. "He's connected to everything. Theresa was his girlfriend—"

"You know, I've had a pretty crummy weekend thus far," Chief interrupted. "Have you still got that dog with you?" Chief's voice crackled with such emotion it caught her off guard.

"Yes," she said tentatively.

"Well, I hope you're taking good care of her." He cleared his throat. "Joe passed away. So we need to figure out who he willed the dog to."

She sat herself down on the metal stool next to the countertop. The dog's owner had passed away? Raven looked up at her as if she didn't have a care in the world. Tears pricked Alexis's eyes. "I thought he was stable."

"He was until someone gave him some of that blasted elephant tranquilizer."

She gasped. What would be the motive for killing Joe? Had it come from the same bottle that had been planted in Nick's hotel room? If she asked, the chief would just tell her to come in again.

Joe had been at the hospital in Boise. Her eyes met Nick's as she tried to piece things together. The back of her mind nagged for attention. Her head hurt from concentrating so hard until it clicked. "The mayor. Theresa said she went out of town with the mayor."

"I've already got Gerald here, Alexis. He practically climbed into a cruiser of his own accord when we were busy trying to get the gunmen rounded up."

"Did you?"

He grunted. "Most of them, but not all. And none of them are talking, so why don't you come in before you get yourselves killed? We can keep you safe here and you can answer a few questions."

"What did Gerald say?" she pressed. "Did he admit to killing Theresa?"

He sighed. "I don't have to tell you a thing, Lexi."

"Chief, you've known me since forever. It's why you can't seem to get my name right." She couldn't resist the dig. "I want justice as much as you do, but I think I have a better chance of getting that outside your station."

He let out a grumble. "Gerald's not talking. He's waiting for his lawyer. The only thing I have to hold him on is a charge of trespassing. I've got a whole lot more that I can charge you with, if we're being honest. So do me a favor and make it easier on the both of us. Come in, and let's figure this out together."

Maybe he was right, and it was time to give up the fight. "Will I be behind bars when we do this figuring?"

Silence answered for a moment before he sighed. "We have witnesses, Alexis."

Cold seeped into her veins. "Wh-what do you mean?"

"Someone in housekeeping at the hotel reported seeing you with the drugs. And management confirmed you left the hotel and returned within an hour in the middle of the night."

"But we didn't!" His words implied more than simple drug possession.

Nick's head and shoulders dropped as he overheard.

"I want to believe you," the chief said, "but the longer you avoid coming in, the worse it looks."

"What about the security camera at the medical clinic?" There had to be something there.

"Nothing. We can't see the door to the employment agency, only the parking lot behind the clinic. Not so much as a stray cat showed up on the footage."

Her heart plummeted. She'd known it was a possibility that the camera wouldn't show the area all the way down to the employment agency, but she'd thought for sure it'd at least show a vehicle driving past. "Do you have a warrant out for me, Chief?"

His two seconds of silence were all the encouragement she needed. He hadn't issued a warrant for their arrest.

"I'm tempted to call your parents," he said, as if she were a teenager instead of a grown woman.

"You go ahead and do that, then." Sarcasm dripped over her words. "You know they'll rush back up here, and it'll be on your head that they'll be put in unnecessary danger." She sighed, knowing she was pushing the boundaries of respectful disagreement. Her parents and the chief were still close friends so she could understand his inclination, but he had to know it would be far worse for them to be there. What if the drug runners put a hit out on them? "I'll think about what you've said and be in touch." She ended the call and stared at her phone as if the solution rested there.

It would be so nice to erase the log of recent calls and pretend it removed the entire day's events, like nothing ever happened.

"I don't have any idea of what we can do next," she said. "If they can't make Gerald talk, then where does that leave us? They have fake witnesses against us, Nick. I don't know how we can win." Her voice rose in pitch despite her effort to remain calm.

The only reason the chief hesitated on the warrant was probably that he didn't want to bother a judge on a holiday weekend, especially because deep down the chief had to know they were innocent. At least, that was her hope. Her hands shook as she dropped her head into them. "We have no proof."

Nick sucked in a sharp breath and tapped the table. "Something's been bothering me. If you're right, and Gerald was the one who killed Joe and broke the glass to kill Theresa, then why wouldn't she tell you that on the message? If I suspected that my mystery girlfriend killed someone and was about to kill me, I would stop keeping secrets. It'd be the first thing on my message. But instead…"

She lifted her head. "It's as if she was still trying to protect him. Or she was hoping that if she kept his secret, then maybe he wouldn't kill her." She swiped on her phone until she came to voice mail and steeled herself to listen to Theresa's message again.

"We need to talk immediately. In person. I got your message. I think you might be in danger, honey. Where are my stupid time cards?"

Nick stood and put his hand on her shoulder before she even realized her eyes were filling with tears. It seemed so ironic that Theresa thought Alexis was in danger when in reality her murderer was a mere step away. She blinked back the tears. "You were right. She didn't mention him at all. Odd, but maybe she loved him so much she didn't want to face it."

"Possible," he answered slowly. "But it's worth thinking about other possibilities. What about the time cards? Doesn't it seem odd that it was so important for her to find the time cards in the middle of the night?"

Alexis stared at him without really seeing him. The phone call had come in the middle of the night, which was why she'd missed it in the first place. Theresa wasn't the most organized person on the planet, but she always got the job done.

None of the small business owners Alexis worked for had ever bad-mouthed Theresa. Her employees had a high turnover rate, but that was to be expected at a temp agency. Most employees came and went without much notice, except Deborah, who was a sixty-five-year-old retired teacher. She just did odd jobs to stay busy.

Alexis actually had taken most of the work for the past six months. After two weeks of crying and moping, her mother had told her she had to go do something for someone else for her mental health. So Alexis had volunteered at the food bank, where she'd met Theresa, who had asked what she was doing with her time while she was in town. And before she knew it, Alexis had her very own rut that she was stuck in. But the worry about the time cards didn't make sense.

"I don't know why they would matter so much," she admitted. "But I know somewhere we can find copies."

He exhaled. "Is it going to involve sneaking around town and ending up surrounded by gunmen again?"

As much as she hated to admit it, she needed him. "If I agree that's a possibility, will I be on my own?"

He handed Raven an apple he'd found in a basket on the counter. The dog seemed to inhale it within three crunches. "Come on, girl," he said as his way of answering. "You're the only one of us trained to track secrets and face danger."

TEN

The temperature of the night air had dropped by several degrees. A chill settled through the flannel shirt Nick wore. He tried to stop the repeated loop playing in his mind: *You're a wanted man.*

He'd done everything by the book to become a respected, valuable member of the community, and for what? If any of this made the news in Seattle, or worse, if he had to call Mom from jail, she would no doubt suffer a heart attack like she had the night his brother passed away. He didn't know if her heart could handle another shock.

He held the leash, but Raven ran ahead and heeled at Alexis's feet instead of his own. He didn't bother correcting the action, though he tried to tell himself it wasn't because he was hoping Alexis would grow to be a dog person.

Alexis opened the side gate and led them to the closest sidewalk. "People might start to come home from the celebration soon, so it shouldn't look too odd to see a couple out for a walk with our dog."

He liked the sound of a moonlit stroll as a couple

with *their* dog. "There's just one problem. Most everyone in town seems to know who you are."

She pointed at a sign in the front yard that said Vote Kendrick for Mayor. "I don't think I'm the only one with that problem."

If they hadn't been on the run, he would have taken it as a compliment. He loved the idea that the town might embrace him. "So, we just keep our heads down when a car passes."

"Wrong. That's big city thinking. Small-town residents always take a moment to look and see if they know the person on the side of the road." She shrugged. "Then they roll down the window and say hello."

He grinned at the thought. "I guess I haven't been living the small-town way. If we ever get out of this, that sounds nice."

She asked him to stay put for a second as she returned the house key underneath the doormat where she'd found it. She pointed to the left. "Let's turn here. This street doesn't get as much traffic. If we stay behind the tree line, we should be able to get back to my house without being spotted. If you see a car, though—"

"Make like a tree and leave?"

She glared at him, but her lips fought and lost. A laugh escaped and she rolled her eyes. "Well, you got the 'make like a tree' part right."

They were going back to her house. He assumed that meant her parents' house. "Why are we going to your place? Do you have the time cards?"

She tilted her hand at diagonal angles as if debating it in her head before answering. "Yes and no. All the temp agency time cards were hard copies."

"As in pen and paper? That's rare in this day and age."

"Exactly. I thought it was odd, too, but Theresa said that a lot of her clients preferred it that way. To be fair, many of the small business owners are getting up there in age and haven't quite embraced technology. At least, that was her explanation. Now, I wonder."

"You don't think Theresa was involved in the drug operation?"

Her eyes widened in the moonlight. "No! She told me it was Barry's preference, as well—he took care of all the bookkeeping and payroll. He said pen and paper couldn't be hacked."

"Barry is the mayor's brother. The one with the investment firm?"

She nodded. "And the reason Gerald struck it big on the stock market. Seems like everyone invested with him after that. Did you?"

Nick had been tempted. Barry came highly recommended, but when Nick had gone in to discuss it, he came away concerned with Barry's antiquated system. After some research, he decided he could manage his practice's finances himself with the help of some expensive software. He might feel different after rebuilding the practice. His fingers itched to call his insurance company, even if they were closed over the holiday weekend.

"So the only reason people invested was that Gerald had some impressive dividends?"

She frowned. "No. Other older folks made out pretty well." She pursed her lips. "Given the drug angle, it sounds suspicious, doesn't it? I worked for him, temped for him and never even blinked an eye."

"So you didn't suspect anything odd, then?"

"No, but I mainly filed paperwork, entered numbers in spreadsheets—"

"So he wasn't totally computer illiterate." He shrugged. "It's worth exploring, at least. Did you invest with him?"

She pressed her lips together. "I have no money to invest."

"Your parents, then?"

"They wanted to, so I wouldn't be surprised."

"How do the time cards work into his paper and pen methods?"

"He puts them in the shredder after he enters them into the software."

Nick frowned. "That doesn't jibe with the 'this way we won't get hacked' mentality. So you have some that aren't shredded?"

"I'm too type A just to hand over the hard copies without digital accountability."

"No," he said with an exaggerated tone and a wink. "You? Type A?"

She smacked him playfully on the arm. He faked injury, but she ignored him and continued. "So I took photographs of each time card with my smartphone before I submitted it to Theresa."

"Was your pay ever inconsistent?"

She shook her head. "No, I never had a problem."

"But the photos are no longer on your phone." He held up a hand. "Let me guess. You import them onto a backup drive every six weeks."

She bristled. "Every week, if you must know, and it's not a backup drive. It's a laptop." She sighed. "I want to have hope that there's a clue there, but you know in all likelihood, it's going to be nothing."

While true, he preferred hanging onto hope rather than the alternative. The pressure from the day and the seriousness of the matter threatened to overwhelm him, as if it hovered on the back of his neck, ready to paralyze him. He needed to capture his thoughts, or at least avoid thinking about them for a while, or he might self-destruct.

Car beams swung around the corner a block ahead. He took a step backward into the shadows and tugged gently on Alexis's elbow to get her to follow him. As soon as Raven saw they were still, she flopped down on the ground like she wanted to take a nap right there. The poor dog was overdue for a nice, long snooze.

The car blared rock music, but they remained silent. How many squirrels and birds made the wide branches above them their home? He could hardly make out any moonlight when he looked straight up. The tree at their backs had to be one of the widest cedars he'd ever seen. His gaze dropped to find Alexis staring at him curiously.

Heat filled his chest. He couldn't look away. "You're beautiful." The words came out in a whisper, so fast he couldn't stop them.

She blinked, and the moment of connection dissipated into the night.

He wanted to kick himself. What was he doing? She'd made it abundantly clear that she had no plans to date anyone in town. She wouldn't be sticking around. He didn't need a surefire recipe to heartache. And yet he found himself growing increasingly attracted to her.

Alexis grew prettier the more he got to know her. The

opposite usually happened as he got to know women. He didn't know what to make of it.

She scoffed, "Everyone looks good in moonlight."

First of all, that wasn't true, but if she thought it was… "Are you're saying I look good?" he asked.

She pressed her lips to one side and rolled her eyes.

"If you're not, I think I've just proved your theory has holes." He couldn't help but flash his best smile.

She put her head down, but not before he could see the smile forming. "Car's gone," she said and strode ahead of him down the street. Raven rushed after her, almost dragging him by the leash. *Who's walking who?*

Alexis looked over her shoulder. "One more block, and then I know a shortcut through a field where we should be safe from prying eyes."

He picked up his pace to match hers. The playful moment had disappeared, and with the reminder that they weren't safe, the heaviness that had hung over him returned. It warred with the peace that at moments calmed his heart. The war of emotions left him exhausted. The grass up ahead looked good enough to sleep on.

She turned left onto a dirt path marred by weeds and grass. The trees around the abandoned field blocked the streetlights in the distance. Only the moon and the stars lit their way.

With concern, he watched Raven walk. "I'll look at her paws the moment we have light. We'll need to check her for stickers."

"You mean goat heads."

Within the first week of moving to the county, he'd tried to take his bike onto the rural roads. People had warned him about goat heads. He'd imagined the road must be littered with goat skeletons and wondered what kind of odd place he'd moved to, until the stickers had punctured his bike wheels and he'd realized they looked like goat heads.

Alexis looked down at Raven. "I'll try to keep an eye on her and make sure she doesn't start limping," she whispered. "You always wanted to be a veterinarian?"

"Um. No. I started in premed, but I could see the writing on the wall my senior year, so I took an animal biology class just in case. Didn't stop me from my path to medical school, though. Didn't even last a semester before I knew I needed to transfer to a vet school."

"You wanted to be a doctor?" Her tone had a measure of disbelief.

"I always knew I wanted to help people, but it became clear I wouldn't be able to handle it."

She tilted her head. "Why? The blood?" She shivered. "Sorry. Obviously, there's blood involved in being a vet. I wouldn't be able to do it. I can't even stand to think about it."

"No." He still remembered getting the news that his grandfather had passed away from lung cancer. His death had been the final straw for Nick. And everyone at the university had figured out he was done before he had. His cheeks heated at the memories. "I couldn't cope when patients made bad choices to the detriment of their health. I couldn't control people."

"I can understand that," she said softly.

"The clients who bring their animals in to me are, ninety-nine percent of the time, good owners who will do almost anything to make sure their pets stay well."

"Don't you have to deal with bad owners sometimes?"

"There are laws on my side in that event. There aren't

any laws that say people have to stop smoking after they've been diagnosed with lung cancer."

Raven lifted her nose and nuzzled his hand. He pushed the painful memories into the back of his mind. "And animals are easy to love and forgive. It seemed like an easy choice to go into veterinary medicine." He lifted his gaze. They were coming to the edge of the clearing. Now that they were visible through the thin line of trees, they would have to be on guard again. He sighed. "I would ask you why you became a lawyer, but—"

Her entire body stiffened, and her stride grew longer. "You've figured out that's a topic I don't like to talk about."

He nodded but let her words hang in the air.

She eyed him right before she stepped in between the trees. "You do look good in the moonlight, by the way."

He stumbled over a tree root as he processed her words. She must have finally decided she didn't want him poking holes in the theory of hers that said everyone looked good in the moonlight.

He caught up to her as she moved onto the sidewalk, but before he could respond with a flirtatious quip, the surroundings took him by surprise. A block away, a hollowed-out shell of a building with a caved-in roof stood as a reminder that, if they couldn't prove their innocence, his entire life would crumble.

"Nick," Alexis whispered. "The silver car that was at the corner before the fire is back on my street."

Alexis stood paralyzed at the tree line. Her insides shook just seeing the car. True, they had no proof it was associated with the fire, but the least the police could do would be to ask the owner of it a few questions. It had to be the same car, but when she called, she would reveal her and Nick's whereabouts. She needed to be sure it was worth the risk.

Nick pulled her back into the shadows. "Call the police."

"You're sure it's the right move?" Alexis envied the certainty in his voice. She used to make quick decisions with confidence. She fumbled to get her phone.

"No, I'm not, but I think at this point, we'd better be safe than sorry."

Alexis stared at him. She wanted to hear him say that if they called the police, everything was going to be all right. Because people who did the right things were supposed to end up having a good life, not to get hauled off to prison for something they didn't do.

It was the very reason she'd never wanted to be a defense lawyer. Somewhere deep inside, she assumed that all accused people were likely guilty or they wouldn't have been accused in the first place. If this was to be the year in which God put a spotlight on every corner of her heart to reveal all her prejudices and misguided notions, she prayed He would just write her a detailed letter instead. The Bible instantly came to mind.

She hesitated to dial the emergency line. After her last conversation, she didn't want to call the chief, either. Jeremy's contact information was at the top of her list. The phone rang two times before he answered. "Jeremy, the silv—"

"Stop calling me," he interrupted. "I mean it. Unless you're ready to have me pick you up or come in of your own accord, I'm not helping you."

"But—"

"You of all people should know that I can't make concessions for friends. The law is the law. Don't put me in this position again." A dial tone sounded in her ear.

"Sounds like that went well," Nick said drily. "Maybe we should take a peek before we call again. It's possible it's someone visiting one of these houses, right?"

"Not very." They would've parked closer or in the driveway if that were the case.

They stuck to the shadows as they crossed the street and neared the vehicle. Over her shoulder, her parents' house beckoned her. The fridge was full of leftovers and cold iced tea and—

A flick of light through the bay window made her breath catch. But it was only for a second. She blinked to make sure her eyes hadn't played a trick on her. She turned around, searching for another source of light. "Nick, did you see—"

Raven barked at the driver's side door of the silver car.

"Shh," Alexis and Nick both hissed at the dog at the same time.

Raven responded by nudging her nose at the bottom of the door and barking again. She sat down, wagging her tail.

Alexis tugged on Nick's elbow as they ran around the end of the car. "Get down," she whispered. "I saw a light inside my house."

Nick groaned. "Call the police now. If they find someone in the house, that'll give them probable cause to search this car. And Raven seems very sure something is in this vehicle."

Alexis dialed 911. "There's a burglary in progress at 1415 Jefferson." She hung up before the dispatcher could ask any more questions. Light reflected on the street underneath the car. "Why can't they train the dog to sniff loudly instead of bark?"

"Let's just pray that the burglar doesn't have a gun."

The light disappeared as fast as it appeared. Nick straightened painfully slowly until he peeked through the windows of the car. "I don't see anyone approaching."

Her heart sped up. "What if he's getting away? He's probably Theresa's murderer."

Nick's eyes widened. "Why would someone be searching your house?"

Her throat seemed to close. She choked out, "To kill me."

Nick blinked, unfazed. "Or?"

"The time cards?"

He nodded. "I like that option better, but how would they know you have some? Did Theresa know you took pictures of the time cards before you turned them in?"

Alexis racked her brain. "One time I forgot to take a snapshot until I reached her office to turn them in. She witnessed me taking the photos. So, yes. She didn't mind. She teased me about it, in fact. It's…it's possible she told Gerald or someone that I kept digital copies. Maybe that's why she was frantically searching for her copies."

"So if our theory is correct, then your nighttime visitor might be after the cards. Theresa said you were probably in danger. It's possible she knew. Maybe that's why she was frantically trying to find her copies of the time cards."

She nodded toward the house. "Well, if that's what he's after, he won't find them in there."

"He won't?"

"No." She chanced a look through the car windows to catch a view across the street. "Most people assume I live in the house. I don't. I have an apartment above the garage."

A beam of light illuminated the kitchen for a brief moment, enough to see a dark figure lurking about the house. "I don't think he saw us," Nick said. "He must have thought a dog in the neighborhood was barking."

The police were on their way. Alexis hoped the cops had sense enough to keep the sirens off when they approached. The light beam went off again.

"Can you see the house from your apartment?"

She nodded. "Let's go get the time cards. If the cops don't get here in time, we can watch and see where he goes." Nick crossed the street with Raven at his heels before she could object.

She rushed after him. "What if he has a gun?"

Nick's steps faltered. "I wasn't going to confront him. I'm hoping he doesn't see us at all."

"I like that plan." Her heart raced faster the closer they got to her parents' house. They crouched in front of the bushes as they slipped past the bay window. While it served her purposes not to have motion-detecting lights at the moment, if she got out of this alive, she would install some herself. Maybe that would've been enough to deter the intruder. Though if he'd murdered Theresa, she doubted it. A chill ran down her spine at the thought.

Nick led the way, but she realized he didn't know where he was going. She tapped his shoulder, and he let her pass him and Raven. Once she rounded the corner, she'd be at the house threshold. The entrance to the garage was almost directly across from the front door. The space in between acted almost like an outdoor hallway.

She held a hand up to Nick to indicate he should stay put and keep a look out while she opened the side door to the garage. Her eyes strained to see more as she watched the front door before she stepped up to the entrance to her garage apartment. She slipped her apartment key from her jeans and inserted it into the lock.

A steel arm wrapped around her neck, closing off the oxygen. She shoved her elbow backward. Her attacker shifted and her arm thrashed into thin air. He pressed harder into her esophagus. Something sharp dug into her right side. She couldn't think straight enough to decipher if it was a gun or not.

A deep voice rasped into her ear. "Where are the time cards?" Something sounded familiar about it, but the panic and lack of oxygen made her thoughts muddy.

His arm went slack as shards of ceramic rained over her shoulder, stinging but welcome compared to the vise around her neck. She sucked in a deep breath. The attacker fell to the ground. Soil and wilted geraniums littered around his face, which was covered by a ski mask.

Nick's hands dropped from the air.

Alexis cradled her neck with her fingers, desperate to ease the tight pain in her throat. "Gun." She could barely get the word out as a croak. Raven barked at the man but didn't move to attack.

Nick stomped on the man's right forearm, so he must have heard Alexis over Raven's bark. The man howled and released the gun. Nick kicked it aside, but the attacker took that moment to swipe at his other leg, and Nick fell back. Alexis lunged and braced Nick with her outstretched arm.

He regained his balance, but when they both turned, the man had disappeared. Nick grabbed her arm and shoved her toward the door. "He might've found the—"

A bullet shot into the night before he could finish his thought. It whizzed past them and found its mark in the headlight of a police cruiser pulling up to the scene. Nick shoved her inside the apartment entrance and closed the door behind her. "Let's hope they realize we weren't the ones who shot at them."

She held on to the possibility that the officers hadn't even seen them since they were in the shadows, but her throat hurt too much to voice it. Sirens sounded in the street. The police weren't keeping their presence on the down low now after being shot at.

"Keep a watch out, I'll be right back." Alexis ran up the steps inside the garage to her apartment. She flung open the door and flipped on her smartphone's flashlight function. There were only two small windows in the back of the apartment, both facing the backyard, but they were covered with blinds and curtains.

From the street, the building likely looked like a tall garage for an RV. That was, after all, its function before her parents had renovated it into an apartment, intending it at one time to be a possible income source. They had no idea that their only daughter, a lawyer, would end up moving back home to lick her wounds.

The furniture fit in the one-bedroom, one-bathroom studio like a game of Tetris. Her desk sat between the table and the bed. She launched across the strip of tile and shoved the laptop into the computer bag. At least she knew someone wanted those time cards, so they had to be on to something. If she could just get a moment of peace and quiet, maybe she would figure out the motive behind Theresa's murder and have proof of their innocence.

She felt before she saw a figure looming in the doorway. Her muscles tensed. Her fingers reached for a glass paperweight as the only weapon she could find. Her beam of light focused on Nick and her shoulders dropped. He was supposed to have stayed put. Her poor heart couldn't handle another scare, and her throat still wasn't ready for her to try talking.

"Please," Nick said, "tell me you still have your parents' car keys."

She nodded and reached for them. Though she couldn't imagine what good they would do when her dad's car was likely still near Theresa's house, or worse, impounded.

Nick rushed toward her and took them from her hand, studying them in the glow of her phone. A grin crossed his face. "The police are searching next door. It'll take them only a few minutes to realize someone is in here. Can we go?"

She nodded and pulled the strap of the laptop bag across her torso. An open water bottle sat on the edge of the desk. She greedily gulped it as she ran after Nick, back down the stairs. The liquid instantly helped ease some of the soreness. "Where's Raven?" Her voice sounded stronger but still hoarse.

"You'll see. Turn off the phone light before the cops notice."

"Those two sentences contradict each other," she whispered. She grabbed his shoulder in front of her as she turned the beam off and descended the stairs. She hadn't been counting the steps and wouldn't know when they'd come to the bottom. As she fell into the space between his shoulder blades, she knew they'd reached the ground.

"Stay here a second." The sound of metal and greasy wheels echoed through the garage. Light from the moon streamed into the back. Nick stood underneath the open garage door that led into the backyard. When her dad had renovated, he'd made it into a drive-through garage so he could easily take his riding lawnmower out in the backyard. Seemed like overkill given they had only a third of an acre, but it'd made her dad happy.

Raven sat in the sidecar of the old Honda cruiser motorcycle. Nick held something in his hands. "Think fast." What looked like a dark ball volleyed into the air. She barely caught it with her fingertips and felt the opening to the helmet.

"Seriously?" she whispered despite the pain.

He threw his hands up at the otherwise empty garage. "Do you have a better idea?"

If she had, she would've argued, but the angry voices of officers yelling spurred her forward. A gunshot rang out but seemed farther away. The burglar was still out there?

Nick straddled the motorcycle and gestured for her to hop on behind him. She slapped on the helmet and adjusted the laptop bag to lie flat against her back. A harness of sorts, made from the pink leash, crisscrossed around the dog's torso and attached to the seat belt Alexis's dad had installed in the sidecar. Instead of a helmet, Raven wore her mom's old white driving goggles.

"Let's hope this starts." Nick slipped the key into the ignition and cranked the handles. It sputtered before it revved to life.

"Go left." She pointed with her left hand over his shoulder before the cruiser lurched forward. Without a backrest, wrapping her arms around his torso couldn't be avoided. She tried not to notice how surprisingly solid the veterinarian was and instead focused on a decision that she would start a jogging routine if they survived.

The bike and sidecar spun into the yard and shot across diagonally to the alley. Except the sidecar lifted off the ground as Nick made the turn. Alexis held in her instinct to scream and fought against the momentum by leaning hard right. Raven licked her arm as she did so, which almost made Alexis let go of her hold on Nick's torso.

He straightened the bike, and Raven's seat settled back on the ground.

Over her shoulder, flashlights darted inside her parents' house, but no beams were directed at them. Surely they had heard the engine, but maybe they assumed it was someone on the street. Though if they had gotten away without being spotted, what about the burglar?

Another gunshot rang out, and gravel sprayed to her right. A police officer wouldn't have shot without at least calling for them to stop. She was sure of it. The silver vehicle sped out from the side street, windows down, lights off. The motorcycle beam caught the man's eyes as he leaned out of the passenger window, but the ski mask still covered the rest of his face.

She squeezed Nick tighter at the memory of what the burglar's arm felt like around her throat. If not for the helmet, she would've buried her face in his shirt until it was all over.

"Turn right," she yelled. The strain hurt, but it was

the only way to be heard. Nick rotated the handlebars and turned into what looked like a long driveway, but Alexis knew better. The small town had more alleys than streets, but the property owners were responsible for maintaining them. The three property owners of this little stretch were the only ones to contribute the money to pave it.

Nick narrowly avoided a trash can. Lights flashed on in different houses. Sirens grew closer. Raven's nose worked overtime in the air as if she didn't have a care in the world.

The silver car revved behind them and another gunshot sounded, this time spinning the trash can into the alley. The burglar had made it to his getaway car but chose to pursue them rather than escape from the police. Why? Her gut churned as she recalled the feeling of cold metal pressed into her side. If it were more important for him to kill them than to avoid getting caught by the police, how would they ever survive?

ELEVEN

Of all the bad ideas Nick had ever had in his life, this by far was his worst. He hadn't ridden a motorcycle since his late teens, and driving with a sidecar proved to be a completely different beast. On a regular bike, he had to compensate with each turn, but with the sidecar, he had to brake and throttle less to turn left and add throttle to make a right turn. The wheels felt squishy and insecure on the gravel, and the trigger-happy driver behind them was enough to make his head explode with stress.

He took the next street without Alexis's guidance, and it ended up being a long driveway. He revved the throttle, jumped the curb and drove diagonally across the front lawn until he came to the next driveway and took the very next right turn. The gunshots stopped momentarily, but he kept his speed as high as possible.

Two turns later, Alexis patted his shoulder. "You lost them. At least for a moment."

His breathing and heart rate weren't sure they should believe her quite yet, but there were no longer headlights in the side mirrors. The library on his right caught his attention. He swung into the parking lot and slipped behind the building into a spot where the overhead lights didn't reach them. He flicked off the ignition, and everything went dark and quiet.

They both breathed heavier than normal. Raven panted happily but stayed still in the sidecar.

"I'll tell you one thing," he whispered. "If somehow I still become mayor, my first act will be paving all those alleys."

Alexis dropped her helmet-covered head between his shoulder blades and exhaled. He'd have objected to the discomfort, but she was either crying or exhausted, so he remained motionless, his hands still on the handlebars.

Raven looked expectantly at him. Nick removed the goggles. He had no intention of driving the motorcycle even two more feet unless they were held at gunpoint again. He scratched behind Raven's ear. "Who's a good dog?"

She panted like she already knew she was a rock star.

The weight lifted from his back. "Yes, you are," Alexis cooed in hushed tones. She reached over and scratched the dog behind the ears, too, something Nick had thought he'd never see. Raven looked so happy, practically smiling as her mouth hung open. If she hadn't been wearing the homemade harness, Nick felt certain Raven would've ended up in Alexis's lap.

The rev of an engine and sirens approached at high speed. Alexis placed one arm around his waist as if they were about to take off again. The warmth from her embrace made his thoughts muddy, though he told himself it was probably more from exhaustion and lack of food.

The passing lights illuminated a newspaper box on the corner of the sidewalk, next to the back library entrance. He blinked but felt certain his and Alexis's faces were plastered on the front page of *The Barings Herald.* He slipped off the motorcycle and rolled it, passengers and all, until it was deeper in the shadows.

Alexis slipped off her helmet and wordlessly helped him untangle the leash knots and remove it from the seat belt. The farther away the sirens became, the more he could relax.

"I hope they catch the burglar," she whispered.

He walked to the newspaper box without her, clicked on his phone and held it close enough to the box that it wouldn't reflect into the night.

The headline read Mayoral Candidate and Disbarred Attorney Accused of Ties to Drug Ring.

He squinted at the first line of the article. "According to an anonymous source, drugs were found—"

Alexis gasped behind him. She fumbled in her pocket, reached around him and placed a few quarters in the slot, then pulled out the paper. Nick straightened. So he finally knew why she didn't practice law, but unfortunately, so did the rest of the town. Judging by her heartbroken expression, this would be news to everyone.

Her own phone illuminated the front page. The second half of the article included a photograph of Alexis and Nick in the back of a squad car. He groaned. That looked bad. The final photograph, while blurrier, showed Alexis and Nick clasping hands on the cliff. It had been right after she'd helped him to standing, but more importantly, who took the photograph? The angle looked to be from above. "Who's the photographer?"

Her wide eyes met his. "I'm so sorry, Nick. I didn't want to damage your campaign."

"My campaign was probably over the moment someone planted drugs in my room. I'm just sorry the media pulled you into this."

She shook her head. "You're not going to ask me if I really did it?"

"Did what? Let an alleged murderer go free?"

"They're twisting it. I broke privilege." Her head hung. "But it resulted in a murderer walking free."

"I figured it had to be something like that since you stopped practicing law. But look at the photo—"

Her jaw and arm dropped, taking the paper with it, as she shook her head. "And that doesn't bother you?"

"Well, I don't know all the details. Would you rather I be upset?" An exasperated sigh escaped before he could contain it. "Look, I'm sure there's a story behind it, but I really want to know who took that photograph of us on the cliff."

"It said anonymous."

"Can they do that? Don't they need our permission to—"

Her eyes flashed with fiery heat. "The photographer didn't need our consent as we were in a public place. You know I wasn't a defense attorney, right? I was disbarred." She barely took a breath. "Still don't care? 'Cause if you really don't, then I'm happy to be your campaign manager." Her voice rose as her words tripped over each other. She threw her hands in front of her, one hand waving the paper. She may have been talking about his campaign, but her tone and the look in her eyes seemed to be saying more. "They may have twisted the facts, but the result is still the same. I'm responsible for a murderer walking the streets of Seattle. The truth is, it'll destroy your reputation because everyone else in this town will care. They'll care a lot."

Nick stared at her as he tried to process her words. "Like I said, I'm pretty sure people will care more about our suspected association to a drug ring. The word is out. We're running out of time to clear our names."

Raven whimpered and pressed herself into the side of Alexis's leg. She slumped. "Sorry," she whispered. "Everything's out of control, and I just took it out on you. I have no excuse."

Even in the moonlight, he could see the fiery shade of red blossom over her neck and cheeks. She dipped her chin. "I've been ashamed so long. To see it in print…"

He lifted the paper from her fingertips. "Maybe I'm more tired than I want to admit, but I find it hard to believe that the woman in front of me who dreams of advocating for the elderly, who babysat and served her community in word and deed her entire childhood, would intentionally let a murderer go. And until you tell me your side—or let me read this article—I refuse to think anything but the best of you."

She took a step closer to him, her eyes cross-examining his features. His heart raced at her closeness. It was pointless to deny he was falling for her hard despite his best intentions.

"Innocent until proven guilty?" she asked.

"Shouldn't it be that way? I certainly wish someone would give me that benefit of the doubt."

She reached out with her right hand and rested it on his shoulder. He glanced at her fingertips and felt her lips brush his cheek. He closed his eyes and struggled not to pull her into his arms. He turned toward her, but she didn't move away.

His left hand slid across her neck and into her silky hair. He bent his head and leaned forward to—

Raven shoved herself between their legs. Alexis blinked as if waking up from a dream and stared at the dog. A soft smile crossed her face.

Never before had he disliked a dog as much as he did at the moment. Although, maybe Raven was trying to protect them both from broken hearts. "I... I guess we should go before they retrace their steps. It won't take them long to find us."

She walked toward the motorcycle.

He shook his head. "I think there's nothing more noticeable than a dog in a sidecar. Did your dad have to go through additional training before driving your mom in that?" He gestured at the scrapes on the side of the sidecar. "It was harder to handle than I thought."

She shrugged. She'd never taken any interest in learning how to drive it. "Actually, it was my mom's motorcycle. Dad wanted to have her drive him around in the town parades so he could wave like those men in the little cars, with the additional benefit of getting to throw candy."

"Like the Shriners?" He laughed. "I wish I could've seen that. Your parents sound like fun people."

They were fun people until she had come home in a depressed funk. She hoped Arizona was treating them right. "You would like them. Dad made a good mayor." She pointed to the line of trees bordering the back of the parking lot. "We'd better move quickly. It's a good five-minute walk back to Joe's."

He cringed.

"I know," she said before he could comment. "It feels wrong to stay at a dead man's house, but he would want Raven to eat, rest and be comfortable. It'll give us a chance to look at the time cards and regroup." She put a hand between the laptop bag strap and her neck with a grimace. Her spine and muscles might never be the same after the past few days.

Nick slipped a finger underneath the strap on her shoulder. She faltered as he wordlessly lifted the bag off her and placed it on his shoulder. How she wanted to kiss him. It probably had been for the best that Raven had interfered. It would've just complicated everything even more. If they ever got out of this, her situation remained the same. There was no reason to stay in Barings. Once her parents' house sold, she'd have nowhere to stay and no job. Falling for him had to remain off the table. Even though he woke up her mind and her heart in a way no one else ever had. He'd proved himself to be trustworthy and a good man.

"I wanted to tell you," she said softly as they walked in the shadows. "Before the story came out. I wanted you to know."

"So tell me now. Unless you'd rather I read about it."

She took a deep breath and focused on the path ahead. "I haven't told anyone but my parents. I've been writing small web articles for different content farms for pennies just so it'd drive the article down in the search rankings. It'd take a while to sort through all the Alexis Thompson hits—it's not a rare name—but you could find it on the internet. Eventually."

"So it's been in the news before?"

She nodded. "I was a patent lawyer, and my client was in a David-and-Goliath-type case." Her lips lifted in a sad smile. "I was going to win. Out of the blue, he told me he had killed his partner. He had faked evidence that made everyone believe his partner had just left the country. He told me every detail." Her stride diminished, and her steps faltered as she recalled everything. "So, after countless sleepless nights, I called in an anonymous tip. Only it eventually came to light that I was the informant."

"Does it really fall under attorney-client privilege when you weren't his defense lawyer?"

"Unfortunately." She sucked in a breath. "But I argued it was the exception to 'prevent, mitigate or rectify substantial injury to the financial interests of another that is reasonably certain to result or has resulted from the client's commission of a crime in furtherance of which the client has used the lawyer's services.'" She huffed. "Can you tell I memorized the rules from the American Bar Association? Basically I argued that if I helped my client in the patent case, he had a good chance of winning substantial money that his partner's family would never receive. Not to mention the wife couldn't get life insurance because everyone thought he'd left her. I felt part of the crime. I couldn't work, I couldn't eat…" Her throat and nose burned with held-back tears.

"You had no idea that would happen. You were a patent lawyer."

His gentle voice and understanding nature weren't helping her keep it together. She refused to let her guard down, so she pulled back her shoulders. "No. But when I entered this profession, I should've been willing to live with the consequences if it did happen. In the state of Washington, at least, they ruled I should've kept my mouth shut. I was disbarred. All of my lawyer friends agreed with the verdict, and worse, the murderer got to walk free. That poor family knows that he did it, and yet he walks free."

He reached for her hand and squeezed. "You were just trying to do the right thing."

She sighed and savored the comfort. "You are a good man, Nick. I can't stand the thought of being the reason you can't be mayor, then state senator, then…"

"Not that it matters, but I don't have those kinds of aspirations."

She gently pulled her hand out of his. "That's what my dad said before he became mayor. He soon realized that he could help so many more people if he had a bigger circle of influence. Everyone realized it. He had a huge support group encouraging him to do it."

Nick folded his arms across his chest and tried not to be bothered that she had pulled her hand back. "So, did he run for other offices?"

She shook her head. "I got into the wrong crowd for a brief time in high school, and he didn't want the press to scrutinize my choices. So he put his dreams on hold until recently. And then… Well, you know." She cringed. "I'm thankful and ashamed all at the same time." She shook the paper in her hand. "Obviously he was right to fear the press, but who knows how much good he would've done for the state if it weren't for me?"

"You can't think that way, Alexis. You can't allow past circumstances to dictate your future."

"Why not?" Her voice took on a steely quality. She was so tired of that clichéd sentiment. The past had consequences, plain and simple. "Isn't that why you're running in the first place? Because you want to do the good that your brother would've done had he lived?"

He cringed.

Her gut dropped. Her words had consequences, too. "Oh, Nick. I'm sorry. I shouldn't have said that."

"No, you're right to think that. It's true."

She closed her eyes, unable to handle the pain that crossed his features. "Even if it was true, I shouldn't have said it that way. You were trying to encourage me, and I got defensive."

"No, you spoke the truth. I can't judge you, because I'm guilty of the same thing. The past has called the shots in my decisions lately. The bottom line is, I've lived with the guilt of being the surviving brother every single day, but I want to honor my brother. For him it was much more than a job. He genuinely wanted to help make the world a better place. So if we get our names cleared and the danger disappears, I'll still run for mayor." He exhaled. "Truth is, I'm scared I won't be able to handle it."

"I have no doubt your brother would be so proud." She tilted her head, wondering if she'd missed something. Nick was more than competent and educated. "Why would you think you couldn't handle it?"

"For the same reason that I couldn't handle medical school."

She exhaled, remembering what he'd said. "Because you can't control people." She struggled with that daily, as well. "You can't make them choose the right decisions. I feel the same way, but it doesn't mean you should give up and stop trying."

The words sounded right, but they didn't entirely reflect her heart. She was falling for this man, hard. Deep down, she wished he'd give up the campaign and his practice, and they could move to the city and pursue what seemed to be happening between them. Why did God have to show her this man who seemed perfect for her but then have his life goals revolve around politics and animals? The two things she could never be a part of.

Raven rushed ahead of them and pulled to the left. They had reached Joe's backyard. Alexis unlocked the door. Raven ran through the house, searching for her owner. Tears pricked Alexis's eyes as she watched.

They both stood in the entryway, motionless, until Raven ran back to them.

Alexis leaned down and rubbed her head. "How do you tell a dog its owner is gone?" Her voice cracked.

Nick took a knee. Raven flopped to the ground for him to rub her tummy. "I have no idea."

Alexis walked through the house and made sure all the blinds and curtains were closed before she flipped on the pantry light in the kitchen. It spread at just the right angle that it hit the circular table without filling the room with light. While Joe's passing hadn't made the news yet, she knew it would circulate through the town by the morning.

She spread out the newspaper and stared at the photographs. Her hands shook as she recalled the feeling of almost going over the cliff. For the briefest of moments, she thought she'd been responsible for Nick's death. She cleared her throat to keep it from closing. "Nick, remember when you saw someone on that cliff above us? Maybe when you thought you saw a gun, it was actually a camera. This had to be shot with a telephoto lens."

He joined her at the small table. "Possible. That's why I wanted to know who took the photo."

She pointed to the byline. "I know Tommy from temping at the paper. I'm calling him."

"It's midnight."

"The news never sleeps."

His lips curled into an adorable smile. "I'm pretty sure that's not a thing."

"I'm pretty sure I've heard it somewhere." She dialed and put it on speakerphone.

"Hello?" Tommy answered.

She turned away from Nick's smirk, knowing he could hear how groggy the voice on the other end of the line sounded. She got right to the point. "Tommy, where did you get those photographs of Nick and me?"

"Lexi?" She could hear what sounded like sheets shifting in the background. "I'm sorry. I had to print it. It's news."

The brutal headline would plague her nightmares, but a quick skim of the article showed it focused on the facts alone. She wondered which editor made the call to print it, though. "I'm not blaming you. I want to know where those photographs came from."

"They're anonymous."

"You must have some idea of where they came from."

"Someone used one of those temporary email addresses with a Dropbox invitation. The Dropbox account deleted after I downloaded it."

"And you printed it without a reputable source?"

"It came with links to some Seattle news outlets and the American Bar Association. Those were reputable enough for us to take the lead. If it's any consolation, maybe it's someone who really doesn't want to see Mr. Kendrick get elected. You just happened to be a casualty."

She shivered at the last word. But it was clear that this was another dead end. "Okay, Tommy. Go back to sleep."

"I really am sorry, Lexi. I hope you'll keep filling in for us in ad copy."

It hit her like a brick. She couldn't. Even if there hadn't been drugs and fake witnesses against her or a group of drug traffickers determined to kill her, something inside had shifted.

Her shameful secret had come into the light, and she was ready to face it. If she and Nick were able to walk freely again, she would go after her Idaho license. And even if the bar association said no, she'd do something…anything that challenged her mind and engaged her heart. It'd taken being in danger to realize she'd put her life on hold.

She opened the laptop and clicked on the file where she kept the images of the time cards. Nick placed a plate of sandwiches next to her. "Peanut butter and jelly," he said.

She almost inhaled one. She'd taken three bites without so much as tasting it. Raven appeared at her side. She tore off an edge and dropped it. "I think the dog approves."

"She certainly approves of you."

"I meant the sandwiches." She eagerly took another bite.

"I know." He leaned over her shoulder and looked at the images. "What are we looking for?"

His proximity made it hard not to focus on the fact they'd almost kissed minutes ago. "Um, I'm not sure. Anything that seems out of place."

"They don't all look the same." He pointed at the

screen. "The copy shop ones look different than the newspaper ones. The heating-and-air shop orders the information in a completely different way than the medical practice."

That fact had never bothered her before. They were different companies with different logos. But the form in and of itself should've been in the same order. "Maybe they had to design their own time cards?"

He straightened and put his fists on his waist. "It doesn't add up."

"Well, there has to be something here if someone was willing to kill for them."

"Did Theresa have a scanner?" He pointed to the right side of each image. "These aren't standard time cards. They have what looks like a bar code, except it's half the size of a typical one. And what are all these project numbers?"

She shrugged. "I never asked. I assume it's the account number for Theresa to reference." The familiar ache in between her shoulder blades returned. She recognized it instantly as shame for not being more aware. She'd missed so much during her time of self-centered pity. "I'm afraid I considered it beyond my pay grade and never asked."

"Too bad you weren't a tax attorney."

"Yeah. I've got nothing beyond a rudimentary understanding. But a certified fraud examiner would!" She grabbed her phone and scrolled through her contacts until she found her old college friend, Victoria Hayes. Correction. Victoria Tucker now. Her dear friend had gotten married to a handsome skydiving instructor named Jeff a year ago in Boise. Alexis still wasn't used to calling her by her married name.

She sent the text message and waited.

Victoria was always quick to respond.

"It's one in the morning now, Alexis. Maybe she has her phone set to Do Not Disturb like the rest of us."

Alexis let her head fall to the edge of the laptop. Time was ticking. She knew the law would allow Chief Spencer to hold Gerald for only eight hours to question him about Theresa and the drug ring since his trespassing charge wasn't likely to stick.

"They picked Gerald up sometime between eight thirty and nine at night, when the fireworks started. Unless the chief finds some other reason to hold him, we have until only five in the morning to find some evidence. Our time is running out."

TWELVE

Nick tossed and turned on the couch. His exhaustion should've meant he could have slept anywhere, but his mind wouldn't turn off. Alexis had pinpointed his unease with his campaign. While he could encourage changes to be made in the town to stop drug use, he couldn't control people. He could provide more resources for recovery and officers in the schools, but it didn't mean that the town's drug problem would be cured. He sat up in a cold sweat. So was it a waste of time?

His brother had to have faced the same issue, but he had seemed to have an easier time compartmentalizing his work and life. Rarely did he ever talk about work, except if Nick had pestered him with questions whenever they were together. From Nick's perspective, his brother's job had seemed more important than his own.

He looked up at the ceiling as the truth hit him. Even before his brother's death, Nick had been looking for contentment and his identity in other places besides the true source. If he could just be more, control more…

Forgive me, Lord. His entire life as he knew it threatened to fall apart. It was about time he put his identity in the right place. Because if Alexis's friend couldn't help them figure out the puzzle of the time cards, Nick was ready to turn himself in. His confidence had to come from the Lord.

Why couldn't I have met her at a different time? Alexis stirred his heart in a way no other had before. He wanted to get to know her better without running for their lives. Not that it would be easy even if their names were cleared. Alexis didn't believe that he wouldn't have other political aspirations. She refused to let them have a chance because of her past. How would he ever convince her that he didn't care about that? He cared more about their future.

He shuffled into the kitchen and put on a pot of coffee. While it percolated, he looked around, hoping to get his mind off the situation. A box of files sat on the edge of the counter with Raven's toys and training items. Raven's name was on the front of the files. He pulled them out, curious if they would contain a clue about Raven's future owner.

Flipping a folder open, he recognized the first set of papers as a copy of her medical report. He made sure his clients left with a set of them after each visit. It lessened the chance of confusion about what he'd said during an appointment if they had his notes in print. Behind that was a log of Raven's training schedule and benchmarks. What must have been Joe's scrawled handwriting was all over the place.

6/15 Works for approval more than toys or treats. Extraordinary detection of narcotics.
8/3 Excels at detection. Other elements of police work don't interest her.

8/15 Training exercise proved she will protect me but refuses to attack others. She's a lover, not a fighter.

Nick chuckled but sobered at the next line written just before the hit-and-run.

9/1 Starting to wonder if Raven would be better suited as a therapy dog.

A brochure on therapy dog training had been paper-clipped to the back of the folder. Nick pulled it out to read it but noticed that Raven no longer lay at the base of the couch. Come to think of it, he didn't remember stepping over her when he got up to get coffee. When was the last time he heard her deep breathing? Maybe that was part of the reason he couldn't sleep well. Had she gone out the doggie door?

He started to walk to the back door when something buzzed. Finding Raven would have to wait a second. He followed the buzzing into the hallway. Through the open door of a bedroom, he spotted Alexis sleeping, fully clothed, on top of the comforter with her arm draped over Raven. Her peaceful face was even nuzzled up against the dog's fur.

His shoulders relaxed, and he put a hand over his mouth so he wouldn't laugh aloud. If she hadn't claimed to hate dogs so much, the image would've been heart-warming more than hilarious. Raven lifted her head and turned to look at him as if to say, *Would you make that buzzing racket stop before it wakes her up?*

He crossed the room and peeked at the offending smartphone on the nightstand. He hated to wake her up, but this was the call they'd been waiting for. "Alexis. It's Victoria."

She sat up in one smooth motion and swung her legs off the bed. Raven jumped off the bed with a harrumph and rested at her feet. Alexis blinked. He didn't take the time to let her wake up fully but handed her the phone. She frowned, put her thumb on the answer button and lifted it to her ear. "Hello?"

"Sorry. Did I wake you?" The voice on the other end was loud enough Nick could hear it. "I thought you said it was urgent. I woke up and saw the tons of messages you left."

Nick glanced at the clock on the wall. Seven in the morning came quickly when you didn't go to bed until two.

Alexis closed her eyes. "Um, yeah. It is urgent." She yawned. "Let me put you on speakerphone."

She pressed the button and rested the phone on the bed. "Okay," Victoria said, "so I'm looking at these time cards. Totally old school. Did you say this guy was an investment banker?"

Alexis looked as if she'd fallen back asleep even though she was sitting up straight.

"Uh, yes," Nick answered.

"Bookkeeping is one thing, but I don't understand how he would be able to keep up with investments and stock markets without being technologically savvy."

"Well, he does have computers," Alexis said. "He just doesn't like them. I'll admit it might be something the police should look into, but he doesn't come across as smart enough to pull anything dodgy."

"Hmm." Victoria didn't sound so certain. "My fraud senses are going off, but without doing a full audit on him, these time cards don't tell me much. Though I did wonder why only some of them have extra numbers."

Alexis stood up. "Extra numbers? What do you mean?"

Alexis ran to the laptop and pulled up the images.

Victoria rattled off instructions. "Check the one for June 20, when you filled in for receptionist at the medical practice. Then look at July 15. Then there's one in August—"

"I see them," Alexis said. She zoomed in on the images. Sure enough, there was an extra set of numbers on each of them listed underneath Project Number. She'd assumed that was a reference for bookkeeping purposes, but it had to be more than that. None of the other time cards utilized the project number section. And even if they had, not all of her time cards with the medical practice listed a project number. She did the same job, though, each time she worked there.

"A code?" Nick asked.

"Maybe," Alexis said. "Or maybe it's something for their personal records. A medical practice would have different paperwork needs."

"Something about it is niggling in the back of my mind," Victoria said over the speakerphone. "I can't figure it out, though."

"Can't figure what out?" a deep voice in the background said.

"I'm on the phone with Alexis. It's Jeff," Victoria said into the phone. "These numbers."

"If they didn't have those extra numbers after the slash, I'd almost think they were GPS coordinates," Jeff said.

"Did you hear that?" Victoria asked.

Nick leaned forward and put his finger on the laptop screen. "These don't look like GPS coordinates to me."

Alexis agreed. The first number had a double digit, a decimal point and a long line of numbers followed by a vertical slash. The second set was a negative double-digit number, a decimal point and a long line of numbers. The third set after the slash was a series of eight numbers.

"There are different ways of listing coordinates," Jeff explained. "Most people are used to seeing the little degree symbol and a set of cardinal directions—north and south along with east or west. We call that the DMS method, but another method is to give latitude and longitude. Latitude always goes first. I have no idea what the third set of numbers would be, though."

Alexis leaned forward. Because of Jeff's skydiving business, it made sense that he would know how to decipher coordinates. Nick leaned over her shoulder and pulled up a browser. He typed in the first two sets of numbers from the June time card.

The first link that popped up said, "Barings, Idaho, Latitude and Longitude."

Nick leaned back and exhaled. "I think we might be getting somewhere. I would've never guessed that was anything other than a project number."

Her heart pounded. That was too big a coincidence to ignore. Jeff had to be on to something.

"If you want to be sure," Jeff added, "there are converters online that will turn it into standard DMS. Then you can plug that into Google Maps."

"So try that and let us know, okay? I'm getting ready

to head out of town. Investigation in Portland," Victoria said. "I'm sorry I couldn't be of any more help."

Alexis passed on her thankfulness as Nick rapidly found an online converter. Within seconds, he'd determined the location. An agricultural sales warehouse on the outskirts of town. She stared at it, slack-jawed. Agricultural sales had nothing to do with a medical practice. But maybe they were barking up the wrong tree. "We still don't know what the third set of numbers could be."

"Let's try the other two extra number sets before we attempt to figure that out. See if the GPS thing was a fluke."

He typed in and converted the first two sets of numbers for the July and August time cards. Each time, they pinpointed an exact business, unrelated to the medical practice. She leaned back, staring at the map.

Nick tapped her monitor. "Okay, if we're running with this theory, we have to figure out the third set of numbers."

She stared at the June time card. It hit her all at once. "A date and time?"

Nick pointed at the numbers: 06240300. "June 24. Three in the morning if you're using military time."

His eyes lit with hopefulness as their gazes connected. "Did we figure it out?" She scrolled to the next odd time card in July.

"July 28 at six o'clock in the evening." Nick tapped the table. "It'd still be light out. That would be bold."

"Maybe it would draw less attention. Look at the location. It's the heating-and-air parts warehouse. Anyone there on a Saturday at that time wouldn't look so out of place. However, technicians might still be in their trucks servicing clients, but I know for a fact they close up shop by three o'clock on Saturday no matter what. I got tasked with locking up once."

Her fingers shook as she pulled up the August time card. Nick entered the coordinates. "That would be—"

She gasped as the location showed up on the browser. "Barings Furniture? I loved working there. Mr. Griggs is the nicest man. He can't be part of a drug operation. There's no way."

"We don't know if he's involved, Alexis. We're not even sure what this is."

"It has to be connected to the drugs and the mayor." She examined the rest of the numbers. "September 3, two o'clock in the afternoon." Her gaze lifted to meet Nick's. "That's today. Whatever it is, it's going down today."

He tilted his head back. Grabbing her hands, he pulled her to standing as if he wanted to jump up and down. "You did it. You figured it out."

"If we had more time cards from the past years, it would help confirm our theory. Gerald came into his newfound wealth a long time ago. So this must have been going on since then." She started to pace around the room. "Theresa always gave me first chance to work at the practice ever since I moved back. It was one of the nicer jobs so I always took it. But if we're right, the code had to be on other time cards of previous temps who worked there."

"So we don't know exactly what it means yet."

"We know enough. These time cards would've gone from Theresa to Barry for bookkeeping. So someone at the practice had to be feeding Barry the time and place the deals were going down. It's almost foolproof because it passes through several hands without any digital trace. It's the real reason Barry insisted on going old school." She held up a finger. "One of the part-time nurses at the practice hates her job. Said she's tired of looking at rashes all day, but there aren't many medical jobs in our town. She might be the contact supplying the numbers through all the temps."

"Do you think the other temps are in danger, then?"

"I hope not. There was high turnover. There are only a few temps who have worked for Theresa the past few months, and they're much older ladies. I doubt any of them felt the need to keep digital records like I did."

"So how is the bookkeeper involved?"

"Gerald and Barry are brothers. Gerald must have been using Barry's so-called investment service to launder the drug money."

He nodded. "Makes sense to me. We'll give this to the police, and they should be able to catch them red-handed."

Her checks hurt from how wide she grinned.

He pulled her into his arms for a hug. She closed her eyes for the briefest of moments, wanting to savor the moment. Because no matter how much she wanted to pursue a relationship with him, she'd come to terms with the fact she never could.

He released her, but only just enough that he could see into her eyes. "I'm glad you got some sleep…with the help of Raven."

She tilted her head. "Raven?"

Laughter shone from his eyes. "You two were pretty cozy on the bed. I think you've made a new friend."

She frowned. He had to be crazy. "I did no such thing. I would never allow a dog to sleep on the bed."

Although, come to think of it, she did dream about wrapping herself in a fuzzy blanket.

"If you say so." He smiled. "Alexis, after we both get some real rest, I'd like to take you out for dinner."

Her heart plummeted. "I can't."

He released her and stepped back, confusion and hurt written on his face. "Why?"

"The problem with lawyers is they talk too much."

His forehead creased. "Why do I feel like you're leading the witness?"

"I made it pretty obvious I liked you, but without a gun pointed—"

His jaw dropped. "Oh, you can stop there." He shook his head as if trying to erase the conversation. "I see where this is going. If you need a gun pointed at you to want—"

"No, you don't know where I was going." Her words rushed out. "After we prove Gerald is guilty, this town will need a mayor. And in a couple years, this state will need a senat—" She let her sentence drop because it hurt to think she couldn't be alongside him. "I can't stand in the way of you changing the world for the better. I won't do that to another good man."

"There's a verse. I might butcher it, but basically it says if I understood all mysteries, all knowledge, had all faith so that I could move mountains yet have not love, then I am nothing."

Her heart stopped for a moment, savoring the words. She knew the passage. "I think that verse is about loving all mankind," she said softly.

He nodded as if he knew, as well. He squinted as he looked up at the ceiling. "There's something in Ecclesiastes. If one man falls, the other will lift him up. But woe to him that has no one—"

She grinned, appreciating his quick thinking. A lot of people couldn't keep up with her, but Nick practically outpaced her. "You're really reaching now, aren't you?" She laughed. "I appreciate the sentiment."

"Okay. Well, this comes straight from the book of me, myself and I. I'm working at trusting God more so I'm not upset by decisions people make that I don't agree with. But please hear me when I say that if the town doesn't choose me as their leader because I want a beautiful, kind woman with a servant's heart, who I think loves this town more than I do, to be by my side, then that's their bad decision. And I could accept that."

Her eyes filled with tears. It was so tempting. He had no idea. But she couldn't do that to him. Not in the long run. He said he could accept it, but what about five years from now? "I can't," she whispered.

THIRTEEN

They crunched on cereal and sipped coffee in silence on separate sides of the room. It sounded like a symphony composed of awkward. Even if everything between them had been peaches and roses, the reminder that Joe wouldn't be returning to finish the milk before it went bad hung over Nick's head.

"If they ever find his next of kin, we should make a donation," Alexis said, as if thinking the same thing. "Can I use your phone?"

"Why?"

"Given my last conversations with Jeremy and Chief Spencer, I'm not sure they'll answer my call."

He doubted that was true but handed over the phone.

She pointed it at the monitor, snapped photos of the time cards and emailed them to the same address the officer at Theresa's office had supplied. *Here goes.* She dialed and pressed the speakerphone function.

The moment the chief answered, the words flew off her tongue, enough to rival any fast-talking auctioneer. She told him how to read the numbers and relayed her guess that it was probably a wholesale drug shipment of some sort to be picked up by drug dealers throughout town.

"That's in a few hours," he said. "I don't have time to get cooperation from agencies in other towns. We don't have a resident DEA or SWAT team, and frankly, you don't have enough evidence in these time cards for me to justify using one even if I wanted to."

Alexis slumped onto the couch. "Please. You know I'm innocent, Chief. I had access to a vehicle. If I were guilty, wouldn't I have fled town? You know in your gut someone killed Theresa and that scout and Joe. They weren't your typical overdoses. Their deaths have to be connected."

He harrumphed. "The hospital footage showed that Theresa entered Joe's room the night of his death."

Alexis's face paled. "You're not suggesting she—"

"It's possible she saw something. The images are grainy, but she argued with a doctor in the hallway who kept his face turned away from security cameras. The Boise Police have yet to find the doctor matching his description."

"Does he by chance look like Gerald?" Nick asked.

"Gerald is bald," the chief responded. "This man is not."

"His brother, Barry, has a full head of hair," Alexis added. "It makes perfect sense. He runs the bookkeeping service. Has the mayor talked yet? He was with Theresa. He has to know something."

An uncomfortable silence settled over the line. "We had to let him go."

"Then you need to follow up on this tip. Something is going to happen today at that furniture store. And what about all those shootouts? Chief, that has to be enough."

He growled something under his breath. "Barry had an alibi. I know how to do my job. Come to the station."

She hung up on him and turned to Nick. "If he's not going to be at the drop-off, we can't prove our innocence. A drug test might prove we weren't taking drugs but not that we weren't in possession with the intent to distribute."

Nick pointed at his phone. "So maybe we film it happening."

"Yes. Now you're talking."

He shook his head. "While I appreciate your enthusiasm, there's no way I'm letting you get within a hundred feet of that furniture shop."

She eyed him and gave him a smile that he was beginning to regard as dangerous. "You said you wanted to help stop drug trafficking in this town."

It was, in fact, exactly what he wanted to do, but he'd never intended to be so hands-on about it, and he still wasn't sure it was the wisest option. He racked his brain for other ideas and came up with squat. "What we need is a good vantage point, and a promise from you that if this doesn't work, you'll accompany me to the safety of the police station. No matter what."

She pulled up the map on her own phone. "Help me find the perfect spot."

"Could you stop checking your phone? You're making me nervous." He peered out the window. "Unless it's to tell me the police are on the way."

She clicked off the screen as Nick resumed his pacing in front of the windows. "Sorry. I'm just checking the time again. Maybe we got it wrong. They're late." She'd never thought that her odd jobs for the temp agency would've been good for more than a low hourly wage. But the office space for lease above an insurance office made for the perfect spot to see the back of the furniture store.

All it had taken was one call to Jessica, a real-estate agent who Alexis had helped set up showings for a couple of times. Jessica was more than happy to supply the code to the lockbox so she could take a peek at the office space. "It's about time you set up your lawyer digs in town," Jessica had said.

Alexis had tried to lightheartedly shut down the lawyer practice idea, but Jessica had merely laughed. "It'll be our little secret. Check it out and let me know what you think."

Raven paced in front of the folding chair. Alexis reached down and rubbed her soft ears.

"She's growing on you," Nick said.

Alexis shrugged. "She's not bad, I guess. For a dog." Tears threatened to overcome her out of nowhere. How could an animal show such undying devotion to someone it'd only recently met? It moved her. "I wonder who will get her."

Raven wagged her tail as if she understood. The hair near the dog's neck spiked as she stiffened. Alexis pulled her hand back, at first wondering if she'd touched Raven's stitches. But she'd been nowhere near the spot. She looked around but saw nothing. The rev of a motor sounded.

"Here we go," Nick whispered, as if the vehicle could hear them. He ducked and lifted his phone to the corner of the window and pressed Record. Alexis leaned forward, keeping her head low but still high enough that she could see through the window as the furniture truck rounded the corner and headed for the back of the store.

"Do you see the police?" She tried to keep the fear out of her voice, but if they couldn't see Gerald or any criminal activity from the window, then they would still be without evidence. Her heart plummeted as the steel door to the store's loading dock rolled up and the truck backed into it. "I didn't see the driver or whoever opened the door. Did you? I really thought the chief would come around, and the cops would be here."

Nick's head dropped, and he stopped recording. "We tried, Alexis. I think it's time to give up."

Raven released a growl that sent chills up Alexis's spine. It sounded more like a mama bear than a dog. She spun around.

"I agree with him." Barry stood at the top of the stairway, pointing a gun at them. With bushy eyebrows hanging low over his blue eyes, a constant five-o'clock shadow, and dark, thick, wavy hair, he would've more aptly been named Harry. "It is time for you to give up, Alexis."

Her insides twisted. "I genuinely didn't think it was you." She shook her head, but her indignation that this man would pose as a friend to Theresa rose past the fear. "Why would you kill Theresa?"

He reared back as if he'd been slapped. "I didn't do that. I would never do that."

"Yeah, and I'm sure you didn't kill Joe, either, or set us up."

His eyes widened. "I didn't kill anyone."

"Yeah, so the police told me." She huffed. "Your so-called alibi. Someone in your drug ring lied for you, huh?"

He waved the gun wildly. Raven made a sound between a bark and a whine. Alexis's breath caught. Maybe she'd gone too far, but if they were going to admit defeat and die anyway, she at least wanted to know the whole truth. Nick took a step forward and twisted his body as if to block her from any bullets. The gesture was enough to make her words run dry.

"Leave Jessica out of this," Barry spat.

It was a good thing she'd been too stunned to speak. So that was how Barry knew where they were. Jessica, the real estate agent, and Barry were an item. Another unlikely pairing, but she felt sure that, like Theresa, Jessica had no idea what kind of man she'd become involved with.

Barry's face turned red. "And she's not part of any drug ring, either. I'm just here to escort you. So shut your smart mouth and do what I say. I don't want to hurt you." He looked at Nick, eyes imploring. "I never wanted anyone to get hurt." His voice shook with emotion.

Alexis turned to Nick, whose face mirrored her own confusion. Barry had the appearance of someone helpless and in sorrow, just as Gerald had.

"What are you and your brother mixed up in?" Nick asked. "Maybe we can help."

"Mind your own business and get moving."

"The police will be here any minute. We told them all about this."

Barry raised an eyebrow. "So you were the reason for the unplanned traffic stop. Well, nice try. All they saw was furniture inside the truck." He gave a pointed look at the dog. "Without a sniffer, they wouldn't find the drugs stashed inside. They gave the men the green light and moved on, which is what you need to do right now."

Her heart sank. No one would be coming to the rescue.

Barry took a side step and waved them out of the office space. Instead of going down the stairs, he pointed them into the hallway to the fire escape. Raven automatically walked on Alexis's left side, on the opposite side of Barry, as they passed him. Any hope Alexis had that the dog had a hero's instinct faded away.

Once outside, she desperately looked for someone, anyone, who could call for help. Barry pulled his gun closer into his side, but no one was on the sidewalk, on the street or in the alley between the buildings. From this vantage point, she could see a small space between the loading dock and the furniture truck, but there was no sign of anyone. Her eyes filled with tears. Why would God give her a desire to advocate for the less fortunate, yet when she needed a defender, leave her helpless?

She tripped on one of the grated steps, but Nick grabbed her arm to keep her from falling farther. She swiped her vision clear. Maybe she wasn't being fair. Events hadn't gone the way she'd thought they should have, but she had never really been alone. Her parents had been there for her when she'd been disbarred, and maybe if she'd been humble enough and let others know, some of them would've been as supportive as Nick. He had been there when her car almost dove off a cliff and when a bullet had been aimed at her. Twice. And maybe God would've defended her if she'd laid down her fear and gone into the station when Nick had asked her to.

"I'm sorry," she whispered to him. "You were right. I should've given up sooner. I should've listened to you."

Nick gave her a rueful smile as they continued to descend the stairs. "Just remember that if we get out of this—" he winked and reached for her hand "—I think I've fallen in love with you."

Warmth filled her chest, but she couldn't afford even a moment to enjoy it.

Nick gave her fingers a squeeze before she pulled away. They reached the bottom of the stairs and crossed the alley. If they were going to die, at least she could face death with hope in her heart.

FOURTEEN

Nick tensed as he opened a nondescript door from within the alley. While Barry claimed he didn't want to kill them, they had no guarantees about the motives of whoever waited on the other side of the door.

The tip of the gun pressed into Nick's back. "Go on," Barry urged.

The back wall was aqua with black letters in the middle spelling Barings Financial Advisors. The name seemed odd, as Barry was the only advisor at the firm. Texturized taupe wallpaper covered the rest of the walls. Two black leather couches were on opposite sides of the room. They walked toward the empty receptionist desk. Maybe if Nick was fast enough, he could dial 911 from the landline.

Barry gasped behind them. Nick spun around. Someone wearing blue surgical gloves had an arm around Barry's throat. The man inserted a needle into the side of his neck before Barry could even struggle.

Barry's eyes went wide before his mouth and body went slack. The man let go of his throat and grabbed the gun from his hand as Barry's form dropped to the floor.

He calmly capped the syringe.

"You," Alexis breathed.

Dr. Tindale smiled. "Here I am."

Nick warred between rage and confusion. "Why? You're a doctor!"

He smirked. "It's a new generation. Operating a profitable drug ring that skates underneath the nose of law officials takes the same professional skills as managing a successful practice."

Alexis shook her head. "You already make—"

"Beans." Spittle escaped his mouth, an unattractive feature for a man who clearly spent too much time grooming his wavy hair. "A dermatologist in a small town that was supposed to have thrived and has only shrunk. Many of the operators I know have—" he shrugged "—decent paying jobs, I suppose. But if I want the lifestyle I deserve, heroin is the future. And despite living in this Podunk town, it's slightly bigger than all the other small towns in the area. A virtual hub."

"Your stuff is deadly," Nick interjected.

"For those who want the bigger high, they have to accept the bigger risk. We use only microscopic amounts for my regular customers. Obviously, Barry wasn't a regular."

Raven took a step toward the man, and then jumped back, barking.

Tindale waved the gun, directing it at Raven. "That dog was supposed to be dead by now. As soon as Joe brought this rat with him to his appointment, I knew it had to go. It was sniffing and barking. Joe tried to lie and claim the dog was still in training, but I knew he suspected me. They both had to go."

"You were behind the hit and run. You were the doctor at the hospital." Alexis put a hand to her mouth as she yanked back the leash to pull Raven behind her. She stood in front of the dog, and Raven sat at attention. "Theresa spotted you there."

"How was I to know they'd come visiting?" The doc shrugged.

"She'd have known it was you who killed Joe," Alexis said.

Nick tried to step in front of Alexis, but the doctor pointed the gun at him. "Stay there. Gerald said he would keep her in line, but it became clear she was a liability. I'm six months away from retiring for good on a Caribbean island. I just need a few more deals. So if you don't want to end up like your friend…" He stepped to the side and gestured for Alexis to move away from the dog.

She shook her head. Dr. Tindale's eyes narrowed. "You should be able to understand, Alexis. You lose your license in one state, it makes it harder to practice in another."

Her eyes widened.

"Yeah, I looked you up the first time you came into my office." He pursed his lips. "If you'd taken the time to know me, you'd have found we have a lot in common."

Bile rose in Nick's throat. "She was trying to bring justice and healing to others. I imagine all you've done is help yourself." Nick fisted his hands.

The doctor held up the syringe. "The first time you see someone die in front of you is the hardest, but—" he waved it a little "—this stuff makes it pretty easy. I sensed Barry's gratitude was waning after I'd taken him from small-time bookkeeper to investment managcr." He sighed. "But the good news is, neither of you has to die."

Nick and Alexis exchanged a glance. What did he mean?

"It's simple," Tindale continued. "Alexis writes a statement that the veterinarian was behind it all." He shrugged and cast a smile at Nick. "You'll have to go to prison, but you understand. It's the only way."

"Then what?" Alexis pressed. "You let me walk?"

"Oh, no. That wouldn't do me any good. No, you'll take over Barry's job. There will be some that won't trust you since you're disbarred, but most people won't bother changing a thing as long as their dividend checks come regularly. Which they will. We'll probably even have them increase a bit to stop questions. Then, if you'd like, you can choose to come with me or stay here in this pit stop."

Nick's breathing grew erratic. He couldn't be serious. What would stop Alexis from turning witness the moment he was out of sight? And forget about being disbarred, she didn't have a background in finance. His plan didn't make sense.

She pointed toward the sign taped to the receptionist desk. "I can't just step into Barry's role. What about the Securities Investor Protect—"

"Do you think people actually check to see if their brokers are members of SIPC or FINRA?" He shook his head. "Hasn't happened yet. People believe what they want to believe."

"Fine. I'll do whatever you want. But you leave the dog alone." She threw her shoulders back. "I'll make sure she doesn't go into detection work."

"Give him the dog and start writing."

She handed the leash handle to Nick and rounded the desk, her features determined. Tindale stayed right behind her, hovering over her even as she sat down in the chair. He dictated everything for her to write down.

Why would Tindale trust that she wouldn't testify against him? The only thing making sense was that he would have something in writing blaming the two of them. There was no way Tindale would let them live. It had to be a ruse.

Alexis sighed dejectedly. She closed her eyes briefly before she signed her name at the bottom.

"Thank you, dear." In one swift motion, Tindale flicked the cap back off the syringe and aimed it for her neck.

Raven leaped in the air before Nick could register what was happening. She tugged the leash so violently it fell from his fingertips.

Raven's jaw snapped onto Tindale's forearm. She whipped her head back and forth and Tindale howled, but the man still managed to hold onto the needle. He screamed as he turned the gun in his other hand toward the dog.

Alexis leaned to the side, horror on her lips. She grabbed the stapler on the desk and smashed it upward into Tindale's arm holding the gun. The gun shifted and went off. A bullet soared through the ceiling, and fiberglass pieces rained down on the floor.

Nick jumped onto the desk. "Hit him in the face."

Alexis didn't need to be told twice. She smacked the stapler hard directly into Tindale's face as Nick wrenched the gun out of the man's hands. Tindale tried to shake the dog off his forearm. "Get him off!"

Nick handed the gun to Alexis. "Point it at him. If he so much as moves, shoot him."

Nick grabbed the man's wrist and squeezed while he pulled the syringe safely out of Tindale's hand.

"Just get it off," Tindale screamed again.

Three men in red hats and shirts with the logo Barings Furniture embroidered on them rushed in with guns drawn. "Police," one shouted.

Alexis did a double take but didn't drop the gun. "Jeremy?"

The man closest to her nodded and signaled the other two men to go around the desk and surround Tindale. She held out the gun for Jeremy to take. "You guys were there all along?"

"Alexis, can you call Raven?" Nick asked, a smile on his face. "She's not listening to me."

Raven's hind legs were on the desk, but she still whipped her head side to side, her mouth firmly embedded in Tindale's arm. "Here, girl."

Raven's ears perked. She dropped fully onto the desk and vaulted to Alexis's side. Nick joined Alexis and put a hand on her back. "Are you okay?"

"The moment I started writing, I knew he was never going to let us go. He was setting it up so it looked like a murder-suicide so he could go on with business as usual. If it weren't for you, Raven and the police..." Her throat closed so she couldn't say any more. She'd never been so thankful.

Jeremy holstered his weapon once the other two officers had Tindale in hand. "We pulled the furniture truck over on a traffic stop. The two drivers had rap sheets longer than my arm. So we took over and helped the dealers in the store unload the furniture. They started pulling out packages of drugs. Must've been hundreds of thousands of dollars' worth." He smirked. "We arrested ten dealers without so much as a bullet fired, and that was my first undercover assignment."

"Good work. Check the doc for more syringes," Nick called out to the other officers as they escorted him out the door. "Carefully."

Jeremy nodded at Nick. "Thanks."

Chief Spencer walked in at that moment and headed straight for Alexis. He reached his hand out and shook his finger at her. "You have caused me more grief…" He pulled her into a surprising bear hug. "I'm thankful you're safe. If anything had happened to you, your dad would've had my hide."

Tears stung her eyes at the unexpected display of affection. She blinked them back. "Gerald and Barry were both working for Dr. Tindale. I think they got in over their heads, but they were still involved."

The chief nodded. "I imagine Gerald will want to make sure the doc pays for killing his brother. He'll come clean." He reached out to Nick for a hearty handshake. "And I have a feeling you'll make a good mayor."

"You think he still has a chance?" Alexis asked. "After the news?"

"You two have been proven innocent." The chief frowned. "You mean because you were disbarred? Pfft. Most of the town knew a year ago."

"What?" She gazed at Nick in disbelief. He flashed what looked like a happy *I told you so* grin.

Jeremy crossed his arms over his chest. "Old news. I think I heard a good ten months ago."

Her mouth fell open. "You all knew? No one said anything!"

"What was there to say?" The chief shrugged. "Did you make a mistake? I don't know. Some say yes. Maybe there was a better way or maybe there wasn't. None of us could say. No one can fault your motivation, though. We just wanted to give you your space."

The whole town talked about and debated her situation?

Jeremy nodded. "Yeah, we figured you'd snap out of it when you were ready. It was none of our business."

She waited to see if he saw the irony of his statement, but he said nothing. A new thought struck her. "Did—did Theresa know, you think?"

Jeremy nodded. "Absolutely."

She gripped Nick's hand for support, to anchor her and keep the tears at bay. Theresa had been the one who offered her a job that proved to be a lifeline in her darkest hours. In fact, there had been plenty of support all around if she'd only seen it. The past year had been a prison of shame entirely of her own making. While the road ahead wasn't necessarily going to be smooth or without consequences, she would shift her focus where it belonged. She would keep looking up for guidance and hope.

Nick dropped down to check Raven's teeth and stitches.

The chief addressed him. "We haven't found a next of kin for Joe. While you were at his house, did you figure out who the dog's owner would be?"

"You knew where we were?" Alexis asked.

Chief raised an eyebrow. "My cousin lives next door to Joe. She saw a dog in his backyard at eight in the morning and let me know." He looked slightly bashful admitting it next to a wide-eyed Jeremy. "Since you'd already called me, I chose to give you a few more hours. Face it, Alexis, there are no secrets in this town."

Nick laughed and reached down to ruffle Raven's ears. "Unless you find a will, there's no plan set in place for Raven's ownership. But I have someone in mind who would be a good fit."

Alexis's stomach plummeted at the thought. The dog had just saved her life, and they were already talking about sending her off somewhere else? "You aren't going to adopt her? Continue her training?"

Nick's eyes softened as he regarded her. "I hadn't planned to. Joe actually thought she might be better suited to something else. Though if we ever find that silver car, I would like to take a crack at it with her."

The chief stuck his lower lip out in thought. "Are you talking about the one involved in a shootout last night? We found it around the corner in a dark spot in the alley."

"Do you have cause to search it?"

"Yes, but we didn't find anything."

Nick grinned. "Let us try."

Nick knew his brother would've been happy that he'd paid so close attention to all the DEA stories he had told. As soon as Raven sniffed the car, she barked again at the spot underneath the passenger seat.

"We already looked there," Jeremy said.

Nick sat in the driver's seat and began pressing buttons in random order. The chief stood at the window, an amused grin on his face until Nick pressed the AC button and pushed the cigarette lighter in at the same time.

A trapdoor underneath the floorboard popped open. Inside were several prefilled syringes, a fake passport with Dr. Tindale's photograph, cash and a bag presumably filled with heroin.

Nick strode over to meet Alexis. She grinned. "You sure you don't want to continue training her for detection?" She took a knee and wrapped her arms around Raven. "You two made an impressive team." Her eyes looked so hopeful, he couldn't wait to broach the subject any longer.

Nick reached into his jeans pocket and pulled out the folded therapy brochure. She opened it and stared at it in confusion. "Apparently Joe thought she would be a good fit for this. There are tons of practical benefits in taking a therapy dog with you when you work with or visit the elderly."

Her mouth dropped open and she stood up. "Me? You had me in mind for Raven?"

In that moment he knew he had made the right decision, but he tried to act nonchalant. "I couldn't adopt her. This girl I've fallen for made it pretty clear that owning a dog would be a deal breaker."

Her eyes lit up. "Did she? Well maybe she might be willing to reconsider."

A motor revved and screeched to a stop in front of them. Nick tried not to groan in frustration at the interruption.

"Mr. Kendrick!" A man leaned out the window. "*Barings Herald.* According to police, you played a part in helping take down the drug ring in town. How do you think this will affect your campaign?"

Alexis stepped in front of Nick. "Hello, Tommy. This incident only proves that Nick Kendrick challenges the status quo and will make this town better for it." She leaned forward. "That's Alexis Thompson, campaign manager."

Nick's mouth dropped. "Tommy, is it? Will you excuse us?"

He led Alexis away from peering eyes. "Campaign manager, huh?"

Her cheeks and neck turned a rosy blush. "If the job is still available." She held up a hand. "I'll do it only on a volunteer basis. I refuse to be paid. And I'll have to work around my other responsibilities like getting certified for dog therapy, applying to the Idaho Bar…"

His neck tingled with the spark of hope. He picked up her hand gently. "Are you sure? It'll probably involve a lot of lunches, late-night dinners, lots and lots of discussions."

She grinned. "You've already convinced me. There's something you should know, though."

"Oh?" His stomach churned with anxiety, knowing he'd already made it clear how he felt about her. If she insisted they'd never be more than friends, he'd respect her decision. He'd hate it, but he'd honor it.

She stared directly into his eyes. "Nick, I've fallen in love with you, too."

EPILOGUE

Three months later

Alexis drove her new-to-her all-wheel-drive Honda CR-V up the hill. After months of driving back and forth to Nick's house to take horse riding lessons—her new favorite exercise—the curves no longer scared her. She could appreciate the beauty of the road, even in the winter. She pulled over to the viewing point.

In the distance, she could see Nick a few feet past the railing, on the bench. Bundled in his blue North Face coat, complete with a knit beige scarf, he looked picture perfect. She tightened the belt on her red wool trench coat and let Raven out of the backseat. Raven looked up expectantly, wagging her tail.

"Go on, then."

Raven bounded into the light dusting of snow toward Nick. The dog was so well trained, Alexis didn't even need to put a leash on her. Alexis followed her and sat next to Nick. "Hello, Mayor Kendrick."

"I got some good news that the K9 grant for the town will be approved." He leaned over and kissed Alexis on the cheek.

Raven released a funny moan like she was annoyed at the display. Nick echoed the noise as if they were having a conversation about it. He handed Alexis a paper cup filled with hot chocolate, topped with whipped cream. "So, how'd Raven do on her first time out?"

After several classes with Raven, Alexis and the dog had been certified as a therapy team. While Alexis waited for the results of her appeal to the Idaho State Bar, she had no reason not to start serving the elderly in town. Today was their first visit at the nursing home. "Are you kidding? Raven was a natural. Everyone loved her."

"So Raven got plenty of affection. Then maybe she can spare some."

He leaned over and placed one hand on Alexis's neck and the other on her jaw. A shiver ran up her spine, and she was pretty sure it wasn't from the cold.

Raven jumped up on the bench and squeezed her way in between them. Nick sighed. "Raven, I lost something out here." He pulled out a glove from his pocket. The dog sniffed it heartily. "Go to work!"

Alexis frowned. "I didn't realize she knew how to go after a scent without being trained for it." Alexis leaned forward and examined the terrain. They could see the entire valley from this vantage point. "Do you think she'll be safe?"

"I won't let her go far. I have a feeling she knows this path well."

True to his word, Raven stuck her nose into the snow near some sagebrush. She bounded back toward them with a black glove in her mouth.

"How did your glove get clear over there?"

It was almost as if Raven had played this game before

with Nick. Before Alexis could ask a follow-up question, Raven dumped the wet glove in her lap. Except it felt too heavy against her leg to be just a glove, and it had an odd shape. Her breath caught. She looked to Nick for some kind of explanation.

He avoided eye contact and pointed at it. "What'd she find?"

Alexis stretched the opening of the glove and pulled out a velvet box. She stared at it instead of opening it. What if she was making an assumption that wouldn't prove true? Maybe it was just a necklace. "Nick…"

He dropped to a knee and opened the box for her. Inside, the square-cut diamond on the white-gold ring glistened. He reached to hold her hand. "Alexis Thompson, when I ran into you that first day, I knew I'd met my match."

She enjoyed the double meaning and knew it was true for her, as well. The last months had been filled with evenly matched debates over nonimportant issues. On the things that were really important, they heartily agreed. She equally loved their similarities and differences.

"My life changed forever, for the better," Nick said. "Will you make me the happiest man in the world and be my wife?"

She wanted to laugh and cry at the same time. "Yes," she whispered. Her gaze dropped to her hand in his. "I'm pretty sure a contract of this sort is supposed to be sealed with a kiss."

He stood and pulled her up with him. He gently brushed back her hair with his free hand and pulled her close to him. "I never argue with my lawyer."

His lips were half an inch away when she pressed her hand into his chest. "I hope that's not true."

"I see." He looked over her head as if searching for something to argue about. "Musicals are just long, drawn-out monologues."

"We'll have to go to one together to prove that's not true," she retorted.

He raised his eyebrows. "Um…it is never okay to be late."

Even though she agreed with him, she volleyed back for fun, "Then why is the term *fashionably late* a thing?"

He smiled and whispered, "White chocolate is better than dark chocolate."

She gasped and playfully hit his shoulder. "Too far!"

His laugh was delicious as he pulled her closer. "I love you, Alexis. I can't wait to be your husband."

She snuggled deeper into his embrace. "I love you, too."

Raven wormed her way between their legs. Nick groaned as he pulled out a dog treat from his pocket. "I'm ready for you." Raven took the treat and flopped down happily at their feet.

"Smart man. She deserves a lifetime supply of treats."

"Is that so?"

"Oh, yes. She not only won over a self-proclaimed dog-hater but also went above and beyond and tracked down the man of my dreams."

Nick looked into her eyes and beamed.

And finally, his lips touched hers.

* * * * *

Katherine placed a hand on his shoulder. "Don't move," she said.

He blinked and she caught a glimpse of sapphire-blue eyes. He let out another groan.

"Just stay still and let me look at your head."

"I'm fine." He rolled to his side and he squinted up at her. "Who're you?"

"I'm Dr. Katherine Gilroy, so I think I'm the better judge of whether or not you're fine. You have a head wound, which means possible concussion." She reached for him. "What's your name?"

He pushed her hand away. "Dominic O'Ryan. A branch caught me. Knocked me loopy for a few seconds, but not out. We were running from the shooter." His eyes sharpened. "He's still out there." His hand went to his right hip, gripping the empty holster next to the badge on his belt. A star within a circle. "Where's my gun? Where's Carl? My partner, Carl Manning. We need to get out of here."

"I'm sorry," Katherine said, her voice soft. "He didn't make it."

He froze. Then horror sent his eyes wide—and searching. They found the man behind her and Dominic shuddered.

After a few seconds, he let out a low cry, then sucked in another deep breath and composed his features. The intense moment lasted only a few seconds, but Katherine knew he was compartmentalizing, stuffing his emotions into a place he could hold them and deal with them later.

She knew because she'd often done the same thing. Still did on occasion.

In spite of that, his grief was palpable, and Katherine's heart thudded with sympathy for him. She moved back to give him some privacy, her eyes sweeping the hills around them once more. Again, she saw nothing, but the hairs on the back of her neck were standing straight up. "I think we need to find some better cover."

As if to prove her point, another crack sounded. Katherine grabbed the first-aid kit with one hand and pulled Dominic to his feet with the other. "Run!"

Don't miss
Mountain Fugitive *by Lynette Eason,*
available October 2021 wherever
Love Inspired Suspense books and ebooks are sold.

LoveInspired.com

Get 4 FREE REWARDS!

We'll send you 2 FREE Books plus 2 FREE Mystery Gifts.

Love Inspired Suspense books showcase how courage and optimism unite in stories of faith and love in the face of danger.

FREE Value Over $20